I0831813

Lady Doreen

by

Edward M. Nebinger

Dedication

This book is dedicated to fighter pilots the world over – past, present and future. They are a unique fraternity and I consider it a great privilege to have been a 25-year active member – and still feel I belong! Once a fighter pilot, always a fighter pilot!

Copyright Notice

Contents

INTRODUCTION

This is a story written by an old fighter pilot, about some very young fighter pilots in WWII. Maybe I should have said "ex-fighter pilot," but there is really no such thing, because once a fighter pilot, always a fighter pilot. I don't know how that can be; maybe there is some kind of mysterious, unidentified bug that bites you when you get hold of a stick and throttle and are privileged to fly a great fighting machine driven by thousands of horsepower (or pounds of thrust), in peacetime or war. Whatever it is, it is a defining moment in your life, and it stays with you long after the engines are shut down for the last time – and you look back and smile, for those are good memories.

WWII was a momentous time in the history of the world. It was a time of great tragedy, but also a time of a storybook ending in terms of a great and ultimate triumph. It was a war fought largely by a very young generation, many of whom went directly from teen-age innocence into the cauldron of war and emerged several years later with a completely different set of values. I was one of those youngsters, who sat in high school while the Battle of Britain was taking place, wondering if the war would end before I could get there. (I'm sure that sounds crazy today.)

Prior to Pearl Harbor, the U.S, Army and Navy had a strict requirement of at least two years college in order to qualify for entrance into their respective Aviation Cadet training programs. However, in 1942, under wartime pressures and the need to provide pilots to man the more than 100,000 new airplanes President Roosevelt had ordered built, that requirement was dropped, providing that the applicants could pass a stiff entrance test. As a result of this, a large group of young kids, just out of high school and eager to join the fight, passed the exam and jumped right into the Aviation Cadet program!

This is the story of two groups of those young high school graduates from opposite ends of our country. One group from Pennsylvania learned to fly in the Southeast Training Command, while another group from California and Washington State earned their coveted silver wings in the Western Training. Command. In 1944 they came together in the 360th Squadron of the 356th Fighter Group in England to join the fight against the Germans during the great invasion of the Continent in June 1944 – through the end of the war in 1945.

This is a memoir filled with the many complex issues they dealt with to win their silver wings in the face of many obstacles, followed by their baptism of fire and some of their ultimate adventures in combat. But this is not just another "shoot em up" tale of fighter pilots at work. These glamorous and healthy young men, wearing Lieutenant's bars and wings at ages as young as 19 or 20, were quick to attract the attention of a host of young girls and it was inevitable that some serious fireworks were set off.

While some of those romances bloomed quickly, flared brightly and flickered out, others endured throughout the war, including one which ended tragically and another which resulted in a dynasty which lives and flourishes in California today. Let me hasten to say - that dynasty was not mine, but that of one of my fellow pilots. I was merely a witness to those events..

Lady Doreen is the story of how that dynasty came into being and the complex series of events which led up to it.

Ed Nebinger
New Fairfield, CT,
April 2013

CHAPTER ONE

A GATHERING OF EAGLETS

Bethlehem, Pennsylvania – March 1941

Ody Thoma and I were sitting in a study hall with a pack of other seniors at Liberty High School in the steel town of Bethlehem, Pennsylvania. We were supposed to be studying, but were surreptitiously reading a special issue of Life Magazine featuring the Battle of Britain, which had taken place in the summer and fall of 1940. When that special issue with its wonderful photos of the young Royal Air Force fighter pilots and the planes they manned appeared on the newsstands, we had quickly grabbed a copy and were eagerly devouring its contents, whispering quietly to each other and passing the magazine back and forth.

Study halls were often held on the second floor of the auditorium, which comprised a large balcony, and that was where we were sitting. The students were required to sit with two seats between them and keep quiet so the rest could study. Of course there were plenty of notes being passed around, as well as lots of teenage hi jinx. Ody and I shared a number of classes and happened to be sitting close together that day.

Pointing to a photo of a German bomber that had been shot down over England, I said, "That's a Dornier 17, which the Brits call a 'pencil bomber' because it has a very thin fuselage shaped like a pencil. It's kind of a neat-looking airplane. I just saw an ad from Megows in Flying Aces magazine. They have a new kit for a flying scale model of the Do.17. Maybe I'll build one."

Ody, who had no use for anything German, snorted and said, a bit too loudly, "Yeah, well I read that it is a piece of crap that is underpowered, too slow, and carries a very small bomb load! Go ahead and build one; maybe you can enjoy setting it on fire and sailing it out of a second floor window!"

At this point, the hall monitor pointed at us and said, "No talking please, this is supposed to be a study hall."

Ody flashed me a weak grin and pretended to go back to studying.

The special edition of Life Magazine traced the buildup to the crucial aerial battles that had raged over England. The Battle of Britain had mounted steadily during the summer months and reached a crescendo in September of 1940, with massive raids of German bombers wreaking havoc on British air bases, military installations, and war production plants.

The German Luftwaffe had great numerical superiority over the Royal Air Force, and Field Marshall Hermann Goering had promised the Fuhrer that he would bring Britain to its knees with his air flotillas. Goering had come very close to succeeding, and at one point the RAF had been down to zero reserves in its defending force of Hurricane and Spitfire fighters.

Then Goering made a crucial mistake. Buoyed by his apparent success, he promised the German people that not a single British bomber would reach the Ruhr (Germany's great industrial valley).

"If one does," he said, "my name is not Hermann Goering; you can call me Meyer."

However, not long thereafter some brave and determined RAF crews, flying the rather ineffective Wellington bombers that the RAF pilots called "Wimpys," penetrated deep into Germany on a night raid and accidentally bombed Berlin, which had not been their primary target. Berlin was much deeper in Germany than the Ruhr Valley, so Goering's boast became a subject of some worldwide laughter. Reports filtered out of Germany that many of the Luftwaffe pilots were now secretly referring to the rotund Hermann as "Field Marshall Meyer."

The raid on Berlin also enraged Hitler. In a ranting speech carried on German radio countrywide, he promised overwhelming retribution. His ending words, referring to the German bombers that would hit English cities, were, "Er kommt! Er kommt!" (He is coming), at which point the German audience in the large hall clapped and cheered wildly.

To describe such a change as fortunate might have sounded outrageous to those taking the punishment on the ground – but in the grand scale of war it was a strategic turning point.

Previously, the Luftwaffe bombers had targeted airfields, as well as specific industrial factories, particularly those producing aircraft. They had also made periodic raids against the line of radar installations established by the British along the south coast of Britain. Though radar was in its early days, British scientists had done some excellent pioneering work, building a line of big towers with fixed antennas capable of detecting approaching enemy aircraft, particularly when the aircraft were in large massed formations.

The raids on the towers were not very successful, but those on the airfields created serious losses. Meanwhile, attacks on the aircraft factories slowed production not only by direct damage but also by keeping the workforce in bomb shelters.

Hitler's decision to conduct a reign of terror on the population of Britain's cities was a serious miscalculation, which had exactly the reverse of the intended effect! Hitherto, many English people, still smarting from their shocking losses in World War I, had questioned

Britain's entry into a new world war. Now, faced with the destruction of their cities and a direct war on the civilian population, they realized that they were dealing with a madman who had to be stopped. British resolve stiffened and the country was unified as never before.

From a purely military standpoint, it was a godsend. The suspension of attacks against the airfields and production facilities soon enabled the production of new Spitfires and Hurricanes to exceed their losses so that the balance of forces gradually began to even up.

Perhaps even more importantly, Goering's switch to massed formations heading toward specific city targets enabled the British ground controllers to gain a great strategic advantage. Instead of maintaining a large number of airborne patrols, they kept the bulk of their defending fighters on the ground until large groups of attacking aircraft were identified and their incoming courses plotted by the radar stations and ground aircraft spotters, both of which were tied in closely to the plotting and control rooms. Now, the British could launch much larger groups of defending fighters that could focus on the attacking formations.

For Ody and me, this was fascinating stuff. Both of us were avid airplane buffs who built model airplanes and read everything we could find about flying. We belonged to the Bethlehem Aero Aces Model Club and during the summer spent our weekends flying free-flight gas models in the nearby farmers' fields in the Lehigh Valley. I was also a history buff, and had devoured stories about the First World War aces such as Eddie Rickenbacker, Billy Bishop of Canada, Baron Von Richthofen of Germany (the Red Baron), and many of the British and French aces.

My overarching ambition in life was to become an Army fighter pilot, and my heroes at that time were the American pilots who had volunteered to fly fighters with the Royal Air Force. A special American unit called the Eagle Squadron had been formed in Debden, England, and the pilots, who had been checked out in either Hurricanes or Spitfires, wore uniforms similar to those of the RAF, with a special Eagle Squadron patch on their sleeves.

Ody Thoma's interest in the war was different. His Greek family had a distinct hatred for the Nazis, as well as the Fascists in Italy. Since the beginning of the war, the Germans and Italians had been placing increasing pressure on Greece to join hands with them, but the Greeks, who had long-term historical ties with Britain, had staunchly resisted. Determined to demonstrate his military muscle, Mussolini had actually invaded Greece in October 1940, but had been met with heroic resistance from the Hellenic Army, which pushed the Italians back into Albania. Now, Hitler was preparing to step in and launch a German invasion of Greece, thereby pulling his Axis partner's chestnuts out of the fire and consolidating his presence in Southern Europe.

Ody wasn't so rabid about becoming a fighter pilot, but he nevertheless wanted to join the Army Air Corps and become a pilot so he could get to Europe and do some damage to those who were attacking the homeland of his ancestors. Ody wasn't his real name – it was Edward Thoma. However, when we studied Homer's Odyssey in English class, Eddie Thoma had been so taken with Odysseus, the hero of the epic, that somebody started calling him "Ody" for short – and it caught on. It also helped to sort out the two Eds – Ed Thoma and Ed Nebinger – as we hung out together frequently and every time somebody called, "Hey Ed," we both answered. Now the problem was solved, and Ody actually liked his new name a lot. I wondered sometimes whether Ody's real middle name may have actually been Odysseus, but I never asked.

The two of us avidly ate up every word we could read about the battles and wondered if the war would end before we could figure out a way to get there and join the fight. It never occurred to us that we might get ourselves killed. I guess that's probably why wars are primarily fought by the very young, who are inclined to jump right in.

The monitor for the study hall was a man named J. Walter Gapp, the school principal, who occasionally volunteered to share that duty. He was a fine man, devoted to the students, but he had some character traits which made him appear as a bit of a "stiff neck," and set him up as the victim of some crazy stunts.

For example, J. Walter was a bug on speaking English very clearly and not slurring any words, probably because a lot of the kids spoke almost gibberish. Sometimes he would stand on the stage and say to the students, "You MusT LearN to EnunciaTE," pronouncing the words with such emphasis that his whole body shook. Kids can be tough on educators trying to do a good job and found this highly amusing, often mimicking J. Walter when he wasn't around.

That day, Ody slyly pulled out of his satchel three small balsa wood gliders and when the monitor wasn't looking, said, "Watch this action," and launched them into the air over the balcony. They glided neatly around several times before sailing down and landing on the stage and seats below.

The kids had a great laugh over that, while J. Walter sought in vain to determine the source. He might have zeroed in on Ody if he had noticed that each of the gliders had "Greek Air Corps" lettered on the wings.

That was a pretty harmless stunt, but there was another one shortly thereafter that was seriously dangerous. The seats in the auditorium were typical, with backs that concealed much of the lower body of the students. A couple of kids got the bright idea of starting to stamp their feet on the floor slowly, but in cadence. Other kids joined in and soon the entire auditorium balcony was loudly booming and shaking with a hundred or more pairs of feet stamping in perfect cadence.

J. Walter, who understood very well the danger of stamping in cadence in any structure, became alarmed and ran around holding up his hands and shouting, "Stop! Please stop!"

A lot of the kids found this highly amusing and stamped even harder, but finally, a few of the smarter ones yelled for kids to knock it off, and, suddenly realizing the danger of collapsing the entire balcony, I jumped up and yelled, "Cut it out, for Christ's sake!" This surprised a lot of people, as I was basically a quiet kid, but generally popular and known as a clever guy, which gave me credibility. The stomping gradually diminished and came to a stop.

The next day, as I was sitting in class I was handed a message on High School Stationery. It read:

TO: Edward Nebinger, Senior, Class of 41

Please report to my office after class today.

J. W. Gapp, Principal

I thought, *Oh, brother, he probably thinks I was the guy who launched those gliders yesterday – but I'm not going to rat on Ody.*

At 3:45 that afternoon I stopped by the Principal's office. Surprisingly, Mr. Gapp greeted me with a smile, offered his hand to shake, and invited me to sit. Then he said, "Thank you for helping me stop the stamping yesterday; that was an important contribution." He paused, then asked, "Why did you jump up and stop it as you did?"

I told him I knew that continuous oscillations such as rhythmic stamping could cause a whole structure to collapse. I further explained that I was interested in scientific principles and had read a great deal about the inventor Nicolai Tesla, who was not only the father of alternating current but had pioneered the study of wave theory and cyclic oscillations, performing many practical experiments to prove his theories. Tesla had actually produced a very small machine that he claimed could bring down a steel-structured building by gradually building up the synchronous cyclic waves until the structure self-destructed.

Mr. Gapp nodded and said, "Excellent, and quite correct. Tesla was a leading proponent of that theory, which has now become recognized as an important factor in the design of modern structures. I'm glad to see you learning things that are not part of our normal curriculum."

He hesitated briefly, then continued, "I wonder if you would be interested in taking a special test that we administer at the Moravian Prep School, with which I have some affiliation?"

Surprised and puzzled, I asked, "What would be the purpose of the test?"

The principal responded, "You obviously have a high mechanical IQ. It is a general IQ test that we give to groups of students, designed to determine more precisely their aptitudes, in order to help develop their path forward in life." He waited patiently while I mulled it over. I was kind of a low-profile kid at Liberty High – certainly not one of the top-notch students who belonged to all of the honor societies. However, deciding I had nothing to lose, I agreed to take the test.

Mr. Gapp said, "Fine, thanks for stopping by. I'll notify you."

I thanked him and walked out, sensing the principal studying me as I departed.

A month later I sat down with a room full of people for a one-hour test of questions with multiple-choice answers. Some of the questions related to subjects I had not yet taken, but by and large, most of them had logical answers if one just thought them out. I had no clue how I did, but the next day J. Walter called me in and said, "You scored highest of everyone on the test," which surprised me! Mr. Gapp then asked what my interests in life were, and I told him I wanted to be a fighter pilot. He smiled and said, "You can be anything you want to be in life."

I left perplexed, but with a greater insight into the character of people like J. Walter Gapp.

That was high school in 1941. Later, with war looming on the horizon, a great many of the students were destined to enter the military. One of the first lessons they would learn in marching drill was that a military unit marching across a bridge can easily bring down the structure if it continues to march in cadence. Therefore, in military units worldwide, whenever crossing any bridge, the person commanding the unit always gives the command, "Rout step," or its other language equivalent, and the troops randomize their steps until the other side of the bridge is reached, after which marching in cadence is resumed.

San Joaquin Valley, California

Across the Continent in sunny Denair, California, another pair of high school seniors, who were destined to become lifelong friends, were brought together by a precipitous event that occurred in the high school gym locker room one day.

A kid named Richard Andrino, of Filipino heritage, who everybody called Andy, had just finished working out on the parallel bars and was changing by his locker when he overheard a loudmouth in the next aisle saying, "Those goddam greasers are hogging all the equipment around here! Between the Mex‘s and Flippos you can‘t get a shot at anything, and when you do there is so much grease left on it that your hands slip off!"

"Fuckin’ A," said his skinny buddy, who Andrino recognized as a particularly obnoxious jerk with a bad case of acne.

Andy was short in stature but built pretty rugged, and could hold his own pretty well in an even contest. But today the odds were stacked against him a bit, as the loudmouth was a pretty big guy who would be no slouch to take on. He also had a reputation as being the dirtiest player on the Denair "Coyotes" football team. Nevertheless, Andy could never be described as a shrinking violet, and found himself shouting back over the lockers. "That's pure bullshit, and you guys know it!" There was a momentary silence, and then Andy saw two heads poke around the corner and stare at him in amazement.

"Jesus Christ," the big guy said, "Here's one of 'em now." He turned to his buddy and smirked, "Watch out you don't slip on the grease in the aisle."

That was just too much for Andrino, who lost his head and launched himself like a cannon ball head first into the gut of the big guy, and both of them went sailing over a bench, ending up sprawled on their backs on the floor.

"Why you sonofabitch!" yelled the big guy, grabbing Andrino around the neck in a choke hold with one arm and squeezing with all his might, while pounding him in the head with his other fist. At the same time, the acne case started kicking him in the side.

Andy was gasping for air and on the verge of passing out when a tall kid named Burwell, who had taken it all in from the next aisle, felt himself compelled to step in. "Let him go! You're killing him!" yelled Burwell.

The guy retorted, "Butt out, asshole. He asked for it and he's gonna get it!"

Without hesitation, Burwell gave the kicker a shove that sent him careening into a locker. Then he grabbed the big guy's arms, twisted him over, and quickly pinned him to the floor, subduing him with a knee in his groin and a hammerlock. Ray, who was top man on the school wrestling team, had nevertheless expected the guy to be a really tough opponent. Surprisingly, he turned out to be relatively soft, and quickly folded his tent when up against even odds.

"Why don't you pick on somebody your own size?" said Ray quietly, letting the guy up and expecting a new frontal assault. But the big guy seemed to have lost his steam and chose not to renew the contest, resorting instead to a lot of swearing and threats, then departed the scene with the skinny kid in tow – spurred on by the fact that the football coach had just poked his head around the corner to see what the hubbub was all about.

Andrino, who was still only half dressed, gathered himself up from the floor.

"You okay?" asked Burwell.

In spite of the fact that he had a half-bloody nose and was pretty roughed up, Andrino grinned and said to Burwell, "Damn, I'm glad you came along. I don't know what the hell I was thinking – that bastard could have killed me! I gotta learn to keep control of my damn temper."

Sticking out his hand, Burwell said, "I've seen you around a lot, but we really never met. I'm Orvil Burwell, but most people call me Ray, as I hate that damned name."

"Richard Andrino," replied the short kid, "but everybody calls me Andy."

The two Californians became good friends thereafter, and found that their respective parents actually knew each other. Andy's parents worked in the vineyards and truck gardens in the Sonoma Valley, while Ray's family had a small spread. His father was in the insurance business and also collected taxes for the city of Denair. The Burwells, who were devotees of fresh farm produce, had probably come into contact with the Andrinos at some of the fairs and fresh produce market events that took place in the valley.

The two seniors soon found that they had some other things in common. One passion they both shared was ping pong. Both were top-notch players, and they soon teamed up as the top dogs at local tournaments.

It was almost comical, as they appeared like a Mutt and Jeff act, with Ray over six feet tall, and Andy just barely five feet four. But in terms of ping pong, they made a formidable pair. Andy, who had extremely fast reflexes, was actually the better of the two, but both had a power style which enabled them to back off about six or eight feet from the table and wham the ball across the net with terrific force, as well as with some vicious cuts. Another thing that Ray and Andy found they had in common was a desire to become Army fighter pilots by joining the aviation cadets.

Both graduated from Denair High with the class of 1941, but soon found out that while the Army Air Corps was ramping up its pilot training to man the thousands of new airplanes that President Roosevelt had called for, the minimum requirement to join the cadets was two years of college.

With that objective in mind, they made up their minds to get two years of college under their belts as soon as possible, and both entered Modesto Junior College in September of 1941, where they continued their ping pong activities, coming very close to winning the state championship the following year.

Hurry Up and Wait

Back in Pennsylvania, Ody and I graduated from high school in 1941. Neither of us was an honors graduate; in fact we were about in the middle of the pack, but really didn't give a damn, as we had a lot of other interests and therefore simply cruised through high school doing enough to get by, but not setting any records.

Our ambition to become Army Air Corps pilots had run into two snags. First, neither of us was eighteen years old, the minimum age to join the Army. Of more importance, however, was the same obstacle that had frustrated Rich Andrino and Ray Burwell on the West Coast; the Army was not accepting anyone for aviation cadet training with less than two years of college, and we had zero! We did not see any early solutions, so we both looked for a job.

Ody found a job in a business operated by one of his family's friends, while I shopped around and was lucky to land a job in a local motorcycle dealer's shop. Actually, luck had little to do with it, as I had acquired a lot of motorcycle repair experience working with my brother, Bob, during my high school years.

Our family had a decent-sized garage on the alley that ran in back of our house, and Bob, who was three years older, had been running a bootleg fixit-type mechanic shop where a lot of the local young guys hung out, working on cars and motorcycles. It was amazing how much knowledge a bunch of young car buffs and grease monkeys could acquire, and there was virtually nothing that guys with a decent mechanical IQ couldn't fix.

As the result of years of hanging out at the garage, I had picked up a goodly amount of that lore. Of course, as one of the young ones I got saddled with a lot of grunge tasks, such as cleaning parts in solvent, fixing flat tires, and stuff like that. However, that was one of the things kids had to accept – and looking at it from the brighter side, I had learned quite a bit about the mechanical aspects of how cars and bikes ran and how to go about repairing them.

Bob never advertised his mechanic business, as our house was in a residential zone, but the grapevine worked amazingly well and business came in the door by word of mouth. The country was still working its way out of the Great Depression, which had been underway since the early thirties. One of the results was that there were lots of old cars and motorcycles sitting in barns and garages in the local countryside, and every once in a while a guy would bring one in so that Bob could give it a tune-up and get it running right.

I was particularly drawn to motorcycles and managed to get checked out on an old Harley that Bob found at a local auction. Bob soon let me specialize in working on bikes, so that by the time I graduated from high school, I was able to strip a bike completely to the frame, remove the engine, and re-install everything from scratch, repairing as appropriate. A lot of the old bikes had been banging away for years and really needed work, but their owners couldn't afford the tab at the pro shops, so the Nebinger backyard garage got the fix-ups at a discount price.

Another skill I learned was spray painting. Most of the bikes that came into the shop were pretty beat up, but it was surprising what a new coat of paint would do. However, it wasn't just a matter of taking a brush and slapping some paint on, as that ended up looking just like what it was – an amateur job.

I talked Bob into buying a compressor and a high-quality Binks spray gun, and we soon learned to use it very efficiently, working as a team. With the engine, tanks, wheels, and fenders removed from a bike, we first sanded and repainted the entire frame with a nice black enamel. Then the fenders and tanks were carefully sanded, after which two coats of primer were applied. This dried into a dull-looking gray finish, which was then wet sanded with a very fine-grit cloth until it felt as smooth as a pane of glass.

For the finish coat, which usually comprised two colors, we first sprayed on a double coat of lacquer for the main color, allowing it to dry thoroughly, then applied masking tape to spray on the trim color of stripes or whatever the job called for. When the masking tape was removed, it looked great, but that was still not the end, as lacquer dries in a slight orange peel finish. For the final step, Bob and I applied rubbing compound and carefully worked every inch of the surface to an ultra-smooth, polished finish. It was as smooth as a mirror and when the complete bike was re-assembled, it looked just like a brand new machine. Bob was fond of saying to his admiring friends, "If a fly lands on it, he will slip off and kill himself!"

While my skills came in handy at the backyard garage, there was not enough business to provide a full-time salary, which motivated me to look for a job with a cycle dealer. The shop that hired me was officially an Indian dealer, but repaired all kinds of bikes. The guy running the shop quizzed me carefully before hiring me, and seemed to like what he heard. However, the proof was in the pudding, and, as might be expected, I had to work my way back up through the parts cleaning and other dirty work jobs before I was given any real responsibilities. The boss soon accepted my skills as a mechanic, but the thing that really solidified things was when he discovered my spray painting skills, as he had no one else with those talents. Thereafter, I performed every paint job for the shop, and also doubled as an all-around motorcycle mechanic.

One of the first benefits of the job was that I bought myself a little 1935 Indian Pony Scout, which the boss had taken in on a trade. While its 37-cubic-inch engine was not exactly a powerhouse, it was a clean little bike and the boss gave me such a sweet deal, I couldn't pass it up. My transportation problems were solved, and I was soon riding both Harleys and Indians on a daily basis. There was one significant difference between the two. Both had a spark advance on one of the handle grips and the gas on the other; however, the two brands were reversed. Harleys had the gas on the right grip, while Indians had it on the left.

I found it curious that I was able to jump from one to the other without ever getting confused. If I goosed the engine when I thought I was advancing the spark, this could have led to some serious problems. I couldn‘t explain it, but apparently some little switch in my head clicked whenever I changed bikes. I didn't realize it then, but this natural ability to adjust my reflexes without thinking would prove to be crucial to the future course of my life.

After high school graduation, Ody and I kept in touch, but we were both busy with our respective jobs and were basically marking time as the war in Europe continued. While the massive air attacks on England had eased off, the war in Europe reached a new level when Hitler launched an invasion of Russia in June of 1941. Frustrated by the U.S. recruiting standards, Ody and I considered going to Canada to join the RCAF, but heard that we would very likely end up as ground pounders – as the non-flyers were called – and that was not what either of us wanted.

Pearl Harbor

The attack on Pearl Harbor on December 7, 1941, solved the problem for a lot of American kids who wanted to be Army pilots but didn't meet the two years of college requirement. In mid-1942, under wartime stress, the Army Air Corps dropped its strict requirement of two years of college for aviation cadets and made an exception for applicants who could pass a stiff written test. Ody and I took the test, scored well, and, after a thorough physical exam, were accepted into the Air Corps as aviation cadets.

In August 1942, we stood with a group of about a hundred others on the courthouse steps in Allentown, Pennsylvania, and were sworn in as Army Air Corps aviation cadets. We expected to report for duty immediately, but were surprised when the officer in charge announced that although we were now officially a part of the U.S. Army Reserve (with no pay), the Training Command was backed up with a large number of recruits and it would be at least seven months before we would actually be called to active duty. In the meantime, we were advised to go on with our civilian jobs while awaiting orders. We went back to work, wondering how long the war was going to last.

A somewhat similar scenario unfolded in sunny California, where the two buddies, Ray Burwell and Andy Andrino, were immersed in their studies at Modesto Junior College. They were sitting and eating their lunch together, chatting and reading the paper to see what was happening with the war, when Andrino suddenly jumped up and said, "Holy smokes! Look at this! I don't believe it! They're dropping the requirements for two years college!"

"You're kidding," said Burwell, grabbing the paper suspiciously, as Andy was a great joker and loved to pull cute little stunts. "Let me see that.." After scanning it, he said, "There's got to be a catch in this; they've been so damned strict about that requirement.."

But there wasn't a catch.. The next morning, the two skipped classes and rushed down to the Army recruiting station in Denair, where, after standing in a line of guys trying to sign up to fight the "Japs," they finally managed to make their way up to an Army sergeant, who actually didn't know much about the new deal for aviation cadets. However, he told them, "I don't have anything on it right now, but when I get a break, I'll call my post to get the details. Let me have a phone number and I'll call you."

Pearl Harbor must have really awakened everybody, because the sergeant was as good as his word, and, displaying a rare bit of efficiency for the Army, actually called Burwell at his home that evening and said, "The newspaper article was correct. Both the Army and the Navy are scheduling times when you can take the special aviation cadet test. Stop by the recruiting station and I will have the schedules posted."

That evening, Andy and Ray were bubbling over with excitement, as they announced the changed situation with their respective parents. Andrino's parents found the whole deal somewhat confusing. They had hoped that, after graduating from high school, their son would join them in the vineyards, and had never been enthusiastic about having him possibly flying war planes, which sounded especially dangerous. However, they loved their son deeply and had scraped together the tuition and expense for his college, with the idea that maybe he would settle down into something safer. Their natural reaction, therefore, was to say, "Well, you won‘t have to bother with that, as you can just finish up your second year."

Ray‘s parents were equally skeptical. His father, who he always called "Pop," was in the insurance business, and therefore naturally viewed everything from a somewhat calculated aspect. He advised taking it easy and finishing out his year at Modesto Junior College before making any more moves.

"Besides," he cautioned, "you don‘t even know if you can learn to fly; you may end up digging ditches as an Army private, so you better get some more college under your belt." He added, "Beating those little Japs won‘t take long, and you need to be thinking about getting a good job after it is over."

Their parents' advice fell on deaf ears, however, and Andy and Ray took the aviation cadet test two weeks later at the county courthouse. They passed with no problem and after undergoing an initial physical exam, both were accepted into the Army Air Corps' aviation cadets program shortly thereafter. In September 1942, they joined a group of about eighty new recruits who were sworn in at a public ceremony. Both expected to leave shortly for their initial training, but, like Ody and me in Pennsylvania, were keenly disappointed when the officer in charge of the ceremony announced that they were now part of the Army‘s Enlisted Reserve, and that their actual call-up to active duty would be delayed due to a massive backlog in the Air Corps training program. They were advised to pursue their civilian occupations while awaiting future orders.

The delay was actually a cause for rejoicing on the part of their parents, who had dished out the money for the college tuition and other expenses, and had expected to see much of it go down the drain. After some family discussions, Ray and Andy decided to continue finishing as much as they could of their second year at Modesto Junior College.

CHAPTER TWO
YOU'RE IN THE ARMY NOW

A Sudden Change of Pace

Nashville Army Air Base, Tennessee

Because the Southeast Training Command had a greater number of training facilities than the Western Training Command, the aspiring cadets on the East Coast received their call-up orders about two months sooner than those on the other side of the country. In February 1943, Ody and I boarded a train in Allentown with a bunch of other aviation cadets, all with orders assigning us to the classification center at Nashville, Tennessee. Everybody was dressed in civilian clothes and carrying some type of bag.

The train ride turned out to be a nightmare. The locomotive and cars must have been sitting unused in some railroad yard for years, as they were filthy from coal car to caboose. Bits of coal dust had seeped in under the windows, so that every place anyone rested an arm, it was instantly blackened. The ancient locomotive belched smoke out of its stack at a tremendous rate, adding to the soot.

The windows seemed to be fastened shut and couldn't be opened, which may have been a good thing as we would have all gotten a face-full if the train went through any tunnels. However, we soon began to pay a penalty for that, as the atmosphere in the cars became stifling.

All of us new recruits were slowly realizing that Army life may not be all roses, as our status was not unlike that of cattle. Consequently, many of us spent as much time as possible standing on the platform between the cars to get some fresh air.

The train chugged its way slowly throughout the Eastern part of the U.S., stopping at dozens of small towns to pick up new recruits. It gradually worked its way south through part of Maryland, West Virginia, then into Kentucky, stopping at many tiny stations in the boondocks, where some real yokelish characters came down to see their sons off to war. At one station in Kentucky, an old woman smoking a corncob pipe peered intently into the train as if she had never seen one before.

Ody and I were lucky we had boarded near the beginning of the collection shuttle, as we were able to get a seat together and stow our bags in the overhead rack. However, as the cars filled up, we finally reached the point where there were no seats left, and guys started standing in the aisle.

As time wore on, even more recent arrivals ended up sitting on their baggage in the aisle, and a few actually climbed up and stretched out on the overhead baggage racks. About every other guy was smoking, and the air inside became so thick that it was tough to breathe.

The train chugged its way to the extreme western end of Kentucky for about five hours, then looped around and headed southeast into Tennessee for about five more hours.

Food? Forget it – aside from a hot dog and a soda, which we grabbed from a vendor at a station, there wasn‘t any. Luckily, each car had a working water fountain. Ody remarked, "If they are trying to toughen us up for the war, it’s not working. They’re liable to kill half of us with S&S – smoke and starvation."

Finally, after we spent a horrible night trying to get comfortable and get some sleep in the sweaty, smoky atmosphere, our train groaned its way onto a siding at a bleak-looking place outside of Nashville. It was some kind of Army camp with barbed wire that made it look suspiciously like a concentration camp. In retrospect, Ody and I agreed that the term was not too far off the mark.

The Sort Out

Nashville Army Classification Center - February 1943

For now, however, a big gate opened and an officer led the pack up a long hill, which was lined with barracks buildings on each side. Wearing our dirty and crumpled civilian duds, we walked slowly up the hill, lugging our bags and suitcases. It was an Army camp, but our gang of new prospective aviation cadets looked like a file of prisoners who had come back from a thirty-six-hour work detail, with dirty faces and deep circles under our eyes.

As we trudged up the hill, a lot of guys in uniforms came out of the barracks and started making cat calls and yelling wisecracks. A couple of favorites were, "You'll be sooorry" and "Ha, ha, say your prayers, sucker" and "Where do you want us to send your remains?" Then there were some really creative ones, which scared the hell out of a lot of guys, such as, "Wait until you get the spiral needle in the left nut!"

Finally, our pack reached the top of the hill and was divided into two lines, each going into one end of a low barracks and coming out of the other end. We noted several ambulances waiting at the other end of the barracks – not a very sanguine sign. As soon as we got inside of the door, we observed two nurses standing on each side of the line. All of the recruits were instructed to roll up both sleeves – and the nurses hit each one of us with four shots in each arm – *bang, bang, bang, bang* – almost like two machine guns.

Clearly those nurses weren't the cutie types wearing their little white caps; they were battleaxes who looked like maybe they would have made a good machine gun crew!

About every fifth guy keeled over and a bunch of GI corpsmen were kept busy hauling them to the ambulances. A couple of those shots burned a bit and one started hurting rather quickly, but Ody and I made it, speculating that maybe those guys who fainted had let themselves get psyched out on their way up the hill.

Next, we were marched in ragged groups to a supply building, where a couple of clerks handed us our barracks bags, took a quick look at us, made their own selections of the appropriate sizes, and started tossing uniforms, shoes, underwear, socks, towels, and other supplies at us at a rapid rate. There was no trying anything on; we just stuffed everything into the bag. A sergeant then counted off groups of forty guys and marched them off to a barracks.

Each barracks had twenty beds on each side, with a single pot-bellied stove in the center of the building. It was quite cold in Nashville in February, so the smart guys immediately headed for a cot not far from the stove. My pal and I were fortunate that we were near the front of the pack when we reached the barracks, and were able to grab beds about five cots down from the stove, an ideal location, as we wouldn't freeze, but wouldn't roast either, like the dummies who grabbed the beds right next to the stove.

Everybody headed for the showers to wash off the grime and began struggling into their new uniforms, which were olive drab and made out of some stuff that was pretty itchy. About a third did not even fit, and guys were trying to get into uniforms that were much too small or vice versa, so there was some trading and swapping that went on, as well as a few outrageous cases where guys were left with ridiculous fits that would have to be changed later.

Before we were even halfway dressed, a different sergeant came in and yelled, "Listen up, everybody. You guys and those in the next barracks are now officially Squadron Eight. Don't forget it." He then started showing us how to make up our beds with square corners, and how to make them sharp and taut enough to bounce a dime on them.

He also arranged for a few guys with ridiculous uniform fits to return to the supply depot briefly for exchanges to reasonable sizes.

The sarge also told us where we could find the mess hall and grab some chow. He further announced that we would be awakened at 0530 next morning and would have exactly ten minutes to fall out in front of the barracks in full Class A uniform; i.e., everything, including necktie.

Squadron Eight managed to make its way in small groups to the mess hall. Ody and I noted the drill; you grabbed an enormous tray, which held at least twice as much chow as a normal plate, then lined up and walked down the GI chow line where the KPs slopped ladles full of the stuff into each of the compartments. It was an incredible amount of food, which explained why most recruits put on about twenty pounds in the first month.

After devouring a large trayful, Ody belched loudly and remarked, "I guess maybe the Army's not gonna starve us after all."

The new recruits gradually straggled back to the barracks and there followed a tumultuous evening with people trying to sort out and arrange things, wisecracks and pillows flying back and forth, all accompanied by a great deal of creative swearing.

We were beginning to learn an old Army axiom – that in every group there are always a few jokers and wisecrackers, and Squadron Eight was no exception. Actually, it probably would have been more boisterous, but some guys were running a slight fever from the shots. "Lights out" was at ten o'clock and nobody had a hard time getting to sleep after the long, tiring train ride, not to mention the effect of eight shots.

It seemed like they had only been to sleep for an hour, when the door banged open, the lights came on with a blinding flash and the sarge was striding up and down in the aisle rapping his stick on bedposts yelling, "Drop your cocks and grab your socks! Fall out in ten minutes."

There was a mad scramble to get into the new clothes, most of which were still poor fits. It was very cold and damp in Nashville at 0530, so everyone was wearing his GI overcoat buttoned up to the top, standing there bleary-eyed while the sergeant called the roll call and everybody responded with a "Here." After some cutting remarks about the sloppy look of the group, he informed us that the mess hall did not open until 0730 and that everyone was free to chow up then, as long as we were back at the barracks at 0845, with orders to fall out again at 0900.

Welcome to the Army! Really clever; wake us up to rush out into the freezing cold at 0540, then turn us loose for almost two hours until the chow hall opened. Everybody went back into the cozy barracks, where most removed their clothes and caught another hour or so nap, while some eager beavers hit the showers and shaved.

The Army didn't waste any time in getting us new recruits started on initial training. We had a couple of sessions in a classroom, followed by a dizzying amount of learning how to march, with basic commands and ceaseless drill. We also learned when and who to salute, which produced some comical scenes, as whenever an officer appeared, people twenty-five feet away were saluting like idiots, not knowing when to drop the salute.

The next day, a couple of guys decided to beat the system at the early morning roll call. Figuring that they were going to be back in bed in fifteen minutes, they skipped putting on all that uniform stuff and just wore their pants, joining the formation with their overcoats buttoned up to the neck.

The sarge, who had seen it all before, called everyone to attention and said, "Everyone remove your overcoats." Two guys were left standing there like idiots, freezing in pants and t-shirts.

The sarge then called the group to attention, dismissed everyone except the two offending culprits, and left them standing at attention in the cold for another twenty minutes before dismissing them. Nobody tried to beat the system after that.

Nashville was a hell of a place. Everything was heated with soft coal, and the air was continually polluted with lots of smoke. Combine that with a very damp and cold climate, and the result was a place that was a perfect breeding ground for colds, coughs, and outright pneumonia.

Nobody knew whether it was true, but the word was that the camp had been built on the very location of the infamous Civil War Berry Hill Concentration Camp, where thousands of Union prisoners perished. It was believable, because when we walked to the mess hall, there was a constant cacophony of coughs and hacks, and the roadway was covered with thousands of bilious-looking splats where people had spit.

After a while, when some of the recruits started getting sick, Ody and I found out that if you went on sick call and your temperature was less than 103, you got some pills, and maybe were excused from duty for a day. To leap over that hurdle and get admitted to the hospital, you had to hit 104 or better. The hospital was packed.

Making The Cut

Officially, the base was termed an Army Classification Center, and its purpose was to sort out the mass of raw aviation cadet recruits into those who were potentially qualified to enter training to become officers. However, there was also a further important breakdown, in which those who were not washed out right away were then split up into trainees to potentially become pilots, bombardiers, or navigators.

Therefore, the drill was to run everybody through a bunch of academic tests, physical exams, and psychological interviews with the shrinks. That was kind of like the first cut. Those who washed out instantly became GI privates. That pack, which proved to be about half, got shipped to places like Biloxi, Mississippi, where the Army had huge bases specializing in training aircraft ground mechanics and armorers of various types, as well as enlisted aircrew members, such as aerial gunners, radio operators, and flying maintenance men – typically called crew chiefs.

After about a week of general orientation and basic training, the two barracks of Squadron Eight began to be shuffled though the sorting out process.

First we got a very rigorous physical exam. Everyone had already experienced one when he enlisted, but this was three times as thorough. All of us aspiring cadets got probed front and rear, and had to stand in a line naked with feet spread, holding up both hands to display that we had five fingers on each hand and five toes on each foot. I guessed that an extra toe or so would have signaled to the docs that there was a problem with your genes somewhere.

Years later, I knew a captain in my squadron who actually had six fingers and six toes all the way around. It was not clear how he got through the system, but he was a graduate of the Citadel, so maybe that had something to do with it. The captain was a very sharp guy who was perfectly normal, sane and well balanced, so apparently the extra toe theory didn‘t always hold up.

A great deal of attention was paid to our vision. There were extensive color-blind tests, as well as tests for depth perception and acuity of vision. I had always had excellent vision and sailed through the regular eye test with 20/20, and also did very well on the depth perception. On the latter score, they had a test where a guy placed a small ruler-like device against the bridge of your nose and gradually ran a little steel ball on a track toward your forehead. We were told to keep our eyes on the ball as long as possible.

Ody had actually done a lot of eye exercises to further strengthen his vision, so when the guy ran the little ball in toward his face, he was able to follow it all the way in until his eyes were virtually crossed. The guy doing the test called out to his buddy, "Hey, look at this guy!" Nobody knew what that test was for, but whatever it was, we aced it. Ody had a little problem with depth perception, but after a recheck was given the okay.

Who's Crazy?

The next day, Ody and I were scheduled to see the psychiatrists, but at different hours. When I walked in, a goggle-eyed civilian eyeballed me strangely and then invited me to sit down. He proceeded to stare at me for about fifteen seconds and then said suddenly, "Did you ever screw your mother?"

I expected to be asked some strange questions, but that one struck me as so absurd as to be comical, and I laughed outright. (Later, I found out that if I had become very angry, it might have washed me out.) Next, the guy pulled out a picture of an airplane and asked what it was. I replied, "That's a North American B-25 Mitchell bomber."

The doctor nodded and said, "Who was Mitchell?"

I had read everything possible about airplanes since I was a little kid, and answered, "It's named after General Billy Mitchell, who believed that you could sink battleships with air power and was court-martialed for pushing his theories too hard in the wrong places – but they now realize that he was correct."

Then the psychiatrist asked, "What airplane do you want to fly?"

I replied, "The Republic P-47."

The doc said, "Why?"

I answered, "Because it has a 2,000 horsepower engine and is the most powerful U.S. fighter."

After some more small talk, I was excused.

Later, back at the barracks, I asked Ody how he made out with the shrink. Ody smirked and said, "That bastard thinks that all Greeks like boys, but I kept my cool, as I knew he was trying to set a trap! Besides, I'm used to that myth." That brought a laugh from me and all the guys who overheard it. As an afterthought, Ody added, "What the hell does he think accounts for the soaring Greek birth rate?"

Coordinated? Ha Ha. Maybe . . . .

Apparently, Ody and I both had gotten past the shrinks, because the next day we were scheduled to begin what were called psycho-motor tests, which were apparently designed to test a variety of skills, including dexterity, balance, logical reasoning, stability under stress, coordination, etc. There were a half dozen of these, which were really a riot.

For the first test, the cadet sat in a chair facing a black box that had a three-quarter-inch hole in the end of it. The test administrator handed the cadet a stylus, which consisted of a rod with a smaller articulated steel rod on the end that was free to bend but had springs that returned it to the straight position. An electrical cord ran from the stylus to the machine. The cadet was instructed to hold his arm straight out, with the end of the stylus inserted into the hole, which comprised a steel ring that conducted electricity. Whenever the rod touched the ring at any point, it made a beep and a counter kept track of the number of touches, which were penalties.

The test administrator got me all set with my arm stretched out and the rod in the middle, then yelled, "Go!" He also turned on a loud noise machine. I was doing my best to keep the damned thing from touching the sides, but it was making a fair number of beeps like a pinball machine, when the guy suddenly hollered into my ear, "You ***must*** learn to follow ***orders***!" This made me jump and set off a new volley of beeps.

Wow, I thought, *this is a bitch. I must be flunking this test.* I walked out of that test very disheartened.

The second test comprised a little cockpit with a kind of stick and rudder, and the cadet was supposed to keeps things straight and level by moving the controls while the cockpit moved around in a squirrely manner. I was fairly comfortable with that one, as I had a few hours of real stick time that I'd managed to get at a local airport before call-up. I wondered, however, how guys who had never sat in an airplane cockpit were expected to have a clue how to work the controls. I guessed it was typical of the paper pushers who invented all of that stupid stuff. I thought I did pretty well on that one.

Whoever thought up the third test obviously took fiendish delight in making people look stupid at something that appeared fairly easy. As in the first test, I was handed a stylus with an articulated end and a wire leading to the machine. Like the other stylus, the end would bend in any direction when you pressed it. However, the target setup was completely different. It resembled a big black phonograph record going around and around, but on one side of the record there was also a round steel disc about the size of a half dollar. When the record went around, the little disc went around with it, but it was on a track that also allowed it to move in toward the center and out toward the perimeter in a continual in-and-out movement.

This time, the test administrator said, "When I say 'go,' try to keep the stylus touching the little steel disc at all times, as you will be penalized for all of the time you are not making contact." Thus, the scoring was just the opposite of that for the first test. "Further," he announced, "you can't cheat by catching up to the little disc and then pushing down to anchor yourself, as that will bend the tip of the stylus and cause it to cut off contact completely, giving you a continuous penalty score for as long as the contact is broken."

The guy began the test and the thing started going around. I gave it my full concentration, but found it to be a real test of coordination skills, as the movement was compound and seemed almost random. The amount of time the stylus remained on the target seemed to be less than half of the total time for the test, and I emerged from that test really worried.

Later that day, at the barracks, I ran into a friend named Stu Rich, who had just come back from the same test. "Jesus Christ," Stu cursed, "I kept chasing the damned thing, but was always about two inches behind the SOB and couldn't catch up!" That got a good laugh, but it also gave me a bit of hope that others had found the test equally challenging.

The final test looked like a piece of cake. I went into a room with six other guys, and we were each seated in front of a board, which held about a dozen square pegs. One side of each peg was red, and the other side was painted yellow. The instructions were to simply lift each peg out, turn it 180 degrees (half a turn), and put it back into its hole. Very easy.

The test administrator gave the go-ahead, and everyone started moving pegs. I started okay, but then the pegs started getting stuck. I turned two only a quarter turn, instead of a half, and then, as that made me nervous, I actually dropped two pegs on the floor. Gradually, each of the other six guys finished and walked out of the room; I took about another thirty seconds before I got them all turned around.

Feeling quite rattled, I walked out of that room certain that I had washed out with my clumsiness. I trudged back to barracks in a dismal mood. That was the last of the psycho-motor tests.

The next day, the results were posted on the bulletin board in the day room, and everyone clustered around ten deep. Ody and I could not get to the board, but heard lot of yells and a few groans. Some were accompanied by remarks like, "Damn it! Navigator!" or "Oh no! Bombardier!"

I finally worked my way up to the board and eagerly looked for my name. My heart leapt into my throat; there it was – under "Pilot Training!" Somehow, in spite of my dismal showing in the last test, I had achieved my life's ambition, the chance to become an Army fighter pilot. In my excitement, I forgot to check for Ody's name, but Ody spotted the name Thoma a short way down the Pilot Training list from mine, and shouted gleefully, "Hey, we both made it!" He grabbed my hand to shake it.

Later, we found out that the square peg test that I messed up was designed to find people for bombardier training. Some idiot in headquarters had decided that because bombsights had little wheels and knobs to adjust when sighting, the bombardier had to be real dexterous with his fingers. Perhaps that had a certain logic to it, but it was not always consistent, as I had played the violin for ten years. Nevertheless, I gave three silent cheers for the idiots.

Kitchen Police

Many more activities took place at the classification center, including plenty of calisthenics and marching drills, which were expected, but one thing everyone hated was getting nailed for KP, which happened twice for both Ody and me. Everybody got his turns at it, and it was a twenty-four-hour drudge detail. They even had some cots at the mess hall, so the cadets could work a complete three-meal shift, comprising lunch and dinner, followed by a grand cleanup and a sleepover. After breakfast, they were finally out of there.

Like everything else in life, there were scams, rackets and ways to beat the system, and some guys were real pros at exploiting every advantage. There were a series of middle-of-the-road tasks, such as cleaning tables and setting up for the next meal, and generally helping the cooks. Ody nailed down a job as a cook's helper and also slinging the hash on the chow line, filling up guys' trays. Maybe they thought that since he was Greek, he was a natural at making and serving food. That was typical of Army reasoning – all Greeks run restaurants, don't they?

One daily task was potato peeling, which in the "olden" days had been done with peeling knives, but had gone modern and was now done by a potato peeling machine, which was nothing more than a big sander in shallow flowing water. I noticed it took the skins off, and in the process also wasted about half of the potato, which probably benefitted the local pigs – but that's progress, I concluded.

Then there was the great automatic dishwasher, which was universally known as the "china clipper." That was supposedly a pretty good job, but those suckers had to put up with so much steam and noise that it was like working in a ship's boiler room.

The fattest job was "storekeeper," as the guy who got that job stood in a lordly manner leaning over the Dutch door to the storeroom, grandly handing out supplies to the working slobs, while he also got to munch his head off on anything that looked good. The old pros, who had done a lot of KP, headed for that job like a shot and usually aced all of the new guys out.

Then there was the worst job of all, "garbage detail," which I got nailed for one time. You not only got to carry out a lot of filled garbage cans but at the end of each shift you had to scrub out every can cleanly and have it inspected, as if you were going to eat out of it!

Laughin'Boy

Maxwell Army Air Base, Montgomery, Alabama

Having made our way through the initial hurdles, we were now officially aviation cadets and got to wear the uniform with the little wings and propellers on our collars and hats. At the end of a month's testing, marching, and physical training, those of us who were still around boarded a train for Montgomery, Alabama. We were beginning to look and feel like aviation cadets, and looked eagerly toward the next phase, which comprised two months of preflight training. It never dawned on us that when we arrived at Maxwell Army Air Base, we would not be just aviation cadets, but would be that lowest order of beings – underclassmen!

A group of upperclassmen met us at the train and lost no time starting the hazing process and putting us in our proper place. Their pet name for the new guys was "Zombies." The next two hours, before we got within the safety of our newly assigned barracks, were a blur of marching, standing at attention, hitting a brace with chin in and shoulders back, sounding off with name rank and serial number, and obeying countless nonsensical orders, all of which we had to jump to carry out.

The last thing the upperclassmen did before releasing us to our assigned quarters was to hand each of us a little booklet, which contained lots of information about Maxwell AAB, including the names, ranks, and positions of all of the currently assigned big brass. We were ordered to memorize all of the names and be able to recite them if asked at the next day's roll call. Years later, I still remembered the name of the squadron adjutant, as I used word association to study up. His name was Bell, and he was the guy who "sounded off."

The days that followed were a mass of activities, much of which were conducted under a barrage of hazing by the upperclassmen. Whenever we were within our assigned barracks, we were safe from hazing, but when we stepped one inch outside, we were fair game.

As Zombies, we had to walk on certain designated paths, called "ratlines," all of which had square corners. Actually, we never walked, but marched at a rapid pace, specifically 140 paces per minute, with eyes straight ahead. At any moment, an upperclassman might order,

"Halt, Mister! Step off of the ratline." We were then fair game for virtually anything.

Ody, who was carrying a bit of chub, was a quick target for one of the upperclassmen. Part of the cadet uniform was a GI belt, which was made of a form of webbing, with a brass buckle that clamped onto the end. Belts were issued in long lengths; the cadets simply cut them off to accommodate their waist size.

That particular upperclassman, eyeing Ody's midriff, called him to attention, took a firm hold of the end of Ody's belt, then called, "Right, face!" Ody swiveled right ninety degrees, and the hazer held fast to the end, tightening it by about two inches. The upperclassman said, "Cut this portion off, print your name and serial number on it, and present it to me tomorrow morning!"

For a couple of weeks, Ody had to suck in his gut just to get his belt closed. Fortunately, by the end of the month, we had all been leaned down by so much running and exercise that his waist had shrunk to about thirty inches.

I became a different kind of target for some of the upperclassmen, as I became known as a "laughin' boy." I was actually enjoying the experience immensely and found it so amusing that I could not keep a smile off of my face.

This resulted in some very special attention, which typically went as follows: "Mister, wipe that smile off of your face!" (I would then proceed to take my hand and actually wipe the smile off, but sometimes ended up with another smile.) The upperclassman would shout, "Mister, I said wipe that smile off your face and don't let me see it again! Now put it in your pocket."

After several such days, I would be stopped again, and the orders would go something like this: "Mister, how many smiles do you have in your pocket?"

"Eight, sir."

"Very well; now call them out and give them close order drill."

My response was: "Smiles – fall in, in close order. Smiles – tensh-hut! Dress right-dress! Ready – front! Left – face! Forward – march! [This was spoken like Ma-harch, with a great exhalation of breath.] Hut, two, three, four... To the rear – march. To the rear – march. By the left flank – march. By the right flank – march. Smiles – halt! Right – face! Parade – rest! Smiles – tensh-hut! Prepare for inspection."

While being a "laughin' boy"got me a lot of attention, I soon discovered that it was a good kind of attention, as there were a few others who often got irritated and lost their tempers. Those guys became major targets and had a hard time all the way through preflight training.

Maxwell Air Base was the great merging pot where all of the aviation cadets underwent two intensive months of special training, designed to refine their military skills while preparing them for actual flight training.

Thus, we began a daily regimen of classroom academics, marching in large formations, and lots of calisthenics, including a great deal of running. The latter was designed to toughen up our general physical condition while leaning bodies down and generally speeding up physical reflexes.

The idea was that if we were going to enter into combat flying, our bodies should be conditioned to contend with the high-altitude conditions and the high G forces that might be encountered.

In addition to organized calisthenics, the squadron began a series of runs, which became longer and longer until they included seven mile runs around the entire airfield. These outings did not consist entirely of running, as the instructor would sometimes call for a walk for a certain length of time before resuming a fast trot pace.

I was a lean and muscular kid who had been conditioned by years of bike-riding and swimming, but some of the guys who were carrying a bit of chub had a hard time with those extended cross-country runs. Some of them would start panting and eventually fall out of formation, at which point they were threatened with being washed out of the program. Ody was still a little bit overweight, as he enjoyed eating, but it soon melted off under the grind, and he had no trouble.

It was never clear how many actually washed out, but we noticed that some were singled out for additional training, and a few were seen running with seat-pack parachutes strapped on, a very awkward situation to say the least.

At that time, all of the radio and lighting navigational aids were identified by aural or visual flashing of code identifiers. Hence, it was necessary for all aviation cadets to learn International (Morse) Code to the extent that they could send and receive at the rate of at least six words per minute. I got a real break there, as I had learned code when I was twelve years old and had spent many an hour taking down messages from the ham radio operators, which could be picked up on my family‘s home radio. This experience really came in handy, as the first day in code training I took and passed the test, which gave me a free period for about a month. With the very busy daily schedule, this was a godsend.

Maxwell AAB was home to thousands of cadets, and once per week the entire cadet corps paraded to military band music, always in sixteen-abreast formations, marching down the main streets of the base, usually with everyone singing the various cadet marching songs. Those Saturday parades always went to the central parade ground where a complete "pass in review" was staged for the commanding general. Distinguished guests sometimes visited the base, and on one occasion we were given the command, "Eyes, right," and there was President Franklin D. Roosevelt, accompanied by Great Britain’s Lord Halifax.

One thing constantly emphasized at Maxwell was the cadet "honor code," which was a carryover from our country's military academies. Thus, offenses such as cheating on an exam or lying to a superior were treated gravely, with punishment quickly enforced.

These practices were basically good institutions, which were not a problem for cadets who simply toed the line. However, on occasion they led to some scenes that seemed to come right out of some kind of "B" movie and were actually downright comical (although one had better not laugh). For example, one night while everyone in Squadron Eight barracks was soundly snoozing, the lights suddenly came on and the command was heard, "Everyone up and fall out in the street in front of the barracks in full Class A uniform [which included white gloves] in ten minutes."

About two hundred sleepy cadets quickly dressed and rushed out to stand in formation. We were quickly called to attention, then given the commands, "Dress, right – dress," "Ready – front," and "Parade – rest."

With everyone standing formally and not a word being spoken, the squadron adjutant called out, "Attention to orders!" He then proceeded to read out a statement, which went something like, "Whereas Cadet __________ has been found guilty of cheating on an exam and has therefore violated the honor code, he is hereby dismissed from the corps, and his name will never again be mentioned in the Corps of Cadets!"

Ody didn't catch the name of the offender, and whispered to the guy next to him, "What was that name?" The guy didn't answer, for obvious reasons, and the subject was closed forever.

Another time, the entire cadet corps was paraded to the central parade ground and a somewhat similar scene took place – only, this time, the offender was actually a cadet officer with chevrons. With each of the squadrons standing at attention, the offending cadet officer was marched to the front, a statement of his offense was read out, and an officer actually ripped off his chevrons, which had already been partially detached.

It was pretty dramatic and I found myself waiting for the next move, which might have been to break his sword in two, or punch a hole through his hat, but that never happened. It all sounded a bit melodramatic and somewhat comical, but in discussing the event later, Ody and I had to conclude that the application of the honor code was highly effective in making everyone better cadets and officer candidates.

"Ginny"

Shortly before completion of Maxwell's training program, all of us cadets (who did not have punishment tours from "gigs" to march off) were granted what was generally known as "Open Post," which meant we had a free weekend and were allowed to go into the local town of Montgomery. Unfortunately, Ody was one of those with tours to work off, so I went into town by myself.

That was a weekend I would never forget. Montgomery was a graceful old southern town, which had at one time been the capital of the Confederacy, and the old Capital building was still standing. After roaming around the town, I decided to go to a local movie and took a seat near the rear of the theater. Immediately after taking my seat, I was entranced by the lovely girl who was sitting directly in front of me with her family.

The movie was some type of comedy and she, her mother, father, and brother were all having a great time, laughing at various scenes. The girl had lovely, curly light brunette hair and a melodious laugh, which rang like the tone of a bell ringer's bell – not one of those high tinkling ones but the kind that sang out. I could not believe it.

While I was not a bold girl chaser, I had known many fine girls in my growing up years, and considered many of them to be special friends. But I had never known one that knocked me right off my feet like this one. I told myself that I was being foolish and to just forget it, as that family did not know me from Adam, and managed to sit through the movie.

Then an amazing thing happened that I marveled about long afterward. As everyone exited the theater, the mother and her two children stopped to visit the restrooms, and, as chance would have it, the father was standing out in the front waiting for them. I had never done anything like this in my life, but my heart leapt into control and I thought, *If I let this girl go out of my life, I will never see her again.*

I had never been a brassy person, but some driving force took command of me, and without thinking about what I was doing, I walked up to the father and said to him, "Excuse me, sir, but would it be possible for me to meet your daughter?"

It was absolutely crazy and I would not have blamed the man if he told me to get lost, but after registering some surprise, and probably a bit of shock, the man turned out to be a Southern gentleman. Afterwards, I reflected that the fact that I was in uniform was probably the only thing that saved the situation, as almost immediately thereafter the mother appeared with the girl and her brother.

After a bit of flustering and asking my name, the man was kind enough to introduce me to his wife and family. It turned out that their name was Power, the lovely daughter and her brother were Virginia and James, and they lived in Prattville, a suburb of Montgomery.

After some small talk, the two parents conferred and (taking pity on the poor fool) invited me to come to their home the following Sunday and join them for dinner, if I could get a pass. I thanked them profusely and said that I would phone them and let them know. They gave me their phone number and we parted with a handshake.

I left there in a daze with my heart in my throat, wondering whether I was crazy, but knowing that if I had let her walk away I might have regretted it all my life.

I also thought, *I have to get a pass for next week, and need to be very careful that I don't pick up any demerits during the week, with tours to walk off on the weekend.* Punishment tours consisted of an hour of carefully walking fifty paces back and forth with a rifle on one's shoulder and an "about face" at each end.

When I told Ody about it, he responded, "Man, you really surprise me. That took a lot of guts to pull that off. What got into you?"

"I can't explain it," I said. "Something just took hold of me and was driving me to do it, and I still can't believe it happened."

Pondering that a bit, Ody pronounced, "I guess when the right girl comes along, nothing else matters. I hope it works out for you." He did not know it at the time, but he was to find out just how perceptive those words of his were.

I weathered what seemed like an eternal week and thankfully managed to get a pass for Sunday. Following the Power's instructions, I took a local bus and was dropped off at a country road intersection, then walked about five hundred feet to the Powers' house, which was surrounded by farm fields. I had managed to pick up a small bouquet of flowers in Montgomery.

I arrived at about 11:30, duked out in my best khakis, brass buckle polished to mirror finish, shoes shined to their best sheen, and proudly sporting the aviation cadet insignias of a little gold wing and a vertical two-bladed propeller. I rang the doorbell, and the door was opened by Virginia herself, which left me a bit tongue-tied in greeting her properly. I then made the mistake of handing her the bouquet, which was a bit of a faux pas, as it should have gone to her mother. However, she neatly picked up the error and said, "Thank you. My mother will appreciate these."

Mrs. Power greeted me in a warm and kindly manner, and I shook hands once again with the younger brother James, whom I had met at the theater. The father came in several minutes later and we all had a nice little exploratory chit chat, after which Mrs. Power excused herself to the kitchen where she was preparing dinner. Everyone was dressed in Sunday finery, as the family had just returned from church in Prattville.

Mr. Power was a tall man with a deep voice and a courtly manner, which had already impressed me at our initial meeting. He immediately recognized that I was quite nervous and did his best to put me at ease by steering the conversation into areas about which I could talk freely, such as my training and how it was progressing.

It was almost a surreal storybook scene. There I was, a Yankee kid from a northern steel town, invading the sacred heart of the Confederacy with my eye on a cherished Southern belle.

The last thing I wanted to do was to come off as a brassy Yankee, invoking memories of the not too distant past. Virginia, for her part, contributed in a polite and lighthearted manner, and her family did their best to make me feel at ease. Clearly, this was an initial test, and I made up my mind to do my best to pass it.

I had told them that my name was Edward M. Nebinger, and they asked what the M. stood for. They found it interesting that my middle name was Montgomery, as Montgomery was the first capital of the Confederacy, and wondered if there was any connection.

I did not know, but explained that my direct ancestors, on both the Nebinger and Montgomery sides, had settled in the York/Lancaster areas of Pennsylvania, and had been with Washington at Valley Forge and Trenton. I suspected that being a "Son of the American Revolution" helped my case, as historical traditions and ancestry were clearly of importance in the Deep South.

I didn't mention, however, that several of my ancestors had been with the Yankee Army in the Civil War.

In a short while, Mrs. Power announced dinner and invited everyone to come to the table. After the father said grace, conversation proceeded in like manner, with a couple of rough spots.

One area that could have landed me in deep water was religion. It turned out that the Power's belonged to the Methodist Church in Prattville, and Virginia played the organ in the church. My family, on the other hand, while basically Protestant, did not even attend church regularly. However, I soon discovered that the Powers, while solid churchgoers, were not zealots, and we moved on to other subjects.

After dinner, Mr. Power invited everyone to join him in a drive to visit the local drug store and soda fountain in Prattville for an ice cream sundae, which sounded like a great idea.

It must have been a Sunday tradition for many people in Prattville, as the soda fountain proved to be a social hub that hummed with conversation, fun, and laughter while people enjoyed their favorite treats. It was a move of genius on the part of the host, which eased the formality and lightened the conversation all around. The Powers greeted many friends, and it was clear that they were a prominent family in Prattville.

Afterwards, Mr. Power said he had to make a brief visit to his place of business. He ran a substantial-sized factory in Prattville, which had actually been the local cotton gin at one time, but had been converted to industrial production and, under wartime pressures, was busily turning out small practice bombs for training purposes. I expressed interest and was invited to come along for a short tour of the factory, while the rest of the family did a bit of window-shopping in town.

Mr. Power asked me quite a few questions about the Bethlehem Steel Company and what my father did there. I explained that my father had been with the company since the twenties and worked in the company headquarters in Bethlehem, where he was an estimator. His job was to prepare the detailed specifications for the precise types and grades of steel to be used on each fabrication job, as well as the exact placement of the rivet holes and other associated parameters. Mr. Power‘s keen interest in the steel industry and its technical aspects suggested that he was probably an engineer.

I found the visit very interesting, but also understood clearly that my host was using the opportunity to further test my character and life experiences.

Dear Mrs. Power,

Thank you for the kind invitation to your home on Sunday as well as for the delicious dinner and the pleasant trip to Prattville which followed thereafter. I enjoyed my visit very much and learned a great deal about life in a small Southern town.

Please accept my apology for the abrupt manner in which I inserted myself into your family circle, and extend my thanks to Mr. Power for his exceptional kindness and courtesy. I assure you I have never done anything as bold as that in my entire life, and I hope that you will accept my motivation as an honorable one. I want you to know, also, that although I am a kid from a northern steel town, my parents raised me to respect the privacy of others, and that my behavior does not represent the norm in Bethlehem, PA.

Frankly, looking back at the situation, it is a wonder that Mr. Power did not toss me into the street – but he is obviously too much of a gentleman for that. Perhaps the fact that I was in uniform saved me.

I also appreciated the friendly manner in which Virginia and James received my visit. It was interesting to learn that Virginia is accomplished enough on the organ to play it at your church, which suggests that her training began at a very young age.

Life in Preflight School at Maxwell Field continues at a hectic but necessary pace. I have always wanted to be an Army Fighter

Pilot, so I am finding all phases of our training interesting. Of course, I am a long way from achieving my objective, as the washout rate in pilot training is very high. However, I have always believed that one can never achieve an objective if he does not at least try.

Thank you again for your special kindness and courtesy.

Sincerely, Ed Nebinger

~~~~~~~~~~~~~~~~~~~~~~~~~~~~~~~~

Aviation Cadet Edward Nebinger
Squadron H-8,
Maxwell AAB
Montgomery, Alabama

Dear Edward,

Well, you certainly know how to spread a little butter to smooth things over. Your "Thank You" letter to my mother was most cleverly written and demonstrated strength of character. In any case, it certainly hit the right mark with my parents, who gave me their OK to correspond with you, should I so choose.

Do I so choose? I think so, as you are certainly different from any of the boys I have known in school or in Prattville.

After our dinner on Sunday, James and I shared a secret laugh at the way you were struggling to cut my mother's steak, but I know that is not kind. In any case, you managed it very well. Momma is a good cook but she always seems to turn steak into shoe leather!

You remarked about my playing the organ in the church and speculated that I got an early start in musical training. You are correct. I had an aunt who was quite accomplished on the piano and she started giving me lessons when I was five. We did not
~~~~~~~~~~~~~~~~~~~~~~~~~~~~~~~~

have a piano at first, but later picked up the little spinet that you saw in our house. After a couple of years my aunt told my parents that I was doing well, and while she played the piano she did not consider herself a teacher. She suggested that I transfer to a teacher whom she recommended in Montgomery. I was with that teacher for about seven years and still see her occasionally, but have more recently transferred my main interest to the organ.

How did I get to play the organ in our church? It happened in an odd way. One afternoon I was visiting our church and the former organist, Mr. Morgan, was practicing on the organ. We talked a bit and I asked him if I could try something on the organ. While there is a basic similarity in the organ and piano keyboards, the many pedals and stops make it almost a whole new world. He showed me a few things and seemed to think I had some aptitude for it. After some further discussion he asked me if I would like to take some free instruction from him, and I jumped at the offer. For a couple of years after that I had an hourly lesson from him at the church, one evening per week.

A year ago he elected to retire from active playing, as he was advanced in age and his health was not good. He recommended me for the post, which is of course an unpaid community service function. There was some concern in our church council about my young age, but upon his recommendation, they accepted me and I have been playing there since. Unfortunately, he died shortly thereafter. He was a kind man and an excellent teacher, and I am grateful to follow in his footsteps. I enjoy it very much, and it adds another meaningful and challenging dimension to my life.

That was long winded. How about you? You seem to have an interest in music. Do you have a musical background?

My Daddy found it interesting that your family has had some association and experience with the steel industry, as he has a technical background. Birmingham, which is our own steel center, is not far away, and while at Bama U. he was one of the students selected to take some special courses related to steelmaking, and also spent some time at the plant.

James and I enjoyed meeting you, and I'm sure my family will invite you again, while you are at Maxwell AAB.

You may write to me at this address, if you wish.

Yours very truly,

Virginia Power

I met Virginia and her family on a few other occasions prior to my departure for primary flight school. On one occasion I sat through a church service while Virginia played the organ in the church. She was an accomplished young high school graduate, and I was encouraged when she looked in the mirror while playing and smiled at me.

That was also the day that she told me I could call her "Ginny," which was the name everyone in Prattville used. We also spent an afternoon in a park and zoo in Montgomery, and on another occasion had a country picnic, in which the Powers introduced me to something that I would have never imagined – pineapple sandwiches with mayonnaise on them. I found them a bit strange by Northern tastes, but had to admit they had a certain appeal.

It was an odd, almost Victorian situation, a far cry from many wartime romances, if it could be called that. All of our meetings were well chaperoned by one of her parents, sometimes accompanied by her younger brother.

It might truly be described as a cautious "arms-length" affair. There were no romantic scenes whatsoever; in fact I never even kissed the girl. However, there was some quiet understanding and magic that seemed to accompany our relationship. Nothing was promised and nothing was said, but she never sought to end our relationship – whatever it was – and when we said goodbye after our last meeting, she surprised me by handing me a little framed color photograph of herself, smiling, with auburn curls and all. That was good enough for me.

CHAPTER THREE

MAGNOLIAS IN THE MORNING

Hawkins Field, Jackson, Mississippi

Looking back at my early training days, I can say with absolute certainly that primary flight school was the essence of flying. It was all stick and rudder, open cockpits with the wind in your face if you skidded, feeling the airplane dance in the turbulence, and sometimes smelling magnolias or other flowers as you climbed aloft in the morning.

After primary, where we learned to take charge of the airplane, all the rest was procedures and increasing degrees of sophistication.

Please indulge me, therefore, if I dredge back from my memory bank some of the exquisite details of that early phase of training and relive once again its romance.

Ody and I were among about eighty of the aviation cadets who had been selected for primary flight training at Jackson, Mississippi. We boarded two large buses, which drove for about five hours before delivering us to our new school.

Our arrival was a pleasant surprise. Our primary flying school was located in the countryside outside of Jackson and was a beautiful facility with the commandant's office, the cadets' barracks, mess hall, and athletic fields all enclosed within a nice white picket fence.

Aside from a flagpole with an American flag flying proudly, it did not even resemble a military facility. In fact, as I later learned, it had been part of Parks Air College before the war balloon had gone up. Directly across the country road that ran by the facility was a small airport, called Hawkins Field, with two hangars and a flight line full of Stearman biplanes. My heart soared when I saw the airplanes, as I had always wanted to fly a biplane – and there they were, waiting!

As new cadets arriving at flight school, we were very much aware of the fact that we would not only be the "underclassmen" but would also be known as "dodo birds," i.e., the lowest order of birds who couldn't fly. We had also been warned that the washout rate at primary flight school was quite high, and that anyone who didn't cut it would be quickly on his way to a large facility at Biloxi, Mississippi, where they trained people for various ground jobs.

All of us new cadets piled out of the bus and were called to attention for roll call and a welcoming address by the Commandant. We were then given our barracks assignments and dismissed, after which an amusing little scene took place.

A salty upperclassman, who was actually wearing a flying helmet and goggles, sauntered up and announced grandly, "Well, well, what a great bunch of dodos. Let me tell you, the last bunch arrived here in two buses, just like you guys. Two months later, what was left departed for basic flight in two taxi cabs!" Everybody laughed – but not too loudly. (Basic flight training was intermediate level.)

The next day, the cadets were issued flying gear, which comprised a cotton flying suit, aviator's helmet, and goggles. We also got our assignments to individual flight instructors, most of whom were civilian pilots. Each instructor was assigned six students, and rumor had it that every instructor had orders to wash out at least two – a rather disturbing thought.

My assigned instructor was Mr. Barnes, a man of about fifty who appeared to be a soft spoken, quiet individual. I did not know it at the time, but I was really not only lucky, but privileged to have been assigned to Mr. Barnes.

The first thing my instructor explained to our little group was that until we soloed, we were not allowed to wear our goggles on the front side of our helmets, unless we were actually in the airplane. Otherwise, all of us dodos were required to wear them backwards; i.e., reversed on our helmets. He then gave each student the assigned time for his first flight, which in my case was two hours hence.

At the assigned time, I met Mr. Barnes in the briefing room and listened carefully as my instructor explained that the Stearman was an open cockpit biplane with fixed landing gear, powered by a Continental 220-horsepower radial engine. He further explained the basic rudiments of flight and told me what we would practice, which was basically straight and level flight, holding wings level and nose on the horizon, then turns left and right, and finally some stalls straight ahead with and without power.

I actually had a few hours in a Piper Cub, which I had picked up on weekends in Pennsylvania. However, I made a point of not mentioning that to Mr. Barnes. I had heard in preflight school that the last thing Army flight instructors wanted to hear was that one of their students thought he was already a hot pilot. No way was I going to shoot my mouth off about that. Let the Army train me its own way.

After showing me how to don and operate (if necessary) my seat-pack parachute, he led the way to an airplane, got me seated, and strapped into the rear cockpit. He showed me how to operate the Gosport speaking tube, which was a pretty crude device comprising a mouthpiece and earphones connected by some rubber tubes. He also acquainted me with the basic controls, and gave one final piece of advice: "If you get sick, you get to clean the cockpit."

Then he signaled to a lineman who jumped onto the left front tire, inserted a crank into a hole in the fuselage behind the engine, and began winding up what was called an "inertia coupling starter." Essentially, it was a flywheel which was revved up to a rapid speed, at which point the pilot yelled, "Clear prop!" Then the lineman pulled a small cable which engaged the starter and cranked over the engine enough to start it.

Mr. Barnes got the engine settled down, taxied to the end of a grass field where he spent a few minutes checking the ignition magnetos, looked left and right carefully to see that the field and flight approach were clear, and took off.

While Mr. Barnes climbed to 2,000 feet, I was enjoying every moment. It was spring, and the countryside underneath was checkered with hundreds of green fields growing crops, and the temperature was quite comfortable. He leveled the airplane, then told me to place my feet on the rudder pedals and take hold of the stick, then follow him as he demonstrated level flight and turns. He explained how to keep the wings level and keep the nose of the airplane basically on the horizon in order to maintain level flight.

After allowing me to practice that a bit, he said, "Now follow me through in some gentle turns and note how I coordinate the stick and rudder to maintain altitude while turning." He then turned the controls over to me and asked me to try some turns, which were relatively simple, although I lost a little altitude in the turns. Then he said, "Okay, I am going to steepen my bank and tighten the turn. Notice that as my bank gets steeper, I have to pull back on the stick to hold my altitude. Actually, as I pull back on the stick, the elevators are helping us turn."

He demonstrated and said, "Your turn; let's see how you do." I rolled into a medium bank and started to turn, but the nose started dropping until I felt the stick start to come back, and Barnes said, "More back pressure on the stick to keep the nose up." I complied and was surprised to feel the way I was being pushed down in the seat by the G forces.

"Okay," Barnes said, "keep her coming around, holding your altitude." I made a couple of 360-degree turns, in which I found myself sawing on the stick a bit as the nose seemed to move up and down on the horizon.

Then he said, "Okay, you are getting the idea. The important thing is that you are making corrections. After a while, you will learn to feed steady back pressure into the stick and hold it steady as long as you want to maintain your turn, then release the back pressure slowly as you roll out of your turn."

After some more practice, Barnes said, "Alright, I have the airplane. Make sure your seat belt is locked and tightened." He then climbed a little higher, made a couple of clearing turns to make sure no other airplanes were around us, and proceeded to wring the airplane out!

He dropped the nose and accelerated to about 150 miles per hour, then pulled it straight up in what I thought was going to be a loop, but at the top of the loop the controls suddenly moved rapidly in every direction and the aircraft whipped into a couple of rapid rolls like it was on greased bearings. For a moment I was disoriented, but found it more exhilarating than anything I had ever experienced!

As Barnes was making his recovery, I noticed that he was watching me in the mirror mounted on the trailing edge of the upper wing. He was probably expecting me to be white-faced, but saw instead that I was grinning from ear to ear, and I yelled into the Gosport, "Wow, that was great! Can we do that again?" (forgetting to call him "sir," as I had been instructed).

Barnes shook his head and said, "Not today. I'll show you some more after you get some stick time under your belt."

My instructor then began demonstrating basic stalls, straight ahead, with and without power, showing me how a wing, which wanted to drop in a stall, could be brought up by proper application of rudder.

Finally, after some further practice, we returned to the field for a landing and he said, "Follow me through on the stick and rudders, lightly, as I make the landing." I did as instructed and felt the instructor‘s controlled movements as he moved the control gently to keep the wings level while gradually bringing the stick back as the aircraft skimmed the landing surface. The landing was three-point with a slight skip on the grass field, but very nice overall. After we taxied in, Mr. Barnes showed me how to tidy the cockpit for the next student, by fastening the seatbelt in place, etc.

As we were walking in, carrying our parachutes, I apologized to my instructor for failing to call him "sir." Mr. Barnes, who was apparently a "good old boy," just nodded and made no comment, but I could see that he was pleased overall with the first lesson, as his new student had not gotten sick, and apparently enjoyed it immensely. I asked him what the name of that maneuver was and he answered, smiling, "It was basically an Immelmann, with a snap-and-a-half at the top." I chalked that up as something I definitely had to learn in the future.

Glory Days

Four of the others in my flight instruction group included cadets named Molnar, Olesky, Perchak, and Sefranek, whose names indicated that they probably came for the same Pennsylvania region I did, and that their names had come off of some alphabetical list.

However, there was also a young guy named Eino Liimitaanen, from Finland, which was interesting, as the Finns were actually fighting on the German side. Unfortunately, the Finns had been virtually forced into that decision by historical events, as Russia had invaded Finland in 1939.

I was reasonably acquainted with what had occurred in the so-called Winter War in Finland, as I had followed the events in the newspaper. The Finns surprised everyone by putting up a hard fight in which the "Russkies" lost a great many men, but finally prevailed by sheer numbers, then settled by grabbing the Karelian Isthmus, which Russia wanted for a naval base on the Baltic.

Eino's father had been one of those who fought the Russians, wearing white garments for camouflage and gliding silently through the forests on skis. The Finns hated the Russians, and really had no use for the Nazis either, but their country had been increasingly drawn to support the Germans as a matter of self defense. Somehow, Eino's family had gotten him out of Finland and into the U.S. Army Air Corps' aviation cadets program, which demonstrated that not all Finns were in agreement with their position in the war, as Finland had historically been a friend of the United States.

Eino and I struck up camaraderie that first day, and I learned how avidly he wanted to become a pilot so he could fight against the Germans. However, on his first flight the next morning, Eino got violently sick and tossed his cookies all over the cockpit, which he had to scrub out after landing. Later that day, I talked to him on the flight line and found him very much discouraged. Although I was a rank amateur myself, I tried to reassure him by suggesting that he would probably get over it in a day or so. Unfortunately, it happened again the next day.

The weather in Jackson was warm and balmy, so that even at a couple of thousand feet, it was quite comfortable in a summer flying suit. After my first two flights, we switched cockpits, with Barnes in the rear one. After reviews of basic turns and coordination exercises, Mr. Barnes placed special focus on stall control and recovery. We went over stalls straight ahead, with both power on and off, then progressed to accelerated stalls in turns.

He also demonstrated how to pull the airplane slowly up into a full power stall and hold it there while walking it by using the rudder on alternate sides to keep a wing from dropping. He then turned the airplane over to me, and I did a reasonable job of keeping the wings level in a near stall condition. I was really surprised at how effective the rudder was in achieving this.

He then showed me how to induce a stall in the airplane during a turn. He said it was essential to be aware of the airplane beginning to shudder, and ease off the back pressure in the turn, applying power to prevent it from flipping over out of control. I took a shot at that and he seemed to be satisfied, saying, "Okay, that was not bad. Now I'm going to demonstrate that if you fly into a fully stalled condition and do not take proper corrective action, the airplane can easily flip over into a tailspin."

Most of the farmers' fields below were rectangular and were, in general, oriented to north/south borders. The first essential thing he stressed was the importance of making clearing turns both left and right before entering maneuvers that could cause the airplane to collide with other airplanes that might be beneath or nearby. Then he said, "Follow me through on the controls, but don't panic, as I am going to actually help make it spin and hold it in the spin for a bit before recovery."

He eased the power back to idle, pulled the nose up slightly, and held it there. At the moment the airplane began to shudder, he kicked in right rudder and pulled the stick straight back, holding the controls in that position. The airplane immediately snapped over into a right tailspin with nose headed almost straight down while revolving like it was on a bearing.

Barnes said, "I am going to keep it spinning for a bit; count the number of turns." I counted to three and noted some rapid and precise control movements, which stopped the spin exactly on the same heading in which we entered it.

My instructor then allowed the airspeed to build up and recovered from the dive, slowly applying power to climb back up. While doing so, he explained, "When the airplane nears a stall, pushing full rudder rapidly in either direction will cause it to snap over in that direction. At the same time, holding the stick full back and full rudder in will keep the airplane spinning in a fully stalled condition until a recovery is made."

He continued, "In order to recover on a desired heading, you need to reverse the rudder a half turn before you want to stop the rotation, and then pop the stick forward to bring the bird out of the stall on the exact desired heading. Recovery is immediate and effective. Actually, if you have enough altitude, you can just let go of the controls and the Stearman will fly itself out, but that is pretty sloppy."

The next day, my lesson actually ran about twenty minutes over, as we reviewed the whole stall regime, including initial entry into spins and recovery. At one point, he said, "Now let's see you do a full stall into a spin entry with a quick recovery." After I made a quick recovery twice in a row, Barnes got interested in challenging me to recover from spins on specified headings.

He made a couple of clearing turns and said, "Now let's see you do a three turn spin to the left, starting on a heading of south, and recovering on the same heading."

I thought that was fantastic stuff and gave it my full concentration. On the first one, I missed my recovery direction by about fifteen degrees, but was feeling pretty good about it overall for a first shot.

My instructor said, "Okay, climb back up and do it again." I climbed back up to 3,000 feet, put the airplane on a heading of south, and was just pulling up the nose into a stall, when he grabbed the stick and yelled, "What did you forget?" Like a thunderbolt, I suddenly remembered I had forgotten my clearing turns and my ego shrunk to the size of a pea. Chagrined, I said, "Sorry, sir," made the required clearing turns, entered the spin, and pulled off a fairly decent recovery on heading.

"That wasn't bad," said Barnes, who took the controls and flew for a few minutes. "You have the airplane. Take me home and show me a good landing."

I took over the controls, looked around, and couldn't find the field. Sheepishly, I said, "I'm not sure which direction it is to the field."

Barnes, who knew very well that I, like all new student pilots, had become disoriented while focusing on the spins, said, "I have it." He took control and rocked the airplane steeply up on a wingtip. There the field was, directly underneath us! My ego once again took a severe tumble and landed in the floor of the cockpit.

Barnes just laughed and said, "You want to learn to keep a sense of orientation of where you are when you're flying. Most airplanes have some kind of navigation aids, but this is not one of them."

I made a decent landing with one small skip, but Barnes was satisfied with the day's work. After we parked the airplane, he said, "All in all, that was a pretty good session. Next time we will review some procedures and maybe try a couple of aerobatics." My heart soared, and I replied, "I will look forward to that, sir."

Modesto Junior College

Modesto, California

Rich Andrino and Ray Burwell were sitting having lunch with two girls in a little pavilion behind Modesto Junior College. Andy was busily jabbering with a cute Filipino girl who came from a barrio called Angeles, in Pampanga Province, quite near to Clark Air Force Base in the Philippine Islands. The girl had come to visit her uncle in California and had been stranded in the U.S. when the Japanese invaded the Philippines in 1942.

This was actually a fortuitous event, as it kept her out from under the Japanese invaders, who did not treat the conquered natives kindly. Further, her uncle, who had been in the U.S. for almost fifteen years, was a successful truck gardener in the San Joaquin Valley, and was able to send her to Modesto Junior College to get a good start on her education, with the longer term goal of her becoming a U.S. citizen.

Andrino, whose parents were both Filipino, could speak a little Tagalog – not very much – but he kept trying it out on the girl, and they were having a good time together.

Burwell, between bites of his sandwich, had his eyes focused one hundred percent on a girl named Lola Almaris, who was hands down the hottest looking chick on the entire campus. A russet-haired gal with bewitching green eyes, she had a shape to kill and didn‘t mind advertising it. She was wearing a skirt, which was not only about two inches shorter than the fashion, but tight as a drum across a fantastic ass.

Ray‘s eyes at the moment, however, were focused on the cleavage of a matched pair of world-class jugs that held his eyes like a pair of magnets. In fact, he was just wrapping up the details of where they would meet for a date that night. Ray had definite plans for getting to at least third base, if not a home run that night. Lola looked like she might throw him an easy pitch that he could knock right out of the ball park.

The pals, however, who had been in two separate worlds, were brought back to earth when both of the girls had to run to an early class.

Watching that fantastic butt wagging as they walked away, Ray sighed and said, "Oh, yeah!" and Andy laughed.

Then, coming back to the present, Ray asked, "Do you think they are ever going to call us up?"

"They better, or this whole damned war is going to be over before we can get there. Our forces are already beginning to close in on the Japs in the Pacific, so it can‘t be too long before they throw in the towel."

Ray nodded his head in agreement. "I‘m ready to go any time – just as long as it isn‘t tonight!" Ray said, raising his eyebrows. Andy laughed and thought, *That guy is incredible – I don't know how the hell he does it – but every good-looking babe that comes along seems to fall all over him! Maybe I better study his technique.*

A week later, they got orders calling them to active duty, and shortly thereafter were shipped to Emporia, Kansas, for initial processing. Apparently, the West Coast Training Command had a somewhat different training approach, as the cadets received ten hours of flying in a Piper Cub, probably to determine whether they had any aptitude for flying at all, before running them through a further battery of tests.

Excerpts from Ray‘s letter describe the situation and also the status of the sex queen, Lola.

Emporia , Kansas *4 April 1943*

Dearest Mom and Pop,

I‘ve been waiting for six years to fly and today I had my opportunity. Boy oh boy, I never had so much fun in my whole life. My instructor took the "Cub" off the ground and I had it from then on to myself. I flew for forty min. and did left and right banks, glides, climbs, and also a stall. Just think, the first time I even flew and did all that. He said I did very good too. Didn't I say I would be able to fly, Pop? Now you'll believe it.

As I said, Squadron A leaves April 17th, so I don't know how much flying I will get. Probably 10 hours. I am living with Richard Andrino again. It sure is swell. I only hope we stick together all the way through. I think Andy did okay in flying.

I still have my civilian clothes. I don't see why I don't send them home.

Gee Mom, would I love to see all of your lovely flowers. You know how I used to love them. But someday I'll be back to see them. I'm just wondering how long it will take for me to get my wings. I don't think it will take over 5 months after I leave here. The hedges and lawns and trees are getting green fast here. Gee, it is a relief to see green things. I tell you there's nothing like California.

Our physical training is stiffer now that we have started flying. We get two straight hours of exercising. Boy, after the two hours are up you know you've been exercising. But I like it because it builds a person up.

You are probably wondering about Lola, the girl I wrote you about. Don't ever worry about the girls and me, Mom and Pop. I wouldn't fall for one gal for anything. I haven't seen Lola for two weeks. She was coming down this weekend but didn't make it. So, do I feel bad? Now I found another one. Take after ol' Pop, don't I, Ha Ha. The only difference is the fact that Pop is married. Ha Ha .

The wind is blowing quite a bit right now. I don't know whether we will fly or not. They said if the wind was over 15 mph they won't let us go up. So I just don't know. Yesterday it was a little windy, but when we got up to 2,000 feet it was very calm.

Well, I guess I'll close. My instructor wants me to write out everything I learned yesterday so I had better get at it. Give my love to everyone and write soon. I haven't heard from you for a long time.

Your loving son, Orvil [1]

While girl troubles seemed to chase after Ray, they were the least of his concerns as he was really enjoying the early part of his training at Emporia – particularly the initial flying he was getting in Piper Cubs. In fact, Ray had quickly risen to the top of his Squadron A flying group and his instructor had provided a very favorably written report, which would follow him to Primary Training School.

Shortly after he sent the letter to his parents telling them how delighted he was with the program, he ran into a totally unexpected snag.

Ray was sitting in the day room chatting with Andy and another friend from Modesto when he remarked. "Man, I have had a throbbing headache all day and it just won't seem to go away. I also feel really tired. I think I'll hit the sack and sleep it off. "

---

[1] Note: His real name was Orvil, which he used in those days, but later chose to be called Ray, which stemmed from his middle name "Loray."

Next morning, however, Ray awoke with a sore throat and a feeling of nausea. Much as he hated to miss another opportunity to fly, he requested permission to go on sick call at the local hospital to check it out, assuming he could join his squadron at the flight line by afternoon. However, at the hospital he got the surprise of his life. After taking his temperature and probing his cheeks and jaw, the doctor immediately ordered Ray confined to an isolation ward and informed him that he had the Mumps, a contagious disease!

This was a bitter pill for Ray to swallow. Now he would fall behind in his training program . Not only that, but Squadron A was scheduled to depart for Primary School in a few days and Andy as well as some other friends from Modesto would go with it.

Hawkins Field

Southeast Training Command, Jackson, Mississippi

Life at the little primary school was actually very pleasant. It was really a civilian flying school, which was being run under contract to the military. There was a minimum of marching and classroom activities, and there was no hazing by the upperclassmen, who were all busily building up flying time or running around with their goggles forward on their heads, demonstrating that they had soloed and were now engaged in more advanced maneuvers and aerobatics. The food, which was excellent, was served by some nice Southern ladies who acted like mothers to the cadets, a far cry from the GI mess halls where they slapped a bunch of stuff on your platter, like it or not.

Evenings were balmy, and twice-weekly movies were shown, with the cadets sitting on the grass and the movie projected onto the side of a barracks that was painted white. One film which was a terrific hit was a new picture called *Casablanca,* starring Humphrey Bogart and an exotic Swedish actress named Ingrid Bergman, which resulted in a lot of people going around saying, "Play it again, Sam" and "Round up the usual suspects."

Then there was the companion film, *To Have and Have Not*, also with Bogart, but this time with a new sexy young actress named Lauren Bacall, who stole the picture. That one resulted in a lot of cadets emulating a sultry voice and saying, "If you want me, just whistle; you know how to whistle, don't you? Just pucker up your lips and blow."

Over the next few days, my Finnish buddy, Eino, was scheduled for two more flights in the Stearman, and both times he got sick again and ended up cleaning out the cockpit. Eino had eagerly joined the cadets in the hope of flying against the Germans, who he despised almost as much as the Russians. However, he was getting increasingly discouraged, as not only was he falling behind in the flight training program but he had apparently developed a psychological fear of flying that was aggravating the situation. I tried to psyche him into just relaxing and enjoying the ride, but I knew in my heart that it was not to be; the handwriting was on the wall.

This was confirmed when, the following day, Eino was dropped from the program and given orders transferring him to Biloxi for training as a ground mechanic. Ody and I bid him a fond goodbye and wished him luck, as a sad but possibly relieved Eino departed with several other washed-out cadets. It demonstrated that sometimes one's fate is determined by factors beyond his control.

Goggles to the Front

My sixth flight was a surprise. We began with a quick review of everything I had previously been taught, then Barnes said, "Let's return to the field and practice some landings." We descended and entered into a basic traffic pattern, Barnes advising, "Now keep your eyes open, as there are other people practicing landings."

I had not had a difficult time with landings, but we made a number of touch and goes in which Mr. Barnes demonstrated some fine points, such as how to handle it if you got a big bounce – the trick was to add a little power to keep up flying speed, while easing the airplane down.

After I made three fairly decent landings, Barnes said, "Taxi over to the edge of the field and stop." I did so, and Barnes said simply, "Want to try it yourself?" I was not sure what he meant until I turned around to see Barnes getting out of the cockpit, with a parting remark before he removed the Gosport from his helmet. "Take her up, fly around for about twenty minutes, and show me a landing that will make me proud."

It suddenly hit me, *Wow, he is soloing me!*

"Yes, sir!" I yelled.

I allowed time for my instructor to get clear, taxied back to the takeoff area, lined up, and pushed the throttle forward. The Stearman accelerated quickly and was in the air almost before I realized it. For the takeoff, I initially had my eyes glued straight ahead, but upon looking to my left I was surprised to notice that another Stearman had also taken off about two hundred feet away and was climbing on a parallel heading. I thought, *Oh, boy, I'll catch hell for not looking around carefully enough before takeoff!*

Anyone who flies will tell you that it is a strange and exhilarating feeling being in the air for the first time with only yourself at the controls; you only experience it once! The flight was otherwise uneventful. I did not make any other crucial mistakes, and made a decent landing.

Mr. Barnes met me back at the parking area, and after watching my shutdown procedure, walked up to the plane, offered me his hand, and said, "Congratulations. Now you can keep your goggles on the front of your helmet." He never once mentioned my faux pas in failing to look around before taking off, and as we walked in together, I reflected once again on how privileged I was to have been assigned to a man of his character.

Life at the primary school thereafter was full of frenzied activity. There were many physical training sessions and the athletic fields were seldom empty, with frequent softball games and track sessions. We had a few general classes, which emphasized basic procedures and techniques, as well as safety. Once a week, the entire company of cadets had a formal parade and "pass in review" in Class A khakis for the commander and any visiting dignitaries – to remind us that we were still in the military.

I was fortunate to have been one of the first of my group to solo and was the subject of some envy by my classmates, as I proudly sported my goggles on the front of my helmet. But as the days progressed, more and more cadets reported to the flight line in the morning with their goggles on the front of their helmets. We noticed, however, that many of those who experienced difficulties were quietly being dropped from the program and sent off to Biloxi to be trained for other non-flying duties.

For a few, like my departed Finnish friend, who really wanted to fly, washing out of the program was a crushing blow, but many others had apparently discovered their own ineptitude for flying and were actually relieved to give it up. I was happy to see that my high school buddy, Ody, who had experienced some problems with stall and spin recovery, had stuck with the program and soloed about five days after me.

"Mellie"

After several weeks, we got a pass to go into Jackson on a Sunday. Without any firm plans on what we would do, Ody and I walked down the country road to a main highway and caught a bus into the city. We stayed on the bus while it made its rounds, to get an idea of the makeup of the city.

At one point we passed the Holy Trinity Greek Orthodox Church, and Ody said, "Look at that! I didn't know they had Greek churches down here!" Then, noticing that the board in front of the church announced a 10 a.m. divine liturgy, he said, "Would you mind if we jump out here so I can pop in and check it out? I can just make it."

"Not a problem," I said. We rang for the bus to stop and both got out at the next corner.

"What's a liturgy?" I asked, and Ody answered, "That's the Orthodox version of a mass."

"Okay", I replied. "I'll hang out and read the paper at that coffee shop over there, and meet you in front of the church."

Ody disappeared into the church for over an hour while I filled up on coffee and strolled around. I waited by the front door of the church as people started streaming out, and believe it or not, here came Ody with two cute girls in tow.

He laughed when he saw my expression, turned to the pair, and said, "This is my friend, Ed Nebinger . "He proceeded to introduce me first to the black-haired one, Melandrea Pappas, who obviously had his eye, and her friend, Deborah Stultz, a cute blonde.

It turned out that they were both first-year students at Millsaps College, some kind of girls' finishing school on the outskirts of Jackson. We chatted for a while and Ody, who obviously did not want to let the black-haired girl get away, said, "Ed and I brought our swimsuits and were planning on finding a park with a swimming pool. Would you perhaps be interested in joining us?"

The two eyed each other and, after giving us a quick once over, apparently passed some quiet signal of agreement, because Melandrea said, "Okay, we will have to get back to the college to pick up our suits and stuff, but I have a car, so maybe we can drop you off someplace near a nice park."

"Sounds like a great idea," exclaimed Ody, as I nodded in agreement.

She led us to her car, a '41 Chevy sedan, and, with Ody in the front seat and me in the rear with the blonde, nosed her way through traffic with considerable skill, suggesting that she was no novice driver. In about fifteen minutes we came to a nice section on the outskirts of Jackson and she said, "There's a good variety of restaurants here, if you want to kill a little time and have lunch. The park is about three blocks down this street, an easy walk. How about if we meet you at the entrance to the park at two o'clock?"

"Great," I said. "This is really very decent of you."

"We'll look forward to seeing you," Ody added, looking keenly at the black-haired girl. We piled out and they drove off, the blonde girl smiling and giving us a little wave.

I turned, gave him a little punch on the arm, and said, "Ody, my man, you are incredible; where the hell do you get it?"

Ody just laughed and said, "All in a day's work." Then added, more seriously, "But I think this may turn out to be a very special day."

We grabbed a hamburger at a local grill and strolled slowly down to the park, which was complete with playgrounds, walking paths with flower beds, and plenty of shady trees with benches to sit on. At two o'clock we were waiting just inside the main gate to the park, but the girls did not show up.

After about ten minutes, Ody started getting a worried look on his face and, scanning the incoming crowd, said, "Do you think maybe they changed their minds?" Having observed the way that Melandrea had kept sneaking looks at him, I doubted it, and said, "I think they'll be along." I was right, as after a few minutes they appeared, and Melandrea said, "Sorry we're late. We got held up by a long freight train at a crossing. We don't see that very often, but I guess the war is ramping up the amount of rail traffic."

The two had achieved quite a transformation from their formal church attire and made a really pretty picture, togged out in tennis shorts and sandals, and showing a goodly amount of leg, which we didn't find objectionable. They wore floral blouses, tied loosely at the waist, and sunglasses. Melandrea had on a straw hat, while the blonde girl, who was about two inches taller, sported a bill cap with MILLSAPS lettered across the front.

The pool was actually a small lake, with a swimming area at one end. It had a couple of great sliding boards that had a constant stream of water running down the chute, resulting in a fast drop with a nice splash at the bottom. The swimming area was not too crowded, and we had a terrific afternoon of romping and playing in the water, intermittently flopping with our towels on the grass where we spent a lot of time firing questions back and forth about our respective lives.

The two girls said that everyone called them Mellie and Debbie, respectively, and invited us to do the same. Mellie revealed that she lived in Natchez, where her father had some form of company associated with shipping on the Mississippi River, but she was not sure exactly what he did.

The other girl, Debbie, was not from Mississippi and lived on Longboat Key on the west coast of Florida, where her father was a commercial artist of some sort. She was not Greek and also not very religious, but the two roomed together and were great friends, so she sometimes accompanied Mellie to the Orthodox Church on Sunday.

That was a memorable day all around. My relationship with Debbie was friendly but platonic, as my interest was back in Alabama, and I got the impression that she probably had someone of importance back in Florida.

For Ody, I could see that it was a different matter entirely. The two spent a great deal of time comparing notes on Greek traditions and other matters in their different worlds, and seemed to be drawn to each other like a pair of magnets, almost unaware of their own obsession.

To her friend and me, however, it was clear that this was not just a casual meeting for them, but an unusual occurrence with potential long-range significance, and we smiled knowingly at each other.

After our swim, we roamed around the park a bit, after which we found a local seafood restaurant where we sat at a table on the veranda, savoring the cuisine and taking advantage of cooling breezes. It was a pleasant evening all around, with lots of lighthearted conversation and funny stories, but we had to cut it short. The girls had to be back at the college by 10 p.m., while final sign-in time at Hawkins Field was nine o-clock, and late returnees were likely to draw demerits and end up walking punishment tours.

We were prepared to grab a bus back to the field, but Mellie insisted on driving us there, as she and Debbie had never seen the facility. It was also clear that neither she nor Ody was eager to see their brief association come to an end. She pulled her Chevy up to the gate at our school, and after some swapping of telephone numbers and other contact details, they rolled off, waving goodbyes.

"Wearing the Airplane"

The days that followed at primary school were a flurry of continuous activities. After several more solo flights in which I practiced the maneuvers we had done, as well as lots of touch-and-go landings, my instructor and I embarked upon a new phase that I really liked – aerobatics, which some pilots referred to as acrobatics. I knew Mr. Barnes looked forward to this phase of training, as I had noted his pleasure that I was thrilled, and not terrified, at those he had performed.

That was a day I would never forget!

Before we got into the airplane, Mr. Barnes gave me some advice about our new phase of training by stating, "Aerobatic flying is not just a matter of recklessly tossing the airplane all over the sky to impress your buddies. Aerobatics performed with precision provides the best all-around measure of your understanding and ability to coordinate the control movements and develop your feel of what the airplane is capable of achieving safely, as well as the limits to which you should not take it. Some of the best aerobatic pilots I have known use the expression 'wearing the airplane,' meaning that you have become one with the airplane and do not have to consciously think about how to fly; it is instinctive."

He then surprised me by saying, "I want to see you approach that stage." Then he said simply, "Let‘s go," and walked toward the Stearman.

That flight was one of the highlights of my life. I was in the front cockpit, and after going through the routine pre-takeoff checks, I took off and started climbing to 3,000 feet. My instructor directed me to head toward an area where there was little routine traffic and was generally reserved for aerobatic training.

As we were climbing, he said, "Okay, today we are going to concentrate on rolls. There are basically four types of rolls that you can perform in the Stearman. The first is a pure aileron roll, in which you simply increase your speed a bit, pull the nose up above the horizon, slam the stick over to one side, and let the airplane roll around sloppily, with very little coordination of controls. Nobody really does aileron rolls, as they are sloppy and uncoordinated. I won‘t even waste time on that; you can try some out yourself later."

As he was making a couple of clearing turns, he continued, "The second and most beautiful of rolls is the barrel roll, in which you coordinate controls all the way through, while maintaining constant positive Gs." He took the controls and said, "I will start out with a slight turn to the right, but the actual barrel roll will be to the left. Watch the needle and ball indicator to see whether I am coordinated all the way through."

He put the airplane into a shallow dive, increased the power, and let the speed build up to 140 miles per hour. He began a nice little smooth turn to the right, then slowly reversed the turn while climbing and continuing to roll to the left, with the nose making an arc over the horizon, then falling through to make a similar arc below the horizon while continuing the roll all the way around to level flight.

The needle showed a constant turn to the left, but the ball remained glued in the middle of its race all the way through the roll. At all times, I was comfortable in the seat, with no sensation of being inverted, as we were continually pulling about one-and-a-half Gs. I tried a couple of barrel rolls, letting the nose fall through too fast on the first, but doing better on the second – although the ball skidded around a bit, and Barnes explained that I had to apply some rudder to keep us from skidding and center it.

Then we got to the real challenge, which was a classic "slow roll." He said, "Check to be sure your safety belt is buckled and adjusted so you have no slack, as you are going to be hanging inverted for part of this roll."

He started by increasing power and accelerating to 150 miles an hour in a shallow dive straight ahead, and then pulled the nose straight up over the horizon while pushing the stick to the left. As the airplane began to roll, he talked his way through: "Okay, as our airplane rolls ninety degrees to the left, I am going to have to push in right rudder to keep the nose up; then, as we go inverted I have to come in with a lot of forward stick to keep us from falling through, while neutralizing my rudder."

At this point the engine cut out – as the gas flow depends on gravity – and it got very quiet, which he forgot to warn me would happen.

He continued, "Now we are coming up on the other side. I must come in strongly with left rudder to keep the nose up, while beginning to ease back on the stick, and now as we continue to roll around toward level flight [at which point the engine came back in with a roar], I neutralize the rudder and use sufficient elevator control to keep the nose on the horizon."

Yeah, while we were rolling upside down, I was not only hanging from my belt but my feet had fallen off the rudder pedals completely! How ridiculous is that?

I told him what had happened and he laughed and said, "Sorry, I forget to tell you the engine always cuts out when we are inverted. Grab hold of the tubing on the side of the cockpit, which will provide enough leverage for you to keep your feet on the rudder pedals. Now follow me through strongly on the controls while I do another one, and give me a little help. The forces on the controls are very strong so you will really have to push hard on the forward stick when we are inverted, or we will fall right out of it."

He proceeded to do another slow roll, while talking me around, then turned the airplane over to me to try a couple on my own. I was surprised at the forces on the stick and rudder, and would have fallen out of the first one while inverted if my instructor hadn't given a strong forward push on the stick to helped me around. On the second try, I made it all the way around – not great, but he was satisfied.

Hearing the Wires Sing

"Alright," he said, "I have the airplane. You can relax for a while and I will talk to you about the fourth type of roll – the snap roll, which is really the most fun. You recall when we practiced spin recovery that when approaching a stall, pulling the stick back will stall the airplane completely, the nose will drop, and we will start spinning in whichever direction you apply rudder. However, it is also possible to stall the aircraft in level flight by an abrupt movement of the stick, and application of rudder at the same time will cause it to snap over into a quick roll. Let me show you."

He increased our speed to 110 miles an hour, then pulled the nose up slightly and suddenly I felt the stick come full back and to the right, very rapidly. The airplane gave a shudder and snapped around in a right roll so fast that it felt like we were on a greased pivot, then stopped with wings precisely level. In the process of the snap roll, both the stick and rudder moved so rapidly in gyrations that I couldn't follow, but the roll was exhilarating. "Wow!" I yelled. "That was great!" (remembering to add the word "sir")."

"Let me explain the control movements, as they are very fast," said Barnes. "When the airplane stalls, you jam in right rudder and pull the stick back and to the right in one quick movement, which will cause it to snap and spin around. To recover, you lead by half a revolution and reverse rudder while you are inverted, then pop the stick to stop it with wings level. I am going to do one more, and I want you to listen for the sound of the wing bracing wires singing, which will tell us it was a good snap roll." He repeated and there was a loud *whang!* sound of the wires singing, which I hadn't noticed before.

He then turned the airplane over to me, and I tried three more snap rolls, of which the first was too slow and did not get all the way around, and the second overshot on the roll. However, the third was a decent snap roll, and I heard the wires give a nice little *whang*. Barnes said, "You're getting it now. You have stopped trying to analyze every movement and are just reacting instinctively."

To polish off the day, we did a couple of quick loops, which were not difficult, then headed for the field. After we taxied in and tidied up the cockpits, my instructor said, "You have a very good aptitude for aerobatic flight, and I want to see you continue to really develop it. Henceforth, when you are flying solo, don‘t let me see you flying straight and level for more than a minute!" That was music to my ears. I grinned and said, "I‘ll be happy to do that, sir."

By the end of the first month, about a third of the group had been washed out and sent on their way, but the remainder were working their way toward a basic goal of completing about sixty-five flight hours of diversified time.

Not long after our first meeting, Mellie and Debbie visited the school and got a grand tour of facilities and flight line. They were fascinated by the flying activities, and Ody and I considered landing in some farmer‘s field and taking them for a ride in the Stearmans. However, after further discussion, common sense prevailed and we decided the risk was too high; if we got caught, we'd be on our way to Biloxi, or worse, real fast.

After a while, whenever Ody could get a Sunday pass, Mellie picked him up (alone) and they disappeared into Jackson. I think they may have gone to church together, but whatever they did, it was clear that they wanted to do it alone.

Several other significant events happened in our flying program. Half way through our training, the only student officer in the class spun in and was killed. It was odd, as all of the class had advanced to spins and spin recovery, but apparently some of the cadets were lacking in confidence and the crash was a cause of some new worries.

I happened to be flying the day the ground crew was picking up the crashed remains of the Stearman, and decided that I needed to reassure myself that I had no subconscious fears. I climbed to 3,000 feet, did a couple of clearing turns, and deliberately put the airplane into a four-turn spin, with nose pointed straight down toward the wreckage. Pull out was uneventful and right on target, which gave me a good feeling. I don‘t know what they thought on the ground, and I never mentioned it to anyone.

We also had an incident where one of the guys in my instructor‘s training group, Olesky, actually broke the entire trailing edge of the top wing by doing snap rolls too fast. Fortunately, he landed safely, with that portion of the wing flopping in the breeze, and there were no major repercussions. With the war in Europe accelerating in severity, the officers in the Southeast Training Command probably figured that our country was going to need fighter pilots with aggressive spirit, and the cadet who broke the wing had demonstrated his.

Two significant landmarks in our training program comprised the twenty-hour and forty-hour checks, each of which the student had to complete with a designated "check pilot" (other than his assigned instructor) in the back seat. The forty-hour check was a full review and demonstration of everything we had learned, with the check pilot sitting "hands off" in the rear. I was so keen about getting mine right that I kept reviewing the sequence over and over in my mind and actually dreamed about it the night before my scheduled ride.

During the flight, I went through the entire sequence and the check pilot said virtually nothing, leaving me wondering what might be in store for me. I needn‘t have worried. Shortly after the ride, as I was waiting in the briefing room, my instructor entered with a smile on his face, saying, "Mr. Johnson just reported that yours was the best forty-hour check he has ever seen."

Wow!

"Congratulations," Mr. Barnes said, offering me his hand. I could see he was pleased and I hardly knew what to say, but fortunately I had enough presence of mind to thank him for all of his efforts in instructing me.

I walked out of there with my head in the clouds, pleased not only with myself but with the knowledge that I had rewarded my instructor for his patience and excellent skills in teaching me. Reflecting further upon it that evening, I was struck with the realization that in wartime, while some are selected for the sharp end of the struggle, there are an equal or greater number of fine people like Mr. Barnes who quietly do their jobs supporting the war effort without medals or acclamation and, in most cases, not even a word of thanks. My admiration for Mr. Barnes and his counterparts knew no bounds.

Miss Virginia Power
Prattville, AL

Dear Ginny,

I enjoyed your last letter very much, and appreciate your taking the time to write, as I know that you have a busy life and many friends in your home town and surrounding areas. Looking back, I am still amazed at the way I inserted myself into your family group and got away with it, only because of your father's generosity of spirit. I swear I never did anything like that in my life, but I trust you understand my motivation.

Please thank your mother for her thoughtfulness and consideration in sending me that great fruitcake, which was delicious as well as nutritious. (Sounds kinda poetic) I shared it with several buddies in my training group - and they asked me to thank your mother for her kindness on their behalf. Just to keep things in perspective, however, please tell your mom that we are not starving and have an excellent eating facility here.

It would be a disservice to call it an Army Mess Hall, as it is manned, or perhaps I should say "ladied" by a group of charming ladies who are loaded with what I guess is old style Mississippi charm. You see, our little Primary Training School was actually a part of a civilian training facility before the war. It has none of the trappings of a military training facility, and even has a white picket fence around it! Nevertheless, sending a home baked cake was a thoughtful gesture and a special touch that warmed everyone's heart and made us all think of home.

Flight training is progressing well and those of us who are still in the group have accumulated close to the required 65 hours of flying time. We will be moving on to Basic Training in about a week, and I hear that we are going to Greenville, MS, which is only about 80 miles or so upriver. There we will move up to a more sophisticated airplane for another phase of training.

I will be almost sorry to leave this place, as flying the Stearman biplanes is a bundle of fun – you can do almost anything with a Stearman! I will also miss my excellent flight instructor, Mr. Barnes, a soft-spoken gentleman of about 50 who is a master of his craft. When they assigned us to instructors it was the luck of the draw, and I came up with an Ace!

Mr. Barnes never says much about himself, but I suspect he has been flying since a very young age and I am sure he has some interesting history. For whatever reason, he still gets a great deal of pleasure out of performing and teaching aerobatics, and as I am also keenly interested in aero, he has taken me under his wing, so to speak, to put a little extra polish on the apple. I have the utmost respect for Mr. Barnes, who is serving his country well in an unheralded role.

My friend Ody, who I told you about, seems to have found himself a serious friend, a pretty black-haired girl, also Greek, named Melandrea, Mellie for short. In fact, they met in the Orthodox Church in Jackson and have been going to church together ever since. Mellie lives in Natchez, MS, and is a student at Millsaps College here in Jackson. Mellie and Ody were worried that he would be shipped off to some far place, but were relieved to find out that we are going to Greenville, which is only a couple of hours away by car, and Mellie has one. I suspect they will see a lot more of each other.

I will close now, as I have rambled on for a while. I don't know what my address will be in Greenville, but I will write a short note after we get established, so that we can continue our dialogue.

As ever, Ed Nebinger

Vultee Vibrators

Greenville, Mississippi

At this point in my training, I had not yet met the three West Coast trainees, Richard Andrino, Ray Burwell, and Bill Crump, but we were destined to soon come together as fellow members of the 360th Fighter Squadron. While we were pursuing basically parallel training tracks in our respective training commands, my own training was phased slightly ahead of theirs.

It was early summer, and Greenville was indeed well named, as everything on the base, as well as the surrounding country, was green and growing. It was a much larger facility than our primary school, a true military base with rows of two-story barracks and a parade ground. The airfield itself had paved runways and parking aprons, and there were long rows of basic trainers on the flight line, with many classes of cadet training underway at different stages.

In the personnel scramble, Ody and I got assigned to different barracks, but they were adjoining, so we saw lots of each other. I was assigned to a room with a guy named Joseph Marmo, who came from New Jersey. Marmo was a great guy, but a real clown, which I will get into later.

After a general orientation session, I was assigned, along with five other cadets, to an instructor named Gates, a young first lieutenant, and was pleased to note that Johnnie Olesky, a good guy from my primary group (of Stearman wing-breaking fame), was one of the five.

The basic trainer we were to fly was a Vultee BT-13, a low-winged, two-place monoplane with fixed landing gear, powered by a 400 horsepower engine. (BT meant Basic Trainer.) Unlike the Stearmans, which had fixed-pitch props, the BT-13 had a controllable-pitch prop, which introduced a new element. Also, instead of open cockpits, the BT-13 had a sliding canopy, which you kept open for takeoff and landing, but then cruised around with it either open or closed, depending on the temperature, etc.

Interestingly, flying gear no longer comprised a flying suit with helmet and goggles, but was actually our khaki military uniform, including the small overseas cap with aviation cadet insignia, perched on one side on our head and held in place by a set of earphones for the radio and interphone. A pair of Ray Ban "Aviator" sunglasses – government issue – topped off our dashing appearance.

That gear, however, came with a certain risk, which I learned the hard way when I twisted my body to check something off of my right wing and, in the process, stuck my head a little too far into the slipstream. *Whoosh!* Suddenly I was without sunglasses, earphones, and flight cap – cadet insignia and all – as they sailed down to the fields below. With no earphones, it was a case of radio-out procedure, in which you entered the traffic pattern, waggled your wings, and waited for a green light from the tower for permission to land. I was able to finesse the replacement of the GI earphones and sunglasses, but had to spring for the cost of a new overseas cap and insignia. I did not make that mistake again.

For some reason, the BT-13 trainer was universally known as the Vultee Vibrator, but I never understood why, as the ones I flew were very nice, smooth-flying airplanes with no vibration whatsoever. Maybe it had to do with the controllable-pitch props, which could get out of adjustment occasionally.

At our first introduction, I thought that my instructor might turn out to be a serious disciplinarian, and was careful to maintain proper military etiquette. I got a huge surprise, however, when shortly after takeoff on our first flight, Gates spotted a farmer with a mule plowing in a nearby field, dropped down, and gave the poor guy a terrific buzz job. He flew about twenty feet over his head, which sent the mule running across the field at top speed, dragging the plow, with the farmer running frantically after him.

Gates threw back his head and roared with laughter, then turned around to see my reaction and found me laughing also. I remembered my primary instructor‘s early antics and wondered whether that was perhaps part of the introductory program, to see how a student reacted. Whatever it was, I knew I had lucked out and gotten another winner.

At Greenville, it was not a case of learning to fly; we all had at least forty-five hours of solo flying plus a lot of instructor time. Rather, basic training was designed to introduce us to some new areas, including night flying, formation flying, and short field landings.

One of the things that I really liked about our training was that they had several grass-covered auxiliary fields within a few miles of the base, and the instructor would sometimes take several of us out to one of those fields. There he would land, while we circled the field. Then he would pull his airplane over to one side of the field and talk to the rest of us over the radio.

Sometimes we would practice forced landings. He would conduct this training by having us fly in a traffic pattern around the field, and then suddenly call one of us and say, "Green two, forced landing – now." The selected student would then have to cut his engine to idle and play his landing by shortening or lengthening his turns, so that he cleared the fence with safe altitude but landed not too far down the field.

We were allowed one clearing of our engine (a short burst of power), so the smart way to play it was to actually plan to be just a little short, then give the engine a nice clearing to pull the airplane around the final turn.

Sometimes we also practiced short-field landings, in which we endeavored to plop it in as close as was safe to the edge of the field without, of course, miscalculating and landing on the other side of the fence.

Flying at Greenville was a delightful experience. While the climate in August was continually hot and muggy, as soon as we climbed to a thousand feet or higher the temperature was comfortable – and most of us flew with cockpit canopy slid back in the open position.

Greenville was located right on the Mississippi River and it was interesting to observe the winding course of the great river. Most of the rivers I had seen had gentle turns and bends, but basically seemed to know where they were going.

Old man Mississippi was another story; he wandered all over the countryside making huge snakelike bends, twisting and winding. There were many sections where the river made almost a complete loop before heading off, and there were also many places where it had actually broken through the levee and created a whole new channel, sometimes leaving behind disconnected half-moons full of water (and mosquitoes, I assumed).

Viewing it from my lofty perspective, it was easy to see why travel on the Mississippi River was an agonizingly slow process, as the actual distance covered was several times that of the straight-line direction it was heading. It gave me a far greater respect for the old-time river pilots like Mark Twain, who somehow managed to keep many hundreds of miles of shifting channels, sand bars, and other obstacles sorted out in their minds.

Night flying was a new challenge, which gave some people a lot of trouble. Prior to going to the airplane, we had to sit in a room wearing red goggles for twenty minutes, the theory being that this would accustom our eyes to the dark.

The theory was a waste of time, as when we went to the airplane we had to turn on some cockpit lights to get ourselves strapped in properly and everything checked before takeoff – so our vision was right back where we started.

For the actual flying, each cadet was assigned a separate flying area and a specific altitude to maintain, which resulted in lots of boredom. We droned around in circles and built up flight time, but had a difficult time staying awake after a long day of other duties. Cadets found various ways to keep themselves awake, including doing an occasional roll or two, so it was not unusual to see a set of lights revolving in the sky.

While the airplanes were equipped with the standard red, green, and white navigation lights, it was sometimes difficult to determine which direction another nearby airplane was travelling. I discovered this to my chagrin on my first nighttime cross-country flight. A number of cadets had been assigned to fly a specified three-legged course, each maintaining an assigned altitude and following certain recognizable lighting features below.

All was well until I arrived at the intersection of two legs and began my turn. Suddenly, here came another set of lights, apparently heading straight at me and at the same altitude.

I dove to pass under him, but the other airplane dove also, so that it almost turned into a game of "chicken," with each trying to outguess the other's move. We passed in what seemed a very close shave, but I will never know how close we came to colliding.

Guitars Help

Speaking of night exercises, there was another type that took place at Greenville. Joseph Marmo, my aforementioned roommate from New Jersey, was a good-looking Italian kid with lots of charm and an easygoing personality. Combine that with his considerable skill at playing the guitar and a good singing voice, and you have an unbeatable combination, at least as far as success with the opposite sex goes. All Marmo had to do was unsling his guitar and strum a few chords and he was instantly surrounded by a circle of admirers, especially female ones. He had a great repertoire, which featured some of the great romantic ballads of the day, such as "In the Blue of Evening" (Frank Sinatra) and "You'll Never Know" (Vera Lynn). However, in between serious songs, he would spice it up with some cute little jingles, all played lightly to appropriate music, such as:

Passengers will please refrain (pause)
From flushing toilets while the train (pause)
Is waiting in the station
I love you (great laughter from the crowd)

And my darling, after dark
We'll goose the statues in the park
If Sherman's horse can take it -
Whyyy can't you?
(Strummmmmmmm) (great laughter and applause)

Marmo quickly zeroed in on the WAC barracks across the field, and sometimes made his way over there on Saturday nights. Needless to say, his batting average with the lady soldiers was out of sight, and he would sometimes appear early the next morning, bleary-eyed and tired, even on days when we had a full day of scheduled assignments ahead of us.

I don't know what ever happened to Marmo, as I never saw him again after basic training. He was a good egg and a fun guy. I hope he survived the war.

Another new and interesting part of our training was formation flying. Lt. Gates started us out by working with each student individually. He would fly straight and level, then tell the selected student to move in slowly on his wing and hold position there. We quickly learned the importance of applying power smoothly and carefully when moving in, as airplanes have no aerial brakes and it is somewhat embarrassing to go sailing past your leader, then bobble around getting into place.

After the initial individual introduction to formation flying, our instructor then advanced to working with two students, one on each wing, and slowly progressing to turns of various types. There was a certain amount of risk for both the students and instructors, as collisions were not unknown and bailouts from two merged airplanes could be difficult.

Some students had a very difficult time with formation flying, but I had always been fascinated by airplanes flying closely together and enjoyed it immensely. Johnnie Olesky and I often flew V formation with Gates, one on each side, with our instructor gradually working us up to steeper and steeper banks, while we kept our eyes glued on his airplane, trying to stay in correct position throughout.

There was a surreal beauty in this, as when you were on the inside of the turn you were looking almost straight up at the other two airplanes and the blue sky and clouds above, and while on the outside of a steep bank you were looking almost straight down at the other planes, painted against the green fields and sometimes the Mississippi River below.

The frosting on the cake for Johnnie and me occurred one day when Gates called us on the radio and said, "We are going to land at auxiliary field number three. Move out just a little bit, but stay right on my wing, as we are going to land together." That was a terrific experience and actually a lot easier than it sounds, as we slowly reduced power and descended to the field, watching the wheels of our instructor's airplane slowly approach the grass, skim a bit, then touch smoothly. All three of us made a smooth landing side-by-side, slowly rolling to a stop.

Lt. Gates then said, "Follow me around singly to takeoff position and line up again on each side; we are going to take off together." We did, and had another new experience under our belts. Thereafter, we practiced formation takeoffs and landings many times.

Quite a few students were washed out completely at Greenville, and toward the end of our second month, another portion, while not dropped from the program, was deemed not to have the aptitude to be fighter pilots and was rerouted in the training program.

Unfortunately, my pal Ody was one of those. His downfall was formation flying, which I enjoyed so much. I don't know whether there was a personality conflict with his instructor or what, but in any case, after a series of poor sessions with formation training, Ody's instructor put him up for an "e-ride," which was a final check flight with a different instructor, who would advise on retaining or dropping the student. The "e" was commonly interpreted as meaning "elimination."

Ody survived the "e-ride" but was tabbed to attend advanced training in twin-engine airplanes, with the long-term goal of assignment to fly either transports or bombers, most probably the latter. The 8th Air Force in England and the 15th Air Force in Italy were losing bombers and bomber pilots at a terrific rate as the war in Europe accelerated, while B-29s were beginning to appear in the Pacific.

In any case, Ody would be headed for a different advanced training base in a week or so. I found it somewhat ironic that students who were weak on formation flying were often sent to multi-engine school, as I had seen many photographs of large groups of bombers in Europe, all flying in close formation and stacked neatly into boxes, where their multiple gunners could provide mutual protection. But the logic of our military planners was sometimes unfathomable.

Miss Virginia Power

Prattville, AL

Dear Ginny,

Just a quick note to say that a lot has happened since my last letter, as the pace of training has really picked up and we are busy all day, then sometimes get scheduled for night flying thereafter.

Johnnie Olesky and I were selected to fly back to our Primary Training school in Jackson, MS, for a short visit – to give the students a chance to see what might lay ahead of them in Basic Training. Our instructor, Lt. Gates, led our little V of three BT-13s as we demonstrated takeoffs and landings from the grass field in close formation. It was quite an honor and a lot of fun.

The other event is that my pal, Ody, has been shipped off to some base in Texas for multi-engine training. Mellie drove up to Greenville to see him off and it was somewhat of a somber scene, as they obviously have serious long-term plans. I was sorry to see him go, as he is the only other person I know here who is from my home town. More importantly however, he and Mellie are a great pair of people.

On the good news side, I have received Orders sending me to Advanced Flight Training at Craig Field, in Selma, Alabama, which is not very far from Prattville, so I hope to be able to see you and your family there.

Have to go, as I have a scheduled class in ten minutes.

Hope you and your family are well.

As Ever, Ed

CHAPTER FOUR

THE WEST COAST TRAINING COMMAND

Goodfellow Army Air Base, San Angelo, Texas

Over a thousand miles away, two other young aviation cadets were whamming away furiously at ping pong balls at a table in the cadet day room at Goodfellow Army Air Base, San Angelo, Texas.

Like their East Coast counterparts, the two Californians had been impacted by the Army's sudden decision to drop the two-year requirement in lieu of satisfactory completion of a special test. They had jumped right into the program, leaving their second year at Modesto Junior College unfinished.

They came very close to getting separated when Ray came down with the Mumps at Preflight in Emporia, Kansas. Fortunately, the whole class was delayed by over a week, due to a backup in the program, and Ray was able to rejoin his class in time to move on with Andy. Now, months later, they were close to completing the basic flying training phase in BT-13s.

The two opponents at the ping pong table were putting on a tremendous show for an admiring group of cadets who surrounded the table, watching their furious play. While at Modesto, both had been ping pong stars, and as a team they had come very close to winning the state championship. Now the two were standing as much as six feet back from the table and whacking curves, cuts, and chops with full force and lots of subtlety, so that balls which clearly looked like they were sure misses were in fact catching the edge of the table and bounding off at odd angles before being returned in force by the other player. The play was accompanied by lots of grunts and yells as they taunted each other good-naturedly.

In terms of skill, they were evenly matched, but their physical appearance was another story. Ray Burwell was good-looking, lean and muscular, and stood about six feet one. In contrast, his opponent, Richard Andrino, was a chunky five-foot-four Filipino kid with a round and smiley face. It was easy to understand why the term "Mutt and Jeff" had followed them from college, where it was first applied.

Right now the game was at a critical point, as they had split wins in the previous two games and this was the rubber for the win. They were at set point, and Ray, who had just grabbed the serve, stood about seven feet back from the table and vowed silently, *I'm going to hit this so hard, it will blast Andy's ass clean away from the table!*

He then whammed a tremendous curve, but Andy stepped forward and deftly caught it with a quick wrist movement that caused it to nick the side of the table and careen off before Ray could reach it.

"Aagh!," yelled Ray. "That was pure luck!" But Andy just grinned and said, "Pure skill."

On the next serve, which was set point, Ray was expecting Andy to follow through with a full force serve, and stood back, rocking on the balls of his feet. Andy picked up the ball and moved casually like he was going to back up for the hit, then suddenly chopped the ball across the net with a terrific back spin, and it stopped dead, dropping on the other side of the net before Ray could reach it.

"You devil!' yelled Ray, but Andy smiled, flexed his muscle, and exclaimed, "Filipino power!" This drew a laugh from the crowd, at which point the two buddies tossed down the paddles and went to grab a Coke.

No Snap Rolls!

Since their call-up to active duty, the fortunes of Ray and Andy had followed a course basically similar to that of Ody and me on the other side of the country. After preflight at San Antonio, they went to primary flight training at Bruce Field, in Ballinger, Texas, another one of some fifty fields across the U.S. that had contracted with the Army to provide such training – which comprised sixty-five hours of flying.

One difference in their training, however, was in the airplanes they flew. Whereas the cadets in the Southeast Training Command largely received primary flight training in Stearman biplanes, most of the Western Training Command schools used Fairchild PT-19 low-wing monoplanes. (PT stood for Primary Trainer.)

The PT-19s were nice-flying little airplanes with two open cockpits, powered by a six-cylinder in-line 175-horsepower Ranger engine, and could perform all of the standard maneuvers, but were not as good an aerobatic bird as the Stearmans. The two friends did not know it, but they were actually missing a delightful part of their training that was popular with the cadets who were lucky enough to fly Stearmans.

Specifically, while the Stearman biplanes could do terrific snap rolls, with wires singing, snap rolls were prohibited in the PT-19, as the airplane had a plywood main spar that had cracked in some earlier flights, causing the wing to fold. Later models of the PT-19 were being fitted with a metal main wing spar, but the rule still stood at the time of Ray and Andy's training.

While in primary flight training at Bruce Field, Ray and Andy had made the acquaintance of another cadet named Bill Crump, who was from Spokane, Washington. Interestingly, Crump had drawn as his primary flight instructor a full-blooded Chinook Indian, who was universally referred to by the cadets as "Chief Iron-ass" (but never within earshot of him).

As Crump later related it to Ray and Andy, whenever he made a mistake his instructor would beat the stick back and forth against his knees and legs, so he would remember not to repeat the error. Bill‘s legs had lots of bruises, and he laughingly remarked to Ray, "Sometimes I wonder if he‘s still carrying a grudge against the settlers!"

However, Crump gained a lot more respect for his instructor when they reached the aerobatic phase of training, as the chief was an absolute demon in the sky, even without the snap rolls, and Crump loved every minute of it.

Ray, Andy and Bill soon discovered that they enjoyed each other‘s company immensely, and as a team could wring the most fun out of Army life – whenever they were out from under the ever-watchful eyes of their instructors and training officers, that is.

Whenever possible, they joined forces in visits to the local town, and as a triad they displayed an awesome power in attracting good-looking members of the opposite sex. They didn‘t know it at the time, but their relationship was to remain in place for the rest of their lives.

In terms of flying ability, all three fell into the category of "natural pilots." They were filled with enthusiasm about every phase of their training and the idea of becoming fighter pilots to combat America‘s enemies.

The trio had sailed through primary training with no major problems, soloing and moving ahead with the leaders of the pack. None of them even came close to a washout, although over thirty-five percent of the class fell by the wayside. However, at Goodfellow Field, an event took place that came very close to splitting up the trio.

Multi-Engine School??

One of the important functions of the basic training schools was to perform a selection and split-out of pilots for different types of future flying. Fighter pilots were sent to advanced training in single-engine airplanes, but prospective transport and bomber pilots were sent to advanced training in twin-engine airplanes.

This was a crucial selection, as the flight instructors recommended further assignment to advanced training in either single-engine or multi-engine based upon the student's general flying ability, as well as his personality. Some pilots were deemed to be aggressive by nature, while others were seen as being more adaptable to flying larger airplanes and managing crews.

Many of the trainees actually wanted to fly multi-engined airplanes, and all they had to do was make that statement and that was where they went. But for young tigers like Ray, Andy, and Bill, who desperately wanted to fly fighters, it was like a sword of Damocles hanging over their heads. Another factor that entered into the selection process, however, was the height of the students, and that is where Ray Burwell ran into a problem. Cockpits of fighters were relatively cramped, so there was a practical limit of height for fighter pilots, and Ray, at six feet one, was borderline. About halfway through the course, Ray's instructor told him he was probably going to be put into the multi-engine group.

That was a crushing blow to Ray, who had always considered that flying a transport or a bomber was like driving a bus, instead of a sleek race car. That night, after he related the day's events to his two buddies in the mess hall, Ray sat staring gloomily into his coffee cup and remarked, "I don't believe it. I've wanted to become a fighter pilot for half of my life, and now I am heading for multi-engine school! It's the end of a dream."

The next day, desperate, and feeling that he had nothing to lose, Ray asked for an appointment to meet with the head of the selection committee. His request was granted. The captain, who was a decent guy, heard Ray's plea and said he would consider it after discussion with Ray's flight instructor.

Ray sweated for two days, and when he was called in again to the captain's office, his heart was in his throat. Ray reported in to the captain, fanned him a smart salute, and waited for the grim news. The captain, who was wearing command pilot wings and had a DFC among his ribbons, returned the salute, smiled, and said, "Okay, you made it. We made an exception for you. Two factors influenced our decision. First, your instructor gave a very good recommendation of your flying skills, but the real deciding factor was that you wanted it bad enough to fight for it."

The captain, who may well have been a fighter pilot himself, offered his hand and said, "Congratulations, and good luck with the rest of your training."

Ray's heart rate jumped and he thanked the captain profusely, fanned him another smart salute, and walked out with his spirit soaring. He was going to be a fighter pilot – provided of course that he made it the rest of the way.

Blooping Sink! The West Coast Gang

January/February 1944

Ray Burwell, Rich Andrino, and Bill Crump stayed together for the remainder of their training program, which was similar to that experienced in the Southeast Training Command except for the geographical locations. After basic training, they went on to advanced training in AT-6s at Moore Army Air Base in south Texas, near the town of Mission, not far from the Mexican border.

For the three, arrival at Moore Field was like entering a whole new world. The field had a number of hard surface runways and was loaded with AT-6 Harvard advanced trainers, as well as a batch of P-40 fighters which they would get to fly, either before or after graduation from the cadets.

However, even though they were now entering advanced flying training, the standards had become even tougher than before, and the Army was washing out cadets for virtually any and all reasons. One would think that having invested so much money and time bringing the students to their present levels of flying proficiency, the training authorities would let up for a bit. Apparently, however, the training command now had so many trainees backed up in the system, they could afford to get even choosier and settle for only those who had been able to fight their way through. The result of all this was that people were being put up for ` e-rides for ridiculous reasons.

For example, there was a little PX on the flight line, but the cadets were told that it was "off limits" during duty hours. Ray knew of one guy in the class ahead of them who was doing well in the flying program, but made the mistake of dropping into the PX for a Coke, and was spotted by one of the training faculty.

He was put up for an "e-ride," failed it, and was washed out of the cadets two weeks before graduation. It seemed like a ridiculous waste of time and money, but the Army was holding all of the cards, and you did not fight it.

Whatever the reason, the discipline had gotten tougher than ever, both in the air and on the ground. The number of ruthless inspections of the cadets' quarters increased dramatically. The inspecting officers went out of their way to find reasons to "gig" people with demerits, so that they ended up walking punishment tours after duty hours.

The quarters at Moore Field comprised rows of very nice stucco buildings with verandas, painted in pleasing colors, and containing little two-room suites, with the cadets assigned two to a unit. Ray and Andy managed to get a room together, while Crump ended up further down the row. Even though Ray and Andy were roommates, they seldom saw each other during the day, as they had been assigned to fly with different instruction units. The only time they spent much time together in quarters was on Saturday mornings, when they shared a ***severe*** inspection.

The inspecting officer would appear wearing white gloves, accompanied by a stooge with a book and pencil. Both cadets stood at "parade rest," like a couple of dummies, while the officer proceeded to reach up to ridiculous places, such as the top of the door frame, run his finger along the top, and find some dust. "Improper cleaning," he'd call out, while the stooge dutifully jotted it down.

After a couple of incidents like that, Ray and Andy went nuts cleaning every niche and crevice they could find. The one that really got them, however, was the sink in their room, which had a faucet washer that needed replacement. No matter how hard they closed the tap, an occasional drop of water would ooze out. Twice, after they had cleaned and dried the sink, a tiny drop of water went *bloop* right after the officer appeared, and the officer called out "Dirty sink!" like the voice of doom.

Frustrated, they came up with a plan to defeat him, which was to stuff the end of the faucet with tissue paper. However, they soon discovered that if it were done too soon, the paper would get soaked and a drop would bloop out. Therefore, their modified plan, which succeeded, was to wait with a wad of tissue in hand until the officer was just leaving the next-door unit, and then quickly jam it up into the tap.

Needle, Ball, and Airspeed

Every morning the cadets assembled in the street in front of their quarters wearing flying suits and caps, and a sergeant marched them down to the flight line, with everyone singing a series of popular marching songs. While there, those not flying were expected to spend every moment studying the various manuals relating to the airplanes or to various phases of training.

As they soon discovered, flying the AT-6s was fun, as they were pretty nimble little airplanes with retractable landing gear and 600-horsepower engines that gave them reasonably good performance. For this final phase of cadet training, much emphasis was placed upon basic instrument flight training, as all pilots will eventually be exposed to a range of weather phenomena and must be prepared to fly on instruments alone.

They were given some time in Link Trainers, which were dummy cockpits with an enclosed hood. The trainers were mounted on a gimbal and were able to change angles to simulate various phases of flight while the cadets flew them on instruments, with an instructor watching and kibitzing.

A substantial amount of time was also scheduled with the student in the rear seat of an AT-6 under a canvas hood, and the instructor in the front seat as observer. They practiced basic radio-range orientation and beam flying, radio compass orientation methods, and were challenged with recovery from unusual flight positions while under the hood.

For the latter, the instructor would fly the airplane, making various maneuvers, and after placing the airplane into an unusual flight position, such as in a spiral, would then say, "You have the airplane," after which the student was expected to recover, using needle, ball, and airspeed and altimeter as his primary flight instruments.

That particular training was extremely critical, as it taught the cadets that while flying in weather, or "blind," as the common expression went, they could not trust their own senses to determine the position of the aircraft.

They learned that there is a condition called "vertigo," which can easily convince a pilot that he is flying straight and level, when in fact his airplane is in a very steep bank or spiral, or vice versa. The instructors pounded into the cadets' skulls the fact that they could not always depend upon the full panel of instruments, but there were three basic indicators that were almost always available.

Therefore, the basic rule, when the artificial horizon and other flight instruments went out, was "center the needle, center the ball, and check your airspeed." This training probably saved the lives of hundreds of military pilots during WWII.

Andy had a sharp example of that on one of his early instrument flights under the hood, and related it to Ray that evening. He was under the hood and his instructor caged the artificial horizon (made it inoperative), made a whole bunch of turns to disorient Andy, then put the airplane into a steep diving spiral and yelled, "You have it!"

Andy didn‘t have a clue what attitude he was in, but saw that the airspeed was increasing rapidly, so he pulled back on the stick to bring it out of the dive, but the airspeed continued building, which he could not understand.

Suddenly, the instructor said, "I have it," grabbed the controls, and leveled the airplane out, then yelled loudly, "Goddammit, [instructors swore sometimes] I knew just what you were going to do!"

The instructor then explained that Andy had failed to first check the needle and ball, which would have told him he was in a steep turn and should have leveled his wings; then, observing the airspeed building, he would have pulled out of the dive and returned to level, stabilized flight. By pulling back on the stick first, Andy had merely tightened the spiral, which under real conditions could have been deadly.

That evening, he and Ray discussed that experience thoroughly and both stored it in their memory banks. That was a lesson they would never forget.

Retractable landing gear was another important new element that was introduced at Moore Field, as all advanced military aircraft would have retractable gear. A couple of incidents occurred during their training. A cadet in their flight unit was flying with instructor aboard, and started to land with his wheels up. Heading down final approach, the instructor said absolutely nothing and waited patiently until the student suddenly recognized his error and went around.

The instructor was a canny guy who allowed the student to remain in the program, but the next day handed him an airplane wheel, tire and all, with the following instructions: "Carry this with you at all times when you are marching to and from quarters. Whenever you stop, set it on the ground. Whenever you move, retract it." That went on for a solid month and was a source of great hilarity in their marching platoon. It was also a very effective method of training.

The designers of the AT-6, North American Aviation, recognized that the airplane would be flown by students who had never before flown an airplane that had retractable landing gear. They had therefore installed a horn, which blew very loudly in the intercom whenever the throttle was closed to near idle position, as it would be prior to landing.

Nevertheless, there was one accident when a student, flying solo, actually did land gear up on the runway, with a loud screeching of metal and sparks flying everywhere. After the airplane slid to a stop he sat dumbly in the cockpit, unhurt but badly shaken, while a training officer, who had clambered up onto the wing, said to him, "Why didn‘t you go around? Didn‘t you hear the tower calling you?"

Believe it or not, the guy answered, "I couldn't hear anything on the radio because that damned horn was blowing so loudly in my ears!"

That incident became a subject of great hilarity among the cadets, but needless to say, the culprit was quickly put up for an "e-ride," and shortly thereafter disappeared from the program.

Night flying was also pretty much a repeat of the stuff they had in basic training. They did, however, have one incident, which, while amusing in retrospect, could have had deadly consequences. A cadet called in for landing instructions, giving the last three of his tail number, then reported, "Army 364 on final approach, gear down and locked."

The tower operator responded, "I don't see you. Flash your landing light." Suddenly the tower operator yelled, "364, pull up! Pull up! Immediately!" The tower operator, searching the sky in the vicinity of Moore Field, had seen that the student was about to land on a nearby bridge, which had lights like the runway, but also had a steel superstructure!

One fatality occurred during night flying when a pilot failed to remove the canvas cover from his pitot tube [2] prior to flight. In certain takeoff directions, there were no lights or other visual cues, as the landscape was mostly ranches and farmers' fields. Consequently, on nights when there was no moonlight or the sky was overcast, it could be black as the ace of spades when they took off, so they had to refer to instruments to climb out properly.

---

[2] The pitostatic tube extended forward of the wing and sensed incoming ram air pressure to operate the airspeed indicator. A small canvas cover was used to protect the opening when the airplane was on the ground, and was an item to always be removed in preflight inspection.

On that particular occasion, the pilot took off, and seeing no airspeed building up, assumed he was stalling and pushed the stick forward, resulting in a dive straight into the ground!

Second Lieutenant or Flight Officer?

While Ray Burwell and his pals were in their second month of training at Moore Field, the Army became concerned that it was graduating too many new second lieutenant pilots and created a whole new grade called "Flight Officer," which was a rank comparable to that of a warrant officer; i.e., halfway between an enlisted man and a commissioned officer. Instead of a gold bar, the new flight officers would wear gold and blue bars.

The authorities decreed that a certain percentage of graduates would become flight officers, so shortly before graduation every cadet was scheduled for a special interview to determine his future rank.

Ray Burwell‘s interview was with a captain, who was an official of the senior training staff. Ray walked in, dutifully saluted and reported as ordered, then stood at attention until invited to sit down. The captain then asked a series of questions, such as, "Assuming your engine is functioning properly, how long a runway will you need to take off in an AT-6 and clear a fifty-foot obstacle?" He also asked Ray how he would handle certain emergency situations. Ray answered to the best of his judgment and the captain made no comment, but then surprised him by asking, "Why do you want to be a second lieutenant?"

Ray thought about it for a moment and decided he might as well be completely candid. He answered, "I didn‘t apply for the cadets because I wanted to become an officer; I joined because I wanted to fly fighters." The captain looked at him in surprise and Ray thought for a fleeting moment, *Oh boy, I probably just shot myself in the foot!*

The captain then retorted, "Oh, so you don't care whether you become an officer?" to which Ray replied, "Yes, sir, I do care. I was just being completely candid with you."

Ray was dismissed.

He became a second lieutenant. He was twenty years old. Both Andy and Bill made the grade too; they must have given the right answers!

Graduation

Toward the end of their training at Moore Field, they had each gotten checked out in the P-40. It was their first ride in a fighter, but they soon discovered that the Curtiss P-40 Warhawks were a pretty tired bunch of old birds.

In fact, Andy had been forced to bail out of his P-40 when the engine exploded and the damned thing caught fire! He landed without injury about thirteen miles from the field, but the fighter was reduced to a smoking pile of junk, which was probably where it belonged in the first place.

In February 1944, after completing all the requirements of the aviation cadets training course, Ray, Andy and Bill all graduated at Moore Field in Class 44B and received their silver pilot's wings. They were also commissioned as second lieutenants in the U.S. Army Reserve, with immediate call-up to continuing active duty.

Moore Field held a formal graduation ceremony for its graduating class. Bill Crump's mother flew down and proudly pinned the new silver wings on her son's chest. While neither Ray's nor Andy's parents were able to attend, they were soon reunited with their sons, as all of the new lieutenants had been granted thirty days leave.

CHAPTER FIVE
SOUTHEAST TRAINING COMMAND

Wings at the Sgt. Major's Office

After completing basic training at Greenville, I joined a group of cadets who were shipped to Craig Field, in Selma, Alabama, for the final phase of our cadet training before graduation and commissioning as second lieutenants. Selma was only about twenty-five miles from Prattville, where Ginny lived, and I had high expectations of being able to visit her and spend a lot more time getting to know her better – and perhaps getting to at least second base, although I was not sure what that would comprise.

However, when I called her house, I was keenly disappointed to learn that she was not even in Prattville and had, in fact, departed for Alabama College for Women, in the Birmingham area, two weeks past. A letter she posted to me while I was at Greenville had apparently been misrouted and did not even reach me until after I was at Craig for some time. However, I did receive an address where I could write to her and had to settle for that, for the time being.

As far as our actual training in AT-6 advanced trainers went, it was interesting, but not significantly different from what we had already learned, except that we were flying faster airplanes with retractable gear and had a higher concentration of instrument training, as well as an introduction to aerial gunnery. It was also a very busy time, with more emphasis upon military discipline, navigation, and precision maneuvers, among other things.

Apparently, with the forthcoming invasion in Europe, training was being accelerated to the maximum. Consequently, we scarcely got a complete weekend to ourselves prior to graduation. Those were the days before cell phones, email, and instant communication everywhere, so letter writing was the primary mode, with an occasional long distance phone call, which did not always reach its intended party.

Before graduation each of us had been awarded a one-time uniform allowance, and the post tailor had prepared for each of us a dandy set of two complete uniforms, in pinks and greens, the large bill hat complete with grommet and insignia, an overseas cap, a short mohair coat for winter wear, and an officer‘s raincoat.

Graduation day for Class 43K was slated for December 5, 1943. A grandstand had been built, with the expectation that we were going to have a formal presentation of our wings, and family members were booked into hotels for miles around. All of the graduating cadets were ordered to report to the base theater at 0545 (believe it or not) and we did so, all decked out in our fancy new officer‘s uniforms.

At precisely 0600, a small group of officers appeared on the stage, including the base commander, a chaplain, and the commandant of cadets. After calling "at ease" (which means "shut up"), they commenced with a Pledge of Allegiance, a short prayer, and a swearing in ceremony, after which we were informed that we were now commissioned officers in the U.S. Army Air Corps Reserve, by order of the President and I don‘t remember who else – maybe the Secretary of War. Everybody cheered and tossed their caps into the air, having made sure in advance that their name was lettered inside of the cap.

The commandant of cadets then made a cute little announcement, which came as a complete surprise to everyone. It went something like this:

"Due to the wartime emergency, we are unable to conduct a formal graduation ceremony, and will use the time instead to get as many of you as possible checked out in the P-40. When you exit the theater, return to your quarters, put on a flying suit, and join your squadron in front of the theater. The sergeant will march you down to the flight line." And then, as a kind of afterthought, he said, "Oh, by the way, when you get a spare moment, stop by the sergeant major's office and pick up your wings!"

Wow, what a reward after almost a year of hard training with the washout sword hanging over our heads every moment. Never mind the parents and families, some of whom had come very long distances. Some high-level Army Training Command planner had apparently gotten the word that the invasion of Europe was imminent and hit the panic button! We might be officers and might be wearing wings (after we picked them up), but it was a stark reminder that we surely were still in the Army!

Air Mail Delivery

Very shortly after getting my wings, I was shipped out to an operational training base in Florida. I never did get the opportunity to visit Alabama College for Women to spend some time with Ginny. However, right before my departure I managed to get a flight in an AT-6, which I flew up to the Birmingham area. Then, dropping down very low, I was able to scout out the location of the college – which looked pleasant with green lawns, shady trees, and students walking on paths between the buildings.

With the engine cut back to idle, I dropped very low, rolled back the canopy, tossed out a sealed envelope, and watched a student run over and pick it up – then I poured the power back on and climbed out of there. The envelope contained my newly earned silver wings and a letter. Printed on the outside of the envelope in large letters was the message:

PLEASE DELIVER THIS LETTER TO
VIRGINIA POWER
WHO IS A STUDENT AT ACW
THANK YOU

Inside the envelope was the following message:

Dear Ginny,

I am shipping out very shortly and took this somewhat extraordinary method of delivering an "Air Mail" message, which I am hoping reaches you. I would be pleased if you would wear the enclosed Wings which are, in fact, the original ones I received in graduation at Craig Field. This gift has a particular significance to me, which I hope you share.

I thought I would get to see you again during my time at Craig but unfortunately it was not in the cards, as the pace of war has placed an extraordinary degree of urgency on the remainder of our training. I assume you are enjoying your time at Alabama College, of which I have had only a brief aerial view, but am told it is a fine place.

If you wish to continue writing, I suggest that you mail your letters to my mother, whose address is shown below. I do not know where I am going and could not tell you if I did know. However, as soon as I am established, I will let you both know. In the meantime, please thank your parents and your brother, James, for their kindness to me.

I do not expect to see you before I ship out, so let me wish you and your Family a Very Happy Christmas Holiday season, and a great year ahead.

Fondly, Lieutenant (Ahem) Edward Nebinger

PS: When I get to my squadron I would like to put your name on my airplane, if that is OK with you.

Kelp Glowing in the Dark

Venice, Florida

Events moved like a whirlwind thereafter. A thirty-day leave, which normally would have been granted to graduating second lieutenants, was canceled. I was ordered to an operational training unit in Venice, Florida, for two intense months of transition and training in Republic P-47 "Thunderbolt" fighters, which everyone referred to as "Jugs," probably because they were kind of fat looking. We practiced all kinds of gunnery and associated combat maneuvers and generally burned up the sky in western Florida.

During this period we had very little free time and were not encouraged to discuss our whereabouts with people. I did manage, however, to get a call through to Mellie Pappas at Millsaps College in Jackson, to catch up on what was happening with Ody.

She told me that after Ody left Greenville, he was sent to Columbus, Mississippi, for multi-engine training, where he successfully completed the cadet program and graduated with Class 43K as a second lieutenant. Mellie had been there for his graduation and had proudly pinned on his wings. Then – surprise, surprise – new Lieutenant Thoma had, in return, placed an engagement ring on her finger, after of course properly asking her permission, which she had instantly granted! She was ecstatic over that, and the two had already placed their families into contact with each other for initial discussions of the nuptials.

However, not much planning could be made at this stage, as the happy couple had only managed to spend a few days together before Ody was shipped off to some base in Texas for transition into B-17 bombers – with the prospect of overseas shipment immediately upon completion of the training.

She also told me that Debbie Stultz had returned to her home on Longboat Key, Florida, for the Christmas and New Year holidays, but would be returning to Millsaps. I gave her the phone number for our operations building, so she could keep me posted on events. The way we were all moving around, it was useful to have her as one central coordinating person that we could all reach.

Several days later, I was surprised to get a call from Debbie Stultz, who said that Longboat Key was only a few miles up the coast from Venice, and that her parents had told her she could invite me and a friend to their home for a beach picnic on the forthcoming Sunday, and she would drive down and pick us up.

That sounded too good to miss and I immediately said, "Okay, that sounds great! These guys are pushing us pretty hard, but I'm sure we can finesse a Sunday. I'll bring a pal; maybe you'll find him interesting. Ha, ha." We made arrangements for a time and place to meet and signed off.

I had met a pilot named Bill Romberg, who was another P-47 jock, and we had flown a couple of aerial gunnery missions together, in which we competed in firing at towed targets with the 50-caliber machine guns in the "Jugs." He was a decent guy who, in conversation, revealed that he was a distant relation to Sigmund Romberg, who composed the *The Student Prince*, as well as other operettas.

Debbie picked us up on Sunday and drove us through Sarasota and out onto Longboat Key, which was a fascinating island that had been joined to the mainland with a causeway. She introduced us to her parents, surprisingly young-looking people who displayed a keen interest in our training, as they often saw the fighters from our base at Venice flying low over the Gulf of Mexico. The island, which was about twenty-four miles long, had miles of unspoiled beaches that seemed to have a whiter than normal type of fine sand.

Their home was located on the beach, but set back, and faced directly west across the Gulf of Mexico. It was a graceful Spanish-style house with a nicely shaded veranda, as well as a broad deck where Debbie‘s father, who was a commercial artist, had set up his easel and was working on a seascape that would be used in some northern journal.

Bill and I took a keen interest in his work, which was very good, and he explained that most of his work was sent to New York publishers for use in various types of commercial advertisements. It amazed us to see how casually an artist of his caliber could make beautiful images come to life magically at the tip of his brush. However, when we remarked on this, he laughed and said, "You‘d be surprised to see how many times I started things that ended up in the trash basket!"

Debbie had also invited another young couple from nearby Sarasota, but they were not able to join us until quite late in the afternoon. The sun was already low on the horizon when the group of us traipsed down to the beach, but the weather was balmy and the temperature of the Gulf waters turned out to be perfect for refreshing swimming.

Debbie‘s mother had packed a bunch of picnic stuff in a basket, including some wieners and marshmallows to roast, so the guys built a fire out of driftwood, of which there was plenty on the beach. (The island was not densely populated in those days, and you could build a fire on the beach and nobody would even raise an eyebrow. Today, the police would undoubtedly appear within five minutes, with dire consequences, including a possible trip to a local hoosegow!)

We sat around the fire laughing, chatting, and roasting wieners as it became dark and a full moon rose over the Gulf. Then the most amazing thing occurred, an event which I have never seen nor heard of since!

The moonlight must have activated some special algae in the water, as magically the entire sea suddenly turned phosphorescent, including all of the kelp visible in the shallow areas. At first we were not sure whether it was harmful, but after determining it was not, swam out, grabbed some of the kelp and brought it ashore where we had a great time rubbing it all over our bodies.

This produced an astounding result, like glowing people from some strange "B" movie! This fantastic event continued for several hours, before waning in the same mysterious way that it had arrived.

It was a monumental end to our last week in America, as directly after that we shipped out to join the war.

Dear Ed,

Well, the "Air Mail" delivery of your letter with the enclosed Wings has caused quite a stir at ACW, which is usually a very quiet campus. In fact, the campus chatter and speculation has been going strong ever since, and I am constantly being bombarded with questions about my secret admirer (which is not so secret anymore.) In fact, it is the talk of the entire campus!

Your letter was actually picked up by a friend of mine who checked my class schedule and came running with it.

My class professors have been very good about it, and a couple of them have actually dropped cute little remarks in class, getting a good laugh from the students. But actually, I am getting a lot of envious looks from the other girls.

The Dean of Students, however, was less sanguine about the whole deal. I heard through the grape vine that he was considering reporting you to Craig Field for a dangerous stunt – but the school administrators apparently talked him out of it. Believe it or not, we heard that the President of our College actually said, "After all, this is wartime, and such things happen." My best girl friend says, "That shows that he has a secret romantic streak in him." Ha

When I told the family what you did, James laughed and my mother said, "Oh, that was very daring. I hope he does not get into trouble." My Daddy just said, "That boy will go far, as he does not let anything stand in his way." That sounds correct to me, as you were very forthright, but proper, in arranging our introduction.

I did not know where to respond, so I sent this to your mother in Pennsylvania, and asked her to forward it to you. If you receive it, you can respond to the address on the envelope.

With regard to the Wings, which are very beautiful, with a soft silver look, I will be pleased to wear them to show my support for the war effort. Ha Ha. Also, I did not know you could put someone's name on an airplane, but if you wish to put "Ginny" on yours, I'll know who you mean. I hope it brings you luck.

I am majoring in Music, with a minor in English Literature.

My family all said to wish you the best of luck, and to tell you that they will include you in their prayers, with the hope that this terrible war will be over soon. I share those wishes.

Your Special Friend, Ginny

CHAPTER SIX

LIEUTENANTS AT TWENTY

(West Coast Command)

A New Recruit Joins The Gang

After graduation the three new second lieutenants headed for Bruning Army Air Base in Nebraska, where they got a checkout in the P-47, followed by two months of operational training, which included a lot of air and ground gunnery training. All three loved the P-47 Thunderbolts, as they were magnificent, one-of-a-kind airplanes, designed by a genius.

Equipped with a monster eighteen-cylinder radial engine, the "Jugs" were huge, powerful machines, which appeared ungainly on the ground, but in the air were surprising agile and maneuverable. Further, they were armed with eight 50-caliber machine guns, four in each wing, giving them fantastic firepower that could instantly destroy any targets in front of them.

To teach them how to operate those guns effectively, quite a few flights were scheduled in which they fired at both stationary ground targets and towed aerial targets.

Interestingly, their training at Bruning also included scheduled skeet shooting sessions at the base's skeet range.

The Army had a theory that fighter pilots benefitted from shooting skeet by learning how to lead their targets. Consequently, each pilot was required to fire a specified number of rounds with shotguns at the base range. Ray, Andy, and Bill really enjoyed shooting skeet as a recreational sport, as all of them had done a certain amount of hunting with their parents as teenagers growing up.

Small game hunting was good in Nebraska and the three friends occasionally were able to borrow a shotgun as well as a Jeep from the skeet range at the base, and drive out into the countryside for some hunting. That led to an interesting event, which was to have long-term consequences.

One day, while sitting in a country diner with the borrowed shotgun, they met a rancher who told them he would be happy to see them shoot some coyotes, as he had some that were really bugging his animals. They chatted and the rancher told them he knew where there was a whole nest of them near a water pump on his property.

Interested, they drove with him to his place where he led them behind some outbuildings and showed them a hole where they lived. "I‘ve been trying to drown them," he said, drawing a bucket of water and pouring it down the hole. Then he dug down and came up with a shovel full of muddy earth in which there were a half dozen tiny mouse-like creatures, which were baby coyotes that still had their eyes closed. He told them he had to get rid of them, as their parents were grabbing his chickens and would soon be harassing his heavier stock.

As he was about to toss them into a bucket of water, Bill Crump asked him if he could have one. The rancher thought he was foolish, but said, "Be my guest. Have ‘em all, if you want." Crump took one and stuffed it in his shirt.

Later, he nursed it with an eyedropper and managed to keep it alive and growing. That baby coyote, which he named "Jeep," was later to achieve a measure of fame with the 360th Fighter Squadron as the only coyote to ever fly five combat missions!

Farmers' Daughters

There were lots of farms in Nebraska, with corn the predominant crop. There was also another excellent crop that Nebraska farmers produced – great-looking farmers' daughters! Apparently, farm life, with plenty of fresh air, good food, and vigorous exercise performing farm chores, produced an inordinate number of pretty girls with healthy (and quite normal) appetites of all types.

The influx of a carefully selected group of equally healthy new second lieutenant fighter pilots resulted in a volatile combination which, given the slightest spark, was bound to create some flash fires, and surely did.

Ray Burwell was a real Romeo, but I don't think he knew it. Tall and good-looking, Ray had a ready smile and a quick wit, so girls were naturally drawn to his charm, like pins to a magnet. The funny part of it was that he never seemed to give a conscious thought to the matter – it just happened. Not only that, he didn't seem to be able to turn one down, so that everywhere he went, new girls popped up, each one more interesting than the last.

When he was first called to active duty, several girls had contacted his parents to find out where he was stationed, so they could write to him. Not only that, but after he arrived at Emporia, Kansas, in his early training program, a girl named Lola was interested enough to want to chase him to Kansas and asked Ray's parents for his new address. Ray encouraged his parents not to give it to her.

More recently, he had sent a letter to his parents in which he expressed concern about another girl named Pat who was apparently chasing him and had made claims of some type. Ray included the following paragraph:

Pat isn't fooling me one bit, and I will never let any girl buffalo me, you may be sure!. It's true I like her quite a bit, but not so much that I can't reason this out. I'll have a lot of time to reason this out when I get home.

It appeared that Ray was going to have a lot of "reasoning out" when he finally got home – but he was actually just getting started!

It was mid-1944, and three young fighter pilots had just finished a grueling year's grind, overcome all obstacles, gained the coveted wings and gold lieutenant's bars they had sought, and were flying what they considered the world's best fighter, the P-47. Life was good and was to be enjoyed. Probably the simplest way to sum up the situation was to say that all three of the young pilots wasted no time in 'making hay while the sun shines,' and left some badly broken hearts behind them.

Meeting Doris

Harding AAB, Baton Rouge, Louisiana - July 1944

After completing operational training, the three were sent to Harding Field, near Baton Rouge, Louisiana, for further processing and to await shipment overseas. That was where Ray Burwell's troubles really began.

They were now considered to be fully trained P-47 pilots and had the expectation that this would essentially be a transition point, where they would await orders shipping them to whatever overseas destination the Army decreed.

Crump's girl and her mother had just arrived for a farewell visit and they took off somewhere. After getting settled in, Ray and Andy found themselves looking for something to do and considered going to

New Orleans, which was eighty miles away. However, upon checking the bulletin board they discovered that one of the big bands was visiting and would be playing for the dance at the Officer's Club on Saturday, which was only two days away. The band was "Les Brown and his Band of Renown" and they were featuring a new and very pretty singer named Doris Day.

It sounded interesting, but neither had a date and the time was too short to dredge one up. Nevertheless, they decided to take it in anyway. Their uniforms had taken a pretty good beating on the train from Nebraska, but they managed to finesse a rush job from the local dry cleaner, so they wouldn't look like they had already been in combat.

Come Saturday night, the club was packed to the gills and the place was jumping. The band was terrific and Doris Day was knocking them dead with songs like "Sentimental Journey," and "Swingin' on a Star" from a movie called *Going My Way*.

Neither Andy nor Ray was a drinker, but they squeezed up to the bar and managed to get something not too lethal. Every table was occupied, but they found themselves a convenient spot by the wall and started taking in the action on the jammed dance floor. Fighter pilots must have been considered good catches by the local populace, as there was certainly no shortage of good-looking girls in the place.

One pretty blonde girl, in particular, who cruised by in the arms of a first lieutenant, caught Ray's eye and he marveled at her beauty and poise, envying her partner. Seeing Ray staring at her, she gave him a tiny smile, then turned her attention back to her partner.

At the end of the number, he noticed that she cast a glance over her shoulder in his direction, but Ray assumed it must be aimed at another friend in the crowd. However, during the next dance, which was a fox trot, she actually turned and stared straight at Ray, then followed it up by turning around and looking at him after she and her partner had taken their seats at the conclusion of the dance.

My God, thought Ray. Is she actually inviting me to ask her to dance when she is sitting with a nice-looking guy? I must be imagining things.

However, the very next time she took the floor, it happened again, and this time she tossed a broad smile in his direction, leaving no doubt about her interest. That settled it. Ray did not know what to expect but figured it was definitely worth the risk, and the next time the couple took the floor, Ray walked over to them and simply said, "Excuse me, may I cut in?"

The lieutenant, who did not appear to be too shocked, looked at the girl, then turned to Ray and said, "Okay, just take good care of her." He handed her over to Ray, who took her hand and said, "Thanks, I will certainly do that."

It was a magical moment; the kind that only happens once in a lifetime, and his success almost left him breathless. He said to the girl, "I didn't know whether your date was going to slug me or what, but I had to find out."

She laughed and said, "Well, he's my date alright, but he is also my brother."

Ray's heart leapt up like he had just taken a shot of adrenalin. He actually stopped dancing, looked straight into her eyes, and said, "Wow!"

She returned the look, said nothing, and suddenly it was like everything stopped and the sound faded, as if someone had turned the volume down and there was no one else around. It was what the French call "Coup de Foudre.[3] " Nothing needed to be said; he simply

[3] Literally, "A stroke of lightning: "typically used to mean "Love at first sight." Ironically, it could also be interpreted as a "Thunderbolt!"

drew her closer and they danced silently for a few moments. After several rapturous minutes, he said simply, "Ray Burwell, Denair, California," and she replied, "Doris Clunan, Baton Rouge."

After that, everything around them dissolved into a state of background music and suppressed senses, which seemed to be working at half strength. They returned to the table where Doris somewhat shakily introduced Ray to her brother, Russell, and another local couple. With their encouragement, Ray called Andy over to the table and they somehow found another chair. Doris said that her brother, Russell, like Ray and Andy, was waiting for shipment overseas. Ray noted that Russell was not wearing wings and was sporting insignia on his collar which were not really familiar, but he thought they must be Intelligence, which later was confirmed as correct.

For the rest of the evening, Ray and Doris danced virtually every dance together, while Russell sat with a somewhat bemused smile on his face, as he recognized that the chance meeting of his sister with the tall, good-looking pilot was far more than a casual affair, and had all the earmarks of a landmark event.

Not to be outmaneuvered, Andy managed to find a cute, petite black-haired girl in the crowd and spent a lot of time showing off his considerable skill on the dance floor, particularly with the jitterbug numbers. While Ray and Doris descended into a world of their own, Andy proved to be far from a fifth wheel and, after bringing his new acquisition back to the table, turned out to be quite a raconteur.

At the end of the evening, Andy and his new friend decided to hang out at the club for a while, and Russell spoke quietly to his sister, who nodded and gave him a hug. Russell then turned to Ray and said, "Look, I have a car and you two obviously are not ready to go home, so I will drive us over to where I am quartered and Doris can take the car."

Ray was overwhelmed with emotion and felt like he was swinging on a star himself! They both expressed their gratitude to Russell for his thoughtfulness, and when Doris drove off, Ray already had his arm around her.

For the next five days, the two spent every possible moment exploring their own very private world together. How deep that exploration went will never be known, but on the fifth day Ray asked her to marry him and she immediately said, "Yes."

Several days later, Ray sent the following letter to his parents:

11 July 44

My Dearest Mom and Pop,

I am not able to tell you my whereabouts except that I am somewhere on the east coast. As to when we will leave for overseas, all I can say to that is that it is not in the too distant future.

I am well and am very anxious to get going. Of course, you can't blame me for that, as there is a war to win, and I want to do my part.

You are probably wondering about the phone call I made to you from Baton Rouge. Yes Folks, you know I've been going with girl after girl and not finding the right one. Well, at last I have. I met her in an amazing manner during a dance at the Base Officers Club. Well, this would sound strange to some people but not to you, it seems that things just happened to bring us together. I went with her for five days and Bingo we were both head over heels in love!

Now, on the Bible, I swear it isn't just another passing fancy. I know because I asked her to marry me and she readily accepted. She is a gorgeous thing and is about the sweetest girl I have ever met. She likes exactly the same things I do and we get along beautifully. Her name is Doris Clunan, but I'm going to change that when I come back from overseas. You'll both love her very much, I have no doubt. She is blonde, 5 ft. 6 in., built very, very good and is a beautiful girl for a wife. I am young yet and understand what it would be like if we were married. I am a pretty level headed kid and personally know that we should wait. We will just have to wait until I return and see what happens.

Doris is going to write you and also send a big picture that we had taken together. Possibly you have heard from her already. I surely hope so. Well, enough for now. I know you will think her a swell choice for a wife. I wish you had one of the pictures that I have of Doris. Everyone that sees it thinks she is beautiful, which is correct.

Tell everyone hello for me and please don't worry. I have all the confidence in the world and now that I have Doris I know everything will be okay.

Give old Pugs a big hug for me, will you? He sure is the world's greatest dog! Write me soon and never fear, I'll always write home.

Your loving Son, Ray

PS: It seems that I am going by a new name now. No one likes Orvil, and frankly I never liked it either, so I have been going by the name Ray, which I took from my middle name Loray. It's easy to remember and doesn't sound too bad. What do you think of the idea?

Two weeks later, Ray, Andy, and Bill shipped out for an unknown overseas destination.

The night before Ray's departure, he and Doris spent an agonizing farewell evening together, with the minutes melting away swiftly and neither knowing whether they would ever see each other again.

Their last week had been a frantic one, with serious consideration given to a quick marriage before a local justice of the peace and many other ideas, but neither wanted their marriage to be an ugly spur-of-the-moment affair. They wanted it to be a solemn and beautiful event that would set the stage for the rest of their lives together. So, in the end, common sense prevailed and they determined to just wait it out, taking events as they came until they could be together again. Their parting, at the railroad station, was a tearful one for both of them.

CHAPTER SEVEN

EIGHTH AIR FORCE

Shipping Out

May 1944

Riding on a British train, I reflected back upon my trip to England. After finishing operational training and checkout in the P-47 Thunderbolt fighter at Venice, Florida, our group of pilots had been herded onto a train, destination unknown, and nobody was allowed to even speculate about where we were going.

What amused the pilots, who were mostly second lieutenants with a few flight officers thrown in, was that everyone had been issued a mosquito net, bug repellent, and an olive drab uniform that looked exactly like infantry GI's. To top it off, we had been issued a pair of those ridiculous leggings that the doughboys wore in WW1, a steel helmet, a gas mask, and a duffle bag. They also checked our dog tags to make sure they were accurate, and made new ones if needed.

Everyone naturally assumed we were heading for the Pacific, as one did not need mosquito netting and bug repellent in Europe. However, the train headed straight for New York, where we were then directed to don every last stitch of the infantry garb, including the leggings and steel helmet, and were told that nobody was to wear any

Army Air Corps insignia of any type, including rank, but especially wings. The next thing we knew, we were being herded up one of a dozen gangplanks onto a giant passenger liner.

How ridiculous was that? What a clever deception plan – the enemy was supposed to think, by some wild stretch of the imagination, that this was a bunch of GI infantry heading for the Pacific to fight the Japanese. Ha, ha. If so, why were they shipping us out of New York, which would require the ship to go all the way around through the Panama Canal, instead of going by rail directly to the West Coast? It was almost comical, as there we were looking like a bunch of 1918 doughboys, heading for the trenches in France. Meanwhile, the guys in the Pacific could probably have used those thousands of mosquito nets, which most likely ended up in trash bins in Europe.

No name was painted on the ship, and nobody knew what ship it was. The pilots were assigned to one of the upper decks of the ship, with bunks to accommodate eight to a cabin. Loading of the ship continued nonstop for another full day, with infantry troops being swallowed up in half-a-dozen decks going right down into the hold.

During this time we weren't supposed to roam around, but I found ways to do some exploring and soon learned that the ship was a British Cunard White Star Liner, but no one knew which one.

In my exploration I discovered a very wide grand stairway that led to a vast main dining salon. Lining the walls were huge paintings showing the various liners of the Cunard Line. Featured most prominently was the Mauretania, sister ship of the old Lusitania, which had been sunk in WW1. Therefore, at first I assumed we were on the Mauretania, but upon comparing that ship to the one we were on, noted that it had four stacks, while we were on a giant three-stacker. After some further research and discussion with the other pilots in our cabin, the group decided we were on the Queen Mary, and somebody who was a ships buff said that the Mauretania had been retired in 1934.

Lady Doreen

Our ship had finally gotten underway and sailed out past the Statue of Liberty, the grand old lady holding her torch high. The word was soon out that the ship was headed for England. Clearly, the charade of the infantry uniforms, etc., had been part of some grand disinformation scheme to fool the ever-watchful enemy about where we were going. However, we concluded that the only ones fooled were our own guys, as it seemed almost ridiculous to think that in a port as large as New York – and considering all of the logistics involved – German agents did not have very good information to convey to their admiralty through one of the many neutral country embassies that contained friends.

Incredible as it seems, we soon learned that there were almost 9,000 men crammed onto that ship, which normally carried about 2,200 passengers. Therefore, the risk of a submarine sinking was a substantial one, and we could not help wondering what kind of panic would ensue if we were actually torpedoed. As it turned out, we did have several submarine contacts on the way across, but some naval ships and a lot of B-24s, along with other patrol aircraft, escorted the ship for about the first thousand miles. We then entered the mid-ocean gap, during which time we went unescorted but were travelling at a very high rate of speed – in excess of 28 knots – so that a submarine would have needed phenomenal luck to get a good shot at us.

Meals were a bit strange on that ship, but considering the number of men aboard I thought they did very well. Because there were so many troops, the ship served only two meals a day, so whenever possible we grabbed stuff for in between. Breakfast, British style, was a bit of a strain for some of the Americans, who had a tough time warming up to kippers and oatmeal in the morning. Personally, I thought the British oatmeal was great – made with whole rolled oats, instead of the flakes Americans use.

As the ship approached the English coast, it was thrilling to see Hawker Hurricanes and Spitfires buzzing overhead and sometimes putting on a show by beating up the ship a bit. It reminded me that I was really in wartime England, three years after having sat in a high school class wondering if the war would end before I could get there.

The ship docked at Liverpool and after a lot of milling around in a huge dockside area, we finally boarded a train filled with replacement pilots, then sat there for hours, probably to make sure everyone was heading to the correct destination. I speculated that, with such a large bunch of guys, about a third would end up on the wrong train.

Any gooom, Chum? *(Artist John Purdy)*

While we were sitting in the cars with the windows open, a pack of British kids started working the train, looking for handouts. Their standard call was, "Any gum, chum?" However, it wasn't pronounced gum, with a soft "u"; their pronunciation of gum sounded like "doom" – hence "Any Goooom, Chum?" The result of this was a veritable shower of chewing gum, candy, cakes and biscuits, and some cigarettes. Those kids knew a good racket when they saw one and thought the GIs were a gift from heaven.

The train finally took off through the English landscape, which we found to be amazingly green. However, it was early May and we guessed that England gets lots of rain in the springtime. After a half day of chugging across the English countryside, many of us disembarked at a town called Shrewsbury, which was very close to the Welsh border.

It was kind of a grimy place that did not look too prosperous, and we speculated that the main occupation might be coal mining, perhaps in nearby Wales. The people were very friendly to the new bunch of Yanks, but spoke with a very thick accent that some of the guys had trouble understanding.

Atcham

We piled out and boarded a string of lorries (we were already picking up English terms), which took us to a nearby airfield called Atcham, where we were assigned bunks in a row of Quonset huts, each of which contained about twenty guys.

Atcham seemed to be a very busy place, with lots of airplanes of many types zooming around overhead and almost everyone on the ground riding bikes. Curiously, the place seemed to be loaded with barbed wire, in those concertina rolls that are used on battlefields, and I wondered why they needed the stuff at all, when Atcham was apparently a long way from the coast and any conceivable type of enemy action. It struck me also that the idea of bikes and barbed wire was not such a hot combination, and in that regard, my speculation proved to be prescient not too long thereafter.

The next day, all of us new pilots were assigned to various flight line units where we were given the lowdown on the situation with regard to enemy action. It was 1944, and while the Germans were still masters of almost the entire European Continent, the days of active raids against England were virtually over. Total Allied airpower now significantly eclipsed that of the Germans so that, other than an occasional German reconnaissance flight, there was little threat from enemy airplanes.

However, closer to the coast, the V-1 "buzz bombs," or "doodlebugs" as the British called them, were a continuing menace, as they were being sent across the Channel daily against targets in England, mainly London and other large cities. V-1s did not have an accurate guidance system, and were thus basically terror weapons that were programmed to fly in a specific direction for a set amount of time before diving into whatever happened to be beneath. At Atcham, we were well beyond typical V-1 range.

The airfield was loaded with P-47s, which were mostly all razorback models, as the newer D-25 models with the "bubble canopies" were all going to the fighting squadrons. Flying was essentially a repeat of what we had undergone in operational training units in the States, except that it was a lot more wild and wooly, with nobody posting regulations about low flying and the like. Young fighter pilots are typically filled with enthusiasm, and at Atcham they often worked some of it off by flying up the valleys in Wales, buzzing everything in sight, and treating the people to some special aerobatic shows. The word was that the Welsh people loved it.

One thing that quickly became clear to us was that England was a mass of airfields. There was a saying, 'Fly ten minutes in any direction and you will find an airfield.' However, there was a similarity in design of many of the airfields, which could turn out to be a problem if you did not pay careful attention to the specific landmarks around your base.

In fact, that very similarity almost got me into trouble one day when I called in for landing and got the okay from the tower. I roared in over the runway and pitched up in a typical landing pattern, which was to pull up in a steep climbing turn and dump the landing gear and full flaps while bending the bird around in a continuous turn almost to landing. It looked really pretty from the ground, as the air in Europe was always very damp, and all of the time you were in the turn there were streamers coming off of your wing tips.

Making a real showy landing, I set it down on the runway nicely and was beginning to slow my "after-landing roll" when I noticed a runway-length marker go by and realized I had landed on the wrong field and was quickly running out of runway. In fact, my Jug went right off the end of the runway onto a grass swale, which continued down a nice grassy bank with no obstacles!

Now, here is the beauty of a Republic P-47 Thunderbolt. That big airplane had a very wide landing gear, and there was a tail wheel which you could disengage. I reached down, unlocked the tail wheel, swung the Jug around with no problem, applied power, and taxied the airplane back up the grassy bank onto the runway.

As I sat there in the cockpit, with engine ticking over, wondering where the hell I had landed, a young RAF ground-crew man rode up on a bicycle and climbed up on the wing. He seemed to be thrilled to be standing on one of the much-vaunted American Thunderbolts. I asked him, "What is this place?" and he told me it was an RAF training base with Miles Masters trainers.

"Where is Atcham?" I asked, and he pointed and said, "About ten miles over that way." I thanked him and waved as he gave me a smiling salute and mounted his bike. Then I taxied back to takeoff position, got a green light from the tower – which was not on my radio frequency – and took to the air.

After climbing up a bit, I gave the field a once-over and discovered that it was an exact replica of my base, except that it was about half scale. I was lucky it had such a nice patch of grass at the end of the runway. Needless to say, I didn't tell the operations people at Atcham that I had been dumb enough to land at the wrong field!

Bikes and Barbed Wire

Earlier I mentioned that everybody at Atcham travelled around on bicycles and all of us new fighter pilots soon joined that crowd, as there were lots of bikes around, which we took over from their previous owners who had departed for squadrons. They were all British bikes, which were tall things with skinny tires, unlike the balloon-tire ones that were the popular type in America at that time. The type didn't matter, though, as they were bikes and they enabled us to get around easier than walking everywhere, as the base was well spread out.

There was, however, one significant difference from American bikes. The brake control was on the handlebars, and comprised a small lever that you squeezed, which in turn caused a pad to press against the front wheel rim for braking. It worked well but took a little getting used to, as we were all used to the U.S. style, which was simply to reverse peddling and push down on the rear pedal. After a short checkout and transition, everyone zipped around with no problem.

That was, however, before our first visit to Shrewsbury. About twenty of us pedaled our bikes to a place by the main gate where we parked them, and a GI truck gave us a ride into Shrewsbury, which, as previously noted, was a grimy industrial town. But nobody was concerned about that, as it was a town and, as such, possessed two particular attractions that had been missing elsewhere: pubs and women.

One thing that Britain was never short of was beer, which tasted okay, but we soon discovered it was always served warm – ice was not to be had. Another thing we quickly learned was that you never ordered a bottle of beer, as every pub was equipped with a row of taps. You simply asked for a "pint" and the pub keeper drew a glass mugful, with a small head of foam on the top.

For guys who preferred a heavier-type drink, Guinness Stout was available in endless quantities. However, for people who didn't drink, it was difficult to find a pub that had any kind of soft drinks. The only substitute was a drink called Shandy, which was a mixture of half beer and half lemonade. However, the local pub-crawlers, who were mostly grimy-looking elderly miners with coal dust embedded into the wrinkles in their faces, considered Shandy to be a drink for women and wimps, and were highly amused to see an American fighter pilot drinking the stuff. The crowd of pilots that I was with did not provide them with much amusement.

With respect to the opposite sex, there was a surprising quantity of good-looking young women in the town, and they were downright friendly to the "Yank fliers," as they called us. In fact, the ratio of women to men in Shrewsbury was about two to one, as most of the local young men were off somewhere in the military services, and had been for a long time judging by the readiness of the girls to throw smiles at the healthy-looking American pilots.

It turned out to be a rip-roaring evening, with the various pubs reaping good business from the Yanks, and the pack gradually splitting into smaller groups as various liaisons were made and people disappeared in many directions. Those of us who remained reasonably sober noticed one thing. The older people in the town, particularly the women, looked with disgust upon some of the women who let themselves be picked up. I heard one of them call after a woman who went off on the arm of a Yank, "For shame, you hussy, when your husband has been fighting with the 8th Army in Africa for two years."

A small subconscious thought crept into my head, *Maybe that is why she went off with him.* But I immediately tried to suppress it.

The GI truck was supposed to pick us up at 11 p.m., but it was at least 11:30 before most of the pack straggled to the meeting place. There are always a few in every pack who either can't hold their booze or make it a point of drinking themselves into idiocy, and in that regard our group was no exception. The ride back was a raucous one, with lots of songs being sung, most of which had some kind of sexual content – a favorite one being:

I used to work in Chicago, in a department store.

I used to work in Chicago, I did but I don't anymore.

A lady came in, she asked for some cloth,

I asked her what kind she adored.

Felt, she said, and felt her I did.

I did but I don't anymore.

This was sung with endless variations, dealing with various hardware store items that the subject lady inquired about – stupid but amusing.

We drove in the main gate, piled out of the truck, and everybody grabbed the first bike in sight and started down the hill toward our row of Quonset huts, which were set in an enclosure surrounded by concertina wire. Most of the pack had sense enough to remember the difference with British bikes, but two of those who had been singing the loudest streaked off down the hill like a shot, trying to beat the pack. They actually did okay in the race and got there first, as they were operating on reflex actions, but their befuddled brains were obviously still back in the States. When they went to apply the brakes, they pedaled backwards frantically to no avail, streaked right past the Quonset huts, and plowed straight into a roll of barbed concertina wire at the bottom of the hill!

There was a pretty bad scene after that, which lasted about half an hour, as the Officer of the Day called the ambulance, then organized a party of the soberest to help extricate the badly lacerated and bleeding pair, who then spent the next week in the base hospital. In wartime, casualties happen, but as the British like to say, "There is always the unexpected."

Booze and Barbed Wire Don't Mix! *(Artist John Purdy)*

Another incident occurred around that time – again the result of too much booze. Most of the pilots were content to hit the sack after a day of flying and other duties, but on occasion a pack would head for town and, as usual, some would arrive back fairly well soused. Our Quonset huts had a light in each end, with individual switches, and "lights out" was typically at ten o'clock. One Saturday night we had just gotten into a sound sleep when suddenly the lights went on with a blinding flash, as four half-drunk guys arrived back at the Quonset after a visit to town.

The guy in the next cot yelled, "Shut that goddamned light off!" He was answered with a lot of ribald comments, such as "Blow it out of your barracks bag." That did not sit too well with the guy in the next bed, who was apparently one of those people who does not wake up in a good mood. Next thing he yelled was, "Put out that f--ing light or I am going to shoot it out!" – and there he was with his .45 pistol in hand!

The light stayed on, and the next thing I heard was a loud "*Blam*!" and the overhead light dissolved in a cloud of sparks and smoke, after which the slug undoubtedly continued through the thin metal roof of the Quonset to who knows where.

Oh, boy, I thought, *this is going to be trouble*, and everybody rushed to their sacks, pulling up their blankets to pretend they had all been sound asleep. Five minutes later, the Officer of the Day entered the hut with a flashlight in his hand, and asked if there was any problem. He was assured that there was no problem, and after flashing the light around a bit, the O.D. never said another word and just left. He had to have known, as you could still smell the smoke from the gunpowder, as well as from the burnt wiring. I guess he was just relieved to know that no one had been shot, and let well enough alone.

Martlesham Heath

After about two weeks in Atcham, thirteen of us P-47 replacement pilots piled into a 6x6 truck and headed for our assigned unit, which was the 356th Fighter Group, located at Martlesham Heath, near the coast in East Anglia. The names of our group seemed to follow the alphabetical listing that I had noticed in the training command, as they were: Gleason, Laviolette, Nebinger, Olive, Peacock, Pleasant, Rideout, Romine, Russell, Servocky, Taylor, Urban, and Williams.

It appeared that once again, in true Army style, thirteen names had been taken off of some list, in alphabetical order, in the same manner as back in the training command. I wondered, sometimes, what happens to guys whose names start with X, like Xavier, or Z for Zilch!

An interesting thing happened on the way to our assigned group. We were riding GI-style in the back of a 6x6 truck and stopped in Debden, where the American 4th Fighter Group was stationed. We did not know it at the time, but the 4th group was to become famous as the top-scoring American group in the 8th Air Force Fighter Command, with over a thousand kills by the end of the war. Curiously, it had also been the home base for the all-volunteer American Eagle Squadron, which had flown Hurricanes and Spitfires alongside the RAF during the early days of the war and the Battle of Britain. As a high school kid in 1940, my heroes had been the pilots who flew with the Eagle Squadron, and here I was, at the very base where they had flown.

Because of its early record and the aggressive spirit of its leaders, the 4th Fighter Group was one of the first to be equipped with the new North American P-51 fighters, which provided them with significant additional range for bomber escort and penetration of enemy territory. While we were there, the group returned from a mission in which they had tangled with a pack of German fighters. They had shot down some Me.109s, but I overheard one of the flight leaders giving a pilot hell for letting another one get away.

I had been admiring the sleek-looking P-51 Mustangs as they were taxiing in and commented on this to some of my fellow pilots. My remarks must have been overheard by one of the squadron commanders, who was wearing lots of ribbons and could have been a former Eagle himself. He came up to me and asked whether I would like to stay with the 4th Fighter Group. Wow. It was a strange moment of decision and I was tempted to say yes, but there I was with twelve of my fellow pilots, all of us trained on P-47s, so I decided to stay with my group. I told him my decision and thanked him for the offer.

I did not know it at the time, but that was a fateful decision. I had passed up the opportunity to become a member of the leading American fighter group – to join instead what would become known as the "hard luck 356th," which ended up with the worst loss to kills record of all fifteen American fighter groups. Years later, I realized that as a member of the 4th, I would either have quickly become an ace or quickly become dead. The 4th group had great leaders who did everything in their power to find enemy aircraft and destroy them. I was later to learn that – while the 356th had some excellent leaders at the squadron level and an excellent Deputy Commander, its Group Commander should never have been assigned to lead a combat fighter group.

The Castle

After several more hours of driving, our group of thirteen arrived at our new base, Martlesham Heath, which was located just outside of Ipswich in Suffolk, East Anglia. We did not go directly to the airfield but were first dropped off at our new living quarters, Playford Hall. I couldn't believe it; it wasn't a hall, it was a fifteenth-century brick mansion, and it actually had a moat around it filled with water and one small bridge!

Playford Hall

While everyone referred to it – American style – as the "castle," it really wasn't a castle at all, but was in fact a brick building several stories high, with many chimneys to support multiple fireplaces.

Clearly, it had been built as a country manor for some of England's aristocracy, but while not constructed in true castle style, its moat indicated that its builders still considered it prudent to incorporate certain defensive measures, as English history was replete with small wars and factional disputes.

Initially, I was assigned to bunk in an adjoining carriage house, outside of the moat, but shortly thereafter was moved onto the second floor, where we had six pilots bunking in one very large room. Bathroom facilities were down the hall and were not too bad, indicating that some modifications had occurred in recent years. There were actually a couple of huge bathtubs, but we soon learned that it was rare that the castle had enough hot water to support a full bath. All things considered, however, we would be living damned plush as compared to the ground pounders, who spent most of their military lives in GI barracks, tents, shot-up houses, and, oftentimes, foxholes in the ground that were half filled with muddy water.

The next day, we were taken by truck to the airfield, which was always referred to as Martlesham, and checked in at the 360th Fighter Squadron, which had its operations in a kind of tarpaper shack instead of the typical Quonset hut. It was equipped with a big blackboard for mission assignments and other data, a teletype machine by which the squadron intelligence officer received the operations orders from higher headquarters and transmitted his "after mission" reports, and a briefing room in which the pilots received final instructions and reported back at the completion of each mission.

We also noted that at the end of our operations shack, there was a little bar, which had the squadron insignia of a flaming sword painted prominently on its front. I soon learned that the little bar did, in fact, do some flaming good business at the completion of each combat mission, following debriefing.

It is a little known fact that combat pilots (and I assume other crew members) were entitled by Army regulations to two shots of whiskey after each mission. Further, that so-called nerve-bracing medicine was officially metered out liberally by Doctor Carey, our squadron flight surgeon, who was the recipient of the booze through official channels.

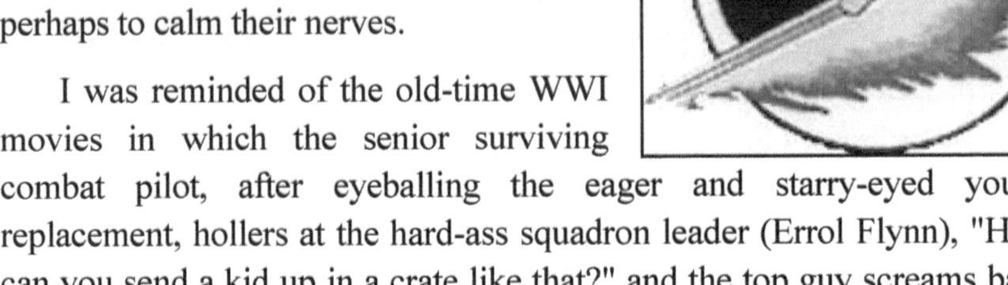

The whiskey was obviously a carryover from World War I when pilots were flying in open cockpit planes in freezing weather and probably needed the stuff to thaw them out a bit, as well as perhaps to calm their nerves.

I was reminded of the old-time WWI movies in which the senior surviving combat pilot, after eyeballing the eager and starry-eyed young replacement, hollers at the hard-ass squadron leader (Errol Flynn), "How can you send a kid up in a crate like that?" and the top guy screams back at him, "THOSE ARE THE ORDERS!"

Speaking of crates, they must have had a goodly number of extra P-47s, or were really hard up for replacement pilots, because shortly thereafter each of us new pilots was assigned a P-47, and we were allowed to paint whatever insignia or names we wished on the side of the bird. Mine was a P-47D-5 model, which was a tired-looking "razorback" [4] with the squadron letter, a big PI, painted on the side, plus my own letter, which was A. Hence, I became PI-A, a set of letters which subsequently carried over to my Mustang after our group switched over to the longer-range P-51D fighters later in the year.

As noted previously, everybody referred to the P-47s as "Jugs." It was never clear where the name came from; some claimed it was short for "Juggernauts," but it appeared to me it was more likely because they were fat, like little brown jugs. In any case, it was a good name.

The ranking squadron officers and a few of the more experienced pilots were fortunate in being assigned to the later-model Jug (the D-25), which differed mainly in that it was equipped with the new bubble

---

[4] Early-model P-47s had a ridge behind the cockpit running to the tail. These "razorbacks" decreased drag but caused a blind spot aft. Later P-47s had a bubble canopy with 360 degree vision.

canopy, which afforded greatly improved visibility, particular to the rear, where an enemy airplane was likely to sneak up on you. The other significant factor was that the later-model Jugs were equipped with water injection tanks that held thirty gallons of water, as compared to fifteen gallons in the razorbacks.

For those who have never heard of water injection, let me say that it was an amazing development, which the new pilots, when initially briefed on it, could scarcely believe! The P-47s were powered by a Pratt & Whitney eighteen-cylinder R-2800 radial engine, developing 2,000 horsepower at full throttle, which on the gauges was 57 inches of mercury and 2,700 rpm. These were very high-compression engines and their high-altitude performance was greatly increased through the use of a special supercharger, which was driven by what was called a waste-gate turbine – essentially a turbine wheel in the exhaust manifold.

Now, for those not in the know, here is the part that is hard to believe. There was a little toggle switch on the top of the throttle, and when the engine was running wide open, a flick of that toggle would send a jet of water into the intake manifolds, which increased the power by as much as 600 horsepower! Unbelievable but true. How was that possible?

The fact was that the R-2800 engines were already burning special 130-octane (anti-knock) fuel, and efforts to squeeze more power out of them by increasing the manifold pressure could result in "detonation," which is essentially a form of pre-ignition that robs the engine of its full-power potential.

How then, you may ask, does shooting a jet of water into the engine improve the situation? The answer is that the water, which is introduced into the intake manifold, enters the combustion chambers as a fine mist, which cools and aids the atomization of the intake mix, resisting detonation by making the mixture burn slower, and thus squeezing even more power out of the great engine!

In practice, when you hit the toggle while running at full power, there was a momentary gulp – then the engine gave a burst of power which was not unlike that which occurs when lighting the afterburners in modern jet fighters. Water injection was great for providing an extra burst of power to get you out of a jam, or to give you an edge over an adversary. However, after running with water injection for fifteen minutes, the engine oil strainers usually showed evidence of fine metal filings, indicating that the extra power was taking its toll on the internal parts of the engine.

One other thing was different in the combat aircraft. All of the aircraft were equipped with new paddle-bladed propellers (four-bladed), as compared to the ones with the narrower blades we had flown in all of our previous training. The huge new paddle-bladed props provided significant advantages in climb and cruise performance, and resulted in additional fuel savings for longer missions.

Another advantage, which we would find out later, was that they increased the ability of the Jugs to turn tighter in a dogfight, as the huge props acted like a big gyro; in fact, you could actually use the quality of gyros known as "precession" to help whip you around dramatically in a tight left turn.

Kesgrave Hall During WW2

The 360th Fighter Squadron was one of the three squadrons of the 356th Fighter Group, 8th Air Force – the other two squadrons being the 359th and 361st, all flying out of Martlesham. We learned later that the pilots of the 359th squadron lived at another country manor called Kesgrave Hall, while those of the 361st lived on the base. Apparently, we had lucked out in our assignment of quarters.

Our squadron commander was Major John Vogt, who, we soon learned, was not only a decent man but also a very competent and stable leader. (Many years later, Major Vogt became commanding general of all of the USAF forces in Europe – USAFE.) The operations officer was

Captain Cota, but Captain Ellingson, a senior combat officer, often substituted for him. Other key members of the squadron staff included Captain "Doc" Carey, our good natured Flight Surgeon, Captain Ragnell, Engineering/Maintenance; Captain Symmes, Armament; and Lieutenant Levy, Intelligence.

Our group of thirteen arrived at the squadron on around May 28. Initial plans called for some additional operational training in England, so for a few days some extra training flights were scheduled, which resulted largely in droning around the beautiful green English countryside in large formations and at very low altitudes, perhaps to give some additional encouragement to the English people that more Americans were arriving daily and that the invasion could not be far off.

Their assumption was, of course, quite correct, and every country road for a hundred miles around was packed with endless rows of trucks, tanks, Jeeps, artillery pieces, and other such pieces of gear, all lined up waiting for the great invasion which would take place at some point, but nobody knew when.

Shortly after arriving at our new base, I was surprised to receive a letter from Mellie Papas, which must have been chasing after me. She wrote to tell me that Eddie Thoma – my pal from Bethlehem, Pennsylvania, her fiancée – was also stationed in England and had been assigned to the 384th Bombardment Squadron, 544th Bomb Group, a B-17 outfit at RAF Station Grafton Underwood. She said that after getting checked out in B-17s in Texas, Ody had actually been temporarily assigned to a B-17 ferry crew as co-pilot at Scott Field, Illinois, where they picked up a factory-new bomber and flew it across the ocean, via Iceland, directly to his new base in England. Thus, Ody had already gotten a nice bit of experience in the airplane under his belt.

Mellie also wrote that as far as their engagement went, both sets of parents were delighted and were busily sending photographs and other information back and forth between Mississippi and Pennsylvania.

However, beyond that, there was nothing she could do except write letters, pray, and wait the war out.

I looked up Grafton Underwood on the map and discovered it was considerably inland, in the west-northwest direction, near a town called Kettering. There was no hope of getting a phone call through to Ody in wartime England, so I sent him a brief letter telling him where I was located and that I would see if I could borrow the group's UC-64 "Norseman" liaison plane to fly up for a visit.

CHAPTER EIGHT
THE INVASION

D-Day, June 6, 1944

Our squadron was slated to conduct another week or so of training for us new pilots, but events intervened. On the morning of June 5, I happened to be talking to Captain Ragnell, our squadron maintenance officer, and he told me that the 356th group had just received a special order to have all aircraft painted with broad black and white stripes by 0100 hours, June 6.

I said to him, "That has got to mean that tomorrow is the invasion!" But he said he didn't think so. I offered to bet him five pounds that tomorrow was D-Day, and he took me up on it.

I won that bet, because the next morning the entire squadron was awakened in the very wee hours and ordered to wear pistols and gas masks. By the time we arrived at the flight line, we could hear thousands of engines rumbling overhead, as hundreds of bombers and transport aircraft were already aloft, heading for destinations somewhere across the English Channel.

The operations briefing map revealed a series of very short lines for penetration points along the Normandy Coast by our three squadrons, and the mission was simply "targets of opportunity;" i.e., hit anything that moved on the roads and railroads, with major emphasis upon armor and support vehicles.

SUPREME HEADQUARTERS
ALLIED EXPEDITIONARY FORCE

June 6, 1944
360th Fighter Squad.
England

Soldiers, Sailors and Airmen of the Allied Expeditionary Force!

You are about to embark upon the Great Crusade, toward which we have striven these many months. The eyes of the world are upon you. The hopes and prayers of liberty-loving people everywhere march with you. In company with our brave Allies and brothers-in-arms on other Fronts, you will bring about the destruction of the German war machine, the elimination of Nazi tyranny over the oppressed peoples of Europe, and security for ourselves in a free world.

Your task will not be an easy one. Your enemy is well trained, well equipped and battle-hardened. He will fight savagely.

But this is the year 1944! Much has happened since the Nazi triumphs of 1940-41. The United Nations have inflicted upon the Germans great defeats, in open battle, man-to-man. Our air offensive has seriously reduced their strength in the air and their capacity to wage war on the ground. Our Home Fronts have given us an overwhelming superiority in weapons and munitions of war, and placed at our disposal great reserves of trained fighting men. The tide has turned! The free men of the world are marching together to Victory!

I have full confidence in your courage, devotion to duty and skill in battle. We will accept nothing less than full Victory!

Good Luck! And let us all beseech the blessing of Almighty God upon this great and noble undertaking.

Dwight Eisenhower

Multiple missions were planned, and by 0430 our first mission was already in the air, heading for the French coast. Apparently, some of the airplanes took off with the paint still wet. All of us new guys were eager to go on a mission, but were worried they were going to keep us in squadron training school for another week. However, things moved swiftly and there was a maximum effort underway, so they kept adding missions and offered to take several of us new pilots on a mission. We cut cards to see who would go; I was lucky enough to draw a queen and was one of those scheduled.

We took off when it was still dark, climbed up above a low overcast, and flew toward the coast of Normandy. On the way, two buzz bombs flew right past the squadron, heading for England, but no one was allowed to break formation and go after them. The Brits, who had special units equipped with the very fast Hawker Tempest fighters, would probably shoot them down before they could hit their inland targets.

Approaching the coast of Normandy, there was a solid deck of clouds beneath us, but we could see continuous flashing that lit up the clouds. This was the invasion fleet bombarding the coast to soften up the landing zones. Nobody knew whether this was a feint or the real invasion, but initial indications were that it was the real thing. In fact, upon reaching the squadron that morning, each of us had been handed a special circular signed by General Eisenhower, which began with the words, "Soldiers, Sailors and Airmen of the Allied Expeditionary Force."

We could not see any of the beachheads because of the cloud cover, but about twenty-five miles inland our squadron found a couple of holes and dropped through the overcast where things still looked pretty dark underneath. The squadron then split up into four flights of four, as we fanned out to probe for targets of opportunity. There was very little traffic on the roads and absolutely no sign of armor moving toward the landing zones. Also, while we had been cautioned to keep our eyes open for enemy fighters, there was not a sign of them. If this was, indeed, the great invasion, Hitler had surely been taken by surprise.

As missions go, that first one was a pretty dull start. The few vehicles on the road, which we shot up, appeared to be civilian ones, and I hoped they weren't French milkmen making their early-morning rounds, if they have such things in France. We also inadvertently flew over a flak tower, which fired at us with small-caliber mg flak, but tracers warned us and we turned back and completely destroyed it.

They scheduled a lot of extra missions that day, and the pace was so hectic that some of them did not even get recorded. However, I didn't get to fly again until June 8, when our squadron put up a maximum effort of six flights of four each, all carrying 165-gallon belly tanks and two general-purpose 500-pound bombs. (The Jugs could easily handle that bomb load and a lot more). While there was some increased activity on the roads leading to the beachheads, they were certainly not packed with armor moving up, making us wonder what the Germans were waiting for.

Later we were to learn that Hitler had held most of his armor back, as he was convinced that Normandy was a feint and expected the real invasion to be through Holland or Belgium. The Allies had, in fact, been very successful with a grand deception plan that had General Patton commanding a large Army directly across the Channel, which Hitler thought would be the spearhead of the real invasion.

German reconnaissance flights prior to D-Day had confirmed that General Patton's army, waiting in East Anglia, did indeed have thousands of tanks straight across the Channel in apparent readiness to serve as the spearhead for the real invasion. However, Hitler never discovered that the army was a complete fake and that the many tanks and support vehicles were in fact made out of rubber and inflated! The American rubber manufacturers must have had some good business out of that.

One thing that had increased sharply behind the beachheads, however, was enemy flak, as every road intersection and railroad yard was loaded with it. We were working over what appeared to be a bivouac area when the guy in front of me took a hit, caught fire, and bailed out. My flight then dive-bombed and destroyed some canal boats, while the rest of the group bombed and strafed marshaling yards, trains, truck convoys, a powerhouse, and a small armored column. That sounds like a pretty good day, but our group of three squadrons lost six planes that day, of which five were due to flak, while one guy dive-bombed an ammunition train too low and it exploded, blowing him up with it. From a tactical odds standpoint, this was not a very successful result.

In the days that followed, the American 9th Air Force, which was also equipped with P-47s, began moving into bases in France as soon as the airfields were captured and cleared. Consequently, our missions began to gradually switch over to escort of various light-bomber groups, as they attacked targets in advance of our invasion forces, as well as some deeper in enemy territory.

"Hard Luck"

June 13-15

Following the invasion, missions continued at a substantial pace. The days became considerably longer and we were using what was called "British Double Summer Time," which meant that it was still light at almost 2200 (10 p.m.). On June 13, we flew a long, uneventful escort mission, which did not take off until almost 1830 and crossed back over the Channel at almost 2200. It was close to 2300 when we shut down engines and dragged ourselves out of our P-47s.

Nevertheless, the next morning we were awakened at 0400 and went on a mission escorting bombers at 25,000 feet to a target in France. I was wingman for the leader of Vortex Blue Flight. It was uneventful, except that we lost the number four man in my flight, Lt. Fred Phillips, who was on his second mission.

On our return from the escort mission, Phillips called Blue leader Captain L'Heureux and reported that his engine was cutting out.

Thinking that Phillips was having a problem with his supercharger, which would only impact the aircraft at high altitude, L'Heureux told him to drop down through the overcast on course, and he would meet him there. They rejoined below the overcast and Blue four tried various ideas to get it restarted, but to no avail; the engine was totally dead. Vortex Blue leader then advised him to continue trying to restart, but if not successful to bail out at 8,000 feet. Upon reaching that altitude, Phillips opened the canopy, rolled over, and dropped out over Belgium. His chute opened okay and he was seen to land safely. He was later reported to be a POW.

Ironically, Phillips' favorite expression, for some reason, was "Hard Luck," and that in fact was the name he had painted on the side of his Jug. While he was reporting his unsuccessful efforts to restart and his intention of bailing out, a voice came over the radio and said quietly, "Hard Luck."

As time went on, we learned that Phillips' engine probably went out due to what was called a "vapor lock." This could happen when you ran a fuel tank out and did not switch to another quickly enough. The engine fuel pumps would greedily suck in a bunch of air, instead of fuel, and subsequently, after you had switched to a tank with fuel in it, the pumps would not be able to pull fuel into the engine to keep it running.

This was a critical bit of knowledge, as we carried external tanks full of fuel that we used up before dropping them, typically either one 165-gallon belly tank or two 108-gallon wing tanks.

In Thunderbolts, fuel conservation was everything, as the big engine gobbled up fuel at a terrific rate; therefore, it was important to use every bit of external fuel before switching to internal tanks. There was a little fuel pressure gauge on our instrument panel, and when a selected tank was running out, the needle would drop once, then go back up, then drop a second time, at which point the engine would cut out.

I don't know how I did it with everything else we were looking out for, but I became very proficient at catching that needle drop, out of the corner of an eye, and quickly switching tanks before the second drop. Those were the little things that could keep you flying, instead of ending up in an enemy prisoner of war camp.

That same day the group flew a second fighter/bomber sweep carrying 165-gallon belly tanks plus clusters of fragmentation bombs under each wing. Major Vogt was leading the squadron, and once again I was Blue number two on Captain L'Heureux's wing. We made landfall near the Dieppe area and split up, with the 359th flying top cover while the other two squadrons looked for targets of opportunity on the ground.

I don't know where the 359th was looking, but about a dozen Me.109s suddenly made a very fast attack out of the sun and kept right on going through us. On the way, one flew right up behind Tex Green, who was one of our number four guys, and blasted hell out of his Jug with 20mm and lots of MG ammo. (The 109G carried one 20mm or 30mm cannon that fired through the propeller hub, and two 13.2mm machine guns in the nose. Some carried additional guns under the wings.) Fortunately, Green was flying a stout Republic P-47, which stayed in the air as a flying wreck and carried him home.

Everybody jettisoned their frag bombs and milled around, with Vogt trying his best to find the Jerries (as the Germans were tabbed), who had disappeared through a low cloud deck. We did not have much success other than one damage claim. The squadron got back to Martlesham at almost 2300, with everyone very low on fuel, as we had been running almost wide open at low level trying to find the German fighters.

I landed with fifteen gallons left, after taking off with 470, plus the frags – a pretty good load. When we got back to operations, everybody caught hell from Group for not keeping their eyes open, and I'm sure the 359th squadron commander heard some fancy words. I was becoming fatigued from lack of sleep after flying three long missions in about eighteen hours. Nevertheless, the next day we took off again at 0530 to escort bombers attacking the enemy ahead of our advancing troops in France.

Castle Clowns & Nose Art

In the time between missions, living at the castle was always interesting, as there are always a goodly number of real clowns and characters among fighter pilots. The big room where I was bunking with five other pilots was no exception, and whenever we were getting ready to drive to the airfield for missions, that room was always filled with lots of levity. A guy across the room, Lt. Roy Bluhm, was one of the so-called "old boys," who had been there for a while.

Bluhm had one peculiarity that amused everyone. For some reason he slept in his birthday suit and would wake up and stroll down the hall, buck naked, to the bathroom facilities, then return to his cot and begin dressing. The very first item he donned was always his white silk flying scarf, followed by underwear, flying suit, jacket, and other assorted gear. Whenever Bluhm was going through this routine, there was no end to the ribald remarks being tossed out, including suggestions that maybe he should put on his armor plate to protect his prized nether regions, etc.

Another of the "old boys" was Lt. Robert Leidy, who was quite proud of being a "Down Easterner" from Aroostook County, way up in northern Maine (where they grew the potatoes), and had the broad twang in his voice to prove it.

I recall one time when he grinned broadly and announced to the room at large, "I got me a day off today and borrowed the Jeep, so I'm gonna drive on down the road fur a piece and pick up my girl. Ha Ha."

Not a bad double entendre for a potato farmer, I reflected. Fighter squadrons are filled with all kinds of characters and hidden talent.

Our group had received a new bunch of later-model P-47s, which probably came from some fighter groups that were switching over to the newer P-51s. However, most of these went to the guys who had been flying the older Jugs the longest.

As a relatively new guy, I was still flying my old razorback Jug, PI-A, which now sported the name "Miss Ginny" on the engine cowling, as well as an insignia that comprised an eagle swooping down and dramatically crushing a swastika in its claws. I probably read too many of those dime airplane magazines before the war.

There were some really imaginative names and designs on the side of our airplanes, and our squadron painter was really good at creating the art that each pilot wanted.

My favorite was the one that Ed Pleasant had painted on his Jug. Ed, who smoked cigars constantly, hailed from Turners Falls, Massachusetts, and was one of the thirteen of us who all arrived at the squadron the same day. He was a good guy with a nice sense of humor.

Along the whole side of his Jug he had painted a skeleton sitting on a coffin, firing a tripod-mounted machine gun. The skeleton was wearing a helmet and goggles, as well as a flying scarf flapping in the breeze, and was smoking a big cigar. As if that were not enough, below the whole deal, Ed had painted in huge letters, "Mayor of Turners Falls."

In spite of the rather grim motif of Ed's insignia, I am happy to say that he survived the war, and Turners Falls must have been proud of him. However, some years later, Ed, who was of Polish descent, suffered a heart attack while visiting relatives in Poland, and died in a hospital there.

I never did find out whether he was really the mayor of Turners Falls – but it was a nice boast on the side of his bird, which must have confounded the Germans who got a good look at it.

Ed Pleasant's Jug

Another friend of mine, Robert Gleason, was a quiet guy who had been assigned a P-47 with the rather unwelcome letters of PI-G, but then added to the insult by having the name "Vicious Virgin" painted on the side of the bird. I don't know the derivation of that one, but many years after the war I met Bob at one of the reunions. He had recently retired after many years flying 747s as a captain for one of the major airlines.

I don't know who he was referring to, but, on that occasion, after reminiscing a bit over a couple of beers, he muttered just three words: "That damned woman!"

I found it interesting that the German fighter pilots had some décor on the side of their airplanes, but nothing compared to the Americans. Perhaps the German pilots were limited by their regulations or considered it unmilitary.

They did not put little American insignias on the side of their airplanes for the ones they shot down. If they had, some of them might have covered the entire airplane, as some of the great German aces who had been fighting for five years (and before that in the Spanish Civil War) had hundreds of kills and had earned Germany's highest decoration – the Knights Cross with Oak Leaves, Swords and Diamonds. The Germans did not use the term "Aces;" they called them "Experts."

Ody Thoma's Last Mission

While we had some losses in the fighter squadrons, we nevertheless enjoyed great numerical superiority over the enemy, and our tours of combat were relatively soft as compared to those of American and RAF bomber crews – and laughable, as compared to the German pilots, who flew until they were killed or promoted to staff positions.

Even though the bombers now had escort almost all the way to and from their targets, they were still the prime targets for the enemy fighter command, which would periodically assemble a large group of fighters to attack the bombers heading toward a sensitive strategic target.

An even more deadly menace for the bombers was the massive amount of heavy flak, which had increased at an almost exponential rate. At the same time, the German radar predictors had become much more accurate in pinpointing boxes of bombers flying in close formation and rained a lethal hail of steel at them.

Unlike the fighters, which could weave to avoid flak, the bombers were forced to fly an absolutely straight and steady line from their IP (Initial Point) to their assigned bomb drop point.

This was vividly brought home to me on July 21, 1944, when I received a Western Union telegram from Melandrea Pappas with the following message:

LT. EDWARD NEBINGER

360TH FIGHTER SQUADRON, 8TH AF

WAR DEPT REPORTS LT EDWARD THOMA KILLED IN ACTION JUNE 20 NO FURTHER DETAIL. BOTH FAMILIES DEVASTATED MY WORLD DESTROYED. PLS TRY TO GET MORE INFO.

MELANDREA PAPPAS

This was terrible news to me, as I had not only lost my Bethlehem buddy but realized how agonizing it must be for Mellie, as the two were so deeply in love, with bright plans for the future. Now that world had come crashing down.

Determined to find out what happened, I got permission from Major Vogt to borrow the UC-61 (a military liaison version of a Fairchild 24 cabin monoplane) to fly up to Grafton Underwood. After about a twenty-five-minute flight, I arrived at a huge base, which, as might be expected, was packed with B-17s, parked everywhere. After landing, I got a ground-crew man with a Jeep to take me to the operations building of the 544th Bomb Squadron where I met with the C.O.

He described what happened. The 384th group had been on a mission to bomb an oil depot in Hamburg, Germany. Ody had been flying as command pilot aboard B-17 BK-Q "Queenie," which was assigned as lead group deputy but was required to assume the lead when the lead group aircraft aborted. Over the target, the aircraft took a direct hit in the nose from 88mm flak, which killed Ody, wounded both the navigator and bombardier, and seriously injured the co-pilot, First Lieutenant Robert Strand. The airplane was a flying wreck, but Lt. Strand, despite his serious injuries, managed to coax it home.

The C.O. of the 544th Bomb Squadron expressed his sincere regrets about the loss of Thoma with the words, "It was a hard loss, but it was a miracle that we didn't lose the entire airplane and crew. Lt. Strand is still in the base hospital and group is recommending him for the Distinguished Service Cross for the exceptional job he did bringing that airplane back."

I inquired whether he knew where Ody was buried. He did not know but said he would find out and that I could check back. I thanked him and returned to the UC-61. Flying back to the squadron, I reflected that Lt. Strand's actions certainly merited the DSC. Unfortunately, my old buddy had received a different type of cross.

I sent a long letter to Mellie and another to Ody's parents, relating as much detail as wartime censorship allowed.

Subsequently, after his recovery from serious injuries, Lt. Strand was, in fact, awarded the Distinguished Service Cross, which is the second-highest decoration, next to the Congressional Medal of Honor. His citation reads as follows:

AWARD AND DECORATION

Robert E. Strand

Distinguished Service Cross

CITATION SYNOPSIS:

First Lieutenant (Air Corps) Robert E. Strand, United States Army Air Forces, was awarded the Distinguished Service Cross for extraordinary heroism in connection with military operations against an armed enemy while serving as Co-Pilot of a B-17 Heavy Bomber in the 544th Bombardment Squadron, 384th Bombardment Group (H), EIGHTH Air Force, while participating in a bombing mission on 20 June 1944, against enemy targets in the European Theater of Operations. During a bombing mission Lieutenant Edward Thoma, Pilot of First Lieutenant Strand's B-17 Bomber, was killed in action. Through his courage and skill First Lieutenant Strand brought his damaged airplane back to his base. The personal courage and zealous devotion to duty displayed by First Lieutenant Strand on this occasion have upheld the highest traditions of the military service and reflect great credit upon himself, the 8th Air Force, and the United States Army Air Forces.

Missing the Invasion – But not the War

Early July 1944

Ray, Andy, and Bill had all missed the invasion on D-Day, as their training had been slightly behind that of my group from the Southeast Training Command. The Army planners had expected that they were going to lose thousands of pilots in the invasion and subsequent attacks, but were pleasantly surprised when the losses turned out to be substantially less than anticipated. The fact was that the ever increasing number of strategic bombing raids on Hitler's infrastructure had a cumulative impact, which, by 1944, had greatly reduced his ability to send aloft massive flights of fighters to attack the Allied aircraft and their invading ground forces.

Even though the Germans actually had plenty of fighter aircraft, their ability to put them into the air had been severely impacted by attacks on oil refineries, as well as the railroads used to carry the fuel to the forward bases in Germany and Russia. The skies over Germany now belonged to the RAF and Americans, who could go where they chose at will, although at selective times the Germans could put together some large groups of Me.109s and FW-190 fighters.

As the invading armies slowly fought their way out of some of the massive German defensive pockets in Normandy, the three friends, all fully trained P-47 jocks, gradually neared their ultimate destination: the 360th Fighter Squadron, where they would join forces with us in the squadron.

Sitting in the back of a GI 6x6 canvas-covered truck, Ray Burwell reflected back over the long and complex journey they had undergone since his parting from Doris on that last day in Baton Rouge. It had been an agonizing time, as the two were completely swept off their feet about each other, and wartime schedules had squeezed their remaining time together at Harding Field into only a few days.

The dramatic event of their sudden engagement had resulted in a whirlwind of letters and phone calls back and forth between the respective parents, as the lovers tried desperately to put together a logical scenario which would allow them to marry.

At first they had considered a quick marriage, but with only a few days remaining before Ray would ship out, it soon became obvious this was impractical. Also, there was the problem of religion to be sorted out. Doris was Roman Catholic and had actually attended a convent school, so her roots in that religion were deep ones.

In contrast, Ray's parents were of some Protestant denomination, and they were not too comfortable with the idea of their grandchildren growing up in the Catholic religion. That was a problem, but not one that couldn't be overcome.

In fact, Ray and Doris had actually discussed a justice of the peace wedding, but both really wanted a formal church wedding, as they considered their romance a lifetime one and wanted to be joined very properly. They also wanted their respective families to be able to witness and take part in the happy event, so, all things considered, the decision was made that they would await Ray's return from overseas. In the meantime, phone calls between the respective families took place, while a series of letters and photographs also flew back and forth.

In the flush of their new romance, the lovers were both having trouble thinking straight, and their resulting giddiness was demonstrated by the fact that Doris had actually sent a letter to Ray's parents and asked his father for permission to marry his son! This was a cause of some amusement for Ray's parents, and they talked about it in a letter to their son. Ray's letter in response referred to the incident as follows:

Dearest Mom & Pop,

June 30, 1944

This may be my last letter to you before we ship out. I trust you got the one in which I set up a code which will tell you where we have been sent. Don't forget to study it.

Pop, I was sure tickled to find out that Doris actually sent you a letter asking your permission to marry me! We are so crazy about each other that neither one of us is thinking right. But as far as Doris asking your consent about marrying me, I understood that the fellow was to get consent from the girl's folks! Ha, Ha, after all I picked her, or did she pick me? Ha Ha. I actually think it was the latter. But seriously, this ol' boy will also appreciate your consent, you may be sure of that.

Doris and I have so many things to sort out in order to begin our married life together. But there is still a war to finish, so we will have to just make our plans to fit the situation as it unfolds.

I will undoubtedly go back to school when this is over, for I want to get a good job and that means more school.

I am feeling fine and am looking forward with great expectations to where we are being sent. Wherever we go, I can assure you that we have had the best training that could ever be provided, and I know we will be flying great airplanes, especially if we stay with the P-47 Thunderbolts, which are fantastic planes.

Well, there are just oodles of things to talk about but for reasons beyond my control I have to finish up. Love to everyone. Write often and keep me informed of how things go with Doris, as overseas mail may be slow and erratic, and I could easily miss letters which come directly from my wonderful fiancé'.

Your loving son, Ray

First Coyote in England

Shortly after that letter of Ray's was posted, the three West Coast buddies – Rich Andrino, Ray Burwell, and Bill Crump – had boarded a train together with a group of other pilots and assorted military personnel, heading for an East Coast port of embarkation.

After about nine smoke-filled hours of switching, banging, and stopping to pick up additional troops, the train arrived at Camp Kilmer, New Jersey, which was a newly opened, massive facility for processing combat-ready troops and officers of all types for shipment to Europe and Africa. Like my own group, they had been subjected to the same masquerade of being issued uniforms to dress like 1918 doughboys, and issued new dog tags, gas masks, and Colt .45 automatics with shoulder holsters.

One thing completely unique, however, was the idea of adding a coyote to the shipping manifest, as Crump, who had nursed his tiny baby coyote into a cute little puppy, was not about to part with his new friend. He explored a number of solutions, including possibly getting a general they had met to bring him along as a mascot.

While the general was accommodating and actually explored the situation, he soon discovered that it was virtually impossible and told them so. The British were very strict about bringing new types of animals into their country and it soon became obvious that there was no way that it could be done legally. He explained this to Crump and also warned him that if the animal were discovered aboard ship, it would be promptly tossed overboard.

Crump, however, was bound and determined to haul "Jeep" with him to Europe – rules and regulations be damned – and came up with an ingenious solution. The gas masks that were issued to everyone were in a square-shaped bag about six inches wide and nine inches high.

Crump decided this would make a great hiding place for Jeep, so he tossed the gas mask into the trash, put some padding in the bottom, and stuffed the little coyote into it. He also cut a small hole in the bottom of the bag so Jeep could stick his nose through to breathe.

Inasmuch as the gas mask bag was olive drab, like everything else they were wearing, there was little chance of anyone observing the little brown and black nose poking out of the bottom, as it blended in quite well.

Shortly thereafter they boarded a train, which took them to a terminal in nearby New York City, where they observed a gigantic two-funnel liner, painted all grey, waiting at the quayside, with many gangplanks in place. There was no name on the ship, but it was obvious that it was the "Queen Elizabeth," an 85,000-ton ship, which was not only the largest passenger liner afloat but also the fastest, at thirty knots.

The officer pilots were directed to one of many lines of troops, all inching their way slowly toward the various gangplanks, each of which was funneling its passengers into one of the many decks. They spent several hours shuffling along, lugging their barracks bags full of gear, while a flock of Red Cross ladies did yeoman service by providing them with coffee and donuts, which must have been supplied by the truckload.

As they got closer to the sloping gangplank, the three were a bit nervous that their ruse for sneaking Jeep aboard could be tripped up if the little guy decided to howl or yip as they were walking up the gangplank to enter the ship.

But Jeep must have inherited an instinctive ability to hide quietly, as coyotes live in a furtive world all their lives and discretion being the better part of valor was written into their genes.

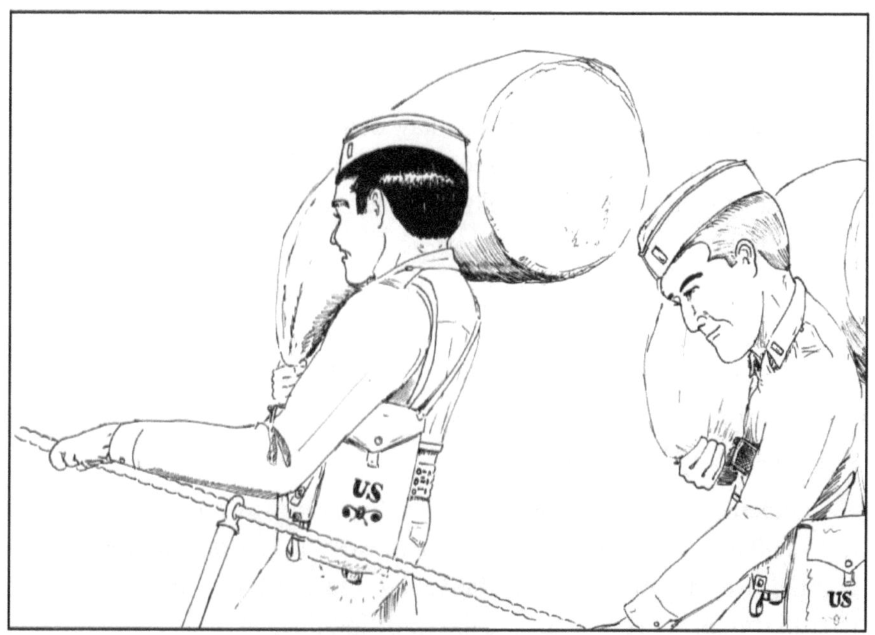

"Jeep" Comes Aboard *(Artist: John Purdy)*

The ruse worked to perfection, but not before some nervous scenes in which the three friends kept up the appearance of normality by engaging in conversation, while the coyote lay quietly in the bottom of the bag. They got aboard with no problem and were directed to a very large cabin on one of the upper decks.

In its original configuration, this cabin, which had its own private bathroom facilities, had probably been a first-class stateroom for two people but had been refitted with fold-up bunks, and now accommodated about twenty officer pilots. The bunks were stacked four high along the walls and were connected together by chains so the complete stack could be folded up by raising the chain.

The three friends speculated that falling out of bed from the top tier could be lethal, and Andy and Ray managed to grab bunks in the two lower tiers. Crump initially got stuck with a third-tier bunk, but after Jeep was revealed and all the pilots made a fuss over him, one of the guys with a bottom bunk generously offered to swap so that Jeep could occupy a sheltered spot under the bottom tier.

While these accommodations may sound like a squeeze job, they were really quite plush compared to those of the thousands of enlisted men whose bunks and hammocks occupied the many decks going down into the hold.

The Queen Elizabeth, which had been designed to accommodate approximately 2,000 passengers in several classes, had gone into service just before war was declared in 1939. As the result of several massive retrofits, the ship had been completely stripped of civilian comforts and converted into a troop carrier.

Unbelievably, as they learned later, the ship was now carrying close to 13,000 troops to Europe. In fact, there were no less than fourteen decks going down into the cavernous bowels of the great ship and it had taken over thirty-six hours of boarding the shuffling lines of troops until the ship was fully loaded. Reflecting upon this, the three pilots wondered what kind of disaster would occur if the enemy submarines were able to sink the juicy target.

As it turned out, they had a couple of submarine contacts, but the huge ship was well escorted and was travelling in excess of twenty-eight knots, which was well above the speed of any submarines, either submerged or on the surface. This apparently deprived the enemy of any success, and the ship made the trip safely.

The two "Queens", Queen Mary and Queen Elizabeth, made hundreds of transits across the North Atlantic but were never attacked by hostile submarines. For which, everybody involved was eternally thankful.

Bill, Andy, and Ray did have one scare, however, which was closer to home for them. As word spread of Jeep's presence, he became very popular and was visited by all kinds of military personnel, including some really cute nurses (which was okay with the fighter pilot lieutenants). Also, the general who Crump had talked to before sailing was on the ship and probably told a few of his big brass friends.

Crump was therefore getting concerned that the word might reach the wrong ears, and as they neared the coast of England, he got the shock of his life. The door opened and a U.S. Army bird colonel entered the room! Someone called, "Attention!" and everyone sprang to their feet.

The colonel said, "I hear there is a coyote aboard. Who owns him and where is he?"

Dreading the worst, Crump spoke up, "The coyote is mine, sir."

"Well, where is the damned thing?" responded the colonel, and Bill pulled Jeep's box out from under his bunk and lifted him out.

Jeep stood still obediently while the colonel eyeballed him. The colonel did not endeavor to pet him but merely exclaimed, "Well, I'll be damned." He then began to tell the pilots of his own unsuccessful efforts to tame one in his native Texas. According to his recounting of his experiences, every time he thought he had made some progress in domesticating the coyote, a chicken or any small animal would walk by, and the coyote would suddenly revert to his primordial instincts and jump on it.

Jeep, however, must have provided some new and favorable perspective because the colonel thanked the pilots and walked out of the room with a smile on his face. Bill never heard another word about it and disembarked in England in the same manner as he had boarded ship, with Jeep's little nose protruding through the bottom of the gas mask bag. I guess the colonel didn't give a damn about the British laws, which was in fact typical of many Americans.

CHAPTER NINE

THE WEST COAST GROUP ARRIVES

Reinforcements for the 360th Squadron

In July, Ray, Bill, and Andy disembarked from the great ship in Scotland, and after spending a few days at various "sorting out" places, including Atcham, finally boarded a 6x6 GI truck which was to take them to their newly assigned fighter squadron.

Finally, on July 14, 1944, the three West Coast friends finally arrived at the 356th group at Martlesham Heath, near the Channel coast in East Anglia, along with a few other replacements pilots. When their allocation to squadrons was being determined, they asked if they could be assigned to the same squadron and were fortunate in having their request granted. All were ecstatic, as after a long period of training they were finally at a combat fighter squadron and all were still together, eager to pitch in and do their bit to bring the war to a successful conclusion.

In a letter to his parents, Ray expressed his pleasure about the whole situation:

My Dearest Mom and Pop

At last I have reached my final destination. I have been assigned to my group and it is really a swell outfit. You probably noticed on my return address I am in the 360th Squadron, 356th Group; Eighth Air Force. I can also say that we are based in

England and boy, are we living in a swell place. Our squadron is staying in a castle away from the field. It must be 200/300 years old and even has a moat surrounding it. We (Bill, Andy, and I) are living in one big room together. We are all lucky enough to get into the same Group and even the same Squadron. Remember the time you told Andy to be sure and stick with me? Well, we did it and it is very exceptional too. But please don't put any of this in the paper unless you say only that Andy and I are in a Fighter Sq. together.

On our way here we stopped overnight in London and what did we see but a buzz-bomb, in fact two. Boy, they really travel. One of them landed about 8 to 10 blocks from us. Wow. Ha Ha. We couldn't see much of the town for they really have a black-out. But we will go again on our days off and look the place over.

Believe it or not I am being a very good boy over here. Ha! I guess it's because of Doris; fact is I know it is. I am still as crazy about her and know I will always feel the same. I hope you are still writing to her.

Speaking of letters, you will be getting a letter from another girl soon. She sent one to Bill's mother too. I don't know what claims she thinks she has on me, but don't pay it any attention. I think you understand.

You remember how I wrote about Bill Crump getting a baby coyote. Well, believe it not, he is here with us. Bill smuggled him aboard the ship in a gas mask bag, which worked great, and got him off the same way. We all helped with the ruse, and got away with it. Jeep even traveled on the train with us after we landed. Sometimes, when the train stopped, Bill would lower him down from the window on a long leash, so he could find a tree or a bush. He was very popular and one time the English trainmen even held up the train for a minute so he could finish his business. Ha Ha. I think I am going to like the English people. Why shouldn't I, my Pop is English too!

I hope all is ok at home. I am fine and things look good over here, don't they. I mean about how the invasion is going. Too bad we missed it, but we are fully trained and ready to join in and do our part.

Tell everyone hello for me. I remain.

Your loving son, Ray

The ABC Gang!

I met the new pilots at our operations shack and found them to be full of questions and raring to go! Ray and I really did not get to know each other well for a while, as he and his buddies were bunking in the carriage house outside of the moat at the castle, which was kind of the overflow place where I had originally stayed before getting moved into the castle proper.

While all of the new guys were eager to get started flying missions, that was not going to happen for a while. Apparently, now that the invasion was successfully underway and our losses in pilots had been less than expected, higher headquarters had decreed that all of the new arrivals should be given some further pre-combat training at squadron level. This comprised many lectures by veteran pilots, filled with "do's and don'ts" and "Watch out for this and that," followed by a lot of droning around and dummy dogfights in English skies, burning up valuable aviation gas.

This was a source of frustration to Andrino, Burwell, and Crump, who, because of their names and the fact that they were frequently together, were sometimes referred to by the operations officer – with tongue in cheek – as his "ABC gang," a term which soon caught on in the squadron.

The word was soon out about the coyote and everyone in the squadron was quite eager to meet and make a fuss over Jeep, who actually seemed to enjoy it and was never unfriendly to everyone. We already had seven dogs at the castle, a really motley collection of types and breeds, and if one lumped in Jeep as a dog relative, that made eight! They were interesting and friendly companions for a bunch of fighter pilots far from home.

In one of the early letters that Ray wrote home to his parents, he inquired about his own dog, "Pugs," and talked about the menagerie at the castle with the words, *Why, this is a dog's paradise!*

Crump had some concerns about letting Jeep roam free, but after a few days slipped his leash and tried him out. The coyote had a great time roaming around the nearby fields, but never dragged home any fresh kills, as far as I knew, so I guess he had passed the test of becoming domesticated. A couple of English gardeners, however, who soon got the word, were not too happy about the strange new animal in England, and there was some genuine concern that a local game warden might put in an appearance.

While the ABC pilots were late arrivals, they lucked out in the assignment of P-47s and all three ended up with nice bubble-canopy D-25 Jugs. The switchover to P-51s within the 8th Air Force Fighter Command was being accelerated and, consequently, the later model Jugs that were being replaced were switched over to the remaining P-47 outfits, of which we were one.

I was still flying my old razorback Jug and probably could have been reassigned to a newer bird if I had asked, but it was clear that we were all going to switch to P-51s within a few months, so I decided to stick it out with old PI-A, which had been a pretty lucky airplane so far. Besides, I had my nice paint job, including "Miss Ginny," on the cowling, and did not see much point in going through a new insignia repainting exercise.

Andy and Ed

The ABC pilots, on the other hand, were in their glory with their new airplanes and were making the most of it.

Andrino had some kind of slinky-looking babe painted on the side of his PI-X, but I never learned her name.

Bill Crump's Jug, PI-W, had a coyote with mouth open wide (howling) and a huge "Jackie" painted on the side. I think that was the name of the gal he worked with in Washington State before joining the Air Corps. Sometimes I wondered why he didn't name his P-47 "Jeep" after his little coyote buddy.

Ray Burwell's insignia, however, was the crowning achievement, as he had the squadron artist paint a huge "Lady Doris" in script on the side of his Jug. As if that was not enough, he also had the artist paint a framed picture of Doris above the name. Ray was really proud of that paint job and went around telling everyone how it really looked like her.

Later, however, after I saw a real picture of Doris, it appeared to me that the artist had missed it by a long shot. She was much prettier than depicted. But as the old saying goes, 'Beauty is in the eye of the beholder,' and Ray was so enraptured by Doris that anyone who didn't see her that way would have been considered crazy.

Burwell's Mustang

(No picture available of P-47 with insignia, but it was the same)

Aside from that, I don't think it ever occurred to Ray that no Brit would ever call his girlfriend "Lady," unless of course she happened to have been married to a Lord. Ha. But in the eyes of the British, Americans are a brash bunch – which we are – but I guess that's what sets us off from the rest.

Tex Green

On July 18, the group flew an uneventful fighter sweep in the Dieppe-Evreux-Dreux areas. No enemy aircraft were encountered and the 360th returned to Martlesham with no losses, only to discover that during its absence, a very popular pilot, Tex Green, had been killed! It wasn't a combat loss; it was a stupid accident, which took place over England.

When I first came to our squadron, one of the first pilots I became acquainted with was a soft-spoken man with the unlikely name of Shirley Green, whom everyone called Tex. A quiet, self-confident man, he was a Texan through and through, and his P-47, PI-U, was called "Lone Star Lady."

Shortly after the invasion, I was on the June 14 mission with Tex, during which our squadron had been milling around looking for ground targets to unload its frag bombs on. We were caught flat-footed with a surprise bounce by about a dozen 109s, and a hot German pilot had made mincemeat out of Green's Jug.

After landing, I walked over to talk to Tex, who had dragged old PI-U back literally shot full of holes of various sizes by the German pilot. It was probably one of their high scoring aces, who did his best to add another notch to his record. However, the German must have run out of ammo or something because he couldn't knock Tex's P-47 out of the sky, in spite of blasting the hell out of it.

That was the experience of many of the German fighter pilots, who found the P-47 an exceptionally tough bird, with incredible survival capabilities. In fact, there was one well-known case where a German pilot fired everything he had, shooting out most of the controls, and turning the American airplane into a flying pile of junk that could scarcely turn, but nevertheless stayed in the air. Frustrated and out of ammo, the German pilot flew up beside the P-47, looked over at its pilot, saluted, and peeled off.

Looking over the damage, Tex smiled and spoke admiringly of his enemy opponent's skill, making light of the whole episode. Tex had been flying missions for quite a while before I arrived and was close to finishing his tour of combat. I admired his "sangfroid."

One day after I got to know Tex better, I chatted with him about ranching in Texas. As a kid from a Pennsylvania steel town, I had never been on a real ranch and innocently asked how big his ranch was. He seemed reluctant to talk about it and replied, "It's about fifty-six sections," probably hoping I would drop the subject. But I pursued the matter by asking how big a section was, and he smiled and said simply, "A section is 640 acres." It didn't really register at the time, but later it hit me. A section is a square mile. Fifty-six square miles! Wow!

Tex was not lost on a combat mission but on a simple training mission, as the result of some stupid clowning around and a miscalculation. Details from the after-accident report read as follows:

18 July 1944

Lt. Green was scheduled to lead an afternoon four ship training flight with some new pilots. Just before takeoff it was discovered that two of the ships would be late in taking off, and arrangements were made for them to join up with Lt. Green over the field. Meanwhile, another 360th pilot, Lt. Wayne Leathers, happened to be flying in the vicinity on a solo test flight and volunteered to join up with Tex and his wingman until the others arrived. Thus, a three ship flight was in close formation when the others joined them. One of the arriving Thunderbolts pulled up sharply in front of the three-ship formation and did a barrel role, which surprised Lt. Green so that he nosed over sharply. His two wingmen lost sight of him and continued straight ahead in a slight climb. Lt. Green then pulled up, apparently watching the ship rolling in front of him. The propeller of Lt. Leather's ship cut the tail off of Lt. Green's ship and he went straight

down, crashing near Woodbridge, Suffolk. Lt. Leathers was able to land safely with a badly damaged propeller, but Lt. Green died in the crash.

The next morning, I was in our operations building on the flight line when I noticed a very beautiful woman standing in front of the building, crying. I called it to the attention of our C.O., Major Vogt, who said quietly, "I better go out and talk to her."

People died in combat situations; such losses were expected. That was part of the business we were in. But Tex's loss was a senseless tragedy of epic proportions, which hurt everyone deeply.

Illicit Cargo

Since the arrival of Crump and Jeep at the castle, the little coyote had developed from a puppy to a very intelligent and alert young animal that was universally liked by everyone. He was extremely good-natured and, despite being handled and roughed about by hundreds of people, had never been known to bite or nip at anyone. His attachment to Bill Crump was complete in every respect, to the point where they had been known on occasion to share Bill's sack in the castle.

Bill, like the rest of the ABC group, had begun his pre-combat training during July, and had spent a lot of time droning around English skies. Often, Bill would bring Jeep down to the flight line and let him stay with his ground-crew guys while he was flying. However, for some time he had been contemplating taking Jeep up with him in his P-47. There were, however, several problems to be considered. First, Bill was not sure how Jeep would react to the G forces that were experienced in fighters.

More problematic, however, was the thought that the coyote would get hypoxia from the lack of oxygen at altitude. All of us breathed oxygen from takeoff to landing. In fact, the microphone for our radio transmissions was actually inside of our oxygen mask. But most pilots could fly up to 10,000 feet without wearing their masks, and many times pilots would take them off at 15,000 to 17,000 feet when descending on the way home, usually to have a smoke. Thus, it was probable that the lower altitudes would not pose a problem, but many combat missions, particularly bomber escort, required climbing to 20,000 feet or higher – and sometimes as high as 35,000 feet.

Thus, Crump found himself looking for an opportunity to give it a try on a flight that he knew would be at relatively low level. His opportunity came on August 14 when a training mission was scheduled as a low-altitude formation flight. What also made it opportune, however, was the fact that the flight of four was comprised of Ray, Andy, and another pilot who was close-mouthed and could be counted on not to blab about it and have the word get back to the squadron commander, who may have taken a dim view of it.

Bill put Jeep in the cockpit and watched him sniff around a bit before settling down on the floor like he was going to take a nap. With that assurance, Bill cranked up the P-47, taxied out with the flight, and took off. The way Bill related it later was that Jeep was amazing, and acted like an old pro at flying. He stayed put on the floor and did not try to move around, and the only time he appeared a little disconcerted was when Bill pulled some Gs on the pre-landing pitch out. He looked up at Crump, who reached down and petted him, after which he settled down even tighter into his spot on the floor.

Unbelievable as it may sound, Bill Crump actually took Jeep on five combat missions in the months that followed. I don't know how he got away with it, but he must have selected the missions very carefully – probably low-level target of opportunity sweeps, and we never heard about it until after they returned successfully. I don't know whether the C.O. or the ops officer ever learned of it, but if they did, there was never an official word of reprimand.

A couple of questions dogged me about Crump's illicit cargo. One of my early concerns was that the little guy might get tangled up with the rudder pedals and get himself mashed, particularly on takeoff, which required a lot of right rudder to keep the airplane on the runway while it accelerated. Apparently, that was never a concern, as Jeep stayed in place.

However, a more serious question was, *What would Bill do if he got hit by flak or by an enemy aircraft and had to bail out?* Did he have a little bag that he would put Jeep into before he hit the silk? Or would he choose to try to belly a badly damaged airplane in, rather than bail out and leave his buddy to go down with the ship?

I never asked Bill those questions. Fortunately, those scenarios never took place, and Bill Crump made it through the war safely, sometimes by a small miracle.

Although I wondered about those eventualities, I never questioned or disapproved, as I had my own episode with illegal cargo.

I had heard of a guy in one of the other fighter groups who had landed on a German Autobahn with his P-47 and successfully picked up a fellow pilot who had been forced to land "gear up" in a nearby field. One day I received a surprise visit at the squadron from a guy who had been a former classmate in my hometown high school. He was now a U.S. Army enlisted man, a sergeant named Gus Savaki, working in SHAEF headquarters in London. I'm not sure how he knew where I was stationed, but maybe if you work at those echelons you can track anybody.

Anyway, Gus showed up at the castle and I took him down to the flight line to show him the Jugs. It was a quiet day, with no combat missions scheduled but lots of local flying, checking out various systems in the airplanes, etc. Therefore, we were at leave to take our airplanes up on a local flight without pre-scheduling.

I was standing by my airplane with my crew chief and armorer, Sgt. Wooley and Cpl. Ott, when Gus asked a natural question, "What is it like to fly in a monster airplane like this?"

I laughed and suddenly a wild thought hit me, *Why don't I take him up and show him?* I said to Gus, "Do you want to take a ride?" He thought I was joking, but I said, "It's been done before. I'll toss out my chute and sit on your lap."

He looked at me in astonishment and said, "If you're serious, I'm game." This astonished my crew, who would never have taken a crazy chance like that.

My parachute was in the cockpit, so I handed it out and Gus parked his butt in the bucket seat. He was a pretty small guy and I was a lean five feet nine, so I knew we could fit. We found a small piece of foam rubber to put on Gus's lap and I climbed in, sat on his lap, and cranked up the Jug.

As we were taxiing out, I told my passenger to squat way down as we went by the control tower. He did and I got clearance from the tower and blasted off. I didn't hear much from Gus during the early part of that flight. It was kind of strange as I was sitting up there pretty high. I never gave much thought to what might happen if we lost the engine or something. But danger is a relative term, and if you were used to getting shot at every time you flew across the Channel, that little caper seemed like a pretty mild deal.

I climbed a few thousand feet and decided to do a little barrel roll. As I pulled it up and around I heard a pretty loud groan from Gus, which suggested that we had better not stay up too long, as it had to be pretty damned uncomfortable for my passenger.

I didn't do any more rolls or high G maneuvers; however, when we descended and entered the traffic pattern I made a normal pitch up, which was about 2.5 Gs, dropped the landing gear and flaps, and bent it around for a landing. All the way around, I could hear a loud groan from the guy I was sitting on. Even with my meager 155 pounds or so, Gus was feeling the equivalent of two-and-a-half times that, or almost 390 pounds, in his lap! No wonder he groaned. I never saw that guy again. If he survived the war and is still living, he is probably one of a handful of people in the world who can claim they rode as a passenger in a single-seat WWII fighter!

Ed with "Miss Ginny"

The ABC Gang "Rounds Up" Targets

The 360th had a couple of interesting missions on September 1. The 356th group was assigned to perform two missions in what was called a "rodeo." I'm not sure where the name came from, but a rodeo basically comprised rounding up and destroying as much of the enemy fighting and support capabilities as possible, using dive-bombing and strafing to maximum advantage.

The Allies had been making good progress pushing the Germans east, with the result that the Germans were building up their defenses in the area of southern Belgium. Consequently, on the first mission, the 360th found some good targets on a major rail line running between

Liege and Namur, dive-bombing and strafing a marshaling yard and a railroad bridge.

The squadron also found a bunch of military trucks moving up on a nearby road, and in the process of strafing them discovered a small airfield with some Me.109s taxiing. Leidy (of Aroostook County potato farmer fame) made a quick attack and destroyed a 109 on his first pass, then came around for another pass, during which time the Jerries got their ack ack cranked up and into action.

Leidy got some strikes on another 109 and claimed a "damaged," but in the process took a 20mm hit and was lucky to get out of there. Once again the good old Jug demonstrated its toughness, and Leidy brought it home without incident.

Finally, after more than a solid month of training and being bystanders for the passing show, the ABC gang finally got a chance to fly some missions.

Bill Crump got the first opportunity on September 3, when the squadron was assigned to fly a three-flight (twelve-ship) rodeo mission looking for targets of opportunity in the vicinity of Aachen, Germany. Major Cota led the squadron, with Bill assigned to fly as Green two in the very experienced Capt. Ellingson's flight.

Arriving at the target area, they found it fairly well loaded with rail traffic, which was a bit unusual as the Germans usually ran their heavy rail traffic at night. With overwhelming air superiority now in the hands of the Allies, running trains in Germany during daylight was a very hazardous occupation; in fact, the standard joke in the squadrons was that German locomotive engineers got an Iron Cross every time they made a daylight run! However, with the Allied armies pushing toward the Rhine, the German Army was moving everything it could forward to bolster its defenses.

Spotting a full train in motion, Ellingson invited Crump to make the first pass, which he eagerly did, hitting the engine first, which spouted steam, then shooting up the rest of the cars. The squadron also found another five trains that day, which they shot up, in addition to destroying more than a dozen military vehicles. It was a good day all around, as the 360th did not lose anyone. However, the squadron took a lot of damage from 20mm flak, as the whole area was loaded with it.

On the way back across the Channel, Crump's engine started cutting out, but he was able to coax the bird to home base. Major Cota told him to land first, which was smart, as Bill's engine conked out completely on final approach and he glided in. Upon examination of the P-47, it was found to have several dozen flak holes, probably from exploding 20mm shells. Any other airplane would probably have packed it in. It was an interesting first mission for Bill Crump.

On September 5, Andrino got to fly his first mission, which was once again a fighter sweep of the territory in front of our advancing armies from Amersfoot to Rheine. Capt. Bluhm (of white silk scarf fame) was leading our squadron, which comprised only three flights of four.

Ray wanted to be with Andy on his first mission, and was disappointed not to be scheduled. However, Andy and I were both assigned to Vortex Blue flight, and I assured Ray that, as number four in Andy's flight, I would look after his little buddy's tail to keep some bad guy from sneaking up on him.

Andy was chafing at the bit to find some juicy targets, but was disappointed. We patrolled the area in the vicinity of Zwolle for almost an hour, but it turned out to be a fairly uneventful mission, as the railways and roads were virtually devoid of targets that day. Our squadron ended up with a few railroad cars strafed, which were probably already junk, and we claimed only three trucks destroyed. It was getting to be a joke in the group that we had been so successful, we were running out of targets. Andy was disappointed, but we assured him that there would be better days ahead.

Motorcycles are Dangerous

Since my arrival at the squadron, I had not had time to look over the surrounding area – other than my regular commutes from the castle to the field, which were usually by GI truck or sometimes by riding an English bike. Therefore, on an afternoon when I was not scheduled to fly, I caught a ride into Ipswich, about three miles away, with the object of looking over the town to see what the local shops had to offer, and possibly grab a beer at one of the pubs and chat it up with the locals.

The town was pretty quiet, as it was a weekday and everyone was hard at work somewhere contributing to the continuing war effort. Also, with wartime rationing, the shops had very little to offer. However, in browsing around I came to a small motorcycle fixit shop, which interested me, as I had ridden motorcycles from a very early age and found them to be a great mode of transport, as well as a lot of fun. I stopped in to see how English motorcycles compared to those we rode in the States, and had a pleasant chat with the owner.

He was a friendly guy who had done some racing at dirt tracks in England before the war, a sport activity that I also found interesting. He was either a really good salesman or I was an easy mark (maybe both), because I ended up buying a nice little BSA motorcycle for twenty-nine pounds.

I don't remember what year the bike was and it wasn't important anyway, as it ran like a seventeen-jewel watch and really eased my transportation problems. Gasoline, which was very strictly rationed for the British, was no problem, as the BSA burned only a minuscule amount, which I could easily scrounge on the base at Martlesham.

I had ridden all types of motorcycles ever since I was about thirteen years old and considered the BSA to be as safe as a little tinker toy. However, when I rode it down to the squadron a couple of days later, I got a different reaction from Major Vogt, who told me it was against regulations and that I was going to have to get rid of it.

Apparently, the Army brass hats were concerned that their pilot officers, whom they had trained over a long period at great expense, could easily be taken out of action by an accident while riding a dangerous motorcycle. The thought also crossed my mind that the subject regulation may have been inspired by the fact that "Lawrence of Arabia" had killed himself crashing on a motorcycle after WWI.

Reflecting back upon the "barbed wire debacle" at Atcham, I wondered whether maybe they should also apply it to British bicycles – but that of course would immobilize half of the 8th Air Force, including ground and flying crews. I rode the BSA back into Ipswich and talked the BSA dealer into buying it back – at a substantial discount.

Tactical Idiocy

September 13, 1944

This was a day I wouldn't forget. Ray and I, as well as Ed Pleasant, were assigned to a flight being led by a captain named Archer who was from another squadron but had been temporarily assigned to the 360th. Perhaps the group brass thought that the new pilots should get the benefit of flying with some more experienced guys; hence Ray, as a relatively new guy, was flying Archer's wing, while Ed Pleasant and I comprised the other element of two.

It turned out that Archer, who was considered to be very experienced, was also very foolish. Good old Archer damned near got our whole flight killed!

We were assigned to escort the bombers, with rendezvous just east of Osnabruck in Germany. Archer was leading Vortex Blue Flight that was stacked on the right side of the 360th squadron, which was in turn the right squadron in our group of forty-eight P-47s. The weather was good, with broken clouds topping out around 18,000 feet. Climb-out was uneventful and we picked up the bombers right on schedule at 28,000 feet.

Major Vogt was leading our squadron and had just started a slow climb to get on top of the bombers for a weaving coverage when my waste-gate supercharger developed a problem and I found myself unable to develop enough power to continue the climb. I called Blue leader and told him my problem.

Vogt heard my transmission and called, "Vortex Blue leader, take your flight and drop down. If your number four is running okay, look for targets of opportunity and continue the mission on your own."

Archer said, "Vortex Blue lead here, roger, dropping down," and began a slow descent. As luck would have it, I just happened to be looking down though a big hole in the clouds and spotted a German airfield with airplanes taxiing on it. Wow, a rare find, as the Germans were pretty canny about concealing their fields. However, they were probably just in the process of launching some fighters to attack the bombers overhead.

I called Archer and said, "There is an airfield directly underneath us and I see fighters taxiing on the runway." At the lower altitude my engine was running normally, with no problems.

Now any other leader with half a brain would have immediately launched a swift attack, without another word, in order to get a surprise jump on the Germans. Not Archer. He made a gradual let-down until we were actually circling above the field at about 7,000 feet, "casing the joint," so to speak. .

Then he announced over the radio (for all to hear – including the Germans) his grand plan: "Okay, Blue flight, we are going to go out about five miles, hit the deck, and come back line abreast."

Great, what a brilliant strategy!

We headed out, made our turn, lined up four abreast, and came roaring back, right on the deck. Meanwhile, it was easy to visualize the Germans yelling, "Achtung! Achtung!" and cranking up every ack ack gun on the field!

In the turning descent, the two-ship element had crossed over, so the lead element was now on the right, and as Pleasant's wingman I was on the extreme left side of the line.

We hopped up over a line of trees at the edge of the field and the Germans sent up a terrific hail of tracers and 20mm stuff. I immediately got hit in the left wing by a 20mm cannon shell, which blew a nice hole in the top of the wing (and also the underside, as I found out later). Meanwhile, I could see the buddy of the German gunner who nailed me firing a twin machine gun at me from a ditch by the runway. I was firing my guns, but could not depress the nose enough to hit him without running into the ground (another Archer mistake, coming in too low), so the guy played tic-tac-toe all over the bottom of my airplane as I roared by.

Fortunately, my good old Jug kept flying and we roared across the field, at which point I noticed that the trees on the other side were loaded with Me.210 and .410 twin-engine fighters, of which one had started burning. It was probably a night fighter field.

Off to my right, I saw an FW-190 taking strikes from one of our flight, but on that single pass every one of us took serious flak damage, two of our flight actually taking bullets through the fuel tanks, which were fortunately self-sealing.

Archer didn't try another pass and we all got the hell out of there with our birds still flying. No question about it – the Republic P-47 was really a fantastic airplane, absolutely built like a brick one. If we had been flying anything else, there probably would have been four burning wrecks strewn across that field.

As it turned out, everybody made it home, but when I landed I discovered that both of my tires had been shot out and I ran off the runway onto the grass before getting it stopped.

The engineering maintenance officer, Capt. Ragnell, came out to check over my airplane, which was a mess, with two huge holes in the left wing, plus lots of bullet holes through both wings, the fuselage, and the tail.

Then he took out his pocket knife, reached into the jagged hole in the wing, and prized off the back end of the 20mm shell which had entered the leading edge of the wing and exploded against the main spar, fusing itself onto the metal. Only a Jug could have taken that punishment without losing the wing. I still have the shell today.

The upshot of that whole mess was that we got only a couple of damage claims on the Me.410s and one FW-190 (although Archer claimed a "destroyed"), while four perfectly good P-47s were out of commission for major repairs for at least a week. I got a whole new wing, horizontal stabilizer, and two tires.

I don’t know how our brilliant flight leader got away with that fiasco, but he did. Some might call it the fog of war. Ed Pleasant and I had another viewpoint. While Archer was making his gallant combat report, Pleasant said to me quietly, "Christ, what a fucking idiot! We’re lucky any of us are still alive. I wonder where he learned his tactics!"

Later, after the photo lab checked everybody’s gun camera film, it was determined that Ray had also destroyed an Me.410 and he got official credit for it. Not a bad start for one of the new pilots.

In his exuberance about the confirmed plane destroyed, Ray described the incident in one of his letters to his parents (although putting that type of information in letters was officially frowned upon). An excerpt from his letter reads:

"Before I forget it, I want to tell you some rather good news. A while back I was on a flight that shot up an airfield in Germany and in doing so I thought I damaged one plane. You know, planes count just as much on the ground as they do in the air. Well, the gun camera film came back yesterday and it seems I not only damaged one but destroyed one as well."

"Not bad, eh? I might get to be an Ace yet. Ha Ha. "

Stanbridge Earls

Maybe it was a pure coincidence but not long after that, Ed Pleasant and I got selected to go to the flak farm for a week. I did not think we looked nervous or were biting our nails or anything, but I guess the squadron had a couple of slots on hand and figured, after assessing the damage, that this was the time to use them.

Anyway, Ed and I were privileged to spend a week at a splendid English estate near Romsey, in Hampshire, southern England. It was a graceful Tudor-style mansion called Stanbridge Earls, which was surrounded by forty acres of lovely English countryside, including two lakes. It was one of about a dozen such mansions employed by the 8th Air Force to serve as rest homes for air crews who were undergoing stressful missions.

Typically, almost every flying crewmember, at some point during his tour of operations, was granted a week at one of these homes scattered throughout southern England. Stanbridge Earls hosted officers only, and seemed to be assigned for use by fighter pilots, as everyone we met was from one of the 8th Air Force Fighter Command groups. However, other homes were assigned for use by officers, as well as enlisted crewmembers from the many bomb groups in England.

The mansion was elegantly furnished in English period style, with a large dining room in which a table accommodated about twenty-four guests. Breakfast and lunch were somewhat informal, but dinner was always completely formal, with all officers in full Class A uniform, including ribbons. Ed and I soon found that we were in rather distinguished company, including some hot shot pilots from the 4th and 56th Fighter Groups.

I also met Captain George Preddy from the 352nd group, who had already run up over twenty kills and seemed destined to become one of our highest scoring aces. Unfortunately, about three months later during the Battle of the Bulge, then-Major Preddy was shot down and killed by our own troops, who fired at him as he was pursuing a German fighter at very low level. He became the top scoring Mustang ace of the war, with a total of thirty-two-and-a-half kills.

Major Preddy is memorialized today with some excellent aviation art depicting his P-51 "Cripes A'Mighty" in action.

Major Preddy with his P-51 "Cripes a Mighty".

Living at Stanbridge Earls was like stepping back to an earlier time in Britain's history, as there were constant reminders of that around us. A broad expanse of lawn behind the mansion had, in one corner, an elegant gazebo constructed of some rare hardwood in an architectural style that clearly suggested it had been shipped from Burma, perhaps by an earlier owner of the estate.

One day as I was watching the English gardener at work, I asked him how he managed to achieve such a beautiful deep green and astoundingly flat lawn. He smiled and responded, "Very simple, all you have to do is roll it for three-hundred years!"

It was indeed a restful place, with lots of leisure activities, such as billiards, archery practice, and bike rides though the lovely surrounding countryside. Ed and I spent considerable time cycling the country roads and visited the historical Romsey Abbey, which was quite close to Stanbridge Earls.

The abbey, which dated back over a thousand years, had been rebuilt a number of times and now comprised a beautiful grey stone church constructed in gothic style, with striking stained glass windows that were boarded up and sandbagged to protect them from damage from a stray enemy missile or bomb.

Although adapted for modern usage as a church, the abbey's massive construction still exhibited signs of its earlier use as a defensive structure, including narrow slits in the walls for firing arrows at attackers, as well as a round fortress-like tower with crenelated wall battlements behind which the defenders had crouched.

We later learned that there was actually a secret tunnel that ran from nearby Stanbridge Earls to the inside of the abbey, so that the earlier inhabitants could quickly escape to safety in times of attack. In the dining room we were shown the secret door, which was the entrance to the tunnel.

Our visit to Stanbridge Earls left us refreshed, and with a deeper feeling for the beauty and the magnificent history of England.

CHAPTER TEN

CONTINUING OPERATIONS

Pictures on a Dresser

Upon our return to the squadron, we learned that a general reassignment of quarters at the castle was underway. A couple of people had completed their tours, which comprised 270 hours, or about sixty-plus missions, and had shipped out, and we had also lost a number of pilots over the past couple of weeks. Consequently, the pilots who were living in the annex outside of the moat were being moved into the castle and some of the guys in the big dorm room, including me, were being assigned to smaller rooms.

Andy was assigned to room with another guy on the second floor, and Ray and I were assigned to a corner room on the third floor – not a bad location, with a couple of nice windows to overlook the moat and grounds. This was a fortunate occurrence, as I got to know Ray a lot better over the months ahead and we became good friends, although not as close as his other two pals in the ABC gang.

Crump was given a small room to himself (and Jeep) right next to ours, which was of mixed benefit. We got to see a little more of Jeep, although the coyote actually spent most of his time in the fresh air outside of the castle. On the negative side, however, we had to put up with Crump's somewhat boisterous activities, such as rat-a-tat-ing loudly with his drumsticks and raising hell in general, particularly after a party.

In fact, any time Bill had a little booze in him, he was capable of turning into a complete wild man. I recall one occasion when after some kind of party, he climbed out his window and ended up swinging from the heavy rain gutter over the moat. We were trying to coax him back in, fearing that the old metal would break and dump him into the moat three stories down, with the potential for sticking him to the mud at the bottom!

The room I shared with Ray Burwell at the castle had a mirror and an old dresser, and two nice pictures sat side by side on it. Ray's picture was of his fiancée, Doris Clunan, who was a very beautiful blonde-haired girl with a look of sophistication about her. I began to understand why, shortly after being assigned his P-47, Ray had gotten the squadron painter to apply the name "Lady Doris" in large script letters on the side of it, together with a framed picture of Doris herself.

Privately I still thought that the picture on the airplane did not do justice to her at all, but Ray thought it was great so I never voiced that opinion.

My own photo on the dresser was that of Virginia Power, whose smile and curly auburn locks had bewitched me from the first time I saw her in Montgomery, Alabama. It was the picture she had presented to me at our last meeting, shortly before she went off to Alabama College for Women in Montevallo, where she was wearing the wings that I had "air-dropped" on the campus after graduation.

I did not have her photo painted on the side of my airplane, but instead settled for a simple "Miss Ginny," stenciled on the cowling, which I thought would meet with her approval. While a fun-loving girl, she was nevertheless a somewhat reserved Southern belle with traditional values.

While the two pictures went a long way toward brightening up our little room, they were, in fact, mute reminders, as neither Ray nor I had received any letters for almost a month. It was understandable, however, as all letters going overseas were routed to one of hundreds of APO numbers, each assigned to a base. But with millions of military personnel moving around in preparation for the invasion, letters were being continuously forwarded, chasing people to their new destinations.

To complicate matters, the U.S. had recently introduced V-mail, by which millions of letters were photocopied into tiny facsimiles that carried the message at a fraction of the original size in order to save weight and bulk in overseas shipments.

Ray had told me about his whirlwind romance with Doris and was filled with ideas about their future together. However, he was greatly concerned, as the last letter he received revealed that she had left Baton Rouge shortly after his departure and had gone off to New York City, apparently with some expectation of actually becoming a "Powers model!" In those days, Powers was the most well-known agency for magazine ads and was famed for its very beautiful and elegant models.

Ray was obviously exhibiting signs of concern, as he referred to the move to New York several times and kept checking his mail daily. He also inquired about possibly sending a telegram but did not even have her new address, so he could only resort to writing to his parents to see if she had been in contact with them.

I think Ray was experiencing doubts about whether he might have turned Doris off with some of his letters. I did not pry into Ray's private affairs, but on some occasions when we sat having a quiet beer together he would open up and I got the impression that he needed to rationalize his own thinking and was trying it out on a neutral party. I guess I was that party, as he knew very well that I would never blab about private things.

However, looking back with the perspective of a lot of history, as well the permission of Ray's family today, I am at liberty to reveal that one basic problem that kept rearing its head was religion. Although both Doris and Ray agreed that they wanted a church wedding, it seemed to be a question of 'Whose church?' Doris had been raised as a Catholic and had attended a convent school. According to Ray, however, she 'did not take her religion too seriously,' and had, in fact, agreed to be married by a justice of the peace.

Ray, on the other hand, indicated that he did take his religion seriously. Combining that with the idea that both really wanted a church wedding, Doris had apparently been left with two choices: Ray's church or none! Apparently he had communicated those sentiments to her. Since then, she had gone to NYC, ostensibly looking for new employment, and letters had become less frequent.

Periodically, a spate of letters would go back and forth in which they both pledged their continuing love for each other and agreed that they would work everything out in the future. Also, Ray had sent her photos of his P-47 with "Lady Doris" on it, which thrilled her, and he also told her that he was planning to have it painted on his new Mustang as soon as the group switched over to them.

One of the firmest pegs in my personal philosophy is 'Never get in the way of anybody's religion,' so I voiced no opinion whatsoever to Ray, except to speak in an encouraging manner about the future with his lovely fiancée. With respect to Ginny's picture on the dresser, I was not even sure that I could consider her my girl. She had given me her picture and was wearing my pilot's wings, but that was as far as it went. Our letters back and forth were also quite proper and relatively formal, and never hinted at intimacy in any way. Curiously enough, I found out later that she was also carrying on a correspondence with my mother, which was a complete surprise to me. Was she checking out my roots and character?

Summing this all up, I guess for both Ray and myself, it was a case of 'Wait and see what develops.'

Operation "Market Garden"

September 17, 1944

After the invading forces finally broke out of the Falaise Pocket, the grand plan was to move north and east on a broad front toward the Rhine River and the Ruhr Valley. However, General Montgomery, commander of all of the British invasion forces, became concerned that his supply situation was deteriorating as the German resistance continued to stiffen. He proposed to General Eisenhower that they consolidate their forces into a single, narrow but very strong thrust, which would punch through to Berlin. To achieve this, they would need to circumvent the northern end of the Siegfried Line by seizing the bridges across the Meuse River and the Lower Rhine. This would then allow the Allies to encircle Germany's industrial heartland in the Ruhr Valley.

To accomplish these objectives, Montgomery proposed very large-scale airborne drops in Holland, with the objective of capturing the bridges to provide a means for a rapid advance by armor. Supreme Headquarters, Allied Expeditionary Forces (SHAEF) accepted this proposed plan and code-named it "Operation Market Garden."

No one in the 356th had ever heard of "Market Garden," but they were soon to find out that the 356th was one of four groups selected to provide over two hundred P-47s to support the effort.

Early in the morning, the group assembled in the briefing room to get the details of the mission. The group had been flying very long missions deep into Germany, but when the briefing officer drew back the curtain covering the target map presentation, the pilots were quite surprised to see only a single, very short red line extending from Martlesham to Arnhem, a few miles into Holland. There was some surprised chatter about, and one wag cracked, "Milk run today," which drew a laugh. But as it turned out, that milk was destined to turn quite sour before the day was through.

The ABC gang had all experienced their baptism of fire and were now considered to be fully capable combat pilots. Consequently, Andrino and Burwell were scheduled, along with Ed Pleasant, to fly in Captain Fletcher's Blue flight, while Bill Crump was to fly the wing of Col. Tukey, who was leading the group.

The briefing officer explained that their mission was in support of a massive airborne invasion consisting of hundreds of towed, troop-carrying gliders, as well as waves of transports carrying paratroops. The primary mission of these forces was to capture and hold the many bridges and crossing points of the many rivers and canals which encircled Holland, so that our forces could drive tanks and armored vehicles forward rapidly.

The big concern, however, was that the bridges would be defended by heavy concentrations of flak. Therefore, the four groups of P-47s had been selected to knock out the flak before the landings. Without question, the P-47 groups had been selected for this task because of their superior firepower of eight 50-caliber guns, as well as their survivability. Each of the Jugs would also carry two 250-pound fragmentation bombs.

As the briefing continued, the pilots found out that the P-47s were essentially to be used for bait, as their orders were to fly around at only 2,000 to 2,500 feet and wait for the enemy gunners to fire at them, then go down and destroy the flak site. It was going to be an interesting day.

My Jug, P-IA, had undergone some flak damage that had been repaired, so I was not scheduled for the mission but was instead slated for a test flight that afternoon to check it out. Thus, Capt. Ragnell, the maintenance officer, and I stood at the flight line watching the group take off at 1100 hours and shortly thereafter were amazed to witness the invading force of hundreds of tow planes and gliders, many of which passed directly over our field on the way to Holland.

It was a fantastic scene, with the sky filled with planes of many types, moving at a relatively slow pace, as the gliders were great lumbering things, not designed for speed but to carry a heavy load of combat troops plus supporting gear. I noticed that some of the transports were towing more than one glider and also that the gliders were of several distinct types. I found out later that the American gliders, Waco CG-4s,[5] carried fifteen to eighteen troops or could handle a Jeep or small artillery piece, while the larger British Horsa gliders could accommodate twenty-eight combat troops with gear or, alternatively, a light tank or artillery piece.

Speaking of Horsas, as we watched some of the British gliders pass directly over our field, the tow cable of one suddenly snapped and it began spiraling down, heading for the runway at Martlesham. Seeing that it was going to land on our field, we grabbed a Jeep and drove out to the runway and waited while it rolled to a stop. Much to our surprise, the doors opened and a couple of dozen Scots in full battle dress with weapons at the ready came boiling out of the glider looking very much like they were ready to take out anything that got in their way! Fortunately, their officer was able to convince them that they had landed in friendly territory or we might have become casualties of "friendly fire!"

---

[5] Unbelievable as it may sound, the U.S. actually built 13,900 CG-4 gliders using at least a dozen manufacturers, a ridiculous and irrational overproduction, which demonstrated how many war industries, once started, ran at full speed, non-stop until war's end. After the war there were thousands of them sitting in depots all around the country, and I actually bought one, war surplus, for $75 (it cost about $21,500 to produce). The wing, which was eighty-four feet in length, had a chord of twelve feet and was covered with 1/8-inch mahogany plywood, while the fuselage, which was of steel tubing, was fabric covered. The amazing thing is that the glider was contained in five giant crates, which were made out of mahogany! I sold the lumber from the crates for $400 and made a dandy utility trailer using aluminum tubing and the giant wheels of the undercarriage.

Later, after the excitement died down, the Scots entertained the spectators with an impromptu show by their prized bagpiper, who had naturally accompanied them into battle.

Meanwhile, the 356th group had proceeded to its target areas near Nijmegen, and the squadrons split up into separate hunting flights. The whole Market Garden invasion turned out to be an unbelievable fiasco of epic proportions. With an illogic that staggers the imagination, SHAEF headquarters had decided to inform the Dutch Underground, which was absolutely riddled with traitors and German agents, that the landings were coming. The Germans not only doubled and tripled the flak but stationed armor at strategic points throughout the area. They even positioned a large number of 88mm guns right on the coast and lowered their barrels to shoot down many transport planes, with gliders still attached, while they were still over the North Sea.

The four P-47 groups, the people in the gliders, and the paratroops were sacrificial lambs to that stupidity, and Market Garden was a defeat which set back the whole Allied invasion by months.

There was no lack of targets, as the Germans launched a hail of flak of all sizes at any airplane that came into range. In the 360th squadron, Ray's flight took the worst pasting. Ray spotted a pill box surrounded by four gun emplacements and in accordance with the briefed procedures, immediately attacked first. He scored a lot of good hits, but in turn, his Jug took some hits from the flak pit.

Pulling up off the target, he realized he had forgotten to drop his frags and decided to make another attack. That pass was almost fatal for Ray, as the gunners had really gotten the range and plastered his Jug in several places, causing oil to completely fill his windscreen so he could hardly see. However, his bombs took out the target and he was able to clear the area, get some altitude, and head for the nearest base in England, which was Manston, right on the coast.

With Manston in sight but still over the sea his engine quit, but with the canopy slid back to see where he was going, he was able to glide in and land downwind. His left tire had been almost shot off and the plane was a flying pile of junk. The 40mm hole in his wing was large enough to crawl into, and the two holes in the canopy were directly behind his head. That's about as close as you can get to destruction and still survive.

Obviously, the Germans, with precise forehand knowledge of when and where the airborne invasion was to take place, had deployed many of their very best flak batteries to the Nijmegen area. While many of the guns had been knocked out, the losses in the 356th group continued to mount.

Almost immediately after Ray departed to drag his battered bird back to England, Fletcher, with Andy on his wing, attacked a flak battery by a bridge northwest of Nijmegen. The gunners must have all concentrated on the lead Thunderbolt because Andy made it through the attack without a scratch, but Fletcher immediately took hits which knocked out his engine and set the Jug on fire.

For whatever reason, Fletcher chose not to bail out, perhaps because he was too low, but instead aimed the burning airplane for a nice flat field and bellied it in. The fire had not reached the cockpit and Andy observed him jump out of the airplane and run to a nearby woods to hide. Observing that the fire in Fletcher's Jug had gone out, a member of the 359th then strafed the downed airplane, destroying it.

Meanwhile, Ed Pleasant's Jug had also taken a good pasting from both 20mm and 40mm, which inflicted major damage, leaving Andrino as the only one of Blue Flight who, by some miracle, had not been hit. Without question, if they had been flying any other airplanes except the P-47s, three out of the four in Blue Flight would have ended up as crashed and burning wrecks. Planners at 8th Air Force had indeed been wise in selecting only P-47-equipped groups for the mission.

Even so, it turned out to be a serious day for the 356th group, which, in addition to many shot up birds that returned to England, lost five P-47s. Flight Officer Tucker of the 360th squadron was shot down and killed, while Lt. Broxton of the 359th squadron was hit badly and his airplane was seen to hit the ground and cartwheel before coming to a stop. Broxton, who sustained only minor wounds, was later picked up by the 82nd Airborne and returned to England. Metaphorically speaking, Operation Market Garden was not a garden of roses for the 356th group!

There was an interesting aftermath to the Fletcher incident. A month later, as several of us were sitting in the fireplace room in the castle playing poker, the door opened and in he walked, sound as a dollar! We looked at him in amazement and were just about to jump up and greet him when he spotted his fancy Wellington boots, which one of the guys had helped himself to, and said, "Take 'em off!"

After the commotion died down, he told us his story. If anyone had made this up, I would never have believed it. A Dutch farmer, who was a member of the Underground, had picked him up and taken him into his house where he dressed him in typical Dutch farmer duds. A week later, a German squad came to the farmer's house and seeing Fletcher standing there, inquired who he was.

According to a pre-rehearsed script, the farmer told the German that Fletcher was his deaf and dumb son. The German looked at him and, believe it or not, left without further comment! Later, the Dutch Underground spirited Fletcher out of the country and back to England.

I suspect that the German knew but decided not to report it. After all, by late 1944, with their country in a shambles from bombing, the Allies advancing on one side and the Russians on the other, most Germans knew they would not win the war and were just eager to get it over with.

CHAPTER ELEVEN

ADVENTURES IN LONDON

A-1 Sauce and the Ugly Americans

Market Garden had taken a serious toll on the 356th group. Over and above the five airplanes that we lost outright, many more had received very serious flak damage. Consequently, during the late September period the group stood down from operations for about four days to give the mechanics and other ground crew a chance to catch up on repairs and maintenance.

Most of us were suffering from sleep deprivation and should have probably just sacked out for a while, but with a couple of free days at hand, some of us decided to forget the sleep – we would go to London and check out the big city. Ed Pleasant, Fritz Rideout, Bob Gleason, and I jumped on a train, all duked out in "pinks and greens," as the army uniforms were called, with shoes shined and belt buckle brass gleaming. The train was jam-packed and we spent about half of the trip standing in the aisle hanging onto straps or whatever we could grab.

On the way, we were amused when an American P-51 from one of the other fighter groups did a pretty good job of buzzing and beating up the train. I wondered if maybe the guy's girl was on the train and he was showing off a bit to impress her. He damned well impressed us; in fact, one pass was so low that I found myself hoping he wouldn't get carried away with himself and hit the train, with disastrous consequences. Almost everyone on the train was in uniform of some sort and they all seemed to get a kick out of the little American show with the Mustang, taking it for granted that this was a normal buzz job. We knew better.

Arriving at the typically smelly station in London, we grabbed a taxi which took us to the Jules Club on Jermyn Street near Piccadilly Square, where we hoped to book some decent rooms for the night. However, the place was filled to the brim, so we ended up taking a cab to some little hotel on the outskirts which was third-rate, but a place to sleep nonetheless. We tossed our bags in, locked the doors, and went sightseeing in London.

London was a beehive of activity, with troops from all of the British colonies and dominions, Americans, and Europeans from many occupied countries, who had succeeded in eluding their Nazi masters and were now in England preparing to help kick the Fuhrer in the teeth.

Ed Pleasant, who was of Polish descent, was particularly pleased to see some RAF pilots and crewmembers wearing the square red and white checkerboard patch of Poland on their uniforms. The Poles, whose country had been savagely destroyed by the Nazis, had a deep hatred for everything German and couldn't wait to wreak vengeance on the enemy.

We were walking by the houses of Parliament speculating about what each building was, when a nice English gentleman stopped, introduced himself, and said he would be happy to answer our questions. After some explanations he offered to take the four of us for a tour of Parliament. We accepted his offer and got a nice personally guided tour through both the House of Commons and the House of Lords.

Judging from the way he was greeted respectfully by many people as we strolled around, I am sure he was either an MP or a Lord, as he was immaculately dressed from head to toe, including a Bowler hat and silver-topped cane. However, with typical English reserve he had introduced himself only by name, omitting any title. In retrospect, I think he was expressing his appreciation to a group of very young-looking American pilots who were there in England helping his country throw off the yoke of the Nazi dictator after almost five long years of going it alone.

Later, we also got a nice tour of Westminster Abbey, which impressed us with its size and magnificence. It was awesome to stand next to the tombs of many of Great Britain's former monarchs, as well as many other special people in England's long history. Some very famous scientists, including Isaac Newton and Charles Darwin, share the cathedral's magnificence. We noted also a special area, which had come to be called Poet's Corner, that contained the remains of many famous writers and poets, including Chaucer, Ben Johnson (who was buried standing up at his request), Robert Burns, Lord Byron, and many others from the rich and interesting history of the British Empire. We also saw the Stone of Scone, which sat under the throne upon which the Kings of Scotland had historically been crowned.

While the cultural tour of London was interesting, the group quickly tired of that and looked around for some excitement in the most interesting form – good-looking girls and booze. With that thought in mind, the four of us hit a couple of pubs but found them to be pretty dull and populated largely by old geezers, as most of the young people in London were hard at work on their wartime jobs.

One thing we noticed in London traffic was that there seemed to be a lot of those tiny little panel trucks with "A-1 Steak Sauce" displayed prominently on the side.

"That looks good," remarked Rideout. "Why don't we find a nice restaurant or a pub with beer and skittles and order a T-bone steak?"

Everybody agreed so we headed for the first good-looking pub/restaurant and checked the menu. No steak. We tried another and the waiter said, "Oh, no sir, I am sorry but there is no beefsteak to be had; whatever is produced is going to the troops in the field." *That's odd,* we thought, *if there is no steak in the restaurants, why all the little A-1 trucks?* We asked a cab driver and he said, "If you want steak, you have to find a black market pub. I can take you to one, but it is quite a way out in the suburbs."

At that point, Pleasant and Gleason bowed out, saying they were going to stay closer to the heart of London and not waste a lot of dough on cab fare, which probably made a lot of sense. However, for Rideout, the pursuit of a steak had become a challenge that he was bound and determined to master. After Rideout engaged in some dickering about the price, the cabbie agreed to take the two of us to a place he knew of in Mayfair.

It was a fairly good drive across London traffic, during which time we were treated to views of barrage balloons flying on cables and operated by WAAF girls, as well as lots of anti-aircraft guns located in small parks or sheltered areas, also manned by WAAFs. The cabbie told us that the girls did everything except actually discharge the guns; a man was assigned to do that. Actually, the AA did not appear to be manned at full strength, which did not surprise us, as the raids by German aircraft, even at night, had become rare since Hitler had abandoned his plan to invade England. Hitler had opted instead to attack Russia, which had turned out to be more than a handful for even the mighty Wehrmacht.

One threat that did continue, however, was the V-1 buzz bombs, or Doodlebugs, as the Brits quaintly termed them. Doodlebug attacks had increased sharply, particularly during the nighttime hours, with London still the primary target. While the British radar stations and controllers had re-oriented their priorities to the V-1 terror weapons and assigned special squadrons of fighters to intercept them, quite a few still succeeded in reaching their target areas. We assumed that some of the flak crews were chowing up and that the guns would be fully manned after dark. We were soon to witness a vivid demonstration of the threat that the V-1 bombs represented.

The cabbie dropped us on a quiet street in the Mayfair area, which seemed to be prosperous looking, and pointed to a door with a little sign which simply said, "Robb's Place." We went in and found it to be a small pub with an equally small dining room manned by a single waiter. We each ordered a pint and asked for a menu. However, when we perused the menu we noticed that we could order fish, bangers and mash (sausages and mashed potatoes), chicken pot pie, or, oddly enough, rabbit stew, but no sign of any beef whatsoever.

Now, I am not a fancy eater and would have been perfectly happy with any of those, but Rideout got really ticked off that the cabbie had done a con job on us. When the waiter came back, Rideout piped up, a bit loudly, "The cabbie told us we could get a steak here."

The waiter looked a little flustered and said quietly, "I don't know anything about that, sir. Perhaps you would like to talk to the manager. Please follow me." And with that he showed us to the kitchen.

It appeared that the manager was also the chef, as a guy came over to us wearing a white cook's outfit, looked us over carefully, got a nod from the waiter and said, "I hear you are looking for some American-style beefsteak. We rarely ever receive any but we just happen to have two rump steaks that are about ten ounces each. They'll cost you dear though. They're the last ones we have."

We said, "How much?" and he quoted a price which would have knocked the head off of most Englishmen – but as the old saying goes, 'Americans are overpaid, overfed, and over here.' (I'll leave out the fourth slogan.) Rideout didn't even wait for my answer and just said, "Okay, let's go for it. I'll take mine rare."

The waiter quietly moved us to a single table in a private alcove, completely out of sight of the other patrons and, in about thirty-five minutes, served the steaks. I have to say that the steaks were absolutely delicious and cooked perfectly, in European style with some type of wine sauce, accompanied by crisped potatoes and Brussels sprouts. Of course there was the inevitable *A-1 Sauce*!

It was truly a fine dinner, but all through the meal I had an increasing sense of being a traitor to my country. *What the hell had I gotten myself into?* I thought. *Talk about the ugly American!* We had been criticizing some of our American GIs, whom we observed acting like complete boors and treating every English girl they saw like some kind of streetwalker – and here we were, the supposed flower of America's Officer Corps, acting like a couple of pigs and breaking British laws while many hardworking English civilians were having a difficult time getting enough food to feed their children properly.

The growing realization of this sin actually turned the food I was eating into some kind of acid reflux condition that dogged me the rest of the evening. I left there with the resolution that this was the last time I would ever participate in such an illicit and selfish activity.

Anne

The Jules Club, which was actually one of fifteen such clubs run by the American Red Cross, was known to put on great dances on Saturday nights. Inasmuch as it was still only 8:30 p.m. when we finished our illicit dinner, we decided to make our way back there and luckily found a bus which took us to Piccadilly Square, which was close to the club's location. Entering, we climbed a stairway, at the top of which was a large coat rack and table that contained about a hundred or so military hats of all varieties.

As a precaution, before placing our hats on the table, we took a pen and inked in our names on the lining inside of the hat. That was probably a good move, but it didn't guarantee that we would ever see our hats again, as we would later learn that the last few guys who left the place usually found that their hats had either disappeared or had been accidentally (perhaps) swapped for another which was either less beat up or a better fit. That was one of the wartime risks you had to take, I guess.

The club was nicely operated by Red Cross ladies in uniform, who did a good job of serving as hostesses to keep the place running in a respectable fashion. They also operated a nice little snack bar, which served sandwiches, donuts, coffee or tea, and Cokes at a minimum price. No booze, absolutely, although it would have been naïve to think that none was being sneaked in. An RAF guy we talked to told us that earlier in the war they had in fact also served what was called "National Beer," but apparently found that alcoholic beverages in an overheated room full of military people was not a good idea. He also said that the beer was lousy anyway.

The dance floor was filled with a lively crowd, mostly Americans in uniform, but also a goodly number of both male and female military from the allied forces of many services and branches, as well as assorted girls in civilian clothes. An orchestra of about ten pieces, made up of British civilians, was trying its best to emulate the sounds of some of the American big bands, but missing the mark by a long shot. However, nobody was concerned about that, as their rhythm was good, the music was loud, and the people on the floor were having a great time dancing to numbers ranging from slow dances and fox trots to swing and jitterbug, and even some fun twenties music like the Charleston.

You had to give the band credit; they were doing their best to provide something for everyone. One of the Red Cross ladies, a really good-looking gal, turned out to be an excellent singer and stepped up to the microphone periodically. I noticed, however, that she was wearing a wedding ring and always neatly fended off any overtures by guys seeking to date her.

Rideout and I plunged right in and danced with a couple of American WACs, as well as some British girls who were apparently not attached to anybody and were just there taking in the action. It was fun but nothing special. Then a curious thing happened. Rideout and I went over to the snack bar, got some Cokes, and set them on a small table.

We were about to sit down when I noticed that one of my shoelaces had become untied. I bent over, retied the lace, and stood up rather abruptly, just in time to knock the tray of tea and cookies out of the hand of a British WAAF who was walking by with it. Two cups of tea and two cookies went flying, some of the tea landing on the girl's arm, and some on another WAAF seated at the next table. The girl gave a gasp and I cried out, "Oh my God, I'm terribly sorry!" and scrambled to pick up the debris. "Please sit down and I'll get a cloth to sponge off your uniforms."

I dashed quickly over to the snack bar where the attendant, who had observed the scene, was already holding a cloth under a water faucet and wringing it out. I thanked her, grabbed the cloth, and dashed back to the two WAAFs, who were sitting together at the next table pulling themselves together.

Handing them the cloth, I said, "That was really clumsy of me; I'm very sorry."

The girl took the cloth, sponged off the spots, which fortunately hardly showed on their deep blue uniforms, gave me a half-smile, and said simply, "Casualty of war, I suppose – not to worry, the tea wasn't hot enough to burn," and her companion laughed pleasantly as she handed the cloth back to me.

"Let me replace your tea and cookies," I said. "How do you take your tea?"

"Plain," the second WAAF replied, and I returned to the counter where the attendant, a sharp woman, had already prepared a second tray and handed it to me with a smiling comment, "No charge. Red Cross to the rescue."

I thanked her and returned to the table with the tray, made a little small talk, then turned to rejoin Rideout who was still sitting at the next table, grinning.

I was still a bit embarrassed by the whole deal, but the thought suddenly hit me that those were two very nice and pretty girls, and on an impulse I turned back to the WAAF table and said to the girl I had bumped into, "Look, I assure you – that was definitely not a ploy to make your acquaintance, but since we have already met, so to speak, would you care to join us?"

I think they were as surprised as I was, laughed, looked at each other, and she said simply, "Okay, thank you."

They brought their tea and cookies over to our table, where Rideout stood up, offered his hand and said, "Fritz Rideout – and I'm not a German in disguise," which got a good laugh.

I followed with "Ed Nebinger," I have a German name also, but my middle name is Montgomery, which is the English side- from my grandmother. I anticipated the question which would follow and said, "I know your'e going to ask me if I am related to your General Montgomery and the answer is that I really don't know, but my father traced us back to the Montgoumerey's who arrived with the Norman conquest, so I guess we are all connected somewhere – but I wouldn't bank on it!"

Everybody smiled and the girl that I had bumped introduced herself, "Anne Wynne-Eaton and this is my co-worker Jennifer Townsend."

We shook hands all around and sat down, at which point there was a momentary pause and I filled in with, "Well, to use an old American expression, it's nice running into you this way," which started things off on a congenial note.

Anne was a stunning beauty with black hair and green eyes, but I had noted when we shook hands that she was wearing a wedding ring, which dampened my initial enthusiasm. Jennifer, while not a classic beauty, was nevertheless a good-looking girl who could easily be described as really cute. She was a dark blonde with hazel eyes, a nice combination which Rideout seemed to find interesting. Both girls were about five feet seven, with slim figures that gave them a sharp look in their blue WAAF uniforms.

Not being too familiar with RAF ranks, I asked them what the single ring on their sleeve signified and Anne replied, "We are both section officers, which is kind of like a flight officer in the RAF except that we don't fly. We do, however, wear a form of the RAF wings on our hats to signify that we are part of that service, and we perform a wide variety of ground tasks to support flying operations."

"Now I know why RAF morale is so high," voiced Rideout. "Too bad the Army Air Corps didn't think of that idea," he added, and we all chuckled.

The band, which had just resumed after an intermission, started out with a nice rhythmic slow number and we all took the floor to explore our respective talents. Anne, as might have been expected, turned out to be a very smooth dancer, light on her feet, and completely responsive to any lead that she was given. I felt pretty good about that first dance, which went well, but my ego took a bit of a tumble on the next, which turned out to be a waltz that somebody had requested. I quickly discovered that I still had the universal American weakness; we were terrible waltzers. Anne, however, was accomplished, as all Europeans seem to be, and slyly took over the lead job while cleverly disguising the fact that she was doing it, so that we actually looked good on the floor.

We returned to the table, ordered some more Cokes, and chatted about our respective jobs and where we were stationed, etc. It turned out that both Anne and Jennifer were section controllers at the major RAF plotting station in Uxbridge on the Western outskirts of London. One thing we found out quickly was that both were completely familiar with fighter pilots of all types, as they had worked at plotting incoming German bombing raids and had vectored the British fighters to intercept them. During the earlier days of the mass dogfights over Britain and the Channel, they had listened intently to the chatter of the British fighter pilots and some of their salty language which filled the radio channels. Clearly, they understood fighter pilots very well.

I said to Anne, "I notice you are wearing a wedding ring. Is your husband with the armed forces?"

"He was," she replied, "but was shot down by a JU-88 over the Bay of Biscay in 1942. He was piloting a Sunderland flying boat during a nighttime anti-submarine mission. His body was never recovered."

"Oh, that is terrible. I hope you weren't on duty in the plotting station at the time."

"Fortunately not," she replied. "Our station at Uxbridge is responsible for RAF Group 11 of Fighter Command. Stanley was with RAF Coastal Command, which is controlled by stations closer to the coast. However, I heard about the loss very quickly, as we do not lose very many of the big flying boats."

It occurred to me that Anne may well have some resentment against fighter pilots, as they had failed to protect her husband's Sunderland that fateful night. Cautiously, I explored the subject by saying, "Aren't the coastal command flying boats given any fighter protection?"

"Yes," she replied. "Typically we have some Beaufighters on patrol near the flying boats and they can easily handle the JU-88s, but the weather was very soupy that night and those Beaus are not radar-equipped. At the time it happened, the Germans had greatly stepped up their efforts to protect their submarines which transited back and forth across the Bay of Biscay while going and coming from their bases on the French Coast to their Atlantic patrol areas. The Germans not only sharply increased the surface flak capabilities of their submarines by installing more anti-aircraft guns but also deployed some JU-88C squadrons, which are equipped with Lichtenstein radar which gives them a fairly good all-weather capability. It was one of those that popped out of a cloud deck and shot down Stanley's airplane."

I made no further comment, not wanting to dwell on unpleasant memories, and simply invited Anne to join me on the dance floor for a slow dance.

She was very quiet; perhaps the retelling of the episode had brought on pensive memories of that time in her life. However, as the dance progressed, she moved closer to me and actually put her head on my shoulder.

I will tell you honestly that I am not one of those guys who seizes every opportunity on a dance floor to get a cheap thrill by pressing his body full length against his partner. However, when Anne laid her head against my shoulder and moved closer to me I felt an incredible erotic sensation that I had never experienced in my life before. I felt myself becoming aroused, and, try as I might to put it out of my mind, my body took control of me and I was a helpless prisoner. Anne felt it too, I could tell, as she said absolutely nothing and we just danced slowly and closely, letting the waves of desire course through our bodies.

Fortunately, that lovely and memorable dance was followed by a kind of quick-step, which gave us both an opportunity to return to some semblance of normalcy. We returned to the table while Fritz and Jennifer were still on the floor and simply sat quietly. Both of us knew that a special moment had taken place and I think we both were recovering from an adrenalin rush. We tried to make small talk, like nothing had happened – but it was no use. Finally I blurted out, "My God, Anne, I've got to see you again!"

She looked me straight in the eyes and said simply, "Yes," and reached for my hand.

The rest of the evening passed by in a rush. I danced with Jennifer but I scarcely remember it, except that every time Fritz and Anne went by on the floor, Anne's eyes sought mine and we locked like two magnets. It was a memorable evening all the way around.

The Jules Club closed at 11 p.m. and we joined a queue for cabs. Jennifer lived in some type of military barracks near the Uxbridge Controller Station, so Rideout simply put her in a cab, paid the fare, and grabbed another cab, saying, "I'll see you back at the hotel."

Anne had an apartment in Kensington. I insisted upon taking her there and she put up token resistance, but it was obvious that neither of us was willing to end the enchantment of our newfound togetherness. It was strange; we did not need to say anything but it was as if we had a form of mental telepathy that communicated our every thought.

That was never as clear as when the cab pulled up in front of her apartment stairs. I looked at her with a question in my eyes, but she simply put a finger across my lips and said softly, "No, but I am not on duty tomorrow and if you would like to spend the day together I would like it."

I kissed her then; it was like molten lava and we both pulled away quickly like we were avoiding falling into it. I thanked her for the lovely evening and said, "I'll pick you up at ten-thirty tomorrow morning; wear your walking shoes." She nodded, gave me a small smile, and stood there watching as the cab drove away. I rode the rest of the way to my hotel in a daze.

"Buzz-Bombs"

The next day when my cab pulled up in front of her apartment, she was standing on the landing carrying an umbrella and a picnic basket. Surprisingly, she was wearing civilian clothes – a delightful flowered frock which flowed nicely over her curves. She looked even slimmer than in uniform, although she was one of the few women I have seen who wear a uniform well. She was wearing flat walking shoes and a large sunbonnet, which framed her beautiful black hair like a Gainsborough. Frankly, I did not know that RAF personnel were allowed to wear civilian clothes while off duty, but I applauded the idea.

We had the cab drop us off at Kensington Park, not too far from Anne's apartment. It was a pleasant place with shady trees, benches, and even a few flowers, although a great deal of the land was taken up by Victory Gardens. Britain needed every bit of food it could grow and not only encouraged everyone to have a Victory Garden but also had a whole corps of women, the "Land Army," that operated farms and performed other homeland tasks while Britain's men were off fighting the war in many theatres worldwide.

It was a delightful morning with fleecy cumulus clouds aloft, which made me wonder about the umbrella. But I quickly concluded thereafter that the English know it is wise to carry an umbrella most of the time.

The first thing Anne did was to reach for my hand, and thereafter there was seldom a moment when we were not holding hands, simply enjoying being with each other and experiencing a quiet moment in wartime London, which seemed to be having a brief respite from V-1 bombs and V-2 rockets.

We ate a nice picnic lunch, which Anne had been thoughtful enough to pack. It comprised some finger sandwiches made out of some type of seafood pate, accompanied by tiny sweet gherkins and a glass of cold tea. It was surprisingly tasty.

However, in retrospect, I believe that anything Anne prepared would have tasted like manna, as I was increasingly captivated by this vibrant woman with such a quiet and polished yet down-to-earth manner. We saved some ends of bread to feed some ducks in a nearby pond and watched two little boys sail their tiny boats while their nanny kept careful watch on a nearby bench.

It was an idyllic scene, with a serenity that almost caused us to forget we were in a war zone. Yet shortly thereafter, we were brought sharply back to reality.

We had exited the park by another gate and were strolling through a nice area in West Kensington when we heard the distinctive sound of a German buzz bomb approaching. "It's a V-1," Anne said. "We track them all of the time. It must have gotten through the fighter screen as well as the outer London AA defenses."

We were in an area of large apartment buildings, as well as some good-sized office complexes, that lined both sides of the street. The V-I approached steadily, making a very loud rumble reminiscent of a large truck with a defective muffler laboring up a steep hill.

"This one could be close," said Anne, "but I don't see any air raid shelters. Let's get ready to flatten ourselves against one of the big buildings."

Both of us knew that as long as we heard the sound of the pulse jet engine there was no danger, but when the engine quit, the bomb would do a wing-over and in approximately eight seconds would contact a ground target and explode.

We flattened ourselves against a tall building, holding hands, and listened to the bomb coming directly overhead, at which point the engine quit and there was a sudden awful silence. I hugged Anne closely, trying to protect her from the blast that we knew was coming.

The explosion that followed was tremendous, with dust and debris filling the air, and the building that was sheltering us rocked on its foundations, making us fear that it would come down around our heads. Fortunately for us, the V-1 had impacted a block away in a cross street, which actually sheltered us from the blast, other than some dusting.

Walking quickly to the scene of the strike, we soon found out that every window for a city block around had been blown to smithereens and the street was a sea of broken glass and rubble, with a huge dust and smoke cloud covering everything. Most shocking, however, was that the entire second floor had been blown out of a building, which turned out to be a hospital containing a children's ward.

Emergency rescue crews appeared from everywhere and the sound of ambulances filled the air. It was obvious that the casualty count was going to be high, but there was nothing we could do and we quickly moved away from the scene to let the crews do their work.

Anne, who was obviously upset by the hit on the hospital, said, "There is a phone box on the next corner. I need to call my Uxbridge Station."

I had never heard of a phone box but soon understood that it was a phone booth. We hurried to it and she checked in. After a brief conversation, she turned to me and said, "I have to report for duty, as one of the section controllers is absent and they are already tracking a major wave of V-1s inbound."

We dashed quickly toward a major intersection and were fortunate to flag down an unoccupied cab. Anne directed the cabbie to her apartment for a quick stop to change into her uniform, while I waited in the cab. Within minutes she appeared, looking sharp in her WAAF duds.

All business now, she asked the cabbie to please take us as fast as possible to her station in the Uxbridge district in the western end of London. The cabbie knew where the station was, but when he stopped at the location I could not see any structure of significance. Then Anne said, "It's an underground bunker."

I assumed I would have to leave her there, but Anne said, "They don't normally allow visitors, but we do have a section for visiting

VIPs and I can get you in if you would like to see the operation," to which I nodded eagerly.

We exited the cab and both Anne and I reached for the fare, but the cabbie surprised us by saying to Anne, "No charge; this one's on me, Luv."

Anne voiced her thanks and quickly moved toward an entranceway. Moving to follow her, I turned back toward the cab, tossed the driver a small salute and said, "You're a patriot!" He called after me in a cockney accent, "Give –itler -ell, Yank!" and drove off smiling.

I dashed after Anne, for whom a guard had already opened the entrance portal leading to a very long stairway that descended deeply underground. On the way down, Anne said, "We're sixty feet underground, so most bombs won't touch us."

It grew cooler as we descended, and at the bottom the stair opened up into a large, brightly lit room that was buzzing with activity, but in a very restrained, business-like manner. Anne quickly directed me to a small visitors' gallery, where I joined some other visitors, primarily military personnel.

The dominant feature in the room was a very large plotting table, which bore the map of the entire Southeast region of England extending to the other side of the Channel. A number of WAAFs wearing ear phones were sitting around a plotting table wielding long rakes, which they used to position markers containing information on various threats and also, I assumed, friendly assets.

I noticed that Anne had already joined the two other section officers at the table. On two of the walls were some very large whiteboards containing information and notices of various sorts, while several RAF officers sat in a raised gallery overseeing the entire operation, also wearing headphones and quietly issuing orders via a small mike.

It quickly became clear that a great many V-1 buzz bombs were inbound toward London and other nearby targets and that preparations to intercept and destroy them were well in progress. The coastal batteries would account for some and a squadron of Hawker Tempest fighters had already been scrambled to pick off those that got by the flak batteries. Tempests, which were powered by a very powerful Napier Sabre H-shaped engine of twenty-four cylinders, were very fast and could catch the V-1s – which were quite speedy – and shoot them down.

Earlier, they had simply flown up beside the V-1s, put a wing under that of the missile, and flipped it up, causing the weapon to spill its gyros and crash. However, the Germans soon tumbled to that trick and cleverly put in a device that caused the missile to instantly explode in flight if the gyro was spilled, which had resulted in the loss of some Tempest fighters and pilots. Now they simply flew up behind, making sure they were far enough away not to be damaged by the explosion, and hosed them with 20mm cannon fire.

An RAF flight officer sitting next to me explained that the British defense system against the V-1s was actually very good, but the Germans had changed their tactics. Instead of sending in individual bombs – which could be easily tracked and shot down – they were now saving them up and then launching a hundred or more in a massive attack designed to overwhelm the defenses and allow some of the terror weapons to get through. That was what was now taking place.

In further discussion with him, I learned that the bunker I was sitting in was known as the "Battle of Britain Bunker" and had, in fact, been the principal controlling point during that epic battle. It had been assigned to direct the operations of RAF Group 11, which contained many RAF Spitfire and Hurricane fighter squadrons and some 20,000 total RAF personnel.

During those crucial days, many distinguished historical figures, including the King and Queen, had visited the bunker, and on

September 15, the peak day of fighting, Winston Churchill had sat there next to Air Vice Marshal Sir Keith Park and asked how many reserves they had. The answer was, "We have none."

During a brief lull in the action, Anne came over to me and explained that she was going to be on duty for at least another three hours and that I should therefore feel free to return to my hotel.

However, I was not about to let this great woman get away from me, no matter how long it took, and said quietly, "Anne, if you don't mind, I would like to hang around and take you home. However, I do not want to create any wrong impressions among your co-workers, so why don't I leave but I will hang out in that café across the street. I'll find a book or something to read."

She looked into my eyes, nodded, and walked away. A couple of minutes later, as I was getting up to leave, she came over, smiled, and quietly handed me a book, saying,

"Sometimes things are very quiet and I find time to read, but not tonight I think." It was Hemingway's *A Farewell to Arms,* a wartime romance.

As I was walking up the stairs, she called after me. "If any of the V-1s start getting too close, run over and ask the guard to let you into the bunker."

It was a full three hours and then some before Anne appeared, and during that time quite a few buzz bombs got through to London. I could hear them exploding at distant places in the city, but none came close to our location.

When Anne finally joined me, I was happy to see her again but noted that she looked tired, and she remarked, "It was a mass attack of more than a hundred bombs. We stopped most of them, but unfortunately did not get them all."

We shared a quiet dinner and a glass of wine in the café, which seemed to pick her up. To this day I still can't explain the feeling that passed between us. It was odd and almost ethereal. There was no need to rationalize why we were sitting together in a small café on the outskirts of London, and neither made pretenses that it was just a casual time that we were sharing. It just felt right sitting there together and I knew then that I loved this incredible woman.

Leaving the café, Anne said that I had spent enough money on taxis and she knew where we could pick up a bus a couple of blocks away. We did that and got dropped off very close to her apartment. This time there was no question as to whether I was invited in. Anne opened the door, settled me into a nice easy chair, went to the kitchen and came back with a bottle of wine and two glasses, which she filled.

We toasted our meeting and Anne came swiftly into my arms. I cannot describe the feeling that enveloped me when I felt her arms around me, and when we kissed it was absolutely a beginning of something wonderful. The feeling that was growing between us was undeniable and Anne said softly, "I have not been with another man since my husband. I haven't wanted to – until now." And she set her wine glass down, took my hand, and led me into the bedroom.

That night was the beginning of my real adult life. It was more than a momentary passion or a sexual adventure; it was a fulfillment and a culmination of everything that had happened in my life to date. And the beauty of it all was that it was shared, completely and without reservation. I could not believe that two people could achieve such a perfect blending, a blending of mind and bodies, and of psyche and physicality, all without any conscious thought of how it was happening – it just was – and it was right in every way. Some time during that night , I cried out, "Oh, Anne, you know I love you!" and she nodded happily and said, "Yes, yes," with tears in her eyes.

I began to talk of marriage, but she said, "No, not yet; I feel it too, but we scarcely know one another and this is wartime." She paused, then added, "I do not want to go through that again. We need to finish our jobs, keep our minds on staying alive, and get this damned war over with first."

Early the next morning I took a heartrending leave of Anne, after making very sure that I had all of her contact information and her working schedule as best she knew, and also that she knew where and how to contact me. I reflected that what Anne had said was correct – our romance was so sudden that we really knew very little about each other. But there would be time for that, and I intended to pursue it at every opportunity.

After some difficulty I caught a cab to our hotel in time to meet the guys, who were grabbing a quick continental breakfast before heading to the train station. Rideout had put the word out about the two WAAFs and they had all written an obvious scenario in their minds, which produced some good-natured joshing.

But I admitted nothing and told them merely that a gentleman does not discuss his affairs of the evening, and I was a gentleman by Act of Congress. Besides, I thought privately, my experience was so much more than a simple nocturnal adventure that I had no desire to have anyone even think that it was less than honorable. To me, it was much more than an affair – it was everything!

Back to Business

As the Allied forces advanced gradually into Germany, resistance by the German forces stiffened, as they were pushed into a smaller and smaller territory. Also, there was an air of desperation about it. Most clear-thinking Germans knew that they had no chance of winning the war and that it was only a matter of time before their leadership must surrender. Nevertheless, the German military was not about to give in without a fight and they still had a lot of highly experienced troops, as well as immense quantities of military tanks, fighting vehicles, and support equipment that had been pulled back from Russia as the German forces retreated.

The result of all this was that the 8th Air Force was kept quite busy during the late months of 1944 and flew a large number of diverse missions, including bombing raids on both strategic and tactical targets, with lots of escorting fighters. Meanwhile, an increasingly powerful 8th Air Force Fighter Command frequently joined the U.S. 9th Air Force in France and Germany, beating up everything in sight in support of our advancing forces.

Ray, Andy and a Superbolt

Consequently, during the latter months of 1944, the 356th group was kept quite busy and often flew missions with five flights of four per squadron, bringing the strength of a normal group mission to sixty airplanes, with maximum efforts going as high as eighty-four airplanes.

I was now one of the more experienced pilots in the squadron and was frequently scheduled. It was an intensive and tiring time of multiple missions, with little opportunity to visit Anne in London. Of course, we conducted a regular correspondence and an occasional phone call, but British phones were as bad as ever, so that was not very satisfactory.

Shortly after our return from London the 356th Group flew a number of consecutive missions with the mission of strafing and bombing ground targets in the general area from Rotterdam to Koblenz on the West side of the Rhine. The Germans had amassed some very strong defenses in the area, trying to stop the Allies' Eastward push, and consequently there were plenty of targets to attack, particularly ground transportation

However, the Germans had moved some squadrons of long-nosed FW-190s into the Koblenz area and these were undoubtedly manned by high scoring "Experts," as the enemy termed its Aces. With the Thunderbolt pilots focusing their primary attention on ground targets they became vulnerable to surprise attacks from enemy fighters and the Germans took full advantage.

In late September the 360th Squadron had a a particularly bad day as two of its flights which had been focusing on ground targets were bounced by the 190s, which shot down three of the P-47s, and wounded a fourth pilot. Lt. Garlent of Green flight was seen to go straight down and crash. This was followed by Lt. Leidy (of Aroostook County potato fame) calling to say he was in a dogfight with four FW-190s, while Fritz Rideout reported that he had been hit by 190s, and that some of his controls had been shot out. He was trying to drag his battered airplane back, but shortly after reported that two more of the FW-190s were attacking him again, after which no more was heard.

Meanwhile, Major Vogt, the Squadron Leader, was frantically trying find the fight to come to their aid, without success. Afterward it was confirmed that Garlent, Leidy and Rideout had all been shot down and killed, while Lt. Romine was wounded but made it back to Martlesham.

Vengeance Weapons

By late 1944 the Germans were having little success with their V-1 Buzz Bombs, as the British had a well-developed defensive screen of fighters and flak. Also, many of their launching sites had been overrun by the advancing allies. However, the Germans had strongly ramped up the launches of their newer V-2 rocket vengeance weapon, against which there was no defense whatsoever – as well as no warning.. It climbed into the stratosphere over England and descended at supersonic speed, its massive warhead producing catastrophic damage if it impacted in a populated area.

On October 11, we flew an early morning mission escorting bombers that hit Cologne and Koblenz. There was no fighter opposition, but we observed three vertical contrails of V-2 rockets going up into the stratosphere and leaning in the direction of England. Upon our return we were sitting in the operations room when, suddenly, the place was shaken by a terrific explosion. We ran out to see what it was but could see nothing. Later, we discovered that a V-2 rocket had landed in a field about a hundred yards from the castle and had blown a hole about twenty-feet deep and thirty-five feet wide in the field, setting a haystack on fire.

Of course, it was not one of those we saw going up, which had long since landed elsewhere, but part of a later volley. The V-2 also blew out the windows in the castle's kitchen, injuring the cook slightly. Later, it became the source of some amusement for the 360th pilots to learn that while the residents of the castle were out on a mission, the cook, who thought he had a nice cushy job, actually earned a Purple Heart that day!

A couple of days later we were scheduled to fly on a repeat bomber escort mission to Cologne/Koblenz carrying two 165-gallon external tanks of fuel. I was flying the wing of Lt. Russell and we were both flying old razorback P-47s, which must have been getting pretty tired.

As we took off side by side, Russell's engine started cutting out and he barely cleared the trees at the end of the field before getting it going properly.

Also, just as I was clearing the end of the runway, one of my external tanks fell off and I went over the mess hall holding full left stick and rudder to keep the airplane flying at 120 miles per hour. Calculating the weight of the fuel at about 8.5 pounds per gallon, I had an asymmetric weight condition of about 1,400 pounds! Fortunately, the fuel tank did not hit anything and did not ignite. I flew out over the Channel and dropped the other external tank, and we both landed safely. However, it could have been a major tragedy with two burning wrecks and a burning mess hall full of troops.

The Germans may actually have been trying to knock out some of the 356th's facilities with their so-called "vengeance weapons." It seems unlikely that the V-2 that almost hit the castle could have been deliberately targeted at us. However, for the last few weeks, the Germans had been sending over a few Doodlebugs regularly every night. They went right over Ipswich and quite often right over the castle at very low altitude. If you went into Ipswich to see a movie, sometimes a "cuckoo" alarm would be flashed on the screen. Nobody would go to a shelter but a little later we would hear it go over.

Lt. Daly, our intelligence officer, called it the "eight o'clock special." One night after a long mission, I must have slept very soundly, as the British flak batteries tracked a V-1 that kept circling around and blew it up. It knocked the radio right off my table, but I did not wake up.

The Germans were well aware of each of the American fighter groups and where they were stationed. We had a little radio at our bar in the squadron operations shack and several times we were amused to hear "Axis Sally," who broadcasted from Germany in English, tell us how they were going to get the "killer cowboys" of the 356th group.

CHAPTER TWELVE
OFF- DUTY EVENTS

Ray Meets Doreen

October 4

Friday's mission was dull and uneventful, and upon landing the squadron discovered that the group was going to stand down the next three days to catch up on maintenance. With a golden opportunity in hand, half the squadron jumped onto the train at Ipswich and headed for London, about an hour and a half ride.

Bill Crump had some form of other duty scheduled, so Ray was accompanied by his little Filipino buddy, Andy Andrino. They chatted about their high school days and laughed about how they had been thrown together by the crazy events in the high school locker room, and how they had discovered afterwards that their families actually knew each other to some extent.

They also reminisced about their college days at Modesto Junior College , where they had achieved considerable renown for their ping pong skills and had come very close to becoming California state champions before enlisting in the cadets in 1943. Ray reflected upon how amazing it was that he and Andy succeeded in going through flight training together, and both beat the odds against the ever-present threat of a washout despite a ton of hurdles. Good luck seemed to stay with them, and both graduated in March 1944 in Class 44B.

Watching the English countryside sail by from his window in the train, Ray smiled as he reflected back on those fun college days. Now, Andy often flew as Ray's wingman and they were closer than ever.

Sitting next to him, Andy was listening to the rhythmic sound of the train wheels clacking across the rail junctions, a sound which seemed to run in sequences of "klick-a-clack-a-clack, klick-a-clack-a-clack." Andy paraphrased this aloud with "Start a second front, start a second front." That was a sentiment that had previously been much talked about in the newspapers and continually pushed by the Russians prior to D-Day. At that time, the Russians had millions of men fighting desperately, while the Germans were still uncontested on the land in all of continental Europe!

Now a second front had indeed been started and Allied forces were well on their way toward meeting the Russians at the Elbe River to put a final nail in the Nazi coffin.

Debarking at an ancient station in northeastern London, they were once again greeted with the urine smell of generations of water closets leaking onto the rail beds and hastened to grab some fresh air and a taxi. There was the usual queue for cabs, but after about twenty minutes they succeeded in getting one and headed for the Jules Club where they were fortunate to get a shared room.

It was still mid-afternoon when they got checked in, so they decided to head over to Selfridges, a large department store which had a surprisingly fine line of goods in spite of wartime shortages. Ray had heard from the guys in the squadron that the store carried Wellingtons and they headed to the department that sold shoes and boots.

They were delighted to find that it was indeed true, and after some browsing and fitting both ended up wearing a shiny black pair of low-cut Wellington boots, a favorite with the fliers in the 8th Air Force. Many were known to wear them on combat missions, even though it was against the rules to do so because if they had to bail out, the boots, which did not have laces, were liable to snap off when the chute opened. But flyers were notorious for not worrying about things like that. They lived mostly for the present – tomorrow would take care of itself.

Emerging onto the street, they strolled along, enjoying the sights and listening to the steady clopping of thousands of hob-nailed boots from the military men of many nations. London was really a fantastic place, and in spite of the fact that it was a daily target for buzz bombs and an occasional V-2 rocket, it was the first place everybody headed to as soon as they got a three-day pass. Consequently, it was a sea of uniforms and a babble of voices in many languages.

Americans, who were sprinkled liberally in the crowds, were fiercely resented by many of the English people, particularly the men, who observed them throwing their money at the English girls, many of whom were not at all insulted by it.

A certain portion of the American GIs were, in fact, obnoxious bastards who took advantage of their situation, and being away from home and all restraints, didn't give a damn about the consequences. Unfortunately, this resulted in all Americans getting tarred with the same brush, and it took a pretty far-sighted Englishman to move beyond it. The much heard expression, 'Overpaid, overfed, and over here!' was sometimes also heard with a fourth attribute, 'over-sexed' (or even ruder versions). One group not present in the London crowds, and which bore a particularly bitter cross, were the men of the British Eighth Army whose women were vulnerable in England while they sweated and fought in Africa.

Strolling past an area of apartment buildings, they heard piano music coming from what appeared to be a below basement walk-down. A sign posted on the railing said simply, CONCERT - MYRA HESS TODAY. Ray, who played the trumpet and had an interest in music, slowed and said, "Why don't we take a look, Andy?"

Andy, who had nothing against music, nevertheless felt that his time could be better employed in London than watching concerts. "No way, buddy, that's not my style, but why don't you check it out and I'll see you back at the Jules Club this evening."

"Okay," said Ray, "I think I will. See you later."

At the bottom of the stairs, he was greeted by an attendant who told him that there was no charge; it was a free concert for the benefit of the servicemen and the local war workers. He ushered Ray to a seat near the front of a small auditorium and handed him a rather crudely printed program. On the way into his seat, he had to squeeze past three people, who comprised a strikingly pretty woman sitting between two older people, probably her parents. Ray was in the process of excusing himself when he accidentally stepped on the foot of the elderly woman, causing her to give a low exclamation.

"Oh, I'm terribly sorry!" said Ray, turning red with embarrassment for having made a fool of himself in front of the audience.

Wincing in pain, but in true British fashion, the woman said, "It's quite all right," and the girl gave him a half smile as if to say, 'It's all right, we understand.' However, the man gave him a look that suggested he was a bit annoyed.

Ray had never really heard of Myra Hess but soon discovered that she was not only a famous pianist but also a "Dame of the British Empire."

Dame Myra opened her concert with Brahms 2nd Piano Concerto in B Flat Major, and played magnificently through the lyrical and challenging work. Because of the length of the concerto, Dame Myra chose to play only the first and third movements. During the first movement, which was an allegro, Ray was rapt with attention, astonished at the skill and power of the world-famous pianist who had given her time to play for the war workers and people off the street. However, at the beginning of the third movement, which was a slower andante, he happened to look over at the girl and was surprised to meet her eyes glancing at him. He smiled, and she nodded, turning away primly.

At the end of the concerto, an intermission was announced, with tea and small biscuits served on a table in the back of the auditorium. Seeing the family at the table, Ray took the opportunity to again express his regrets by saying to the woman, "That was terribly clumsy of me. I hope I haven't done any damage to your foot."

"Not at all," said the woman stoutly, although Ray had noticed her limping slightly on the way back to the table.

For the first time, the man spoke, more kindly now, "Not to worry; casualty of war, you know," and they all laughed. Then, as if to put Ray further at ease, he said, "You Yanks are doing a good job against the Germans, and we appreciate it."

"Thank you, that's very kind of you to say that, sir," responded Ray, "but your men have been carrying the load all alone for a long time."

"Yes," said the man, and a look of pain crossed the faces of the family, causing Ray to wonder what he might have said wrong.

Ray's consternation showed in his face, but the girl hastened to add quietly, "My parents knew some of the pilots who flew from a nearby base during the Battle of Britain. My Mum often had some of them at our house. One of our favorites was a Hurricane pilot who was shot down and killed."

"Oh, I'm sorry," said Ray, looking at the mother. "I'm beginning to understand what it is like to lose some good friends, as we have already lost some. But I guess that is the price we have to pay to keep tyrants from stealing our freedom."

"Yes," said the father quietly. "It is."

The mother nodded soberly.

A small hand bell announced the end of the intermission and they all returned to their seats, this time the family standing politely while Ray moved into his own seat.

Dame Myra started the second half with a very popular wartime work, "The Warsaw Concerto," followed by Claude Debussy's two "Arabesques," both delightful and melodious works of genius.

Glancing lightly at the family, Ray could see that they were enjoying the program as much as he was, and on two occasions his peripheral vision suggested that the girl was looking over at him while ostensibly addressing her mother. The program finished with the sprightly Spanish Caprice of Rimsky Korsakoff, and the applause was loud and continuous, causing Dame Myra to take repeated bows to acknowledge the acclaim.

As the audience began to file out, Ray found himself looking longingly at the girl and her family, as if a friend was going out of his life. But as he approached the door, he saw them having a small discussion and was startled to see the man turn around and address him, "Look here, Leftenant, you seem to be a decent fellow, and it just doesn't seem right to run off like this when there are guests in our country."

He held out his hand and said, "Let me introduce myself; I'm Herb Bolton and this is my wife, Ivy, and my daughter, Doreen. We live in Ipswich, East Anglia."

Ray was surprised but found himself to be inordinately pleased. He smiled and stuck out his hand, saying, "Ray Burwell, Denair, California; I'm happy to meet you." Then he added, "I don't know whether I am supposed to say this, but I am stationed just outside of Ipswich at Martlesham Heath airfield."

"Oh, we know it well," said Mrs. Bolton. "That is where many of the Battle of Britain boys were stationed during the Blitz. We often had them at our house." Then, looking at Mr. Bolton, who gave a slight nod in confirmation, she said, "I don't know what your schedule is, young man, but if you are not occupied next Saturday we would be pleased to have you come to our home for dinner." She added, "It's nothing very fancy, but I think we can manage," and the girl smiled encouragingly.

"That's really very nice of you," said Ray. "I don't know what our mission schedule is, but I promised my flying buddy, Andy, that our next day off we would take in a movie that is playing in Ipswich. I actually came to London with him this time and I don't think I should leave him on his own again."

As he said it, he could not help but note the look of disappointment that passed on the girl's face, and he felt for a second that he was making a great mistake. But the mother came back quickly with, "Well, perhaps your friend would like to join us; if you are both available, we would be happy to have him."

"Well, thanks, that's really very kind of you," said Ray. "Let me sort it out when I get back to the squadron and I will call you to confirm."

"That's fine," said Mr. Bolton. "We live just outside Ipswich and you can catch a bus from Martlesham to our place, which is only about four miles. I can give you the details if you can make it." He handed Ray a card, saying, "Here is our number; you can ring us anytime, but the sooner the better so that my wife can plan things."

"Thanks again, I would very much like to come," said Ray, glancing at Doreen. "Let me see what Andy has to say."

"All right, I hope we will see you again," said Mrs. Bolton, smiling, with the man giving a slight nod. They strolled off, with the mother giving a small smile and the girl sneaking a quick peek back at Ray – who felt the eye contact like a bolt of electricity.

Wow, said Ray to himself, *I can't believe it. Andy better not drag his feet on this or I'm going to kick his butt!* Then he had a momentary flash of guilt as he remembered Doris, but it didn't dim his enthusiasm as much as he might have expected.

That evening Ray ran into Andy in the snack bar at the Jules Club and told him about the invitation. Watching Ray's face as he told about it, Andy could see that he better play ball and quickly assented.

Their trip back to Martlesham was uneventful and they returned to the squadron to find that the mission schedule had been more or less routine. The debacle at Arnhem had set back the Allied timetable by as much as two months, and the Germans were being stubborn in resisting Allied forces. Consequently, the 360th flew several more rather uneventful missions that week, after which Ray and Andy managed to finesse a free Saturday from the operations officer.

On Saturday morning he called the Boltons, and Doreen answered the phone; she sounded happy to hear from him. When Ray said they were planning to come, she said, without any pretense whatsoever, "I'm glad; it would have been a shame if you couldn't make it."

They chatted a bit and she gave him directions to their house, signing off with, "We will look forward to meeting your friend Andy."

The Boltons

October 8

Saturday afternoon Ray and Andy caught the Ipswich bus outside of the main gate, which took them to a station in the center of the town. They had the address of the Bolton's house but decided that the easiest way to get there would be to grab a taxi. The queue was very short for a change, it being late afternoon. (Apparently the taxi business heated up later in the evening.)

After a relatively short drive, the cabbie pulled up at a house sitting directly next to a golf course. The driver announced grandly, "Here y'are Leftenants; maybe you should have brought your Bobby Burns woodies."

They laughed and Ray said, "Maybe next time," and paid the fare plus a generous tip, which sent the driver off with a smile and a "Thanks, governor."

As the cabbie drove off, Andy turned to Ray and said, "They really do talk just like in the movies."

There was no doorbell but Ray rapped the clapper a couple of times and Mrs. Bolton answered the door, with Doreen standing directly behind her. They exchanged greetings and Ray introduced Andy to Mrs. Bolton and Doreen, who then invited them to come in and meet the rest of the family.

Mr. Bolton, who was reading a paper and smoking a pipe, stood up, somewhat reluctantly it appeared, but after being introduced to Andrino, shook his hand and said, "Sit down, sit down and join us. We are just having some tea and biscuits; my wife makes very good ones," to which Mrs. Bolton responded, "Well, they are nothing special but I guess they will do for a starter."

Just then a young girl walked into the room and Doreen said, "This is my younger sister, Cynthia; she is sixteen."

The girl smiled impishly, said "Hello," and after eyeballing Ray, switched her look directly to Doreen, who actually blushed a bit. (She would never admit it, but after their return from London where they met Ray, she had reported excitedly to her sister, "Oh, Cyn, we met such a handsome American officer who is a fighter pilot at Martlesham. He was dressed in his uniform of greens and pinks. So dashing!! – and he is coming here for dinner!")

Everybody sat while Mrs. Bolton poured tea, and Mr. Bolton started the conversation off with, "How's the war going?" Ray told him that things had quieted down over the past week, but there was a feeling that the Germans were massing their strength for a new push to stall the Allied offensive, as their forces that had been withdrawn from

Russia were now being compressed into a smaller and smaller defensive perimeter.

Mr. Bolton told them that he knew that feeling, as he had been in the trenches with the Northumberland Fusiliers for over three years during WWI. He went on to say, "We had those quiet periods sometimes, which usually meant that the Germans were building up for some new mischief. The Jerries can be sticky when they set their minds to it."

Andy said, "I can't imagine what it must have been like standing in those muddy and cold trenches month after month."

Mr. Bolton responded, "It was not only cold enough to chill your bones, it was wet constantly and no matter how much grease you rubbed on your boots your feet were usually wet! But I think that was actually what saved my life, as I developed a bad set of hammer toes and was in hospital a couple of times when we had a big push and lost a lot of men."

Andy and Ray looked puzzled about the "hammer toes," but Mr. Bolton hastened to explain he thought that was what the Yanks called "trench foot." He went on to say, "It was kind of a miracle that I made it through alive without any battle wounds, just a few toes."

Ray said, "I think what we are doing is really soft, compared to what your men went through in that war!"

The modesty of that statement surprised Herb Bolton, who had gained a poor appreciation of the Yanks he met during that earlier war, and caused him to respond gracefully, "Well, I don't think I would want your job either. I like to keep my feet on the ground, hammer toes and all," which brought a laugh from all.

He concluded by saying, "Why don't you call me Herb, and my wife is called Ivy." The two pilots repeated their first names and everyone shook hands again.

Ivy Bolton joined the conversation, "Herb, that is the first time I've heard you talk about the trenches in years." Then, turning to Ray and Andy, she said, "My husband is usually very quiet about his life, but he is quite skilled. He is a bricklayer and a construction man, and has lots of other skills. Herb can do anything; he even built a little radio set when we were younger – he also built this house, and earlier in the war made a bomb shelter in the back yard."

Turning to her husband, she followed with, "Herb, why don't you show the lieutenants the house and grounds while Doreen and I work on dinner, so our American guests get an idea of how a typical English family lives."

Herb muttered something like, "Well, I don't know how typical we are, but I can show them around."

He gave them a tour of the house, which was a nice six-room villa constructed of frame and bricks, not pretentious but well-built and nicely situated with golf links in both the front and back of the house. It comprised a two-story building, with the living room, dining room, and kitchen downstairs, and two large bedrooms, one small one, and a bathroom upstairs. He explained how he had been very lucky to find this piece of ground in such a nice, private location, where they did not have to rub up against close neighbors. He also showed them their substantial Victory Garden with shady trees rimming the property, and pointing to a beautiful white lilac tree next to the garden, said, "When the weather is nice, we sometimes have breakfast out under that shady tree."

Andy and Ray complimented him on his home and pleasant surroundings and they returned to the living room where, shortly thereafter, they were all invited to come to the dinner table.

Doreen and her mother placed the main dinner entrees on the table and took their seats. Mr. and Mrs. Bolton sat at opposite ends of the table, while Ray and Andy were seated directly across from Doreen and Cynthia. They bowed their heads and Mr. Bolton voiced a very brief statement of grace, after which all said, "Amen," and the ladies began serving.

Dinner comprised a very large chicken pot pie with a tasty crust, accompanied by dumplings, Brussels sprouts, and carrots. Ray and Andy knew that the family had dug into their food rations to produce such a nice meal, so while neither of them was particularly fond of Brussels sprouts, both accepted a healthy serving of everything.

It soon became evident that Mrs. Bolton was a talented cook who had learned how to do a lot with relatively little in wartime England, as the dinner was delicious. She explained how both the carrots and Brussels sprouts came from their own garden, although it was late in the season. Herb Bolton provided the final touch by producing a bottle of white French wine, which they had apparently been saving for a special occasion – and this was it.

Conversation flowed freely. Ray and Andy told them of their life in sunny California, describing the lush vineyards and fresh produce that grew for miles around in the San Joaquin Valley. They also talked of their parents and their occupations in that verdant area, and watched the envious expressions on the faces of people who had been living with wartime scarcities for almost five years.

To put that into perspective, Cynthia, who had been eleven when the war started, said that she could not remember what a banana or a melon tasted like!

Not wishing to prolong a sensitive topic, Ray turned the conversation to the Boltons and their war experiences. Mrs. Bolton talked about some of her war jobs. Lodgings for workers had become very scarce, so over the war years she had taken in several war workers. These had included an airman who was a radio technician who worked for one of the radio locator stations.

All of the fighters and bombers, as well as the air/sea rescue service, relied heavily upon these radio locator stations along the coast for what were called DF (Direction Finding) steers to help guide them, particularly during bad weather – of which England had plenty.

She had also boarded two forestry workers; one of whom was a channel islander from Jersey who managed to escape when the Germans took the islands. She also described some of her many war help activities, including making dolls for the children of servicemen at Christmas, a job she loved.

It turned out that Doreen, who was nineteen, worked as a receptionist and secretary to a captain who ran the National Farmers Union in Ipswich, Suffolk. Production of food in England was very carefully controlled and monitored, as much of the nation's food was imported.

Earlier in the war the German submarines had come very close to closing a stranglehold on the island, but had been defeated by the Royal Navy and those of the dominions, which were later joined by the U.S. Navy and Coast Guard after Pearl Harbor.

Nevertheless, the drive to produce as much food as possible continued. Doreen also emphasized the importance of the "Women's Land Army," which had enlisted thousands of young girls and women who tilled the land and performed all manner of farming tasks to fill in for the workers who had been taken into the military services.

Throughout the dinner and the evening, Ray and Doreen had been quietly sneaking glances at each other while trying to maintain a posture of normal polite conversation. However, it was not until later, when the family took a quiet stroll out to the yard, that Ray found a moment to talk to her.

The attraction was mutual and neither made any pretense of hiding it. Ray asked her for a date and she replied that the local Red Cross Club had dances on Friday nights from 7 to 10 p.m. Ray said, "Great, I'll call you," and Doreen smiled and said very honestly, "That would be nice."

Later, as they were taking their leave at the door, Doreen said quietly, "Invite your friend to come along and I will bring Cynthia with me. She is only sixteen, but I can see that Andy is not only a nice, fun guy but also a gentleman who would not take advantage of her." She was correct and astute in noticing that.

First Date with Doreen

October 13, 1944

A week after that first visit, Ray and Andy rode the bus into Ipswich and walked a short distance to the Officer's Club building where the Red Cross dances were held. As they greeted Doreen and Cynthia in front of the club, they could hear a band already playing and noted that it was doing a good job with American swing-style music. However, they were surprised to note that before being admitted, everyone had to pass through a brief interview with the Red Cross personnel, who actually asked some personal questions.

Doreen explained that the American Red Cross wanted to maintain the propriety of its dances by screening out undesirables, such as "ladies of the evening," and therefore labeled its dances "By Invitation Only," which gave them the option of refusing anyone they chose. They also had a strict rule: No alcoholic beverages of any kind. Those rules were okay with Ray and Andy, as neither was a heavy drinker, and they noted with pleasure that they and the Bolton girls were passed through quickly with a smile and a friendly word.

The dance floor was surprisingly crowded and the music was eminently danceable, with the band playing all of the great tunes of the big band era. The musicians did a very capable job with the music of the various big bands and seemed to have a special interest in emulating the unique style of Glen Miller, which was called "doubling the lead," with clarinet over a saxophone. It just so happened that Glen Miller and his band were in England at the time, entertaining the troops and planning to go to Paris, which had been liberated and was trying its best to return to pre-war gaity. [6]

Both of the Bolton girls were excellent dancers and neither had any trouble adjusting to the somewhat more casual American styles for a variety of slow dances. When the band stepped up the pace to swing and jitterbug, however, the Americans were in a class of their own.

The British girls and guys loved it, as it represented a form of freedom which not only dictated letting go of their inhibitions but also allowed them to toss aside their wartime stresses and just enjoy life. Ray was quite competent in this area but Andy, whose skill and footwork were dazzling, was a master, as he had demonstrated back in Baton Rouge on the night they met Doris. Cynthia surprised her sister at how quickly she picked up the beat under Andy's strong lead. She seemed to have a natural aptitude for the rhythm.

However, Andy also soon zeroed in on a nice-looking unaccompanied girl with an intriguing and exotic Asiatic look – perhaps half Chinese or Malayan. The two shared a number of dances and moved like a syncopated piece of machinery on the floor. Andy didn't bring her to the table, however, as that would have been rude to his date, but undoubtedly a connection was made there.

Sitting quietly with Doreen, watching Andy and his partner on the floor, Ray had a strong flash of guilt, as his memory was swept back to

---

[6] Unfortunately, Glen Miller would lose his life a short time later. On December 15, 1944, he flew in a U.S. Army UC-64 Norseman to join his band in Paris. The airplane disappeared over the Channel and was never seen again. Many years later, it was revealed that Miller's plane was probably the victim of an accident that occurred when an RAF bomber squadron aborted its assigned mission due to weather over the target area and returned to England, jettisoning its bomb load over a designated North Sea area. One of the gunners reported seeing a light plane spin in far below, probably struck by one of the hundreds of bombs that were jettisoned into the sea, over which the Norseman was flying at a low altitude.

that eventful first evening with Doris, to whom he was pledged, and here he was sitting with a pretty English girl. However, he quickly rationalized to himself that he was not committing a sin. After all, it was not a violation of a commitment to simply share a pleasant evening with some very nice company.

Nevertheless, when he danced with that nice company and felt her moving next to him, a lot of his senses were awakened and he knew that he wanted to spend a lot more time with this lovely girl.

The Wild Frontier

With the winding down of the long British Double Summer Time days and the lull in scheduled missions during the conversion of the 356th to a P-51 Mustang group, the number of leisure activities and parties jumped up dramatically. Ray and Andy had a thing for hunting, and managed to borrow a couple of shotguns to see if they could scare up some pheasants in the gorse of a nearby field. I did not have a shotgun but was invited to traipse along. Game turned out to be very scarce, but the one thing they did manage to scare up was a nearby farmer who came charging out and threatened to report them to the local game warden.

I don't know whether it was not hunting season or if they were on private property, but some heated words were exchanged, after which I was surprised to hear Andy say loudly and pointedly to Ray, "Well, if he is going to report us anyway…," to which Ray answered, "Yeah, that's right," – at which point the whistleblower hastily said, "Now wait a minute," and took off at a run across the field, apparently convinced that the crazy gun-toting Americans were going to either work him over or perhaps even use the shotguns on him. Andy and Ray sounded like a well-oiled team! Of course, it was all a fake (I think), but I guess our reputation preceded us, as there were lots of American cowboy movies floating around in Europe.

Out behind the castle there were some big fields that, for some reason, were loaded with rather large jackrabbits (the British called them hares). Sometimes, when things became boring at the castle, some of us would go out and see if we could nail some of them with our government-issued .45-caliber automatic pistols.

Most of us had qualified as experts with the weapon in training, but anybody who has fired one of those things will tell you it is damned difficult to hit anything with it, unless the pistol is carefully aimed and a round slowly squeezed off. But it was a lot of fun trying to hit one of the rabbits, as they were very fast and would jump unexpectedly.

I made the mistake of going hunting with Bill Crump one day, who demonstrated once again why he had earned the name "Wild Bill." Every time a hare was spotted, Bill would go into an instant shooting spree, blasting away shot after shot and sometimes swinging the pistol wildly as the rabbit changed course.

After concluding that I was liable to end up as the hare, I made it a point not to go hunting with Bill again!

We also had some pretty wild parties at the castle. Earlier I mentioned the mission whiskey, of which two shots per pilot were dished out by Doc. Carey at the conclusion of each mission. However, it was not necessary to drink it; you could get chits for it and save it up. Therefore, some guys saved up their chits for parties, and a few non-drinkers also contributed their chits, so that booze flowed pretty freely during those occasions.

I recall one occasion when the cooks in the castle managed to come up with a couple of decent-sized roasts, which were absolutely rare in wartime England. Somebody rigged up a spit behind the castle and the roasts were put on.

Bill Crump and Jeep at the Castle

While waiting for the meat to cook, everybody played a crazy game that would be called "helicopter" today, but there were no helicopters then.

To play the game, you take a broomstick or some other piece of wood, hold it up over your head and while looking straight up at it, turn around ten times as rapidly as possible. Then you lay the stick on the ground and try to step over it. Nine out of ten people will never make it over the stick but will take off in a wild tangent while trying to get their balance and wind up crashing into things and other people. It is a barrel of laughs and gets better with a little liquid stimulation.

Somewhere in the midst of that game, Crump decided that we needed more light to brighten up the scene. Damned if he didn't come up with a ten-gallon can of GI gasoline. He poured it into the moat and tossed a lighted match in after it. *Whoosh!* Flames leaped fifty feet into the air, circling the whole castle as the gas moved around the moat. Meanwhile, Crump, with Jeep trailing behind, was doing an imitation Indian war dance.

Fortunately, the castle was built of bricks, so no damage was done, but a number of the neighbors appeared, worried about what the crazy Americans were doing now. I am sure the local fire marshal must have also heard about it and talked to the C.O., but Crump never mentioned catching an official chewing out for that incident.

The English people were actually very friendly to the American pilots, as they recognized that these very young men were risking their lives daily in the war effort and were therefore willing to cut some slack for them letting off some steam. Also, fighter pilots were accorded special status in England, as they had saved the country during the Battle of Britain.

Kesgrave Hall, where the 359th squadron lived, also saw some pretty wild parties. I was not there but heard about one episode in which, at the height of the evening, some clown came up with a live hand grenade and decided, while standing on the balcony, to create some fireworks by pulling the pin and throwing it as far as he could into the surrounding brush. His pals all ducked down and waited for the blast, but it didn't go off!

The 359th C.O. heard about it and ordered those guys to get out there and find the damned thing, if it took all night. A bunch of them were out there looking for it on hands and knees with candles and lighters for over an hour, but couldn't find it! Finally, somebody came up with a hand grenade with the pin still in it, which the C.O. promptly confiscated. I never did confirm this, but rumor had it that one of the pilots had quietly gone back to the base and gotten one someplace.

CHAPTER THIRTEEN

INTERLUDE

Playing Tag With Jets

Over the previous week, we flew several more missions escorting bombers, which hit Cologne, Kassel, and Magdeburg. Apparently our troops were making a determined effort to take these areas and wanted to soften them up as much as possible. However, the weather was terrible and each time we had to climb to over 30,000 feet to get above the clouds.

On October 22, we went 425 miles into Germany and never once saw the ground. There were no enemy fighters, but my flight, which had been holding a steady course for a few minutes, almost got a direct hit from flak at 28,000 feet, right through the overcast.

The enemy 88mm flak batteries were getting very good and their radar predictors could track a target at its exact altitude and predict where it was going to be – then an entire battery would fire at once, bracketing the target. On that occasion, flak landed all around us, but fortunately nobody was hit. When the tracking batteries got close, the smartest way to avoid being hit was to turn into the last burst, as the next one would be someplace else.

They must have had a squadron of Me.262 jets stationed near Dummer Lake because quite often we would see them at a distance, waiting to pick someone off. We heard that the jets were manned by the most experienced German fighter pilots, many of whom were wearing the Knight's Cross, which was awarded to those with thirty or more kills (the Germans called them "victories"). On November 1, our squadron chased three and could not catch them, but we observed one sneak up on a P-51 and shoot it down in the distance.

The Germans also had some squadrons of long-nosed Focke-Wulf FW-190D (Dora) fighters, which had previously been stationed in France where they were sometimes known to the Americans as the "Abbeville Kids," but were probably also manned by very experienced German aces. They had been moved into Germany (we suspected the Koblenz area) after the Allies advanced. The long-nosed "Dora" models were powered by a twelve-cylinder inverted Vee engine, which was liquid-cooled and delivered more horsepower than the radial engines in the earlier FW-190 models. Consequently, they had much better performance, particularly in terms of speed, climb, and dive.

The next day we were flying at 25,000 feet, escorting bombers in the vicinity of Dummer Lake, when we observed some activity high above us. Suddenly, a twin-engine aircraft came at our flight head-on, at terrific speed. I saw him coming in silhouette but was not sure of what type aircraft it was and held my fire. The aircraft flashed directly under and slightly to my left, and I clearly saw the pilot sitting in the cockpit of a beautiful slate-colored Me.262! Andrino, who was number three, cried out, "It's a blow job!" which was the somewhat quaint term he used to describe the jets.

Our flight racked around so hard after him that we stalled out and had to recover while the jet disappeared far below, outdistancing dozens of American P-47s that were frantically trying to catch him. He was probably trying to make it back for a landing at his airfield, where the Germans sometimes patrolled the fields with FW-190Ds to fight off

American fighters and keep them from attacking the jets while they were taking off or landing – their most vulnerable time.

Jeep Gets a Military Funeral

October 28

Over the past months, Jeep had become quite a celebrity, not only with the pilots and ground crews but also with the school kids in the local village. Bill Crump, who had taken Jeep on some combat missions in his P-47, also took him everywhere he went, riding in a Jeep or on a bike, with Jeep tucked under his jacket. On some occasions, he even rode in a taxi. After the kids in the local village heard about him, they started coming to the castle to visit and watch Crump play with the coyote, then gradually warmed up to the point where they would join in the frisking and playing.

Word of this soon rippled through the entire village, and the kids talked about it so much at their school that the headmaster actually invited Bill to bring the animal to the school. Crump appeared at the school dressed in full flying gear, expecting to meet a few kids, but was surprised when the headmaster invited him to come to the auditorium, where he demonstrated Jeep's friendly personality before the entire student body.

The kids had a great time petting Jeep and it was the talk of the school for a long time after. The local officials, including the game warden, had at first been alarmed about having a new species of wild animal in England, but apparently after observing his behavior close up, were willing to let the little guy stay in peace.

Fighter pilots, who had saved England in 1940, were popular with the English people. Also, the officials probably reasoned that there was not another coyote in England, so there was no danger of Jeep mating with another coyote and populating England with a whole new species.

Bill kept Jeep on a tether attached to a long wire, which allowed him to traverse a good-sized territory by the castle. On October 28, he returned to the castle and found Jeep missing from his leash. Reasoning that he might have gotten loose and gone to the village to visit some of the kids, Bill rode his bike into the village and asked around. He heard only that Jeep had been seen following some kids. Bill began to become alarmed, as Jeep had never stayed away long before, and organized some search parties.

A short time later, Jeep was found. He was lying on a path just off one of the local roads. Apparently he had been hit by a military vehicle, was gravely injured, and had wandered off to die.

Crump was totally shocked and angered at the driver who had been stupid enough to hit him and was not even considerate enough to stop and check the animal. With tears in his eyes, Bill organized a military funeral for his little pal. One of the pilots made up a little casket, and a grave was dug near the castle. An honor guard composed of seven pilots plus the C.O. was drawn up, everybody carrying their .45 automatics, and the group chaplain officiated.

Unfortunately, neither Andy nor I were present, but we got the details later and visited the little grave.

Reportedly, our squadron flight surgeon made an impromptu eulogy, praising Jeep as a patriotic Native American who had flown five combat missions in support of his country before dying an honorable but untimely death.

The coyote, wearing dog tags that identified him as "Jeep NMI [7] Coyote," was lowered into the grave, while Ray Burwell played "Taps." There were supposed to be three synchronous volleys over the grave, but it didn't go off too smoothly, as a couple of the pilots forgot

[7] (NMI) No middle initial.

to chamber a round by pulling back the slide. Consequently, the initial volley was a bit ragged, but Jeep was nevertheless interred with full honors.

Believe it or not, the next morning, as no combat missions were scheduled, Bill organized a flight of four P-47s to fly over the grave in the traditional "missing man formation." The formation of four flew slowly over Playford Hall and one airplane pulled up and out, symbolizing the missing man. Then Crump made a low-level high-speed pass over the grave, pulled up, and did a couple of victory rolls, in honor of Jeep.

It was all very melodramatic, and typified one of the true incidents that take place in a real wartime scenario, but which – to use the idiom – is stranger than fiction. In retrospect, I wondered where the twenty-one slugs from the three-volley salute ended up, as the American pilots did not have blanks in their pistols.

Beautiful New Mustangs

During the past six months, the 8th Air Force Fighter Command had been gradually switching its P-47 groups over to the new North American P-51 Mustang fighters, which provided a significant advantage in long-range penetration. With the additional range, bombers were now being escorted all the way to their targets and back, which sharply cut down their losses from enemy fighters.

The 356th was actually one of the last to convert, but during the October/November time frame a lot of brand new P-51s were delivered to the group, straight from the factories in the States. The new Mustangs were sleek-looking birds with long, slim noses that housed Rolls-Royce (Packard-built) Merlin, twelve-cylinder, liquid-cooled in-line engines, as compared to the monster radial engines on the Jugs, which gave them a fat but powerful look.

However, no missions were being flown with a mixed group of fighters, as there was a tremendous amount of work to be done by the ground crews before the Mustangs were considered ready for combat. Most of them had been shipped across the ocean on the decks of freighters, partially dis-assembled, with assembly completed at some facility close to the landing port. Our ground crews therefore had to first ensure that the complete assembly had been made properly.

The fighters also had to be brought up to combat readiness standard, with the six 50-caliber guns carefully tested and bore- sighted in ground pits to ensure that when they were fired, the 50s would strike exactly where the gyro-stabilized gunsights were showing the aiming point on the target. Finally, each of the new airplanes had to be painted with the group colors, which were a brilliant design of red and blue diamonds on the long noses, plus a candy-stripe spinner on the propellers. The 356th group had, without question, the sharpest-looking nose design in the 8th Air Force Fighter Command, which perhaps made up for the fact that our P-47s had been the only 8th Air Force fighters with plain noses; i.e., no color at all, except different-colored tail fins to differentiate the three squadrons.

Inasmuch as the new P-51s had as little as two hours of running time on their engines, each of the pilots was scheduled to break in his engine carefully (called slow-timing) by flying a total of ten hours at various power settings over England, between scheduled combat missions in the P-47s.. That was actually a fun time, as it gave us the opportunity to acquaint ourselves with the airplane and its characteristics, as well as test its maneuvering capability in some mock dogfights with other airplanes.

We found the Mustangs to be very maneuverable airplanes, with a light feel on the controls and capable of turning quite well. (In a pinch, dropping about fifteen degrees of flaps helped.) We could beat almost everything else in the sky – except a Spitfire, which could turn on a dime. If we picked a mock dogfight with a Spit, therefore, we always made sure we had an initial advantage of either speed or altitude before we jumped him. It was easy to understand why Goering's fighter pilots were frustrated by the RAF during the Battle of Britain. Some RAF wag actually wrote a little poem commemorating Goering's perplexity – based upon a true episode:

"Spitfires"

Oh, to be in England, Now that War is there
To jump into our Spitfires and catch a bit of air
What fun to hear the "Scramble" and dash out to your kite
And know the mighty Merlin will roar with all its might

We'll slip the sticky bonds of earth and climb into the sun
Then wait up there quite sneakily, to catch the wily Hun
How really very jolly, when his bombers are unescorted
We'll settle his hash right quickly – the fastest yet recorded

Now Goering's in a lather, when he steps down from his train
His losses are quite troubling and he's under quite a strain
He lines up all his aces and tells them once again
How men like him fought mightily when he flew with Richthofen

He tells Galland they're 'feiglings[8],' the deadliest of words
And here's the answer that comes back - from the one who wears the "Swords[9]"
"Herr Reich Marshall, you know my men are Deutschland's greatest fliers
So if you hope to win the war, then get them all Spitfires!"

(Note: This poem was written, tongue in cheek, as a tribute to Pilot Officer John G. Magee, Jr., 412 Squadron, RCAF, who penned the famous poem, "High Flight." I think he would have chuckled, as it was one 20 year old fighter pilot to another.)

---

8 *Cowards*

9 German fighter pilot slang for one of Germany's greatest decorations. Adolf Galland, Chief of German Fighter Command, veteran of the Spanish Civil War as well as WW2 wore the "Knights Cross with Oak Leaves, Swords and Diamonds." The German pilots called the Oak Leaves "cabbages" and the Swords "Knives and forks."

Adolph Galland

In checking out in the new Mustangs, one characteristic we had been well cautioned about was the amount of torque produced by the Merlin engines in the long noses of the airplane. We joked that you needed a strong right leg to fly the airplane, as it was necessary to feed in the power slowly while accelerating for takeoff to keep the airplane on the runway. Of course, after the airplane got up to speed, the trim tabs took care of the changing torque.

At the completion of my ten hours of slow-time in my new Mustang, I decided to see how fast it would go, on the deck, wide open at 61 inches of Mercury manifold pressure and 3,000 rpm. With a full combat load of armor plate, plus 1,880 rounds of 50-caliber ammo, my bird clocked exactly 361 miles per hour. [10]

The Farmers' Meeting Room

After their first date at the dance in Ipswich, Ray met Doreen for a second date. They went to the Odeon theater in Ipswich and watched a relatively new and very popular movie called *The Constant Nymph*, a complex drama about Lewis Dodd, a frustrated Belgian composer (Charles Boyer) who can't seem to find anyone who appreciates his work. What he does find, however, is Tessa, a beautiful fourteen year old, one of four daughters of a friend (played by a very young Joan

[10] This may sound surprisingly slow to those who have viewed the Reno Air Races in the post-war years, where P-51s attain speeds of 500+ mph. However, those special racing versions are much lighter airplanes with all combat gear removed, and have the advantage of many aerodynamic refinements, as well as souped-up engines.

Fontaine) who falls desperately in love with Lewis, although he doesn't seem to either know it or appreciate it. Lewis has his eye on another whom he marries, as she is older, more sophisticated, and rich – the latter two attributes apparently being quite important in advancing his career.

Predictably, the film ends in tragedy, as unfortunately Tessa has another (real) heart problem from which she dies, just as Lewis finally realizes he has made the mistake of his life. The film had a great cast, including Peter Lorre, Alexis Smith, Brenda Marshall, and Charles Coburn, and was supported by a lovely musical score by Erich Korngold, who later composed many wonderful scores for films, such as *The Sea Hawks* and *Robin Hood.*

Ray and Doreen found the drama gripping and entertaining, as the dramatic scenes and great acting led to some tears and a great deal of hand-holding, which moved them even closer together. As an amusing side note, the film was widely known, tongue in cheek, throughout Britain, as "The Constant Nympho," which perhaps added to its popularity.

Emerging from the theater, they wanted to go someplace and sit, but the evening had turned quite cool, so sitting on a park bench wasn't too inviting. They would have been welcome back at the Bolton home, but both wanted to spend some private time together. Doreen, who was secretary for the National Farmers' Union in Ipswich, gave a brief thought to the members' room where planning conferences were sometimes held and where the farmers could meet and talk. It was a cozy room, furnished almost like a home, with armchairs and a nice gas fireplace.

At first she dismissed it from her mind, but as they walked hand in hand and the chill soaked into her bones, she could not help reflecting about those comfortable chairs and that warm fire. *No one is there in the evening,* Doreen thought. *What harm would it do?* However, another thought entered her mind: *Would Ray consider this an overly bold suggestion from a proper young lady?* She already had strong feelings for this man and did not want to jeopardize their relationship.

Finally, taking her heart in hand and throwing caution to the wind, she mentioned the idea to Ray, cautiously suggesting the possibility of them stopping in to warm up. Ray jumped at the idea; what young man would not? "Wow, that sounds like a great idea – but will you get in trouble with your boss?"

Doreen said, "Well, we would not stay long and the office is always closed in the evening, so what harm would it do? Besides, I am getting chilled to the bone and there is even a teapot and I could make us a nice cuppa."

That was the clincher; they walked the short distance to the office, noted that no one was present, and Doreen opened the door. She put on a single light, made sure the blackout curtains were closed, and lit the gas fireplace, which produced a soft glow and immediately began reducing the chill. Ray, who voiced his pleasure over the whole deal, plunked himself into an easy chair while Doreen went to the little cabinet, pulled out a tea canister and pot, and set about making tea.

Other than on the dance floor, Ray had never really held this woman in his arms, but when he did, and when they kissed, the gas fireplace was not the only glow that was lit that night. This lovely woman, with her soft speech and quiet manner, had unwittingly thrown a little sand into the gears of Ray's long-term plans with his American fiancée.

For Ray's part, he considered that he was only spending a quiet evening with a pretty English girl, but he was still true to his sweetheart in the USA.

PART FOURTEEN

BEAUTIFUL NEW MUSTANGS

First P-51 Combat Mission for the 356th Group

November 26

In late November the group finally got the O.K. to formally switch to P-51s, and scheduled its first combat mission. This was the big day for the 356th Fighter Group. It was also Ray's first mission in the P-51, although he had already spent ten hours flying his new airplane breaking in the engine by slow-timing it.

Three squadrons of forty-eight brand new Mustangs worked their way down the taxi strip toward the end of the runway, continually "s"-ing so that their pilots could look alternately from side to side to see where they were going, as it was impossible to see over the long noses that housed the twelve-cylinder Rolls-Royce Merlin engines.

The American jocks had to ride their brakes hard to keep the birds from running away, and silently cursed the habit of the Merlins to load up if idled too slowly. *Why the hell is it,* reflected Burwell, *that the Brits can idle the Rolls-Royce Merlins in their Spitfires at about 800 rpm with no problems, but the Americans' Packard-built Merlins had to be idled at 1,500 rpm on the ground or the plugs would foul up badly and could cause the engines to conk out cold on takeoff – the worst possible time for it to happen.* Ray concluded that it probably had something to do with the 100-130-octane fuel used by the U.S. Mustangs.

Lining up two by two on the runway, each pair of 'Stangs ran up their engines and were waved off in turn by a flagman at the side of the runway. Some of the flagmen that handled that job were not too smart and stood too close to the whirling fourteen-foot propellers. Ray had personally witnessed one flagman strewn across the runway like mincemeat when a Thunderbolt fighter lost a brake during run up and slewed suddenly to the right.

Easing their power up to 61 inches of mercury and 3000 rpm, the sleek birds accelerated quickly and were in the air with gear coming up into the wells before they crossed the end of the runway. Immediately after takeoff, Ray's leader made a turn to a heading of 090 degrees, eased power back to climb settings, and started a gradual climb on course.

Winter was slowly gripping Europe in its clutches and was capable of producing some nasty flying weather, particularly in England where ground fogs were frequent. Almost immediately they entered some low-hanging scud, and Ray stuck closely on the right wing of his leader, as it was damned dark in the clouds that day. Reportedly, the tops of the clouds would only extend to around 15,000 today, which was a comforting thought, as he hated those long, slow climbs through the soup.

Ray was privileged to be flying as element leader for the deputy group commander, Lt. Col. Don Bacchus, who was leading today's escort mission. Colonel Tukey, the group commander, who had finished his tour, had gone back to the States on leave but was scheduled to return and take command again. In the interim Bacchus was group commander, which pleased everybody – all secretly wished that Tukey would find another job in the States.

As Ray sat on the acting group commander's right wing, he admired the row of seven swastikas painted on the side of the lead Mustang. Don was a good guy and an aggressive leader. Too bad the 356th didn't have a few more of his caliber.

The fighter groups in the 8th Air Force, of which the 356th was one of ten, had a relatively crude but effective system for climbing though the clouds with large formations of airplanes. The way it worked was that, whenever possible, the two elements of a flight would join into a finger four before starting to climb through the clouds on a designated course. The next flight took up a heading five degrees to the left of the lead flight, while the following flight steered five degrees to the leader's right. The fourth flight took up a heading of ten degrees left of the leader's course, etc.

The net effect of this was a large fan with gradually diverging spokes. Theoretically, if everybody stayed on course, there should be no mid-air collisions. However, that was a big joke, as the squadron had on several occasions observed flights popping out above the clouds on the opposite side of the leader from where they were supposed to be, indicating that somehow they had strayed off course and crossed in the soup.

Curiously enough, Ray had never known of a mid-air crash occurring during climb-outs. He had, however, known of several cases where wingmen stalled out and spun out of the overcast, sometimes managing to bail out and sometimes not. Climbing through the soup on somebody's wing was pretty nerve racking, particularly when there was a lot of turbulence and the clouds extended very high – sometimes over 32,000 feet.

The fighters were always heavily loaded down with external drop tanks or bombs, and the climbing speeds were not far above the stalling point. Wingmen sat staring at their leader's wing and fuselage, jockeying throttles to stay right close. If the leaders made any turns in the soup, the guys on the inside would get distinctly uncomfortable as they found their speed dropping closer to stall, their sticks got loose in their hand, and they started bobbing up and down.

Even worse was the risk of getting disoriented, where wingmen could develop an overpowering sensation of being in a steep turn when they were, in fact, straight and level – a condition known as vertigo. If vertigo reared its ugly head, the best bet was to trust the instruments, and Ray had developed the habit of sneaking an occasional quick peak at his artificial horizon to make sure that he was not confused about his flight attitude.

There was some chop in the clouds today, but all in all, it was pretty good flying weather. At about 14,000 it become noticeably lighter in the clouds and, predictably, they popped out into bright sunshine at about 15,500, with a solid deck of clouds underneath as far as the eye could see.

The flights were spread out a bit but reasonably well in place. Don made a gradual turn to the left so that the various elements of the widespread formation could close on his lead without too much throttle jockeying. Then, with everyone fairly comfortably in place, he set course for the rendezvous with the assigned Third Bomber Division of B-17s.

They were to intercept the bomber stream on course in the vicinity of Kassel, Germany. The orders were for the 356th to escort the bombers to the targets, the oil refineries at Hanover. There they would be relieved by another bunch of Mustangs from the 4th Fighter Group, which would take off later and proceed directly to their rendezvous.

The three squadrons of the 356th today comprised forty-eight airplanes in total, consisting of four flights of four P-51s each per squadron. For maximum efforts, the group could put up as many as eighty-four airplanes, but today's effort was considered a "normal" mission.

Climbing though 17,000 feet with the Dutch coast in sight, the 'Stangs began to do a bit of wobbling and dancing as their respective two-stage superchargers kicked into high blower, giving an extra surge of power – and the pilots adjusted their throttle settings to stay in good formation. The supercharger blower controls worked automatically off of an aneroid, which was pre-set for about 17,000 feet pressure altitude, but the actuation varied slightly for the individual airplanes. It was actually comforting to watch the airplanes shift and bob as the second stage of the superchargers kicked in, because it was an assurance that the blowers were working correctly.

Approaching Holland, Don called for "battle formation," and the group spread out into a much wider formation that would allow each of the elements of the formation to cover the tails of the other members and to obtain maximum maneuverability, should they be bounced by the enemy.

Up ahead, a few bursts of enemy 88mm ack ack laced the sky harmlessly. The big flak guns seldom got hits on the fighters, but it was nevertheless wise to weave a bit in order to throw off the radar predictors, which tracked the flight in order to aim the big guns. If one continued on a dead straight course, a good battery could begin zeroing in, even at high altitudes. Accordingly, the individual squadron leaders made a small turn of five or ten degrees in course every few minutes or so.

Ray reflected once again how lucky he was to be flying fighters. The poor suckers with the bombers had to fly steady courses, particularly on their final target runs, and the flak was often lethal for them.

Sitting on Don's wing, Ray reflected on the status of his leader, whom he admired greatly. Many in the group felt that Don Bacchus should have been the group commander instead of Col. Tukey. The latter, a full bird colonel, had been group commander for over a year, during which time the group's record for enemy kills sagged to one of the worst in the 8th Air Force.

Tukey, who was privately known to the pilots as "Colonel Turkey," was a disciplinarian who fancied himself as a "book man." That might have been well and good in a headquarters unit, but it had no place in a fighter group. Everybody knew that Tukey's style of bomber escort was to sit right over the top of the bombers and never budge to sniff out enemy aircraft.

In contrast to this, the real aggressive and effective commanders would sweep out in front of the bomber stream as far as a hundred miles ahead, breaking up the enemy fighters who were forming up ahead of the bombers to make their attacks. The Jerries didn't really want to tangle with the fighters, as their prime objective was nailing the bombers that were mauling their cities. However, when forced into it, they would dogfight the Americans.

There were some really hot pilots in the Luftwaffe with years of experience. However, they were usually greatly outnumbered in the air by the American fighters, which now had a deep penetration capability and could reach any point in Germany. Consequently, those that did not get shot down in the ensuing melee would drop their belly tanks and quickly use up their fuel, after which they would be forced to land, giving our bombers a clear field.

Colonel Hubert Zemke of the 56th Fighter Group, a Thunderbolt outfit, developed one particularly effective tactic. Knowing that the German ground plotters were directing their fighters to form up ahead of the bomber stream, "Hub," as he was known to his group, would send his squadrons ahead with flights fanning out in what became known as the "Zemke Fan." The first flight to spot the Germans would radio his position and the group would rapidly close on the enemy fighters.

With this kind of leadership, no wonder the 56th was the leading Thunderbolt group in enemy kills! To further emphasize the aggressive spirit of that great leader, Zemke had actually been known to take his group over Berlin and call out to the Germans over the radio, "Come up and fight!"

Tucked in on the right wing of the squadron leader, Ray sneaked a peak at his fuel selector to make sure he had it on external tanks. It was wise to burn at least a portion of the eighty-five gallons that sat in a tank behind the cockpit, as the weight of the fuel caused a dangerous aft center-of-gravity condition during violent maneuvers.

However, it was also crucial to switch to external tanks as soon as possible in order to conserve the precious internal fuel for the long mission ahead. P-51s carried 270 gallons internally, plus 108 gallons more in each external drop tank hanging under the wings. The drop tanks were made out of paper mache, which was light, cheap, and effective, and the tanks were normally dropped during every mission.

Mustangs typically burned about sixty gallons an hour. Therefore, with the external tanks, this was enough fuel to fly for up to eight hours if managed properly and nothing exciting happened. However, if contact with a significant number of enemy aircraft occurred, the commander would order, "Drop tanks," and the remainder of the mission had to be made on internal fuel load.

Complicating the situation, of course, was the fact that during a dogfight the Merlins would be running wide open and gulping fuel at an alarming rate. The most serious consequence of this was that the U.S. fighters could run short of fuel and be unable to escort the bombers the required portion of their route.

The Germans knew this well, of course, and made every effort to fool the escort fighters into dropping tanks as early as possible, as their real objective was to knock down the bombers. Therefore, there were always one or two Jerries stooging along very high, tracking the formation, reporting it to the controllers on the ground, and occasionally making a pass at the tail-end Charlies.

Today, as the group climbed through 24,000, they spotted the usual pair of Me.109s, sitting up at about 32,000. Bacchus coolly called to the 360th leader, Major Vogt, whose squadron was closest to the German fighters, "Vortex Squadron, keep your eyes on those guys and everybody stay off the radio."

He was not going to be suckered into dropping tanks early. Should the Jerry fighters make a sneak attack on any of the group, the nearest flight would simply turn into them, engaging them head-on, and drop tanks only if necessary.

Sitting about 150 feet out to the right of his leader, with head wagging back and forth to cover the sky, Ray reflected upon the time that Don had managed to nail a couple of the German spotter planes with a clever trick.

At that time the group had been equipped with P-47 Thunderbolts, each of which carried eight 50-caliber guns. Don had ordered four guns removed from each of four T-Bolts and had the crew set up the manifold pressure regulators so that the lightened airplanes could pull about three extra inches of manifold pressure, giving each of the Thunderbolts a significant gain in horsepower.

Bacchus dubbed these four fighters the "Superbolt Flight," and on the next high-altitude escort mission sandwiched them in the middle of the high squadron. As expected, shortly after the group had crossed into Germany, two Me.109 spotters appeared at about 35,000 feet and began to dog the group. Don deliberately had a couple of tail-enders hang back a bit and watch the 109s sniffing around. When they got a little careless and moved in closer, Don called, "Superbolt Flight, drop tanks now!"

The four Superbolt pilots punched off their tanks, nailed their throttles to the wall, and hit the toggle switches on the top of their throttles to activate the water injection. The result of this was four lightened Superbolt fighters pulling about 2,700 horsepower each and climbing like homesick angels!

The surprised Germans were nailed before they could figure out what was happening. One was blown to smithereens and the other pilot bailed out at a high rate of speed. Thereafter, the Jerry spotters had grown more cautious.

Twenty minutes later, the group was at 27,000 and approaching rendezvous. The two German fighters had strayed off somewhere and many contrails – most probably the bombers' – had been sighted at eleven o-clock high, all heading straight into Germany. Major Vogt, whose squadron was positioned high on the port side, called, "Vortex leader here, big friends in sight."

"Roger," said Don. "Look sharp, everybody." He started a gradual turn to the left to initiate a weaving pattern back and forth across the bomber stream.

Several hundred B-17s came more clearly into sight, each pulling a wide swath of four individual contrails, one from each engine, which merged into one giant trail behind each bomber. The net effect was so many vapor trails that the entire area of the sky was being painted in white swaths like giant paint brushes drawn across the blue sky. 'An aluminum overcast,' the fighter jocks jokingly called it. But the sight of hundreds of American bombers boring into Germany to drop their deadly loads on the Third Reich was an impressive one, which conveyed a sense of serene but latent power.

The bombers were dropping chaff occasionally to throw off the radars that guided the flak guns, and the stuff was floating down, twinkling with reflected light. Chaff was a simple but effective invention, consisting of slips of aluminum foil cut to very carefully designed lengths to jam the frequencies of the radars. Sometimes the 8th Air Force even employed some of the very fast Canadian-built de Havilland Mosquito twin-engined fighters to fly in ahead of the bombers, drop the chaff, and get out of there. Masses of the stuff floating down worked surprisingly well for routine flak batteries. However, over the target areas there were usually so many flak guns that fired in box patterns that some of the bombers were bound to get hit. Consequently, losses in the bomber groups were still high, not only in lost airplanes but in substantial numbers of injuries to crews from flying bits of metal.

As his squadron crossed above the lead squadron of bombers, Ray could see the gunners poised in the wide open hatches on both sides of their airplane, 50-caliber guns poised for action. *Poor bastards*, thought Ray, *freezing their asses off at sixty degrees below zero. Heated suits or not, that is just too damned cold for human beings.* Compared to them, the Mustang drivers had it really fat.

Approaching Kassel, the bomber stream made a turn to the north for its second leg of the planned route. The bombers never bored directly to their targets but were carefully routed on a couple of diversionary legs in order to keep the Germans guessing about the final objective and thereby lessening the reception to some degree. Regardless, as the bomber crews had noted, the reception committees in Hunland always seemed to be damn well prepared, a fact which had given 8th Air Force planners cause to wonder whether their carefully planned and secret target plans were not, in fact, being tipped to the Nazis through covert means. However, that was a problem for the brass at the other end. This was the here and now, where the hot metal flew.

Shortly thereafter a lone Me.262 twinjet fighter appeared about 5,000 feet above the formation, cruising along and undoubtedly reporting on the route to the German ground control. "Lampshade here," said Bacchus. "Watch that guy." And forty-eight pairs of eyes tracked his progress. Don knew that it was futile to try to nail the jet, as it was at least 150 miles per hour faster than the Mustangs and could streak away with no problem.

The sight of one or two of the jets was fairly common by late 1944, and the groups knew how to deal with them. Basically, they were ignored unless they got too close. Occasionally, however, the 262s would try to pick off one of the tail-end Charlies, and their 30mm cannon had in fact made quick work of a few careless stragglers.

Today, everybody was staying well up in formation so that cross coverage was good. Should the jet elect to bounce one of the flights, the squadron commander would simply order the flight to turn into it, making it a head-on contest against twenty-four 50-caliber machine guns – not good odds for the German jet.

Fifteen minutes later, the bombers made their final turn onto a straight course toward Hanover. This was the worst time for them, as the flak also intensified and the straight course made it easier for the ground gunners. Suddenly, Vogt, who had eagle eyes, called, "Lampshade, it looks like many bandits forming up at about ten o-clock high."

"Rog, I have them," said Don. "Everybody, drop tanks now!"

"Vortex squadron, stay close to the bombers – Farmhouse fan left, Chinwag fan right. Buster!" (That was the signal for max military climb power.)

The lightened Mustangs surged ahead, climbing in an enveloping action to trap the enemy fighters. The Germans were very high, almost 36,000 feet, and had apparently spent a considerable time climbing to get a jump on the bombers. There was a pack of at least a hundred of them, and their seemingly haphazard weaving contrails were somehow reminiscent of a bunch of wiggly silverfish.

The two sets of adversaries closed rapidly on each other and it soon became obvious that they were going to meet head-on. "Heads-up everybody," called Don, and suddenly the sky was filled with fighters and both the Germans and Americans had their hands full trying to avoid collisions. Ray got off a snap shot at a Jerry with no visible effect, then had to pull up sharply to avoid a head-on. Off to his right, he saw a Mustang and a 109 merge head-on, resulting in a long streak of flame and pieces of debris floating down.

Don made a hard pull up to the right and tacked onto a pair of two camouflaged 109s. Oddly enough, the German wingman was still carrying his belly tank, and Don's burst not only blew off the left wingtip but set fire to the belly tank, sending the Jerry spiraling down. Don edged right to get a shot at a second Jerry, who suddenly flicked over and dived straight down, with Don hard after him and Ray struggling to stay behind Don to protect his leader's tail.

Unfortunately, Don's dive after the Jerry was so precipitous that Ray's airspeed indicator went well beyond the redline and the Mustang began vibrating badly. Suddenly he heard something break (he later discovered it was the landing light in the leading edge of his wing), pulled the throttle back a bit, and eased the dive. As a consequence, he lost sight of Don, who had blended into the landscape far below.

Damn, he thought, *Bacchus is going to have my ass for this*, as he pulled back up into what remained of the melee above. Most of the fighters had disappeared from sight. Suddenly he found himself closing rapidly on the tail of an airplane that was heading directly into the sun and was silhouetted. He thought, *It's a 109*, and, setting his gunsight on the airplane, was just ready to fire when the thought crossed his mind, *Maybe it's another Mustang*, causing him to hold his fire. In the meantime, he had been running at full throttle and was closing rapidly on the other aircraft. As a result, he sailed right up beside the bogey, which turned out to be a beautiful robin's-egg-blue Me.109 with black crosses on the wing.

There followed a comedy of errors, as the startled German fighter pilot looked straight out at a Mustang sailing by his right wing. Quickly, the German chopped his throttle and tried to slide behind the American, whose momentum was rapidly carrying him ahead.

Not to be outdone by this maneuver, Ray did a hard pull up with a violent skid to the right, and then turned back into the German. The result was a quartering head-on pass, with Ray actually passing directly in front of the German's candy-striped propeller spinner, and for a split second found himself looking directly into the barrel of a 20mm cannon mounted directly in its center. Fortunately, the German, who was probably in shock, did not fire at that moment, and there ensued another quick scissor pass, after which the Jerry fighter escaped by diving straight into a large bank of clouds and was not seen again.

To the north, the bombers had plastered the refinery at Hanover and the resulting black smoke was billowing up beyond 40,000 feet. Ray finished the day by joining up with a couple of other stray Mustangs and limping back to Ipswich short of fuel, chagrined about his failure to make an easy kill. Don Bacchus, who had polished off the second German close to the deck, was pretty magnanimous when Ray apologized for losing him in the scrap.

"It's okay," he said. "I damn near pulled the wings off of my bird in the dive. I'm really not sure whether I shot the bastard or he broke up from the dive!"

All told, it had been a good day for the 356th group, which bagged twenty-two with three probable, for a loss of five.

Later, after checking the tail-end silhouettes of both Mustangs and 109s carefully, Ray reflected, *Dammit, why wasn't I smart enough to remember that Mustangs don't have a tail wheel hanging down as that Me.109 did?*

He also wondered who was flying that beautiful blue Me.109. It must have been a very high-ranking officer, as German fighters are normally painted with camouflage or are slate gray. He wondered if he had missed a golden opportunity to shoot down a German general!

Prelude to the Bulge

In early December we entered a relatively quiet period. I flew a number of missions with the entire ABC gang. Crump was nominally assigned to a flight led by Captain Borelli, a long-time veteran, while

Andrino, Burwell, and I were usually assigned to a flight led by Captain Hockmeyer, a quiet but competent leader. Thus, many times, Andy, Ray, and I were flying within a few feet of each other, alternately assigned as wingman to Hockmeyer or element leader, or wingman to each other. It is a good feeling to know that you are flying with competent people who will do the right thing in a crunch.

The weather in early December was very poor, with continuous fogs and heavy layers of clouds, so on most occasions we had to climb through thousands of feet of clouds, with visibility as low as 75 to 100 feet, and eyes glued onto the leader or the element leader (if you happened to be flying number four), and oftentimes not breaking out of the clouds until well above 25,000 feet. Most of the missions were bomber escort to the target, then withdrawal.

On December 6, we had a long-haul escort job to Leipzig, with Andy as number two and Ray on my wing. We were deep into the mountainous and wooded land in Germany and saw plenty of snow. There was not a German fighter in sight, but cruising at 32,000 feet it was sixty degrees below zero, causing my aileron trim tabs to freeze up – not a serious problem but it made the control forces on the stick a bit harder. Once I put my gloved hand about an inch from the top of the canopy and it started steaming, like dry ice.

The extreme cold had given the 8th Air Force groups some trouble because a bit of moisture on the 50-caliber gun solenoids could cause them to freeze up and not fire. The groups had experimented and found that applying ethylene glycol to the solenoids (which is what we used for coolant in our engines) would usually cure this problem.

Another very serious problem that we had to watch for was the oxygen regulator freezing up, which could cause one to get anoxia and become unconscious in a couple of minutes. One pilot in the 356th had gone straight in from 35,000 feet and not uttered a word on the way down. The suspected culprit was anoxia.

Bad weather also posed a serious problem in getting back onto the ground at the end of missions. Those were the days before instrument landing systems, and we had nothing whatsoever, except our eyeballs, to get us back to terra firma. Martlesham had a big mortar set up at the approach end of the runway, and sometimes when there was a very low overcast somebody would pull a chain that fired a very big parachute flare straight up – hoping they did not hit anybody. That worked, but there were some ridiculous moments, with people coming out of the overcast at angles of ninety degrees to the landing runway and having to bend it around at one hundred feet while the people in the control tower ducked and counted their rosary beads.

The mission to Leipzig was over five hours, and when we returned to England almost the entire country was completely fogged in. On that occasion the whole group had to make a landing at a very long and wide emergency landing strip on the coast, and we were only able to get on the ground because of an emergency procedure called FIDO. (Fog Investigation and Dispersal Operation)

It was an amazingly crude yet effective system. Long ditches had been dug on both sides of the large runway and large pipes laid in the ditches to accommodate gasoline, which would be sprayed into the air along the length of the runway. Hundreds of thousands of gallons were sent through the pipes and actually lighted, producing a massive glow that burned off some of the fog and could be seen as a glow from above.

Our group split up into squadrons, then flights of four, which took turns flying over the approach end of the runway – at which point each Mustang peeled off sequentially at fifteen-second intervals, made a 360-degree circuit, dropped landing gear and flaps, and headed for the glow.

It worked exactly as planned and everybody got onto the ground. However, there must have been some close shaves, as when I broke out of the fog over the end of the runway, I looked to my right and there was another Mustang also landing about 150 feet away! We were told that FIDO was an idea conceived by Winston Churchill, but I have never confirmed this. Thinking back on it after years of flying with sophisticated modern landing systems, I continue to be amazed that we did not have burning wrecks strewn all over the English countryside!

The Germans were actually pleased with the continuing bad weather over the Continent. Unknown to SHAEF, [11] they were quietly preparing for a major surprise advance into the Ardennes Region of Belgium, developing into what would later be called the "Battle of the Bulge."

Many of their highly experienced armored divisions had been pulled back into Germany, and a secret buildup for the giant thrust into Belgium was already underway. Once again it was to be the oft-repeated scenario of a major attack be\ng planned through a so-called impenetrable forest, in this case – the Ardennes.

History is replete with such fiascos, and for some reason the military tacticians never seem to learn that impenetrable forests and swamps often turn out to be a quick route around the enemy and that virtually nothing is impenetrable in modern warfare. Of course, the Germans were being especially careful with the use of camouflage so as not to reveal their buildup and stir up a hornet's nest of American and British Fighters.

Last Mission with Ray and Andy

On December 14, the Battle of the Bulge opened with a complete shock to the American forces in Belgium, who were suddenly confronted with hundreds of Panzers crashing through the forest, heading for the Channel ports before anyone even new they were coming. German soldiers from a special forces group under the command of Col. Otto Skorzeny travelled with the first wave. Mostly all language specialists,

[11] Supreme Headquarters, Allied Expeditionary Forces

they were dressed in American uniforms, spoke good English, and had the mission of capturing strategic points, as well as creating confusion amongst the Americans, a plan which succeeded very well for several days until the Americans got wise to it.[12]

The weather over the Ardennes was completely socked in for over a solid week, preventing any of the 8th or 9th Air Forces from providing any meaningful defensive support. Consequently, the German forces made major gains in their massive thrust into Belgium, and the Americans had resorted to slugging it out with the enemy, tank to tank and soldier to soldier.

During the first few days, 19,000 American soldiers were killed and the thrust produced a great bulge in the American lines, which later gave the battle its name, the "Battle of the Bulge." However, the rapid advances that the experienced German armored divisions made into Belgium were finally slowed by some heroic stands by Allied ground forces, coupled with the fact that the rapidly advancing German armor had run away from its own supply train and was running short of petrol and ammunition.

---

[12] In the early sixties, when I was a liaison officer to the 3rd German Korps in Koblenz, Germany, I knew a German Major Friese who had been on this assignment, and who had also helped rescue Mussolini from a mountaintop hotel in Italy where he had been imprisoned by his own people. He was also a veteran of the Russian campaign, and told me how they had operated very effectively when the German forces were advancing rapidly into Russia. All of the Russian bridges had been mined and had guards at both ends. In order to prevent the Russians from blowing the bridges, Skorzeny's Special Forces, dressed as Russian peasants, would run down the road to the bridges and cry out to the guards in Russian, "The Germans are coming! The Germans are coming!" - then quickly shoot down the guards before they had a chance to detonate the explosives. Major Friese and I actually teamed up on a III Korps (NATO) field exercise – and won a gold medal. Curious how the wheel of history turns – yesterday's foe is today's friend!

On December 23, the skies over Europe finally cleared, with visibility as much as a hundred miles in some directions. The 8th Air Force was increased to massive strength to help drive the nail into the coffin of the German attacking forces. In a single mission, the 356th group sent aloft one of its largest efforts of the war, each of the three squadrons putting up six flights of four P-51s, for a total of seventy-two aircraft.

Major Wood led the 360th squadron, and Captain Hockmeyer led our flight, which included Ray, Andy, and myself. The mission comprised a fighter sweep from Belgium to the Coblenz/Strasbourg area under what was called "MEW Control" – essentially long-range radar to help locate enemy aerial forces. Apparently, the German Air Force was lying low, in the face of massive Allied airpower over the Continent. Other than some Me.162 jets that we sighted in the distance, the mission was generally uneventful.

Meanwhile, the 9th Air Force, which operated mainly tough P-47 Thunderbolts, was wreaking havoc on the German armored forces, which were now vulnerable from the air. The veteran Panzer divisions that had been withdrawn from the Eastern Front now encountered tremendous destruction, which literally broke the back of the German resistance.

Thereafter, the German military was steadily pushed back into smaller and smaller territory, with Allied forces advancing from the West and the Russians closing from the East, where they would finally meet the Americans on the Elbe River.

Anne Visits the Castle

The squadron had a full complement of pilots, so that some of us who were close to completing our tours of combat were not scheduled for the next several days. Taking advantage of this, I called Anne to see if she could join me at Martlesham for the Christmas holidays. Operations at Uxbridge had slowed considerably; the Doodlebug attacks had dwindled as their sites were overrun. V-2 attacks continued, but the British could do nothing to combat them. Consequently, Anne had no problem getting several days off and agreed to a visit.

On the afternoon of December 24, I picked her up at the Ipswich railway station and brought her out to the base in a taxi cab. Anne, who was wearing civilian clothes (including nylon stockings that I managed to get sent from the States), looked really ravishing and got her share of approving looks and remarks from the gang at the castle.

Unfortunately, neither Burwell nor Andy was there. They had flown a mission together that morning, but immediately after landing Ray had grabbed a bike and pedaled into Ipswich to spend the holidays with Doreen and her family, while Andy also mysteriously disappeared – probably to meet the little oriental-looking girl he had met at the dance. Andy was very close-mouthed about such things. I wanted Anne to meet Doreen and Ray, as well as Andy, but that would have to wait for a later occasion

On Christmas Eve we had a grand party in the big fireplace room at the castle. The cooks had surprised us with a really decent dinner featuring a large ham basted with a delicious sauce, as well as a medium-sized turkey with gravy, as we had a couple of Jewish pilots in the squadron. I was surprised to see the turkey, as I thought the only time they sent them over was for Thanksgiving. For accompanying vegetables, we had sweet potatoes (which I did not think grew in Britain), a kind of squash that the British called marrows, and, of course, the inevitable Brussels sprouts, which grew profusely in the European climate.

Personally, I liked Brussels sprouts, but our previous C. O. absolutely despised the things and on one occasion remarked, "If you are ever going to crash in a British farmer's field, be sure to pick one which is growing Brussels sprouts!"

To top off their culinary masterpiece, our squadron cooks conjured up a dessert de resistance that comprised a lemon meringue pie, as well as a traditional plum pudding topped with cherries and peach slices. We speculated on how many precious eggs the cooks must have whipped into the meringue, as typically they handed you one egg for breakfast 'because fighter pilots needed the special nourishment to keep their eyesight sharp.' Ha! Some halfway decent coffee, accompanied by a bottle of good brandy that appeared from somewhere, topped off our magnificent feast.

A few belches – Arab style – were heard, registering appreciation, and a special delegation was sent to the kitchen inviting the cooks to join us for a Christmas Eve drink. The consensus was that our kitchen staff was demonstrating good morale, perhaps led by the cook who had earned the Purple Heart while enjoying his cushy job when the V-2 almost took out our castle!

Somebody had dragged in a rather straggly looking tree of some sort; I'm not sure what it was but it wasn't an evergreen; also, we didn't have any lights. No matter – it was a tree and everybody pitched in and found little treats and what-nots to hang on it, so the place assumed a decently festive look, aided by a nice fire crackling in the big fireplace. Unfortunately, we did not have a piano, as a couple of the pilots had some skill on the keys; it was always good to get a group around a piano and sing fighter pilot songs, most of which were ribald, but nevertheless amusing. However, we had a record player with some big band music and that helped a lot with the atmosphere.

Anne danced with a number of the guys who would have loved to ace me out of her, but Anne was very sweet about that and deftly fended off all overtures while not hurting anybody's feelings. This was a special girl and we had a very special relationship, which I knew was going to last.

Late on Christmas Eve, Don Bacchus visited the castle, as he did each of the squadrons. I introduced him to Anne and they chatted for a bit. Later he said to me quietly, "Anne is a classy English girl; you might want to hang on to her," to which I answered, "I plan to, Colonel, but both of us want to get this war over before taking things any further."

I reflected, *What a nice guy, and a great group leader, completely different from our present one.* I heard later that he married an English girl.

As Anne and I danced to that great big band music once again, I felt that thrill course through me, just as it had at the Jules Club the first time we met, which was simply the result of holding this woman in my arms. The thought also occurred to me that while I was sorry Ray was not here to meet her, his absence left the corner room on the third floor of the castle all to us!

Later that night we found a quiet place and exchanged Christmas gifts. We already had small pictures of each other from previous visits, but Anne presented me with a beautiful framed picture of herself in her RAF uniform, which I immediately placed on the bureau in the corner room of the castle. I had long since quietly removed the picture of Ginny and had written to her explaining in a gentlemanly way that I had met someone else. She had understood, as we had no commitment except a friendship, which I knew would continue afterward.

My gift to Anne was some Chanel that I had found in a London PX, as well as another two pairs of nylon stockings, which I had asked my parents to send. To British women, those were more valuable than gold. One other gift I gave to her was a pair of pilot wings. It wasn't an engagement ring, but it was the next best thing.

On Christmas morning we planned to visit the airfield, as a morning mission was going out. Inasmuch as it was a military facility, Anne wore her RAF blue section officer's uniform, in which she looked like a classic recruiting poster girl. We had hoped to meet Crump and Andy, who were both scheduled, but when we arrived the Mustangs were already taxiing out. We caught a ride out to the taxiway with the maintenance officer in his Jeep and were just in time to wave to Crump and Andy as they taxied by in PI-W "Jackie" and PI-X, with the slinky babe on the side.

I never gave it a thought at the time, but that was the last time I was ever to see Andy. We had gone back to the castle and were there in mid-afternoon when the flight returned. Word soon reached the castle that the 360th squadron had lost two P-51s to enemy aircraft that Christmas day. While patrolling near the Rhine, the group had been vectored by MEW Control to the Bonn/Cologne area where they intercepted a group of thirty-plus FW.190s, shooting down three of them, then also encountering about ten Me.109s, shooting down another three.

However, neither Andrino nor Lt. Heubner from the 360th squadron had returned. One of the group's pilots witnessed a P-51 chasing an FW-190 very low, and observed the P-51 hit a tree and disintegrate. However, no one knew which of the two it was. While it was not much consolation to our pilots, the 360th squadron was credited with three of the six shot down. Our operations officer, Capt. Ellingson, got two, and Ed Pleasant took down one, plus three more damaged claims by our pilots.

I reflected on the irony that while both sides observed Christmas, its message of 'Peace on earth, good will toward men' had been mutually ignored that day.

CHAPTER FIFTEEN
THE LAST YEAR OF WAR

Ray's Dilemma

Andy had been Ray's buddy, his constant companion, and his confidant. However, with Andy's loss on Christmas day, 1944, Ray and I spent more time together – that is, when he wasn't with Doreen. Ever since their second date back in October, he seemed to have entered into a state of mounting confusion and needed someone to share his thoughts with.

He and Bill Crump were friends and flying contemporaries, both working toward their ultimate captaincies and a slot as a designated flight commander. However, they were not as close as he and Andy had been, so Ray, who knew I wouldn't blab around, shared his problems with me. He told me of his wonderful second date with Doreen – how they had sat together before a cozy fire in the Farmers' Meeting Room in Ipswich, and how that room had become their secret trysting place. Of course, he did not discuss what went on during those evenings, nor did I wish to know, as that was entirely their own business.

Apparently Doreen's family welcomed Ray as more than a casual acquaintance, and he spent more and more time at their home, often staying overnight when he was not scheduled and had a forty-eight-hour pass. I also noticed that he had started spending a bit more time chatting with the cooks in the kitchen at the castle, so I suspected that some chow may have been secretly re-routed to the Bolton kitchen – a worthy cause in wartime England, where people had to stretch their food coupons to the limit and some food treats that we took for granted were totally unavailable. After all, Americans were all 'overfed' anyway!

What I found somewhat amusing was that while he continually praised Doreen, telling me what a really sweet girl she was, he also maintained the stance that his true love lay back in the USA with his fiancée, Doris, whose picture stood on the dresser next to that of Anne.

When that picture arrived, along with a letter and a fruit cake from Doris, he shared the cake around and also showed her picture to everyone, talking about how beautiful she was. To quote Ray, "Every fellow who saw her picture instantly fell in love with her!" I had to agree that she was beautiful, but I was not one of those who lost his head over her.

Ray had been at the Bolton's house when I brought Anne to the castle for a Christmas visit, so I did not meet Doreen until New Year's Eve when he brought her to the castle for our big bash. We sat together at the party and I found her to be a very likeable, down-to-earth girl with a sweet personality. Ray had indeed described her well and I could understand his interest.

Doreen had brought her seventeen-year-old sister, Cynthia, with her to the party, but appeared to be having some second thoughts about it, as there was a lot of booze being consumed. In fact, at one point she got a bit annoyed at Crump, who offered a glass of straight bourbon to Cynthia, and Doreen stepped in to put the brakes on that. I gave her a silent *Bravo* and knew that we were friends.

After New Year's, the saga continued. Whenever Ray was not scheduled for a mission or other duties, he jumped on a bike and pedaled four miles to "Weatherelm" (which was what the Boltons called their home), where he was apparently treated like one of the family. Also, whenever he had a Friday night free, he and Doreen dashed off to the Red Cross dance in Ipswich, followed, I assume, by their usual tryst at the Farmers' Meeting Room.

Ray told me that one night they almost got caught by her boss, who stopped by the office while they were there. Hearing the key turning in the lock, they quickly shut off the gas fire and hid behind a table, but there was still a soft glow in the fireplace, so it was obvious someone had been there.

Ray thought the British captain had to have known something was afoot but intentionally did not push the issue. Although many British people were offended by some obnoxious Yanks carrying on like boors in England, by and large the English people – who had an innate sense of fair play – were willing to cut some slack for those who were there fighting our mutual enemies.

In my acquaintance with Ray, I had noted that he was a firm believer who never used the Lord's name in vain, yet was never ostentatious about his beliefs. As time rolled by and he spent more and more time with Doreen and her family, he became increasingly conflicted in pursuing his distant romance with his fiancée, Doris.

From the occasional remarks he dropped, I got the distinct impression that one of the factors muddying the waters was religion. I never asked what his particular religion was, but it must have been one of the Protestant sects, as at one time he had alluded vaguely to some kind of revelation that had taken place during his high school years. Also, he mentioned that both he and Doris wanted a church wedding at home, but then followed this up with the statement that although Doris had attended a convent school, she was still "a practical girl" and they would be able to work out some satisfactory compromise.

I was completely neutral on the matter, but my interpretation (with all due respect to my flying buddy) was that the compromise would have to be in favor of Ray's religion.

After the New Year's Eve party, I got the impression that a serious crisis was taking place in his life. After a particularly long and grinding escort mission, we were sitting sharing a beer together at the castle and he starting talking like he needed to get something off his chest.

"I'm sure anxious to know whether Doris got that job in New York. If by three months she hasn't obtained one, she will go back home. Personally, I think she will get it. Boy, she's got what it takes – there is no doubt about that." He paused, then said, "You know I really get some wonderful letters from her. She still feels the same toward me and I'm sure I do likewise. The thing I have to watch out for is that I don't get in too deep with my pretty little English girl." Ha, ha.

After another pause, he continued, "You know something I noticed about my gal over here – she looks a heck of a lot like my mom. Boy, what a coincidence!"

One thing I knew about Ray was that, while he was not a mama's boy, he sure loved his mom!

Next thing I heard was that, on January 8, Doreen sent a letter to Ray's mother telling her they had fallen in love with each other! Not *she* had fallen in love - but *they*. Somewhere along the line, some kind of a promise had been made, but Ray hastened to write to his parents and assure them that he was *just having a good time with the little English girl and was being careful not to get too serious*.

As if to re-assert his devotion to Doris, he had a big picture of himself made up and sent it to her. Significantly, he also had his P-51, PI-D, painted with "Lady Doris" across the side of the nose, and once again Doris's picture was displayed above it, just as it had been on his P-47.

That must have been the straw that broke the camel's back, because shortly thereafter a deep freeze set in with regard to the Bolton/Burwell connection. Ray made no more visits to the Bolton house or to the Red Cross dances, and there were no phone calls to Doreen.

The War Continues

Ray's stalemate continued for a least a month, during which time we flew a number of interesting missions. German strength was clearly diminishing as the bombing of their country continued unabated and their military forces were compressed into a smaller and smaller area, with the Russians advancing on one side and the Allied forces on the other.

On the other hand, the 8th Air Force Fighter Command was stronger than ever, with lots of airplanes and pilots. Almost all of the fighter groups in England had been converted to P-51s or P-38s, while the entire 9th Air Force, which operated in the newly occupied territories in France, Belgium and Holland, was equipped with many squadrons of P-47s.

The Jugs, which had demonstrated their ability to survive under severe enemy fire, were the ideal airplanes for the job. Thus, the "air to ground" mission had been almost entirely turned over to the 9th Air Force, while the 8th Air Force Mustangs and Lightnings were flying largely bomber escort missions or radar-controlled fighter sweeps to clear the skies of enemy aircraft.

With plenty of new P-51s and pilots, the 356th was now sending more than sixty aircraft aloft on every mission – a number that might previously have been considered a maximum effort.

However, the German Air Force, while vastly outnumbered, was far from out. Their squadrons had been re-organized with more FW.190s, including the newer long-nosed FW-190Ds, replacing the less effective Me.109s. These units were commanded by a remaining fringe of the German aces, most of whom were highly experienced from years of war, with dozens of "victories," as they termed them. But these German aces were faced with a problem of increasing seriousness; replacement pilots were arriving with less and less flying time under their belts and many of them held ranks as low as corporal. The new replacements were herded aloft, surrounded as much as possible by the old pros, but their life expectancy was very short.

With regard to the Me.162 jets, Hitler had made a very bad mistake in assigning the jets to a bomber role, the worst possible usage, and Reich Marshall Goering, who really knew better, had gone along with his boss. Finally, after a couple of years of continual urging by Gen. Galland, chief of German fighter forces, Hitler finally relented and allowed Galland to establish a number of Me.262 squadrons, manned almost entirely by the most experienced and highly decorated German fighter pilots.

These men made valiant efforts to utilize the great performance advantages of the jets to harass and shoot down the American bombers and fighters. They had made short work of a number of American aircraft, particularly stragglers, which thus became fair game for the jets to make a quick attack and escape before a shower of American fighters came down on them.

If the jets had been used in this role earlier in the war, they might well have been an important factor, but now, with the skies belonging to the Allied air forces, the odds were greatly stacked against them.

The Me.262s, which were obviously much faster than any propeller-driven fighters and also had a lethal four-30mm cannon, nevertheless had a couple of Achilles heels. Jets were in their infancy and often had mechanical problems, which could cause them to flame-out on takeoff or during a crucial dogfight. A flame-out could also be caused simply by too rapid a movement of the throttle.

The jets also had very short range, and had to execute their attacks quickly, then get back to base and refuel. This was a real problem as sometimes American fighters were waiting over their airfields to nail them during their vulnerable final approach and landing.

Several of their very experienced pilots were killed while landing. Col. Johannes Steinhoff, a German ace with more than nine-hundred missions to his credit, was one of the key organizers of the new jet "Squadrons of "Experts." During takeoff for a mission to attack bombers with rockets, his jet hit a pothole that sheared off a gear and caused it to crash. In the resulting fire, his helmet melted and fused to his scalp, while his eyelids were completely burnt off. Miraculously, he survived, after spending two years in hospitals, and later became one of the generals in the post-war German Air Force.

On February 14, the 356th group flew a sixty-eight-plane escort mission to the Koblenz and Frankfurt areas, during which they ran into several groups of FW.190s and were also harassed by the German jets. Neither Ray nor Bill made any claims, but the group shot down seven FWs without a loss. The group also shot up a bunch of locomotives and railroad stock.

A few days later, the 356th group mounted a sixty-Mustang mission, during which the three squadrons split up. The 360th squadron, of which Ray was a part, picked up bombers in the Brussels area and escorted them to Hamburg and back without enemy fighter contact.

However, the 361st squadron, which made a fighter sweep over southern Germany, had a big day. A couple of its flights found three fields with aircraft on them and destroyed eleven, while damaging five more.

Astonishingly, another flight came upon eight Fieseler Storch (Stork) liaison planes in the air and shot down six, while the other two scampered off somewhere for their lives. What six liaison planes were doing in the air at one time was a mystery, unless it was a primary training field or perhaps some high-ranking Nazi officers trying to make a dash to Switzerland!

After the group landed and was debriefed, Burwell, who was nearing the end of his tour of operations, almost had a fit when he found out how many had been bagged while the 360th squadron was having a peaceful joyride to Hamburg and back.

"Why the hell is it," he ranted, "that whenever we run into a pack I am either not on the mission or someplace else? I want to knock down my share before this war is over!" That brought a few grins from the other pilots – but not much sympathy.

Visit to Anne's Home

In mid-February, I completed a twenty-five-hour extension to my tour and asked for and received a three-day pass prior to assuming new duties at group operations. I was now also wearing railroad tracks on my shoulders, and they felt good. Per some advance planning, which Anne and I had coordinated, Anne managed to get several days off from her WAAF controller duties, and we made the most of it.

Unlike Ray, we knew exactly where we were going and were completely comfortable with it. Per our agreement, we never considered marrying while the war continued, but Anne said she would like to use some of the time to have me meet her parents. Whenever a girl asks a guy to meet her parents, that is surely a sign that things are going in the right direction.

Anne told me that her home was in a small village called Wormley in Hampshire, near Basingstoke, southwest of London, and served by the Wormley and Whitley railway line from London. She thought it best if we got an early morning start from London, so I took an afternoon train from Ipswich to the station closest to Kensington. After negotiating the usual twenty-five-minute wait in the queue, I caught a cab to Anne's house, where we spent a wonderful evening and night together.

It was not just a matter of going to bed with this wonderful woman but the opportunity to sit and spend quiet time together. Although we had been to dances and parties, we actually had spent very little of that high-quality time together learning the details of each other's personality, such as likes and dislikes – the little things which make up life's complete picture.

Our evening together also provided an opportunity for Anne to give me some information about her family so that I would more fully appreciate meeting and associating with them during our visit.

Anne told me that she had two living parents, both in their fifties, with whom she was very close. She had no siblings. Her father had been a captain in Intelligence in WWI and now was engaged in something to do with banking and commerce in Southampton, but she did not provide any details. He was also serving as a member of the local Home Guard. Anne said he did not like it very much and almost every time her father donned his Home Guard uniform he was heard to mutter something like, "Damn Hitler and his gang!"

Anne also explained that, even though there was no longer any threat of an invasion, the Home Guard might be on guard at the railway station, as they sometimes manned checkpoints to screen out surreptitious enemy agents. She added that while many dismissed the Home Guard as a joke, that was quite unjust, as a great many of them had been in the trenches in WWI and knew very well how to handle weapons. Many resented having to do it again, she exclaimed, and followed with, "Woe betide anyone they thought was a German!"

It sounded like her father was aware of the jokes that were made about the Home Guard and had passed on some of his resentment. I did not blame him, as he was another of those millions of volunteers who gave their time and service unheralded and uncompensated during the war.

Anne described her mother as being perpetually busy in local charities and community affairs, including the church committee and the Hospital Home Aid Society, which did all manner of services to help the recovering troops as well as civilian patients.

When she talked about her mother, she smiled and said that if the Germans had invaded, her mother would have said to the Panzer commander, "You can't leave your tank there." I had noted that Anne, who was basically a quiet, reserved person, could also be a very good "take charge" person when the situation demanded it. I reflected, *The apple does not fall very far from the tree*, and I looked forward to meeting this family.

The train on the Wormley and Whitley line left the station at 0830 the next morning and chugged its way through the English countryside for about an hour. Unfortunately, the weather was quite cold and foggy, so we were deprived of admiring the landscape, which was a bit bleak in February anyway. I reflected that springtime is the time to see England, when everything is a fantastic green and birds are singing everywhere. However, in wartime, you did not get to pick and choose; you grabbed your opportunities when and where you could.

A light drizzle had been falling for the past forty-five minutes, so we alighted at the small Wormley station wearing our raincoats, with me holding Anne's black umbrella over us. We did not see any Home Guard (maybe German agents didn't travel early in the morning or in rainy weather), but shortly thereafter a somewhat tired-looking gray sedan pulled up to the station, the horn gave a weak bleep, and Anne's father stepped out to greet us.

He was a nice-looking man, about five feet ten, with sandy hair, a medium build, and a healthy-looking complexion. He was wearing a rain cape and a soft floppy-brimmed hat that reminded me somewhat of an Aussie hat, or maybe something you wear on safari.

Anne stepped quickly to the car, threw her arms around him, and hugged him warmly with her head on his shoulder, reminding me of our first close dance and demonstrating that she had great love for this man. Before she could untangle herself and introduce us, he smiled at me, stuck his hand around her side and said, "James Radcliffe."

I grasped it firmly and answered, "Ed Nebinger ."

From the first moment, it was clear that association with Anne's father would be easy and pleasant. While he was clearly a self-possessed man, he was also very much easygoing and down to earth, just as Anne herself was. He opened the boot and put our bags in, then held the car door while we jumped in.

Anne opened the conversation with "How's mother?"

He responded, "Oh, she is as busy as ever with her usual bagful of things with the Ladies War Aid and other charitable activities. They are presently collecting knitted sweaters and such for a visit to the wounded veterans at the Basingstoke Hospital."

He laughed and added, "Between my Home Guard and her activities, sometimes we are like two ships passing in the night!"

After just a very short drive we turned into the driveway of a stately three-story Georgian house fronted by a large expanse of lawn, which was green even in February. He pulled up in front of a lower section, which was a small wing on the left side of the house, got out of the car, and opened a single-car garage, then pulled the car into it, explaining, "This is part of the original house, which was built back in Elizabethan times. It's been through a number of evolutions, from a coach house and stable to just a coach house, and now a place to park 'Jezebel' here, which is what we call my little car."

I asked what kind of car it was, as I had never seen one like it. Patting the steering wheel, he replied, "'Jezzy' is a 1938 Alvis; she doesn't look like much and gets a little cranky once in a while, but basically gets the job done, so in fairness I am trying to keep her out of the rain and nurse her through this damned war – until we can upgrade."

Anne smiled and said, "Oh, Father, you know very well that you couldn't bear to be parted from Jezzy – she's one of our family."

To which he laughed and said simply, "Yes, I suppose you're right."

He grabbed our bags out of the boot, handed me one, and motioned us through a side connector door that led to a small mudroom/vestibule where Anne parked her umbrella and we hung our raincoats on pegs. I noted some of her father's Home Guard equipment, including a British-style steel helmet with some kind of insignia on the front, a gas mask, a webbed belt, and a pair of foul weather boots. He saw my interest and said, "No weapons here – we keep them hidden elsewhere."

He then opened another door to a hall and called, "Claire, we're here," at which point a large wooly dog rushed up to Anne and nuzzled her, with stub tail wagging.

Anne threw her arms around him and cried, "Shep, you old ruffian, good to see you," ruffling his coat briskly.

She turned to me and said, "This is Shep, who guards our house," and she laughed. "His coat is nice and dry today, but when he goes out in the rain or snow, we have to make very sure he has a real good shake and a dry-off in the mudroom before he gets into the main house – or it would be a disaster."

At this point, there was a sound of quick footsteps and a nicely dressed middle-aged woman rushed forward, threw her arms around Anne, and bubbled breathlessly, "How are you, my dear? So nice to see you again – you look a little tired. Have those nasty Germans been robbing you of your proper sleep?"

Anne laughed and said, "Well that is a lot of questions, Mother – but first let me introduce you to Captain Ed Nebinger , who is with the 8th Air Force at Martlesham Heath, over near Ipswich."

Anne's mother, who was a handsome woman, slightly taller than her daughter, looked me straight in the eyes, smiled, and put out her hand, saying – somewhat formally, "How do you do," then followed it up with, "Very nice that you could visit us. Anne has written to me of some of your adventures with the V-1 bombs; I'm glad you were able to help keep her safe."

I shook her hand and responded, "Thank you for inviting me, Mrs. Radcliffe. I'm happy to be here, as Anne has told me quite a bit about her parents and home, which is quite beautiful. With regard to the V-1s, I think it was somewhat the other way around; she really knows how to handle the buzz bombs."

Mrs. Radcliffe then led us into the parlor, which was furnished in a rather plush and comfortable-looking period style, matching the architecture of the house. We sat together on a small sofa near a fireplace in which a small fire was crackling. It felt really good, as the weather outside had been bone-chilling.

Anne's mother excused herself to the kitchen, while her father drew up a side chair, pulled out a pipe and, before lighting it, invited us to smoke. I had never known Anne to smoke and wondered if perhaps she did, but she said, "Neither of us is a smoker, Father, but please go ahead," and I nodded.

He picked up a small wooden taper from a box on the mantle, stuck it in the fire briefly, then applied it to his pipe, which he drew on contentedly while settling into his chair like all was right with the world. I could see that he was very pleased to have his daughter home for what I surmised was a rare visit during the press of war.

Anne's mother reappeared, accompanied by a matronly looking woman, who set down a tray containing some small biscuits, a teapot and cups, and proceeded to serve us a welcome refresher.

Mrs. Radcliffe then sat down and asked me about my home in America. She found it interesting that I lived in a town called Bethlehem. I told her that there were lots of jokes about it back in Pennsylvania – such as cute little cracks one might hear if he inadvertently left a door open and a cold draft blew in: "Hey, were you born in a stable or what?"

Everyone laughed, but Anne's father said that he did know about the great Bethlehem Steel Company, as he was involved in shipping and had seen quite a lot of steel structures marked Bethlehem Steel, and was also aware of ships turned out by the Bethlehem-owned shipyards.

They also found it interesting that my middle name was Montgomery. I explained that I had no idea whether I might be related to Britain's General Montgomery but that my ancestors had migrated to America in the early seventeen-hundreds.

We talked about the Revolutionary War, and they found it fascinating when I explained that my direct ancestor had served in a Pennsylvania regiment and had been with Washington's army. However, that ancestor's father-in-law was a Tory (American style) who actually fled to New York City and joined Lord Howe after being accused of spying for the British. That gentleman, the Tory, had been very well landed but had his property seized by the colonies and placed into chancery. At the end of the war, most of the Tory properties were returned to their former owners, but my ancestor had gone to England and died, so his property was juggled in the courts for many years but never recovered.

I had gotten only a short glimpse of their home as we were driving in, but remarked about the elegance of its architecture, which was quite beautiful. Mr. Radcliffe responded, "This house, in fact, has its own direct connection with your Revolutionary War," and went on to explain. "The original house was built in about 1603 and was Elizabethan in style. However, over the next two centuries it underwent a number of rebuilds, the major remodeling taking place just before your Revolutionary War, when it emerged with an almost complete Georgian architecture. At that time it was first acquired by the Radcliffe family and was in fact occupied by Colonel William Radcliffe, who was commandant of one of the Crown's regiments fighting in America. Colonel Radcliffe returned to this house, raised a large family in it, and it has been passed down successively to his descendants ever since."

"What a great story!" I exclaimed. "I am a history buff and also find myself drawn to architecture, which I think I would like to study if I survive this war."

When I said that, Anne, who had been very quietly listening to the conversation, perked up, looked at me, and remarked, "I did not know you had those interests, Ed, but I guess we have had little opportunity to talk about much except the war and our respective jobs in it."

Anne's mother, who had intuitively picked up the sense of our deep commitment to each other, remarked encouragingly, "I think that would be a great field of study, and after the war I imagine there will be a great building boom to restore all of the structures that have been destroyed, as well as to provide homes for a new generation of returning service people."

Her husband jumped in with, "That's probably true, but the question is: Where is the money going to come from? This crazy war has not only killed millions but has used up everybody's treasure. And for what reason? To stop a couple of madmen!"

Everyone knew he was right – but we would just have to take it a day at a time and see where life took us.

Following a light lunch, Anne took me on a tour of the house, which was quite interesting, as the place was dripping with history. In fact, it had a kind of musty and old but not unpleasant smell, a subtle reminder of it long lifespan.

Basically it was a three-floor, multi-room structure, rectangular in shape, with eight fireplaces, of which four were in the downstairs corners, with four smaller ones distributed among the second and third floors. Originally, of course, these had been the only heat, but as Anne remarked, "They didn't do much for the third floor, which in earlier days housed the servants. Now the entire third floor has been closed off, as have most of the fireplaces. We now have central heat from a coal-burning furnace in the cellar, which distributes it through some grills and ductwork – but not too efficiently."

She added, "So we frequently use the main fireplace to stay cozy – and everybody sleeps pretty cool."

When she said that, we happened to be standing in the entrance to a bedroom on the second floor. She looked at me and I knew exactly what she was thinking, and knew also that it would never be cool with this woman.

I reached over, pulled her close, and we kissed, hungrily. Then, seeing me eyeballing the bed, she pushed me away, smiled and said, "Don't even think about it!"

As we were descending the main staircase, she stopped and said, "Have you ever seen a priest's hole?" I said that I had read about them in history books and novels but had never seen one.

"You are standing on one," she said, and showed me how to move a small panel that allowed two of the steps linked by a hinge to be lifted and rotated, revealing a small boxlike compartment.

I looked in and said, "That doesn't look big enough to hold anybody."

She smiled and replied, "That is exactly what you are supposed to think. Searchers knew very well where many of the secret openings were typically located, but if they opened this one, they would find only some small treasures that the owners had secreted here. However, the real priest hole is concealed by a second secret panel at the rear of this chamber."

She pointed and said, "The boards are somewhat warped and it has not been opened for some years, but there is actually a large chamber which was equipped with a bed, a small altar, and other comforts, that could house a priest for days."

Anne added, "The owner, prior to the first Radcliffe, was Catholic, and had this built after the 1605 gunpowder plot to blow up the House of Lords, kill King James I, and put a Catholic girl on the throne. The plot failed, but caused great outrage. Parliament ordered a massive hunt for the priests and their followers countrywide. This stairway was part of the original Elizabethan house, but was strengthened and maintained in subsequent remodeling for its historical value."

Our tour continued and she commented, "The servants are now down to one kind lady, whom you met, who helps my mother in the kitchen. She is our only live-in. Mother also has two women from the local village who come in for half a day each week to help keep the place cleaned up. In the spring and summer, of course, everybody pitches in with the Victory Garden."

The rain had stopped so Anne said, "Would you like to meet Blaze?"

I said I did not know who Blaze was but would be interested in anything she wanted to show me.

Anne took me into the mudroom, scrounged up some rubber mud shoes, and led me out a back door. I was surprised to see a very large garden area surrounded by a hedge with a long shed-like building at the end.

Anne hastened to explain. "This is mother's Victory Garden." I was amazed at the size of it, which must have been at least half an acre – and behind that another field which appeared to contain a small orchard.

Awed, I said, "Wow, how can she do all this?"

Anne laughed and said, "As you have probably noticed, my mother is a super organizer. She heads the Village Victory garden committee, and groups of volunteers come here to work the garden. They grow produce for our own tables, and the committee also provides large quantities of fresh garden vegetables and fruit to several of the nearby hospitals – all without charge, of course."

As we trudged toward the outbuilding at the rear of the enclosure, she continued, "Prior to the war, this section comprised a series of very formal and beautiful gardens. At one time, many years ago, there was even a maze, which we called the 'Enigma,' made out of very tall, closely grown hedges. Of course, that was all torn up early in the war, but we will bring it back one day – after Hitler's in his box."

Pointing to the outbuilding, she said, "That was previously our stable but is now largely devoted to gardening implements and storage containers for the Victory Garden."

At that moment, as we neared the outbuilding, a horse with a big white mark on his forehead stuck his head out over a Dutch door in his stable, nodded it up and down, and greeted Anne with a small whinny.

Anne reached into her pocket, pulled out two carrots, and handed me one, saying, "Here, meet Blaze; maybe you can make a new friend."

The horse was obviously delighted, and we took turns feeding him bites of carrot while Anne related, "This is fox hunt country, and before the war, the Wormley Hunt Club held regular events – red coats, foxes and all. My father was even the Hunt Master for a while. At the time, we had three horses, all good jumpers and hunters."

The "him" turned out to be a "her," as Anne explained that Blaze was a nine-year-old mare. She had been a great jumper and a hunter, a favorite of the family, so even though they had to let the others go (to the military), they were able to keep her as a retired family pet.

She added, "Blaze is delighted to get some occasional exercise while serving as a mount for either of my parents, who are both good riders. We also use her to plow up our garden in the springtime; she actually enjoys it."

Holding up our open hands to show Blaze we had no more carrots, we bid her goodbye and walked around to the front of the house. It was largely of brick construction and I noted that it had nine large double-casement windows, each with leaded six-over-six panes.

Eight of the windows were evenly divided on each side of a formal entrance portico and foyer, while the ninth, which had a rounded crown, occupied the space above the entranceway. Most of the glass in the windows was clearly very old and wavy, and I marveled that they were able to preserve so much of the original elegance of the home.

That evening we had a pleasant dinner in a candlelit dining room, with warm conversation all the way around and absolutely no strain. I felt very comfortable with these people and grew to understand and appreciate more fully the wellspring from which Anne's strength of character, integrity, and quiet beauty stemmed.

Anne and I had been assigned to adjoining rooms on the second floor, each equipped with elegant period furniture, comfortable down-filled pillows, and featherbed coverings, and we parted after a relatively chaste goodnight kiss.

Without question, each of us was keenly aware of the other's presence a few short feet away, but we also knew that neither would violate the trust our hosts had shown to us – our doors remained firmly closed.

The following morning, after a hearty country breakfast, we said our goodbyes to Anne's mother, and her father drove us to the station to see us off. Both of us had to return to duty that day, so we parted with difficulty at the London station, where Anne, who had a uniform with her, took a cab directly to Uxbridge, and I switched to another train heading for Ipswich.

All the way back I reflected on the quality and beauty of that special visit, and my heart ached as the train bore us farther and farther apart.

Decision Time

The Bolton/Burwell standoff continued for well over a month, during which time Ray was very quiet and moody. He never came right out and said that he and Doreen had split up, but the situation was obvious and he sure wasn't happy about it. Every once in a while, particularly at mail time, he would break out with some comment like, "I haven't heard from Doris for over a month. One letter in a month isn't very good, is it? For the life of me, I can't figure it out. How can I write to her when I don't even know where she is?"

What he didn't say was, 'I haven't heard from Doreen for quite a while either.'

Around February 20, Ray's ship was scheduled for a routine bore-sighting, which was a procedure whereby the ground crews realign the guns so that they fire exactly where the gunsight is indicating (providing the range is correct).

Ray, who was eager not to miss any more opportunities to run up a score before the war ended, decided to go down to the firing pits to see that it was done properly, and invited me along. I don't know whether it was the setting, with nobody around except ground crews who were busily working on the guns, or what, but suddenly he opened up with a torrent of agony.

"Ed, I want to ask your opinion on something. I guess you noticed that Doreen has not been around for a while. Well, the fact is that we had a falling out over Doris. You know, if you go with a person for quite a while, you become attached to them." (fidgeting) "Well I guess that has happened to me. Doreen and I have gone steady for over four-and-a-half months now, which is the longest I've gone with anyone in my life. She is in love with me I guess, but not once have I led her on in any way. She knows I'm engaged and I haven't lied to her about anything. I think she has hopes of my falling for her and I'll admit it is very possible. We've had some wonderful times together and I'm not kidding.

"My worst worry is this: When I left Doris, I was sure I was in love with her and it's only because I am away from her, and many memories are fading, for we weren't together long enough, that I think maybe I don't love her. I might be the most miserable guy in the world if I brought Doreen home with me and discovered I still wanted Doris. I don't know how the heck I am going to make up my mind – for Doreen is over here while Doris is three thousand miles away."

Bang! *Bang*! Two quick shots rang out as the armorers fired two of the 50s at the target. We looked to see how closely the rounds hit to the mark.

I thought he was finished, but he took another breath and continued, "Anyway – Doreen wants me to break off my engagement with Doris, for she says it isn't fair to her and I quite agree. But I don't want to – or I should say I haven't done so. It's strange that of all the millions of beautiful and lovely girls in the USA, I have to meet up with a little English girl.

"I know that if I were a smart fellow, I wouldn't even think of getting married until I am about twenty-five years old. I know I fall for a girl too easily – especially one that is in love with me. If I was actually sure that Doreen is in love with me, it would simplify things very much. See what I mean? Well, I'll have to make up my mind pretty soon, but I don't see how I am going to do it. Any suggestions?"

Wow! What a pile of stuff to dump on somebody! The last thing in the world you need to do is get in the way of somebody's romance – which is almost as bad as getting in the way of their religion. But my friend was asking for my advice and counsel. *Why me?*

Then I thought, *Maybe he sees how quietly my relationship with Anne has proceeded, with never any questions or controversy.* It was just there and it was right and we both knew it and that was all there was to it.

Taking my life in my hands, I said, "Ray, I understand your agony, but I do not believe that another party can determine what is best for two people. It just happens between them or it doesn't."

I hesitated, then continued, "You know, Ray, I have never known Doris and have only a short acquaintance with Doreen and would never presume to judge either. However, I noticed one thing that you said which intrigues me. You said you were not sure that Doreen is in love with you. I imagine that she is, but the real question you need to ask yourself is simply this, 'Am I in love with her?' If the answer to that is 'Yes,' and it feels good all the time you are with her, then everything else will simply fall into place, as it is meant to be."

He didn't say anything and seemed to be musing, so having concluded my amateur sermon, I said, "Cheer up, Ray. You've been lucky in war, you will probably be lucky in love. Let's go get a beer and drink to luck!"

On a Friday night in early March, Ray suddenly took a taxi into Ipswich. He usually rode his bike if he was going to the Boltons, but my guess was that he was heading straight for the Farmers' Meeting Room for a long-awaited "tete-a-tete" with Doreen.

Late the next afternoon, I walked into our room in the castle to see him busily tearing up pictures of Doris, including her beautiful professionally made color photo, which had stood on the bureau. In its place, sitting proudly beside that of Anne, was a dandy new framed picture of Doreen.

The clouds and the storm had moved on, the skies had cleared, and it looked like fair weather ahead! Ray and I looked at each other; he gave me a broad grin, and I said simply, "Congratulations, Ray," and shook his hand.

I wondered what was going to happen to the "Lady Doris" on the side of his Mustang – but didn't ask.

The Fortunes of War

Since our return from the visit to Anne's parents' home, I had spoken to her briefly several times on the phone, but we had not met again in London. She had told me that with the Allied advances, the V-1 attacks had dwindled down to almost nothing and that she and her fellow Controller Jennifer Townsend were scheduled to attend a retraining course, beginning March 12, for potential reassignment to other duties.

On March 11, Lt. Levy, the intelligence officer at the 360th squadron called me and said he had received an "urgent" message for me to call Section Officer Townsend at the number provided. After several abortive attempts I managed to get through to Jennifer at the Uxbridge plotting station. She greeted me, then said, "I'm almost afraid to ask this, but is Anne with you?"

I said, "Why no, I haven't seen her for about two weeks."

She responded, somewhat shakily, "Oh, God, I was hoping she was there with you. She was off on March 8th, but has not reported in since, and we are both slated for retraining beginning tomorrow. We have called her apartment and no one answers. We even sent someone over there and got the super to unlock the place, with the thought that she might have fallen or something. She is not there and nothing has been disturbed; we don't know what to think! We also called her home in Wormley, and they have not seen her since your visit, and the police have no record of an auto accident."

I was beginning to get nervous, imagining all sorts of crazy things. We exchanged ideas and agreed that Anne was too sensible a person to go AWOL; it was not even conceivable.

Finally, Jennifer said, "Our people are quite concerned and are continuing to investigate; if you hear from her, please call me or the officer on duty at this number immediately. We agreed and hung up, after which I immediately called Anne's apartment several times. The phone just continued to ring.

My heart was in my throat and I considered getting permission to immediately rush to London. But I soon realized it was probably better that I stay where I could be reached with any news.

The next afternoon Jennifer called me again. I picked up the phone, hoping to hear that she had been found and there was a simple explanation. But Jennifer was in tears as she told me that they believed Anne may have been involved in a V-2 strike at Smithfield Market on March 8.

My heart almost burst at that news and, hopefully, I asked where she was hospitalized. Jennifer sobbed and said, "Oh, Ed, it was a direct strike on the market and there were hundreds of casualties. All of the hospitals have reported in and she is not among the injured! Let's hope and pray that one of the reports was not complete. The devastation was terrible and there could be as many as a hundred dead!"

Two days later I received the confirmation that I dreaded. Several military personnel had been among the killed and wounded, and RAF investigators had found a witness, a woman who had spoken briefly to Anne at Smithfield Market, then left shortly before the V-2 struck.

The witness said that Anne had been preparing to join the meat queue, which was a long one, as Smithfield Market offered special cuts not generally available elsewhere, and also offered very advantageous prices. The V-2 had apparently impacted within feet of the queue, and known dead were already over one hundred.

That evening I sat in our room staring at the picture of a beautiful woman in RAF blue on our dresser, and silently raged at the Germans for their dreadful weapon that targeted civilians and descended faster than the speed of sound, giving no warning to allow people to seek shelter.

Over the past year I had seen death and destruction on almost a daily basis and in many forms. But that was by and large remote, almost like watching machines die, rather than humans. Even the losses of Andrino and Ody Thoma, which I felt deeply, could be rationalized to some degree by the fact that they were both engaged in active combat – in fact trying to do harm to the enemy.

But the loss of Anne was so personal and so outrageous that I felt it with all of my senses and to the depth of my very soul; in fact, it dominated every waking moment of my life.

This fine woman, who I loved deeply, had already lost a husband in the war and had spent several years of her young life helping to defend her countrymen from death and destruction from incoming bombers and V-1 bombs.

And now, to be robbed of her life by an incredible ten-thousand-to-one or greater shot seemed to defy all logic and rationale, and I lay awake night after night trying to grasp the fact that it had really happened.

I reflected silently how really stupid wars are. In every case they start out with both sides striving to hit only military targets, but then, inevitably, descend into a bestial business where so-called civilized nations end up incinerating thousands of civilians, including women and children.

Ten days later I sat with Anne's parents in a special RAF memorial ceremony in a chapel near Uxbridge. The chapel was packed with RAF personnel – a sea of blue, a testimony to the respect with which Anne was held by her fellow officers. There was no coffin, no remains, only the memory of a special person.

Ray and Doreen had managed to send a floral tribute, not an easy task in wartime England, and the flowers resided with others in the front of the chapel. Anne's mother was quietly somber, but her father and I sat with tears running unashamedly down our cheeks, and he said softly, "God curse those damned Germans!"

At the train station, we hugged each other closely, all aware of what might have been, and knowing that we would probably never meet again. I watched their train start off, and I waved slowly as they moved out of my life forever.

A month later, Jennifer called and said that Anne had been posthumously awarded the Military Medal "for sustained devotion to duty while under hostile fire."

The medal, which had been previously awarded to several WAAFs who had been killed in attacks on command stations, was the highest decoration that could normally be awarded in the RAF for sustained gallantry that did not involve flying duties.

Ray and Doreen Go to London

In early April, Ray's flight got a couple of days off and he announced that he was going to go to London and was taking Doreen with him. Ray said he wanted to buy a new Battle Jacket,[13] as Crump had been down the week before and got a dandy one for only eight pounds.

They also planned to spec out the situation with regard to marriage.

---

[13] * The short-waisted formal uniform jacket, previously known as the "Eisenhower Jacket," as General Ike had been the one who originated it. Eight Pounds equated to about $35 at that time.

When they returned, Ray sent a letter to his parents explaining the situation:

14 April 1945

My Dearest Mom & Pop;

An awful lot has happened since you last heard from me. I might as well come right out with it and probably it is no surprise to you. Doreen and I have decided to get married before I leave and I have already put my application in. Oh don't worry about it now, for I have thought and thought the matter over carefully and I know I won't regret it. We were going to wait until I went home but events changed our mind.

We went to London yesterday to the American Consul to find out how long it would take Doreen to get over to the States. They said that if you are married it is possible that she can come over about the same time I do or maybe a month or two after. Well, we asked about a Fiancée and they said the US government doesn't handle them and they have to go by an English shipping co. You see, the government will pay your wife's fare on the boat over from the point of embarkation to the final destination. Isn't that swell.

Anyway we went to the largest shipping co. in England, main office in London, and they said it might take up to a year to get over there, so bang! That was enough. We decided to get married before I leave. I will cable you when I find out exactly when.

The policy is this. It usually takes two months for the application to go through but I'm sure we can get it through long before that. It's a cinch; it hadn't better be too long for this war is going to fold up very soon and the Group will undoubtedly move out. The application has to go from our Gp. C.O. up through channels to General Anderson and back. Then we show this okay to the preacher who will marry us. Gosh I always wanted to be married at home, at least near enough so my Mom & Pop could be there, but it looks like this war is disrupting everything. We just have to take what comes and get along the best we can.

I can honestly say this, Mom & Pop. Doreen is a very intelligent girl and I know she will be a big help to me in the years to come. I feel twice as strong with her beside me and I have no doubt that we will get along beautifully. After you meet her you will see how sweet she is and you'll see why this guy fell in love with her.

You have asked a lot of questions, and I will answer them later, but I am trying to get this finished and get one off to Doris. I haven't written her for nearly two months now and my last letter to her wasn't a very happy one for I hadn't heard from her for over a month when I wrote it. So undoubtedly she knows we will never make a go of it. I'm sorry I haven't written her sooner but I'll get it off tonight. I will not tell her I am getting married but merely that I am breaking off with her. So don't you tell her either. It would only make it worse for her.

My captaincy hasn't come back yet but I definitely know I am getting it. By "coming back" I mean it was put through to higher headquarters but as yet has not officially been announced. Isn't it swell though? Just think, a Captain, married, and overseas getting $469.00 a month. Boy won't I be able to save the dough. And will I need it. When Doreen comes over I will be there and I will acquaint her with the country and she can stay with me as long as I am in the States. I only hope she gets over while I am on my leave so I can be with her when she meets you. Gosh am I anxious to show her off. So Folks don't let that worry you either. We will be happy as long as we are with each other. You know everything is going to be different for the little Darling.

I finished my tour but have the 25 hours extension to finish. Gosh it doesn't look like I will for we haven't had a mission in ages. It seems there are practically no more targets left. Oh well, I shouldn't mind. Ha. Ha.

All for now. Sorry I waited so long to write but I've been so busy thinking. All my love to everyone.

Your loving son, Ray

The Proposal

Ray did not mention it in his letter to his parents, but one other very significant thing happened during their visit to London. At their visit to the American Embassy, they had been told that if they were just engaged, they would have to arrange for a British shipping company to bring Doreen over, and that might take as much as a year. On the other hand, if they were married, Doreen would not only be sent to the States at government expense but it might require only a few months.

That settled it. They were going to marry in England and let things sort themselves out from there. To talk it over, they strolled over to St. James Park. It was a pleasant early spring day; the grass was greening and birds were singing.

They sat on a park bench under a big tree to take in the scenery and to enjoy the moment. Ray was thinking how lucky he was to be sitting and holding hands with this wonderful girl, when suddenly it occurred to him that he had never formally asked her to marry him! Yes, they had talked about it; that was why they were here in London – but never a formal proposal.

On an impulse, he stood up, took his hat off and turned around, took her hand in his, and dropped to one knee. She looked at him in surprise and started to tell him that he was going to soil the knee of his uniform trousers when he blurted out that he not only loved her very much but that he was crazy about her – and would she marry him?

She gasped and just started to respond when suddenly a bird overhead dropped a full bomb load directly onto Ray's head! Ray felt it splatter onto his head and cried aloud, "Oh, my Lord, this is unbelievable!" – and started apologizing to Doreen while cleaning up the debris with his handkerchief. "NO! NO!" cried Doreen. "That is good luck!"

Oh, that means good luck!. *(Artist: John Purdy)*

Ray looked at her like she was trying to excuse his embarrassment, but she hastened to assure him she was telling the truth. "That is absolutely good luck. Ask any Englishman!" Then she finished her statement with, "And yes, darling, I will be the happiest girl in the world to be your wife – the sooner the better!" In their excitement, they both forgot that Ray had not presented her with a ring. He did not even have one and would have to take care of that later.

An Unexpected Obstacle

After much agonizing about it, Ray and Doreen finally set their minds firmly on getting married in England while Ray was stationed there. The war was winding down and would soon be over, but there was no way to know what would happen to Ray when it ended. His fighter group might well be re-equipped with very long-range fighters to escort the B-29s, and shipped to the Pacific.

Therefore, in early April 1945, Ray bit the bullet and filed a formal request for permission to marry, in accordance with Army regulations. However, the formal request would have to go through 8th Air Force channels for approval, which meant that it would first have to be approved by the 360th squadron commander, then forwarded through the 356th group, and finally to Brigadier General Anderson, who commanded the 67th Fighter Wing of several groups.

According to the regulation, the prospective bride was required to submit three letters of recommendation from good sources, attesting to the fact that she was of good character, etc. Accordingly, Doreen produced three such letters from the vicar of her church, the secretary of the National Farmers Union, Suffolk Branch (where Doreen worked), and a close personal friend, all of whom attested to her excellent character and integrity. These letters were then forwarded to a military chaplain who, in accordance with further regulations, assembled a small board of officers and reviewed them, signifying approval.

While it might seem like an Army regulation forbidding personnel to marry without official permission was oppressive, there were actually sound reasons for it. First of all, the military did not wish to encourage a flock of fly-by-night marriages, many of which would be the result of ill-considered liaisons. It may not sound kind, but the reality was that there were plenty of women in every country who would jump at the chance to marry an American, get instant citizenship, and a free meal ticket in the States for the rest of their lives, and therefore go to any means to engineer such a scheme.

Frequently, such marriages resulted in serious problems, which were destructive to military morale, not just for the impacted spouse but also for those who were expected to work with an individual whose mind was not fully on the job they had to accomplish. The 8th Air

Force was not in the business of running ob/gyn clinics and nursery schools. That's why it hadn't allowed the troops to take their families overseas with them in the first place, and it wasn't fair to allow some troops to start a new family overseas while the families of most held down the home front.

Further, in the particular case of military flying officers, the services had spent a great deal of time and money training carefully selected men to become finely honed fighting machines, and did not wish to see that focus destroyed by an ill-conceived marriage, with potential adverse consequences in combat.

However, there were some exceptional cases that warranted consideration and appeared unlikely to have an adverse impact upon the individual's combat performance. Ray's case was one of those and, as expected, his squadron commander, Major Wood, immediately gave his approval, offered his congratulations, and patted Ray on the back.

Wood, who was an excellent officer and an inspiring leader, held Ray in high esteem as one of the future leaders of the squadron. He was also well acquainted with Doreen from her various visits to Martlesham, and knew that she was an intelligent girl of fine character from a solid English family – an all-around excellent choice.

As the C.O. signed the paper, however, he cautioned Ray about jumping to conclusions, as the approval still had to clear through two more channels. Ray was optimistic, however, and when he visited the Boltons that night, he reported joyously that the first steps had been taken and potential approval was in the works.

Several days later he received an order to report to Col. Tukey at group headquarters.

At the appointed time, dressed in a spotless Class A uniform, Ray reported to 356th Hq. and told the colonel's secretary that he had an appointment. After verifying it with the colonel on the intercom she told Ray to go in. Ray marched up to Col. Tukey's desk, fanned him a correct salute, and said, "Lt. Burwell, 360th squadron, reporting as ordered, sir."

There was a moment of silence during which Tukey glared at him – then said, "Burwell, do you think you were sent over here to fight this war at your own personal convenience?"

Burwell was stunned! Tukey had started right out in a completely hostile manner. *What possible reason did he have for that?* Ray had done his job eagerly and was not a squadron foul-up but a solid combat fighter pilot with a good record.

Puzzled, he replied, "I'm not sure what you mean, sir. I am very happy to be in the 356th group."

Tukey's attack continued: "Do you think that marrying some chit of an English girl is going to improve your performance? Every one of these local girls is looking for an all-expense paid trip to the USA; can't you see that? What's the real situation, have you got her pregnant?"

Ray gasped, turned red as a beet and replied, hotly, "She's not a chit of any kind. She is my fiancée, she is a fine person, and she is not pregnant!"

Unable to contain his anger, he added, "I consider that an insulting statement." (omitting the "sir.)

"Well, listen - mister. You can be insulted all you want, but your request is denied! I am not having my pilots distracted from their duties by this kind of nonsense. Stand at attention while I am talking to you! Further, if I hear any more about it, you can forget about any future with this group – and that includes your promotion to captain! Is that clearly understood?"

Shocked and dazed, Ray could only mutter quietly, "Yes, sir," to which Tukey replied sharply, "Very well; dismissed!"

Seething inside, but completely a captive of Tukey's power structure, Ray fanned him a reluctant salute, turned, and walked out.

He returned to the squadron in a complete funk, but when he went to tell Major Wood about it, discovered that the C.O. was already aware, as somebody at group had phoned him with the details.

Wood made no comment, except to advise quietly, "You'd better let things settle down for a while and don't try to fight him. Why don't you take the rest of the afternoon off and go explain it to Doreen. Maybe you'll find another solution."

That night, at the Bolton's home in Ipswich, Ray related the day's events to Doreen and her family. In an uncharacteristically strongly worded statement, he concluded, "That bastard! I have never been treated like that since I got my commission. He acted like I was some kind of cadet plebe the way he talked to me!"

Mrs. Bolton, who was very fond of Ray, simply laid a hand on his shoulder, and Herb Bolton, who was usually a very quiet and reserved individual, surprised him by saying, "Some of them big brass have heads like balloons and can cause a world of trouble for the fightin' men."

Mr. Bolton knew what he was talking about, having been called up at eighteen to spend long years in the trenches with the Northumberland Fusiliers during the first war. He considered it almost a miracle that he had made it through alive.

Both Doreen and Ray found themselves smiling at her father's remark, as Herb had actually not liked the Yanks in that war. Doreen remembered him telling his family about how arrogant the Yanks were when they arrived in France in 1918, "Big cigars hanging out of their mouths, saying, 'Where's the shootin' gallery?"' and he had replied, "You'll soon find out!!!" Poorly impressed by that experience, he had strongly encouraged Doreen and Cynthia to avoid the Americans!

Clearly, he had been won over to support one Yank, and Ray agreed that he had hit the nail right on the head about the group commander. Nobody in the 356th group really liked Tukey, and most thought that he should never have been allowed to command a fighter group. Ray wondered if that may have been the source of his antagonism – he probably was aware of his own unpopularity and was subconsciously striking back at the young tigers in the group.

Ray and Doreen, realizing that they had met with an obstacle, nevertheless knew that it would not stop them, so both went quietly back to their jobs, knowing that eventually they would find a way to spend their lives together. Meanwhile, Ray moved on with fighting the war.

Strikes on a Jet

On April 18 Ray flew his sixtieth combat mission of WWII. He thought it might be his last and wanted it to be a meaningful contribution to the war, and in that respect he was not disappointed.

He was leading the 360th squadron, escorting several boxes of B-26 bombers on a relatively short-range mission to bomb the underground fuel storage tanks at Neuberg, Germany, when about a half-dozen FW-190s tried to get into position for a successful attack on the bomber squadron. The 360th was able to break up several attacks, but shortly thereafter two Me.262 "Stormbird" jets appeared high above and made a high-speed pass at Ray's flight from the rear.

Ray called "Break left!" and his flight turned head-on into the jets.

That was the best strategy in combating the jets, which had a vast superiority in speed and would never try to turn with the Mustangs. The four 30mm cannon of the jets were lethal if you took a hit. But by turning his flight of four directly into the jets, it was a case of eight 30mm cannon in the two German jets against twenty-four 50-caliber guns in the Mustangs.

The jets broke off the pass and Ray got a quick ninety-degree deflection shot at one, while continuing to turn and fire at him as he raced away at tremendous speed. He was lucky enough to get a few strikes on the jet before it went completely out of range, and later, after the lab checked his gun camera and confirmed the hits, he was given credit for a "damaged" on the jet. It gave Ray a good feeling and he thought it would not be a bad way to end his combat tour of operations, as even getting strikes on one of the German jets was fairly rare.

The next day, Ray Burwell's captaincy came through, surprising him, as Col. Tukey had threatened to hold it up. However, Tukey, if he had actually sought to delay it, had apparently been unsuccessful, as the 8th Air Force's standard policy was for eligible officers who completed a tour of combat and applied for a twenty-five-hour extension to be promoted to the next highest grade. Ray had filed for an extension and was now about halfway toward completion.

Last Mission

As it happened, Ray actually flew two more missions. One on the nineteenth, while over five hours in duration, was uneventful. However, his last mission, on April 25, was one which would remain in his memory bank for the rest of his life

The 356th was assigned to escort B-17s from two of the 8th Air Force bomb groups, which were to attack the Skoda Armament Works in Pilsen, Czechoslovakia. The mission was very unusual in several aspects: The enemy knew they were coming, as the Allied High Command had deliberately passed a warning to the German authorities so that the Czech workers would have time to take to the bomb shelters. Further, the target was very deep in enemy territory, and, surprisingly, the B-17s were scheduled to bomb from only 20,000 feet, instead of the usual 25,000-30,000.

The 359th squadron was assigned to fly top cover, while the 360th fighters were assigned as the low squadron, with orders to remain at only 12,000 feet prior to the bomb drop, probably so they could intercept any enemy fighters climbing. The problem was that the Mustangs used a lot more gas at the lower altitudes, as the pilots could not lean the engines as much at those heights.

Although Ray was now actually the senior 360th pilot, the squadron was led that day by Lt. Dunn, an experienced combat pilot who was slated for promotion at the completion of the mission. As ordered, they picked up the bombers in the vicinity of Frankfurt, Germany, and escorted them all the way to the target. Cloud cover in the target area was 8/10+, and the bombers had difficulty locating the target. They had orders not to drop unless they had positive identification, as the authorities did not want innocent Czechs in nearby Pilsen to be killed.

In the first two passes over the target area, the bombers failed to make positive ID on the Skoda Plant, and a lot of time and fuel was eaten up circling around. Finally, Dunn radioed the bombers and said that their escorts were low on fuel and could only hang around for one more run. Fortunately, the third run was successful. All of the bombers dropped with good results, and the pack headed out, minus three B-17s that were seen to go down in the target area due to very heavy flak.

The squadron was very deep in enemy territory and shortly thereafter pilots began calling that they were really getting short on fuel. On a relative scale, Mustangs were actually very good on fuel burn, averaging about sixty gallons per hour, which could be stretched a bit by reducing propeller rpm while increasing manifold pressure with the throttle. The P-51 carried 270 gallons internally, plus 108 gallons in each of the two drop tanks, for a total of 489 gallons. That sounds like a lot of fuel, but a significant amount is burned on takeoff and climb out, and on this particular mission they had been underway for over six hours, much of which had been spent milling around at low altitudes. Consequently, it was not surprising that many pilots began reporting that they did not think they could make it back.

Dunn did the smart thing. He headed for occupied territory and asked everybody to keep their eyes open for a field on the Continent. They found one, a 9th Air Force base with a squadron of light bombers just about to take off. With the runway in sight and tanks running dry, there was a frantic free-for-all to get on the ground.

Everyone made it. One pilot's engine actually quit on final approach and he glided in. Meanwhile engines conked out on Mustangs scattered all over the field. Ray hit the deck with about twenty gallons left, gasped a sigh of relief, and wondered what might have happened if the squadron had run into a pack of Jerries on the way back.

The commander of the 9th Air Force base hollered on the radio for the squadron to "Get the hell off of my field" so he could get his bombers in the air, which was greeted with a few catcalls and remarks like, "With what?"

Frantically, they got the P-51s out of the way and the bombers took off, after which the 9th Air Force found enough fuel to give everybody about a hundred gallons each, and the squadron took off and returned to Martlesham Heath uneventfully. That was Captain Ray Burwell's last combat mission in WWII.

After the pilots had completed their debriefing and mission reports with Lt. Levy, they were letting off some steam at the bar when Major Cota, the operations officer, came over to the bar and said to Ray, "Stop by the C.O.'s office when you finish your drink, Ray."

Major Yannell, who had recently taken over the squadron, met him at the door saying, "Nice mission, Ray; congratulations on finishing your tour! Sit down; I have something I want you to read."

He then handed him a letter and sat quietly smiling as Ray read it. It was a letter signed by Gen. Anderson, Headquarters, 67th Fighter Wing, 8th Air Force, granting Ray permission to marry on or after 14 June 1945!

HEADQUARTERS 67TH FIGHTER WING
APO 557 AAF Station 372
U. S. Army

A-A C-C-2

30 APR 1945

291.1

SUBJECT: Permission to Marry.

TO : Captain, Orvil L. Burwell, 0711944, 360th Fighter Squadron, 356th Fighter Group, AAF Station 369, APO 557, U. S. Army.

THRU : Commanding Officer, AAF Station 369, APO 557, U. S. Army.

1. Pursuant to authority contained in paragraph, 3a, Circular 41, Headquarters European Theater of Operations, U. S. Army, 17 April 1944, your request for permission to marry is approved.

2. You are hereby granted permission to marry Miss Doreen E. Bolton, 342 Foxhall Rd., Ipswich, England, on or after 14 June 1945, when the two months waiting period as required by paragraph 6c, Circular 41, Hqs European Theatre of Operations, U. S. Army, 17 April 1945, will have elapsed.

3. The original and one signed copy of this letter will be presented to the appropriate civil or ecclesiastical official in the United Kingdom from whom the securing of civil or ecclesiastical authorization to marry is required. The original letter will be left with said official. On the signed copy of this letter you will obtain a notation by the appropriate official of the date and place of marriage, which copy with notation will be returned to your immediate Commanding Officer for file with your appropriate record as a permanent part thereof.

Edward W. Anderson
EDWARD W. ANDERSON,
Brigadier General, U. S. Army,
Commanding.

OFFICIAL:

Michael J. Fitzgerald
MICHAEL J. FITZGERALD,
Captain, Air Corps,
Adjutant.

1 Incl: Application for Permission to Marry w/allied papers.

Married in Rushmere Church
on 16 June 1945
[illegible]
— Vicar.

Ray was so shocked that he thought he must have misread the letter. He looked at Yannell, then reread it and said, "How can this be? Col. Tukey said he would not approve it. Do you think he changed his mind?"

Yannell said, "I don't know, but I think you better just let sleeping dogs lie. You have what you need."

Somebody at group had quietly forwarded a copy of Ray's request to marry to the 67th Wing. Whoever it was would never admit it, but clearly Ray had a friend there. Yannell, who was a career officer and a good fighter squadron leader, was privately amused and had his own candidate as to who it might have been but would never voice it to anyone.

It was probably Lt. Col. Don Bacchus, deputy group commander, who had commanded the group briefly during Colonel Tukey's absence during a visit to the States. Don was not only an ace with nine kills, he was the type of aggressive leader that the 356th needed, and was popular with everyone. He had specifically asked for Ray to fly his wing on the September 22 mission when the group had scored big.

Yannell secretly hoped that Don Bacchus would inherit the group at some point, get his Eagles, and move them forward in terms of enemy kills, etc.

CHAPTER SIXTEEN

KICKED OUT OF THE GROUP

Tukey Makes Good His Threat

In the 8th Air Force chain of command, Col. Tukey, the Commander of the 356th fighter group, reported directly to Brigadier General Anderson of the 67th Fighter Wing, and when he received a copy of the letter authorizing Ray to marry "on or after 14 June 1945," Tukey flew into a complete rage, but could do nothing to stop it. However, he was able to make good on his threat to kick Ray out of the 356th group!

In early May, Ray received orders transferring him to the 3rd Gunnery and Tow Target Squadron at Wrentham Hall, Thetford, effective May 5, 1945. Tukey had actually initiated the action to get Ray transferred out shortly after the interview in which Ray had lashed back at him angrily.

When Ray opened those orders, he couldn't believe it. Tow Target Squadron! A non-combat unit! Ray had been warned to expect some serious retaliation from Tukey, but this was a humiliating assignment for an experienced combat fighter pilot, and Ray was crushed. The war in Europe was winding down and would soon be over, but Ray wanted to be part of a fighter squadron the day the last shot was fired.

It was not to be. Tukey was able to pull it off because there was actually a surplus of fighter pilots in the group. The training commands in the States had been operating at full speed for several years and a flood of trained fighter pilots had been arriving steadily in England. The initial expectation, prior to the invasion, was that the 8th Air Force would lose thousands of pilots, but it didn't happen. Also, by late 1944, the Luftwaffe had been beaten down from years of fighting, and now, with the Russians squeezing them from the East and the Americans and British from the West, they were hopelessly outnumbered. Many of their great aces were either dead or had been moved into higher positions.

The Luftwaffe actually still had plenty of aircraft, as the German Todt Organization had done a magnificent job of moving fighter production into caves and hidden areas where they were able to continue producing in spite of massive bombing by the RAF and Americans.

However, two other serious problems plagued the Luftwaffe. As their losses mounted, their pilot training program had fallen seriously behind, and replacements were arriving with less and less flying experience.

Even more serious was the shortage of aviation fuel, as the Allied planners had made a concentrated effort to destroy refineries, as well as the rail networks that were needed to transport the fuel. Consequently, the Luftwaffe's strategy was to husband its resources while waiting for a big raid with juicy targets, then send a big pack of fighters aloft to nail as many bombers as it could.

Hitler had failed to exploit his great tactical advantage with the Me.262 jets, which were about a hundred and fifty miles per hour faster than prop-driven fighters, and failed to order enough production of them to assemble large groups. Consequently, they typically operated in twos and threes, manned by the most experienced German fighter pilots, flying very high and looking for an opportunity to pick off a stray bomber or fighter.

Towing Targets

Two days later Ray reported in to the 3rd Gunnery (and Tow Target) Flight, which was located inland at Thetford, Suffolk, about fifty miles north of Ipswich. It was a relatively quiet airfield, with a runway of unusual length, and the first thing Ray noticed was a motley assortment of airplanes of many types, including a strange-looking two-seater bird, which he later found out was a Vultee A-35 Dive Bomber. He noted that there were no P-51s, but there were a couple of A-20 Havocs, a B-26, a UC-61 – which was a light civilian Fairchild 24, adapted for military liaison/utility – and finally, a half-dozen P-47s, mostly razorbacks.

The P-47s caught his eye and he reflected, *Maybe this won't be too bad, if I can get to fly the good old Jugs.*

The living quarters, which turned out to be in a large manor known as Wrentham Hall, were somewhat similar to those at Martlesham but not quite as distinctive and unique as a moated castle. On the whole, not half bad, as military quarters ran. After dropping off his gear, he was surprised to learn that they actually had a couple of functioning showers, which was something that was definitely lacking at Playford Hall. (At the castle you got to climb into a giant bathtub, which was great whenever they had some hot water available, but that was not very often.)

The next day, Ray reported in to the 3rd Gunnery and Tow Target Flight and met the commander, Major Brennan, and his operations officer, Capt. Whitehead. They greeted him in a friendly manner and welcomed him into the unit. He noted that both were sporting DFCs – the major's was of the British variety, which was a lot harder to earn than the U.S. equivalent. Capt. Whitehead then invited Ray to sit down and began explaining the mission of the squadron and how they operated.

Early in the discussion, Ray interjected, "I did not even know we have target squadrons in England. This may be a silly question, but why do we need them when everybody who comes over from the States is already fully qualified as a fighter pilot and has had gunnery training? If they need practice, why not let them go practice on some real targets across the Channel?" It was a rather blunt series of questions and actually not too tactful, but Ray had a habit of cutting right to the chase.

The captain, who was not offended and had been asked that question before, smiled and replied, "There are a couple of reasons. There is a large backlog of replacement pilots, and rather than keep them sitting around, we are providing gunnery training to help them keep their edge. The war here is definitely winding down but is still going strong in the Pacific, so we expect many of the pilots to be transferred to that theatre of war. I don't know whether you know it, but in the States, the development of the P-47N and the P-51H models is well advanced, and both are special very long-range versions. The B-29 force is steadily increasing and the new fighters will be able to escort them all the way to Japan."

"That's amazing," said Ray. "We don't get much news about those kinds of special developments. Maybe I'll end up flying the new Mustangs in the Pacific, which would be okay with me."

But as he said it, his mind flashed back to another matter, and he silently wondered what might happen to Doreen. *I'll just have to take it one day at a time*, he thought, *and see what happens.*

That evening he met some of the pilots assigned to the units and found them to be generally good guys, who had come from various fighter squadrons in England. However, one thing he noted was that virtually every one of them had been sent to the 3rd Gunnery Flight after committing some kind of cardinal sin, either real or imagined. In short, their stories had an eerie similarity to Ray's own experience, leading Ray to the conclusion that assignment to towing targets was the equivalent of being assigned to a penal battalion in the Russian Army, except that on the Russian front the guys in penal battalions were sent into the toughest battles as the first wave of an attack, while the Americans' situation was just the opposite – they had been pulled out of combat. But they were making the best of it, and Ray was determined to do the same.

Ray spent a couple of days learning the ground workings of the target towing business. One of the reasons for the long runway, he found out, was that about a thousand feet of steel cable led from the target towing aircraft to the target, and it was all stretched out nicely on the runway, prior to takeoff. The target itself was comprised of a mesh type of fabric and was ten feet high and thirty feet long. There was a steel bar at the front of the target, with a heavy lead weight on the bottom side, so the target would fly vertically.

The technique for getting the target into the air was for the tow pilot to get his airplane off the ground, with gear coming up, pick up good flying speed as soon as possible, then zoom up to keep the cable and target from dragging past the end of the runway. The landing, of course, was the reverse, with the pilot holding slightly higher altitude on his approach, and landing well down the runway so the target did not drag through any trees, etc. Targets were never dropped, although there was a release in the cockpit for the pilot to drop the target, in the case of an emergency.

Ray, who had practiced gunnery at his operational training unit, was familiar with the method of scoring. If four pilots were scheduled to fire on the same aerial target, the noses of the 50-caliber bullets would be dipped in colored wax paint, with each of the pilots assigned a different color. The projectiles, of course, were straight ball ammunition, not tracers or API [14], which were used in combat loads. Hits on the target always produced a smear of color, so it was then easy for the training people to count hits and compute relative levels of pilot proficiency.

The next day, Capt. Whitehead handed Ray the flight manual on the A-35, saying, "This is one of the airplanes we use for towing; familiarize yourself with the basics and this afternoon I'll give you a checkout in the bird."

Ray sat down and learned that the Vultee A-35, which had been designed to be a dive bomber, was a monster two-seater airplane weighing over 16,000 pounds, powered by a Wright fourteen-cylinder radial engine with 1,700 horsepower. For combat, it was designed to carry four 50-caliber guns firing forward, two in each wing, while a gunner had another fifty mounted on a ring-mount in the rear cockpit. Ray reflected that 1,700 horsepower definitely sounded underpowered, as it probably needed that much power just to drag its own weight plus a couple of thousand pounds of bombs or other combat load into the air.

He also learned a bit about its history, which was very poor. The Vengeance, as it was called, had been originally ordered by the French, but with the fall of France in 1940, most of the production had been transferred to the British under lend-lease. Although the airplanes were used to some extent by the British and their Empire allies in Burma and Southeast Asia, they were found to be sluggish and underpowered, and were so universally unpopular with the pilots that they were soon relegated to secondary tasks, including towing targets.

In his checkout that afternoon, Ray developed an instant dislike for the airplane. Even though the five 50-caliber guns with which it had

---

[14] Armor Piercing and Incendiary

originally been armed had been stripped for its target duties, it still flew like a fat cow.

Crump Flies In for a Visit

On May 5, Crump, who had completed his tour of ops with the 360th squadron and was also sporting his captain bars, flew into the base in PI-W "Jackie" for a quick visit before heading to the States. In his usual flamboyant style, he did a quick buzz job of the field, followed by a few rolls and an Immelmann, before landing. He might have gotten into hot water over that, but no high brass were present at the base and everyone knew the war would be ending in a day or two.

Ray, who had just landed an A-35 with a target, met him at the flight line, where they shook hands and pounded backs, grinning. "What the hell kind of airplane is that?" said Crump, gawking at the two-seat monster that Ray had just stepped out of.

"That's a Vultee Vengeance," laughed Ray, "probably the worst pig of an airplane I have ever flown. Can you imagine this thing in combat? Believe it or not, it came with four fifties firing forward, plus a gunner with another one in the back seat!"

"What a joke," said Crump. "That wreck wouldn't last five minutes in Germany!"

"Yeah," said Ray, "and would you believe it was built for the French to use as a dive bomber before they cashed in their chips? No wonder they lost the war!"

They lunched together while Burwell introduced Crump to some of his fellow tow pilots, and Crump brought him up to date on events at the 356th group. The big bomber mission to Pilsen had probably been the last true bombing effort by the 8th Air Force. Since then, they had flown a couple of missions escorting B-17s that were dropping leaflets over Germany, so Ray had not missed much.

Other than that, Lt. Pidwell had crashed and completely wiped out PI-P "Mary Jane" while on a training mission over England. His flight was off the coast over the North Sea when his engine suddenly made a *whoomp* and started smoking badly.

Pidwell called for an emergency landing and got a DF steer to a base near the coast. He had part power and thought he had the field made, but before he could drop his landing gear the engine literally exploded and quit cold. He was too low to bail out, so Pidwell was forced to belly in, gear up, in a farmer's field, crashing through a dirt embankment before coming to a stop.

He escaped unhurt and ended up having dinner with a kindly farmer and his wife while waiting for the ambulance and crash crew to arrive. Pidwell had been within three hours of completing his combat tour, and reflected on his good luck that it had occurred over England instead of enemy territory, where he would be sitting as a POW.

Crump, who had finished his tour, was scheduled to depart for the States in a couple of days, but told Ray that the 356th group was already planning a monster victory celebration, and was hoping he could catch at least part of it. He suggested that Ray find a way to make it to Martlesham and join in the celebration, then jumped into his bird and blasted off, Crump style, with a couple of parting rolls shortly after gear up. Burwell watched with a pained expression on his face as Crump disappeared into the afternoon haze.

The War Ends

The war ended officially on May 8, 1945, and most units throughout the theatre stood down, until the situation clarified itself. Ray was able to borrow a Jeep from the 3rd Flight motor-pool and drive down to the 360th where a terrific celebration was underway at Playford Hall. He stopped at Ipswich on the way and picked up Doreen. They walked in the door of the castle and found everybody already half blasted, with booze flowing like there was no tomorrow.

Doc Carey, the flight surgeon, had dug into his carefully guarded supply of mission whiskey, and was applying it liberally to all wounds, real and imagined, while many bottles of Scotch and assorted other booze appeared magically from other sources. It was also a sendoff for Crump and Lt. Ciocci of the squadron, both of whom had officially finished their tours and were heading for the States.

Another important event occurred while Doreen and Ray were visiting the castle for the celebration. Ray presented her with a beautiful engagement ring, which actually comprised two rings in white gold, with one main diamond and eight smaller ones on each side. Doreen was thrilled – and amazed at the quality and beauty of the set!

Even though London's diamond district was well established, the war had interrupted normal trade channels and made it difficult to obtain quality jewelry there.. However, Ray had secretly ordered the ring set from a New York jeweler his father knew, and had it sent to Denair, after which his parents sent it to Ray – a long process. Unbelievable as it may sound, the rings were custom-made and would normally have cost five-hundred dollars, but were actually obtained at a substantial discount due to family connections!

That party continued for almost two days, with various people popping in an out, including quite a few girlfriends that appeared miraculously from everywhere.

Sometime during the wild festivities, some clown got a pair of boots and dipped the soles in black paint, then proceeded to make a set of footprints which went up the sidewall of the big fireplace room, across the ceiling, and down the other side. It was a good stunt, but Ray and Doreen wondered what the owner of Playford Hall would think when he finally got his castle back after the 356th returned to the

States. The Americans would probably pick up a good tab for that, which fell under the category of "collateral damage."

During the three-day celebration of VE Day, Ray stayed with the Bolton family. Mrs. Bolton's letter to Ray's mother evokes poignant memories of that event – long past:

May 13, 1945

Dearest Mrs. Burwell,

So many thanks for your very nice letter received today Sunday 13th. We are having some beautiful weather. Ray has been spending his leave with us and he looks better for a change and a rest from his military life at the drome. I wish you could just have seen him and the girls, Doreen & Cynthia, having breakfast out in the garden in the shade of a white Lilac tree.

We have a nice little lawn at the back of the house where we spend most of our time in the very hot weather. I also have a little family of 10 chicks in a little pen on the lawn, which all love to watch.

Ray got very burnt today. It is really very warm weather for May. I know you must be so relieved to know that your son will not have to fight any more. Yes, dear, we were all at a concert pitch, waiting anxiously for the signing of the peace, and we heard it on the wireless. We had just pinned a flag on to our wireless pole.

You see my husband had to lower the pole to put the flag on when Doreen came running out to say there has just been a special announcement. Germany has surrendered unconditionally. So we hoisted the flag at once. Everywhere is very pretty with all the flags. The people have been celebrating for the rest of this week. Heaps of bonfires burning, with Hitler as the hostage.

My husband's name is Herbert William. He is a tradesman in the building's trade, a bricklayer. Our family are mostly agricultural workers, as you know Suffolk is a farming district. Those were the good old days when we could have a pig cured and hung up in the larder. I expect those days are gone for good now, the modern houses are not big enough to store much in. I love cattle and to be on a farm where there is plenty of milk and eggs. I make Ray a nice cup of Ovaltine and I mix the yolk of an egg with it. He says "This is Good."

We have some good times together. You would love to see them both, just a boy and girl in love and so excited about planning their wedding. We will send you every little detail of it we can.

Doreen was so thrilled when Ray presented her with the beautiful double set of Engagement Rings, which Mr. Burwell was so kind to order custom made from a New York jeweler. It was a great help, as the war has completely interrupted normal jewelry trade here. Please thank him for us.

We shall be very happy to know Doreen will be loved by you and Mr. Burwell. You will be mum and dad to her I am sure, dear. Ray and Doreen are both intelligent so I am sure they will help each other as they go through life. Their wedding will be a real English one in a little country church. Our parish is Rushmere. Rushmere is a little village. I have enclosed a picture of the interior of the church.

We live three miles from the drome that Ray did some of his missions from. It is the drome that the boys went from too, to fight the Battle of Britain. It all seems like a dream to me now that the war is over here.

It is wonderful when I think of the hundreds of thousands of aircraft, both English, American and German that have passed over us and we have not seen an accident with one of them. The Germans all went over our areas to get to London.

We can see the sky line over the coast and it was never without a searchlight at night for all of the five years of war. We have seen and heard guns every night too. Now it's Peace, perfect Peace.

So here's wishing the very best of luck from yours lovingly.

Ivy B. Bolton XXXX

Friendly Fire?

May 1945

The gunnery students flew in from various bases and units throughout England, flying mostly P-51s, with a few P-47 razorbacks. For target practice, only the center or inboard pair of 50-caliber guns were armed, and typically the students were limited to exactly two hundred rounds per gun, giving them a firing time of only about fifteen seconds. Therefore, the wisest plan was to fire a series of very short bursts, rather than trying to hose the target.

The process was pretty much routine. The tow plane would drag the target out over the nearest large body of water and, after checking to be sure the area was clear of ships or small craft, the tow pilot would radio the students to begin their runs.

Typically, the tow plane would fly a straight course at about 8,000 feet, maintaining reasonable cruising speed. Each student would begin his pass by flying on a parallel course, slightly higher and forward of the target. He would then make a turning "s"-shaped dive, put the pipper of his gunsight on the target, and begin to fire in short bursts in a classic deflection shot, while curving in on the target as his angle to the target decreased. If the gyro-stabilized gunsight in the P-47 or P-51 was working correctly, it would automatically calculate the correct amount of lead in order to hit the target.

However, it was a lot more difficult than it sounds, as the airplane bounced around in turbulence, and the target, while actually quite large, appeared like a very small rectangle in the sky. Oftentimes, pilots were surprised to discover that they had not gotten a single hit on the rag! It was a matter of concentration, smooth flying, and firing small bursts only when the pipper was stabilized on the target.

While life for the tow pilots was generally a dull grind, there were some incidents that served to remind them that there was an ever-present element of danger, even in their mundane occupation.

All of the trainee pilots were carefully briefed not to hold their firing pass too long and end up firing at a very small angle. However, it was frequently noted, when scoring the hits on the ground, that a few pilots consistently fired at a very low angle, resulting in bullet tears as long as eight inches in length in the target fabric.

While this, in itself, might have signified an aggressive fighter pilot simulating swinging directly behind an enemy aircraft to get a kill shot, it was definitely not a desirable practice when working with a "friendly" tow airplane. The fact is that firing at a very low angle could result in the 50-caliber projectiles hitting and cutting the steel cable in front of the target.

The 3rd Gunnery Flight actually experienced this one day when an over-eager P-51 jock shot the cable off and the target stopped dead, directly in front of his airplane! The pilot, a second lieutenant from the training unit at Atcham, was fortunate to survive that incident, and later related his reactions:

"It scared the hell of me! I was just getting off a nice firing pass, when suddenly the target stopped directly in front of me and the damned thing got big as a house. I thought I was going to hit it and frantically jammed the stick forward, pushing about three negative Gs. I managed to dive narrowly under it but heard a very loud bang in the tail section of my Mustang. The airplane flew okay and I had no trouble landing. However, there was a hell of a dent in the vertical fin where the steel bar and lead weight from the front of the target hit and luckily bounced off."

That pilot didn't realize how very lucky he was. The steel bar and lead weight comprise a very large chunk of metal. Had it hit the canopy, it would have gone straight through, bulletproof glass and all, and that pilot would not have been around to tell about it. Equally bad, had he flown into the thirty-foot target, it could easily have wrapped around the Mustang, negating any opportunity to bail out, with equally serious consequences.

Ray, himself, had an experience one day when he was towing with a P-47, and a P-51 pilot actually shot the cable off *one foot behind his airplane!* After everybody got on the ground and the situation was assessed, there was a serious flap about it, and thereafter trainees were given a warning and threatened with potential court martials for repeats of that incident. Ray, who rarely used the Lord's name in vain, said to the guy, "Jesus Christ, did you think my bird was sporting black crosses?"

The guy apologized and ate so much humble pie that Ray actually felt sorry for him, smiled, and lightened the situation by saying, "It's okay, I've had lots closer ones than that anyway."

The Silver Lining

Target towing was pretty much of a bore after flying combat missions, but Ray soon discovered that there was actually a silver lining in his new assignment. Ray's letter from General Anderson had given him permission to marry Doreen "on or after 14 June 1945, when the two-month waiting period required by Circular 41, Hqs. European Theatre of Operations, U.S. Army, will have elapsed," and that was only a little over a month away.

Initial preparations for their wedding were already underway, with a tentative date set for June 16, 1945. However, with the end of hostilities, no one knew what was in store for his former organization, the 356th group, which could very well be alerted for shipment to the Pacific. On the other hand, the 3rd Gunnery and Tow Target Flight was unlikely to make any sudden moves and would keep him close to his future bride. No one knew how long it would take for war brides to be shipped to the States.

Thinking back over the tumultuous last few months, Burwell smiled to think that Col. Tukey, with all his vindictiveness, had actually done him a big favor. Ray had been able to fly combat missions with the 360th squadron until almost the last day of the war, and Tukey had not been able to hold off his promotion to captain, as he had threatened. Now, not only was he going to be able to marry, but he had a good chance of remaining close to Doreen into the foreseeable future. Ray chuckled over this and said, "I can just imagine Tukey tearing his hair out in frustration. I wonder how a damned fool like that could ever become head of a combat fighter group.

Ray was able to drive down to Ipswich on most weekends, where he stayed with Doreen's parents. In return, whenever Doreen had the time off, she took the train to Thetford and Ray finessed a place for her to stay close by at his quarters.

On one occasion Doreen brought Cynthia with her, and Ray, who was pretty much his own boss now, decided to take them for a ride in the little UC-61 Liaison plane. Unfortunately, Doreen, who had never been in an airplane before, started to get air sick from the turbulence and Ray had to get the airplane on the ground in a hurry. No more UC-61 flights.

The Wedding

June 1945

Doreen began plans for the wedding, riding her bike into the village (as she didn't drive) to meet with the vicar of the Rushmere Saint Andrew church, Church of England, just outside of Ipswich. It was a beautiful and quaint little stone church in an ancient, picturesque setting. It had an arch-shaped door with two spiral-shaped stone columns, which supported a little entrance portico. The vicar explained the standard procedure which called for the "banns of marriage" to be announced ahead of the wedding.

Ray and Doreen duly provided the detail of their marriage planned for June 16, 1945, and the banns were read out on three consecutive

Sundays prior to that date. The traditional reading of the banns concluded with the words, "If anyone can show any just cause or impediment why these two should not be joined together in holy matrimony, may they now declare it." No one objected.

As Ray and Doreen sat in the church together for the third and final reading of the banns, Ray whispered quietly to Doreen, "It's a good thing that Col. Tukey is not a member of the parish!" Doreen gave him a look and a good nudge in the ribs, which made him smile.

Obtaining proper wedding attire was difficult in wartime England, as clothing coupons were very scarce. However, after asking around and running an ad in the local newspaper, Doreen and her mother came up with a very pretty secondhand gown that was not only in good condition but an amazingly good fit, so that no alterations were required. It comprised a fitted antique white brocade with tiny buttons down the back and a heart-shaped neckline.

Wedding days are noted for their missed cues, mishaps and sometimes downright disasters, as the principals are typically and understandably quite nervous about the whole affair, especially without rehearsals. Doreen's wedding had its share of bloopers, but when looking back over the years at its wartime setting, its aura of spontaneity, charm and outright joy, it brings a smile to one's face.

Doreen had two bridesmaids, her sister, Cynthia, and her best friend, Gwen, for whom they rented blue satin dresses with an overlay of lace. However, when Doreen and her mother went to pick them up the day before the wedding, someone had "washed" one of them and it had shrunk the hemline! But there was no time to change, so they just had to make the best of it. At the wedding Doreen noticed that Gwen looked a bit lumpy – but who was commenting? Doreen had a beautiful lace veil with fresh "orange blossoms" – an English tradition – and a very large bouquet of pink roses, which were very hard to hold – especially with shaking hands!!

Their wedding day was blessed with delightful sunny weather and a pleasant temperature. Twelve officers attended, most of them from Ray's old 360th squadron. Ray's best man was Captain Don Hall, a friend who had grown up with him in Denair, California, and who was a pilot flying bombers with the 8th Air Force. He had been stationed less than fifty miles from Martlesham, but Ray had not known that until recently. For the wedding, Ray flew him in with the UC-61.

A wedding car with big white ribbons came to pick up Doreen and her parents from Foxhall Road. The wedding party arrived at the church a little too early while the organist was still going through his repertoire, having not yet gotten to the "Wedding March." However, Doreen's father took hold of her arm and started down the aisle, taking such large steps that the organist was struggling to catch up, and they arrived at the altar before the march could be finished!! Not to worry – it was a wedding and such things always seemed to happen in some way or other.

In her own words, Doreen described the wedding, the reception, and the honeymoon as follows:

"We had a regular church service, with hymns, but at one point the organist was playing a hymn and the audience was singing the words of the next song. Mum laughed and said quietly to my father, 'Maybe they think the war is still on!' Ha, ha. It was a traditional and beautiful ceremony. We said our vows...so much in love…Ray slipped a beautiful gold wedding band onto my finger….and we knew that everything would be forever as we believed this commitment was ordained by God and would hold us together...!! And it did!!!

"We had a reception at the Crown and Anchor Hotel in Ipswich... My father wasn't very good at speeches so we told him he would give the wedding toast to the bride and groom. Very nervously he stood up and said, "Toast to the bride and groom," so quickly we couldn't understand what he said!!! Then my mother stood up and talked and talked and talked until I gently pulled on her arm to indicate, "Okay, that's enough.

"Our three-course lunch was delicious. We all gave some more short speeches – Ray and I and the best man, Don Hall. We had a great wedding cake, which Ray had gotten the chef at his base in Thetford to make up, then Ray had flown it into Ipswich in the UC-61. As my new husband and I stood at the cake ready to cut it, he turned to the guests and said, 'You know, all the way down final approach I was worried that I would bounce or drop it in. But I knew that if I did, Doreen would kill me, so I made the smoothest, slickest landing I ever made in my entire life!' That got a round of applause and laughs all around.

"We took pictures outside the church and I was presented with a small P-51 model my best friend's son had made!!!! A nice surprise!!

"After the reception I went home to change but forgot my little cosmetic bag, which held my beautiful red lipstick. It was Sunday and everything was closed! My first day married and I was without ruby lips! Ray said, 'I don't care, you are beautiful anyway,' which was nice to hear from my new husband.

"We said our good-byes and headed for the train leaving for London at 3:00...the wedding had been at 11:00am.... We were off to the south of England – Torquay – for a week's honeymoon!

We had beautiful weather at a great hotel on the coast; Ray had planned everything. He even talked the owner into a room when she had told him they were full!! "We are on our honeymoon," he said.

Our week could have been a disaster, as one day Ray ran full bore to dive into the ocean off the pier...the tide had gone out, leaving only a shallow strip of water! It was a miracle that he chose to do a shallow dive, and by the grace of God he came out of it all with only a grazed nose from skimming the ocean floor – along with a grazed ego! No broken neck!!!!!!!!

EPILOGUE

The 356th Fighter Group remained at Martlesham Heath until November 4, at which time it returned to the U.S. and was inactivated at Camp Kilmer, New Jersey, on November 10, 1945.

During World War II, the group was the hardest hit, with the highest ratio of losses as compared to enemy aircraft destroyed claims, of all 8th Air Force fighter groups. It earned a Distinguished Unit Citation for actions on September 17, 18, and 23, 1944, in support of Operation Market Garden in Holland.

Richard Andrino

Following the dogfight on Christmas day, 1944, Andy was one of two pilots who did not return. One of the group's pilots witnessed a red tail P-51 chasing an FW-190 very low, and observed the P-51 to hit a tree, crash, and disintegrate. However, no one knew which of the two it was. Red tails were our squadron colors, but we had lost two airplanes that day, so the question was – which one?

After the war ended, captured German documents revealed that both Andrino and Heubner had been killed on that Christmas day. Andy was seen by a minister to crash near

Koblenz, after hitting a tree. He had been chasing an FW-190, which pulled up sharply to avoid the tree, but Andy hit it, cartwheeled, and crashed. The minister, who later conducted Andy's funeral, said there were no dog tags, but the plane was identified as PI-X and by tail number 415307.

Ironically, in 1960 I was stationed right in Koblenz, as liaison officer to the III German Corps, which had become an important part of NATO. Had I known of this report, I would have certainly looked up the minister, if he was still alive, to get further details and to visit Andy's grave.

Some time after the war ended, Andy's parents arranged for the transfer of his remains to the U.S. Andy now rests in Turlock Memorial Park, Turlock, California; Plot 499, Block 20.

Every Christmas day, as we sit down to our Christmas dinner, we fill a wine glass and drink a quiet toast to those who are no longer with us. Andy is one of those who is very much in our minds.

Bill Crump

Ray and Bill

Following the end of the extension to his tour of combat, Captain Bill Crump spent a considerable amount of time on detached service, ferrying fighters to various destinations in Europe. In 1946 he was released from active duty and initially went to work in a shipyard, then later became a flight instructor and airline pilot with a small flying service in Everett, Washington. Bill was recalled to active duty in the Air Force in 1948, assigned to a troop carrier squadron, and shortly thereafter flew C-54 cargo aircraft in the Berlin Airlift.

Bill remained in the Air Force through the completion of a twenty-three-year career, during which he rose to lieutenant colonel. Oddly enough, he spent most of his career flying transport aircraft in the various troop carrier squadrons, essentially what would be called Military Airlift Command today. Notable incidents included flying Bob Hope as well as Les Brown and his Band of Renown from Frankfurt to Berlin in 1948. Les Brown's "Band of Renown," by the way , is the same one which was playing at the Officer's Club in Baton Rouge the night Ray Burwell met Doris Clunan.

During the early fifties, Bill was command pilot on Douglas C-124 Globe Masters, the largest cargo aircraft in the world at the time. I think he must have hated that job, as it was about as far as you can get from flying fighters – more like driving a locomotive.

After retiring as a lieutenant colonel in 1967, he became quite a celebrity in and around his hometown of Edmonds, Washington, and the surrounding area. He bought two Cessna Aerobat aircraft, had them painted with all manner of stripes and decorations, and flew them in many regional airshows, performing aerobatics before the audiences.

In 1988 he became one of the pilots flying the P-51 "Miss America" at the Paine International Air Show and other such events. Bill said that his re-checkout in the P-51, after forty-three years, was easy, as it all came right back to him.

In 1990 he was invited to visit Sweden, where he was privileged to meet the Queen of Sweden in commemorating a flight in which he and some other pilots secretly delivered some Mustangs to the Swedish Air Force in 1945, shortly before the end of the war. Two years later he returned to Ipswich and visited Jeep's grave, where a prominent memorial plaque still remains behind Playford Hall (a private residence today.)

As a local celebrity, he appeared in many public events, including being assigned as parade marshal in a Veteran's day parade and carrying the Olympic torch for a short distance in its passage through Washington State, prior to the 1996 Atlanta Olympics.

Bill never married his high school sweetheart, Jackie, for whom his plane was named. He married a girl named June Sorensen, who had been a fellow student at Edmonds High School in Washington. She and Bill raised four sons during the time they were moving around in the Air Force. His son Bob Crump helped provide details for the publication of this book. Bob said that his older brother Terry was a Cobra pilot in Vietnam, and joined his father as a recipient of the Distinguished Flying Cross.

Bill died in 2008 and is sorely missed by his many friends and family. He is memorialized in the book "Wild Bill," by British author Shaun Crump – no relation – as well as on wildbillcrump.com, which provides additional interesting detail about his colorful life.

"Ginny"

After returning to the States, I was assigned to Craig Field, Selma, Alabama, as an instructor pilot. Inasmuch as it was not far from Alabama College for Women, I took the opportunity to stop by and visit Virginia Power at the college. It was a pleasant meeting. We smiled and shook hands and she gave me back my wings, which were the ones I had air dropped to her on the campus – what seemed like an eternity ago. We laughed when we talked about that incident and the campus buzz that it created. She was still a very pretty girl with curly brunette hair – but the magic was gone.

We both knew that it was for the best, as our meeting had been an aberration in the first place and we lived in two different worlds: She was a southern belle ensconced in her community and its church, while I was a guy from a Yankee steel town. Not only that – but the war had changed everything. A short two years ago, I had been a kid with his head in the clouds, seeing a damsel on a pedestal. Since then I had not only experienced the cauldron of war and grown up but had known the love of a woman from another world – a woman who had given her life to her country and would forever remain in my memory.

We parted, wishing each other well and knowing that we would always be friends, with fond memories of the time we had spent together.

Ray and Doreen

After returning from their honeymoon, Ray and Doreen found a place near Thetford and settled down to wait for transportation to the States. Gunnery training at the 3rd Gunnery Flight gradually slowed, as the various fighter units were successively deactivated and sent home. Hopes of Doreen being shipped home with her husband soon evaporated, as it became clear that the war brides would have to wait for all the troops to be transported before their turn came. Considering the amount of military personnel still to be shipped, this suggested a wait of at least another four months, which turned out to be a good estimate. In fact, at one point in late 1945, ten thousand aggravated British war brides staged a protest march through London, but Doreen was not one of them.

Finally, in early November 1945, Ray was alerted for shipment and was temporarily assigned to the 359th Fighter Group, which was one of the remaining groups of the 67th Fighter Wing. After an agonizing parting from Doreen, who had returned to Ipswich to live with her parents, Ray boarded a truck for an eight-hour ride to a port and subsequently sailed on the Queen Mary – along with thousands of troops and several fighter squadrons. Ray reported that, ironically, Colonel Tukey was one of the passengers on the ship – but made no further comment.

On November 11, 1945, the nine pilots in his stateroom were awakened at 0530 to view the Statue of Liberty. They stood with hearts in their throats and tears in their eyes as the grand old lady emerged from a fog bank and greeted them gloriously in full sunshine with welcoming torch held high! Ray said, "It was worth waking up so early; I wouldn't have missed it for anything!" Coincidently, it was Armistice Day!

Ray flew directly to a processing camp in California, where he was deactivated and became a civilian once again. Shortly thereafter, he learned that Doreen was pregnant, which stimulated him to get busy making a place for his new family in the States. He began by attending insurance school, and then joined his father in the business in Denair. Next, he collaborated with his parents, who had generously offered to build a small wing onto their house in Denair, with the expectation that the newlyweds would live there until they got their lives sorted out.

Finally, on March 6, 1946, Ray received a long-awaited telegram advising him that Doreen was sailing on the S.S. Brazil, a full four months after his departure, and would be arriving in NYC on March 13. The ship was filled with war brides of all nationalities, many of whom were pregnant. Consequently, there was a lot of seasickness aboard the ship, but fortunately, the seas were relatively serene, so it could have been worse.

Doreen travelled across the U.S. by train. At one little town, where the train made a planned twenty-minute stop, she got off the train to quickly buy a new dress for her arrival, and almost missed getting back on board in time. Arriving in California, she expected to change trains in Fresno for the final leg to Denair, but was surprised when Ray (in full uniform) greeted her in Fresno. At their initial meeting, Ray came up behind her and threw his arms around her. To quote him, "Boy, was she surprised!! And she looked great for being five months pregnant!!!" After a long kiss and giant hugs, they headed to Denair on the train together – where a big gathering was awaiting them.

They lived initially with Ray's parents in Denair, where Julie Doreen Burwell was born in April 1946. They later moved to a house in Turlock, California, where Sharon Suzanne Burwell (who actively collaborated on this book) was born March 27, 1949, followed by David Loray Burwell on June 14, 1950.

Although he was successful in business, the itch to fly military aircraft was ever-present in Ray, so he soon became a "weekend warrior," flying various trainers with the Reserve at Castle AFB, Merced, California. However, with the advent of the Korean War, he was recalled to active duty and ordered to Reese AFB in Texas, for upgrading into jet fighters. Doreen and the children accompanied him in what turned out to be an eight-year succession of bases, mostly in Texas, in which the growing family never once lived on base but rented a series of houses off-base.

Doreen soon learned that being a successful mother and wife of a career flying officer in the States had its challenges and required adaptation skills, perhaps not as challenging as those she and her parents had undergone during the war, but nevertheless, a full-time job.

During a two-year assignment at Bryan Air Force Base, Texas, Ray became an instrument instructor, teaching all-weather flying skills. Among his students were many pilots from the Danish Air Force.

In 1955 he was ordered to the 514th Fighter Interceptor Squadron at RAF station Manston AFB, England. This was the very base where Ray had crash-landed after getting his P-47 badly shot up during Operation Market Garden in Holland. Doreen was delighted with this assignment as it enabled her to spend time with her family in Ipswich after an eight year separation. She could once again savor the unique qualities of England, for which she was understandably homesick. Ray and Doreens' children, now 3, 5, and 7, could also experience the love of their grandparents and the traditions of England.

Ray flew ahead, going first on a short period of temporary duty to Denmark, where he continued to train Danish Air Force pilots. Doreen followed with the family on the long journey by train and then the flight across the Atlantic on a Military Airlift Command C-54. She was met by a Colonel who informed her that Ray had been in a bad Jeep accident on the way to meet her, but was not seriously injured. In the wee hours of the morning he arrived with smiles and hugs, still wearing the bloodstained shirt and with 20 stitches he had received from the hospital! Nevertheless, they were all delighted to be re-united and happy to be back in England again.

Ray enjoyed the tour of duty in England thoroughly, as the 514th group was initially equipped with F-86F swept wing (day fighter) jets, but subsequently transitioned to the F-86D radar-equipped models for all-weather interception as part of the NATO Defense Forces. Ray reflected how much better it was flying trans-sonic jets of our own, instead of trying to catch 150-mph-faster Me-262s with propeller-driven fighters.

Following two more three-year assignments at Western bases, Ray was ordered to Vietnam in 1964, where he spent two years on the operations and planning staffs of various liaison squadrons. In the process, he flew one hundred missions as an airborne forward air controller for strikes on enemy positions.

Sometime in the midst of flying those missions he found time to train a number of Vietnamese Air Force pilots. He was very proud of that achievement and became very close to his students, who then joined the ranks of the airborne forward air controllers. In return, Ray was awarded a pair of Vietnamese Air Force Wings, which were personally presented by General Ky. The Vietnamese pilots also presented Ray with a beautiful inlayed piece of artwork, showing the history of their country, as a memento of their time together.

Lt. Colonel Burwell in Vietnam, wearing both USAF and Vietnamese wings

Upon his return, he spent the last two years of his career in a staff position at a radar station in Corvallis, Oregon, from which he retired as a lieutenant colonel in 1967.

Ray was happy to settle down with Doreen and the family, and transitioned quickly back into civilian life. Initially, Ray became a Real Estate broker in Auburn, California, while Doreen also obtained a license and worked with him at the office.

Following a very successful three-year stint, they purchased a 160-acre ranch in Northern California with his son-in-law, and spent the next fourteen years there. This was one of the happiest times in their lives, during which the kids all grew up in the ranch environment, which they loved.

In 1985 Ray finally retired to the golf course – his "fourth career," following military officer, businessman, and rancher – and spent a great deal of his time at the Vista Valley Country Club, Vista, California. Doreen describes that period as "eleven great years!"

During the many years that elapsed after the war, the 356th Fighter Group held a series of annual reunions at various locations, but my wife and I did not attend any for fifty years. In the early nineties, we finally went to one which was held at a restaurant called "The 356th Fighter Group," in Canton, Ohio, where pictures of Ray's Mustang with "Lady Doris" painted prominently on the side were displayed.

Doreen was not there, but Ray quickly assured me (as if I didn't know) that Doris was not the one he had married. I had always assumed that when Ray promised Doreen that he would get rid of all of the pictures of Doris – that this included taking the *Lady Doris* off the side of his airplane, but he never did , so I guess the airplane went into the deep sea bearing that label![15] I never learned why he didn't remove

---

[15] ***Incredible as it may sound today, after the war ended it was determined that it would be uneconomic to return all of the U.S. warplanes to the states, and they were dropped by the thousands into the deep sea, where they have been corroding away ever since. Many of the bombers and fighters were factory new, having never flown a single combat mission!***

it, and never asked him. Maybe he thought it would bring him bad luck if he changed the name. Who knows?

Ray Burwell with the author, September 1944

In 1999, we met Ray and Doreen at a 356th group reunion in Portland, Maine. That was Col. Tukey's home turf and, sure enough, there he sat, while he and Ray glared at each other and Doreen smiled at him sweetly. After the reunion, we drove to Connecticut, stopping on the way to visit the beautiful First Congregational Church in Bennington, Vermont, behind which the poet Robert Frost and his family are buried.

Doreen loved the beautiful architecture of the church, with its raised pulpit from which the minister could survey his flock. She chatted with the custodian and won him over, so that he even arranged for the organist to play especially for us – a stirring performance in a wonderful setting. Oddly enough, Ray did not seem to have much patience with the colonial traditions. Maybe they didn't have enough California in them!

Ray and Doreen spent a night with us at our home in Connecticut. When we parted, Ray said, "Well, I guess I won't see you again, Ed," and he was right. In November of 2001, Ray passed away from heart failure in Santa Rosa, California, after landscaping yet another three-quarters of an acre there, including a sixteen-tree orchard and a little golf course. He played nine holes of golf *one* week before he passed peacefully in the night!

He is buried at the San Joaquin Valley National Cemetery, Gustine, California. Ray's decorations and awards include:

Distinguished Flying Cross
Air Medal with eleven Oak Leaf Clusters
European-African-Middle Eastern Campaign Medal with six Bronze Service Stars
American Campaign Medal
World War II Victory Medal
National Defense Service Medal with one Bronze Service Star
Air Force Reserve Medal with Hour Glass Device
Air Force Longevity Service Award with four Bronze Oak Leaf Clusters
Air Force Outstanding Unit Award
Vietnamese Service Medal with two Bronze Service Stars
Republic of Vietnam Commendation Medal

When I heard of his passing in 2001, I was reminded of a stanza from the poem *Reluctance*, by Robert Frost (1874):

Out through the fields and the woods
And over the walls I have wended;
I have climbed the hills of view
And looked at the world, and descended;
I have come by the highway home,
And lo, it is ended.

The Burwell Dynasty

Ray is gone, but the dynasty that he and Doreen built in sunny California is very much alive and growing. Doreen Burwell truly deserves the title "Lady Doreen," as she is indeed that. A grand white-haired lady who is still pretty, she is surrounded by no less than three living children, eleven grandchildren, and nine great-grandchildren.

Doreen with her children (left to right) Sharon, David, and Julie
Taken in 1964, while Ray was in Vietnam

Each year we receive a special Christmas card from her, always accompanied by a lovely recounting of what the past year has brought and the blessings which have been bestowed upon her and hers. It was those cards that inspired the writing of this book, as she and Ray represent fully what author Tom Brokaw has entitled "The Greatest Generation."

Doreen is today as bright as a shiny dollar, filled with enthusiasm, and has a wonderful sense of humor. In chatting with her about their romance and Ray's visits to her home during their courtship, she recalls with delight many comical incidents from the war years, as if they were yesterday.

Recently, we talked about the "Lady Doris" on the side of his airplane, and she said, "It was an issue at the time it was painted and a "wake-up call" for me. I broke it off in my mother's back yard, gazing into his eyes, professing my love for him and said, ' It's either me or her!' While he never actually promised me he would get rid of it, I had hopes, but did not press the issue, as many people believed it was bad luck to change the name of a plane or a boat. In any case, the name was still there when the plane went into the sea." Then she laughed and said, "I don't care, as I had him for all those years – and they were wonderful ones!"

In addition to the help provided directly by Doreen, I am greatly indebted to her daughter Sharon Justin (nee Sharon Suzanne Burwell), who has been a constant source of accurate information and actually supplied me with almost one hundred of the original letters that went back and forth between Ray and his family, as well as the two lovers and their respective families. She exhibits the same bright spirit that I remember in her mother and my old flying buddy.

Sharon Justin's own words best describe her mother today: "Doreen is now a healthy and young eighty-eight year old. She lives in the Oakmont Community Village on three-quarters of an acre. Dad made sure she was well taken care of and she is very content to live out her years in this little bit of paradise here in Sonoma County, better known as 'Valley of the Moons.' My dad planted sixteen fruit trees, and together they turned this property into a very unique garden.". "Mom also is active in her church and sings in the choir. She is known as the dog evangelist as she walks 'Lovee' throughout Oakmont spreading good cheer and telling others what a wonderful life God has provided for her! You know those British girls…everyone loves their cute little accents. I think that is what caught my dad's eye and ears so many years ago during WWII!!"

Doreen Burwell (white haired) with the Burwell Dynasty in California, 2013

Playford Hall

Following the war, Playford Hall went through several sets of owners, who invested considerable sums restoring it to its former grandeur. This is particularly evident with regard to the beautiful landscaped gardens and pathways which now occupy the land where the 360th pilots partied and hunted rabbits with their .45 pistols. Most recently, Playford Hall was listed as an eight-bedroom late Tudor with an offering price of 3,250,000 Pounds.

Republic P-47 "Thunderbolt" – The Forgotten Airplane

As the history of World War II has been written, rewritten, and augmented, it is commonplace today to read, again and again, the statement, "The P-51 was the best fighter of WWII." Unfortunately, there are three words missing from that statement. It should read, "The P-51 was the best *long-range escort* fighter of World War II."

What you almost never read about is the Republic P-47 Thunderbolt, which was, hands-down, the best air-to-ground fighter bomber of the war – bar none! During the 1944 period, the 356th group, as well as the other P-47-equipped groups, did yeoman service supporting the invasion and the subsequent advance into Germany. As the Germans slowly retreated from Russia, they pulled back more and more of their armor and flak batteries into an area that was increasingly compressed as the fighting went on. The result was a concentration of flak that was not only much denser but had become much more accurate – as the enemy's aiming and tracking systems had been greatly improved and the Germans were able to employ their most experienced and skilled gunners to protect their vital targets.

Almost every P-47 in the 356th group was hit multiple times, typically absorbing 20mm and 40mm hits, as well as multiple machine gun bullets, which would have knocked a P-51 out of the sky. P-47s did not usually burn, but Mustangs did. I can state this with some authority, as I flew a second tour of combat in Mustangs with the Eighteenth Fighter Group Korea in 1950-51. We lost twenty-five percent of our pilots KIA from ground flak, which was only a fraction of what it had been in Germany.

P-51s were not a good air-to-ground airplane. A single slug in the intercooler or the ethylene glycol would either set the airplane on fire or cause the loss of that vital cooling fluid. In the latter case, the common wisdom was that the engine would cook itself and stop in about seven minutes. I personally have had two P-51 wingmen shot down while strafing, both flamers. In fact, in Korea, you could shoot yourself down, because in the early missions in Korea we were firing ball ammunition, and the slugs would bounce off of the rice paddies and you could easily pick one up in the intercooler under the belly.

The P-47 was a magnificent, rugged machine. Its eight 50-caliber machine guns had terrific destructive force and would knock a large moving van right off of the road with a tap of the trigger. On one occasion a locomotive with tender, which was running at full speed to try to escape, was on the outside of a curved section of track and was knocked clean off the track onto its side by one short burst of eight 50s!

The P-47 was the only fighter I have known which could clip a foot-thick telephone pole off with a wing and fly home with a nice round dent in the wing (back to the main spar), sometimes trailing hundreds of feet of wire behind. The big Pratt & Whitney R-2800 engine was really two 9-cylinder radials, joined back to back with a common crankshaft, that could take incredible punishment and keep running. Loss of a single cylinder was fairly commonplace, and on one occasion a Jug in our squadron flew back with two cylinders completely shot off, piston rods flailing in the air, and oil spewing everywhere. The airplane also had good self-sealing fuel tanks and frequently had slugs go right through the tanks and still flew home.

It is noteworthy that the 9th Air Force, which flew from the Continent and had an almost total air-to-ground mission, was equipped with only P-47 fighters. Viewing the whole deal in perspective, I estimate that if we had been flying Mustangs during the intensive 1944 period, about sixty to seventy percent of the group would have been shot down.

Don't misunderstand me, I love the P-51, which was a great airplane, but just want to get the facts straight.

Acknowledgments

This book could not have been written without the wonderful support provided by Doreen Burwell herself, as well as her daughter Sharon Justin (nee Sharon Suzanne Burwell), who provided me with almost one hundred of the many letters written by Ray Burwell and his parents, as well as by Doreen and Ray during their courtship and subsequent marriage. Both searched unstintingly through a mountain of correspondence and photos, from which I selected the nuggets that support the story of this book. Throughout the period of authorship they were a constant source of good-natured encouragement and support, supplying material that I could never have obtained elsewhere, while laughing and enjoying the recalling of events long past.

Other technical detail regarding Bill Crump and "Jeep" was generously provided by Bill's son, Bob, and was also drawn from the book "Wild Bill Crump" by British author Shaun Crump (no relation), with whom I briefly corresponded after the war, providing a small amount of material about the squadron.

I also wish to acknowledge the excellent contributions of the following individuals in the preparation and publication of the book: Professional Copy Editor Diane Alena, who did yeoman service in keeping my pen from straying too far; Artist John Purdy, for his amusing sketches; Art Director Jill Karas Simpson, for her creative work in designing the eye-catching cover art; and last but not least, Stuart Slade, distinguished author of eleven novels, for his excellent advice and professional help in the layout and publishing of the final copy.

Debt of Gratitude

I also owe a particular debt of gratitude to my wife, Marge, for her forbearance and support during the many months in which I spent a great deal of time immersed in my thoughts and pounding away on my computer at what she good-naturedly referred to as "my post." During this period of gestation I was kept generously supplied with cups of coffee and snacks to, as she put it, "keep the creative juices flowing."

Growing Up In A Pennsylvania Steel Town During The Great Depression by Edward Nebinger. This personal memoir looks back at the years before World War II. They represented a time when the U.S. was struggling through the Depression, but people never gave up and instead made the best of what they had. Above all, the Bethlehem Steel Company was the second largest steel producer in the world, and the U.S. was the leading industrial power on earth. Now that great industrial base is largely gone, having moved to other Continents, with Bethlehem Steel among the first of the industrial dominos to fall - an event of tragic proportions. 238 pp, paperback $22.95, E-book, $9.95

Alexander's Generals. Conqueror of the known world whose Macedonian phalanx deafeated all who dared challenge it. Now, poisoned at the peak of his power by an unknown hand. Who shall succeed him? On his death-bed, Alexander left his empire "to the strongest." In doing so, he condemned the vast empire he had ruled to a catastrophic series of civil wars as his generals tried to carve out empires of their own. As old friends and allies turned on each other in a deadly struggle to prove themselves "the strongest" a bitter and relentless blood-feud cuts them down, one by one. Alexander's generals never realize that their deadliest enemy is a man they believe to be already dead. 424pp, paperback $24.95, E-book $9.99

The Long Patrol by Michael J. Kozlowski. On one level, "The Long Patrol" is a description of how the world's first truly operational submarine was designed and built. As this part of the story is methodically unveiled, the characters of Horace Lawson Hunley and the Confederate military officers who backed him come to life and step off the pages of the book. This book is an indispensable social history of the Confederacy during its slow death, the author showing how the loss of the Hunley was made inevitable by this decline. 278 pp, paperback $24.95, E-book $9.95

To Barbary's Far Shore by by Michael J. Kozlowski. In 1805 the fledgling government of the United States of America asked its Marine Corps to do the impossible - to march hundreds of miles across hostile desert and force the Bey of Tripoli to release the crew of the frigate Philadelphia. Eight

Marines, under the command of Lt. Presley O'Bannon proceeded to do the impossible. The Tripoli expedition is famously remembered in the first lines of the Marine Corps Hymn. This book tells us why. 396pp paperback $26.95, E-book $9.95

United States Strategic Bombers 1945 – 2012 by Stuart Slade. A definitive resource from Defense Lion Publications detailing the evolution of the United States Strategic Bomber inventory; from the Boeing B-29 Superfortress in World War II through the B-2 Stealth Bomber. A look at the future for the next generation of United States Bomber is also included. 320 pp, paperback $26.95, E-book $9.95

Air Operations 1958 Lebanon and Taiwan, By Jacob Van Staaveren, Robert D Little and Wilhelmina Burch. Air Operations in the Taiwan Crisis of 1958 and Air Operations in the Lebanon Crisis of 1958 were prepared by the USAF Historical Division . This book is a compilation of those reports with substantial additional material that updates and complements the original material. 127 pp paperback $14.95, E-book $9.99

Air War Vietnam Plans and Operations 1961 – 1968 By Jacob van Staaveran & Stuart Slade. This first volume covers the birth of the American involvement in the Vietnam War from the arrival of the first advisors to the peak of troop deployment numbers. 525 pp paperback $34.95, E-book, 9.99

Air War Vietnam Plans and Operations 1969 – 1975 by Elizabeth Hartsook & Stuart Slade. This second volume describes the search for a negotiated end to the conflict and the final defeat of South Vietnam. 547 pp, paperback $34.95, E-book, $9.99

Close Air Support in Vietnam by Ralph A. Rowley. This historical study deals with U.S. Air Force close air support operations within the Republic of Vietnam. with emphasis on tactics and techniques. 182 pp paperback $19.95, E-book $9.99

Forward Air Control in Vietnam by Ralph A. Rowley. U.S. Air Force forward air controllers flew in support of U.S., South Vietnamese and Allied ground combat units during operations against enemy forces. As the Vietnam war ground on, the enemy threat became more dangerous and the role of the Forward Air Controller expanded. This historical study pays tribute to the men who performed these dangerous roles with such courage. 334 pp paperback $24.95, E-book $9.99

Mad Cats – The Story of VP-63 by Kernan Chaisson. This collection of stories is from the members of VP-63, who served with the "MAD Cat" through almost three years of World War II. It was their work that gave birth to the Magnetic Anomaly Detector (MAD) that today, is carried by almost every ASW aircraft throughout the world. 254 pp, paperback $24.95, E-book 9.95

Tactics and Techniques of Electronic Warfare in Vietnam by Bernard C Nalty. Electronic countermeasures support for the air war against North Vietnam included stand-off jamming, Wild Weasel operations, the use of self-protection pods, and the employment of chaff. Using all these techniques, Linebacker II saw the B-52s of Strategic Air Command facing the most effective air defense system the Soviet Union could provide. The B-52s won. 182 pp, Paperback $19.95, E-book $9.95

The Air Force and the National Guided Missile Program 1944-1950 by Max Rosenberg. The Air Force and The National Guided Missile Program 1944-1950 provides an invaluable insight of the era that gave birth to the modern art of war. 150 pp, paperback $14.95, E-book $9.95

The RF-101 Voodoo over South East Asia 1961 – 1970 by William H. Greenhalgh. The Voodoo pilots photographed objectives all the way to the China border, surviving anti-aircraft fire, missiles, and MiG interceptors – and suffering losses. Truly, the pilots of the RF-101s had a deadly dangerous job, and this history of their achievements pays a much-deserved tribute to their skill and fortitude. 122 pp, Paperback $14.95, E-book $9.95

The Evolution of Aircraft Carriers By Scott MacDonald. Edited and reconstructed by Curtis "Monty" Nebinger. The Evolution of Aircraft Carriers is a compilation of official U.S. Navy documents, essays and photographs that takes the reader on a journey from Eugene Ely's first flight from the USS Birmingham to the building of the first carrier from the keel up and continues on for over 50 years of world naval aircraft carrier and aviation history; ending just after the completion of USS Enterprise CVN-65. 279 pp, paperback $24.95, E-book $9.95

The Big One by Stuart Slade. Europe is being torn apart by a war which nobody can win. Nazi Germany occupies Europe from the Pyrenees to the Volga. In the East, Russian and American troops fight to stop the German Army from breaking through. In the West, American carriers prowl the Atlantic, hurling their midnight-blue fighter-bombers against any target they find. Nothing can stop the madness. America has one last hand left, a plan to bring the war to an end in a single terrible blow. 213 pp, paperback $19.95, E-book, $9.95

Winter Warriors by Stuart Slade. One great German offensive has broken through the Russian defenses leaving an Allied army trapped in the frozen waste land of the Kola Peninsula. While the armies try to survive the bitter cold opposing ski-troops fight a vicious private war to dominate the ground between by their armies. Desperate to break the deadlock, the German Navy sets sail in an effort to destroy the convoys that keep the allied troops on Kola alive. And so, an epic naval battle brews in the icy waters of the North Atlantic. In the midst of the fighting, a U.S. Navy railway gun crew, Russian railway engineers and Siberian ski-troops come together in a desperate battle to save the great guns from the advancing German troops. Behind the scenes, in a war-weary America, another political battle is being fought, one in which a supposed friend can be as deadly an enemy as any found on the Kola Peninsula. 400pp, paperback $24.95, E-book, $9.95

High Frontier by Stuart Slade. Living and working in space is man's greatest challenge. The conquest of space will guarantee man's survival. Yet, there may not be enough time left. On Earth, one empire is collapsing under its own weight and there are those in its government who would prefer to suffer utter destruction rather than defeat. Another is trying to repair the damage from previous blunders and rebuild its relations with the rest of the world. Will humanity have time to scale The High Frontier? 236pp, paperback $22.95, E-book, $9.99

A Mighty Endeavor by Stuart Slade. The unthinkable has happened and a theoretical possibility has become an ugly reality. Britain is out of the war. The Commonwealth is on its own. How can it survive when its military, economic and political center has been stripped away? In a world that is suddenly filled with unexpected enemies and unlikely friends, the Commonwealth has a desperate struggle on its hands. Just to survive will be hard enough. To survive and win is truly A Mighty Endeavor. 420 pp, paperback $24.95, E-book $9.95

Conrad's Eye by Stuart Slade. Conrad Lorenz, Inquisitor - A soul eternally damned, doomed to wander the Earth. His salvation will only come when he has saved enough of those wrongly accused to redeem his soul from the guilt over the innocents he once condemned. For those wrongly accused and in desperate need, there is one last hope for justice - that Conrad will cast his eye upon their case. 464 pp, paperback $29.95, E-book, $9.95

All these books are available from our website
www.lionpubs.com

www.ingramcontent.com/pod-product-compliance
Lightning Source LLC
Chambersburg PA
CBHW030821310726
48980CB00006B/579/J

9781939335326